Yurei **Attack!**

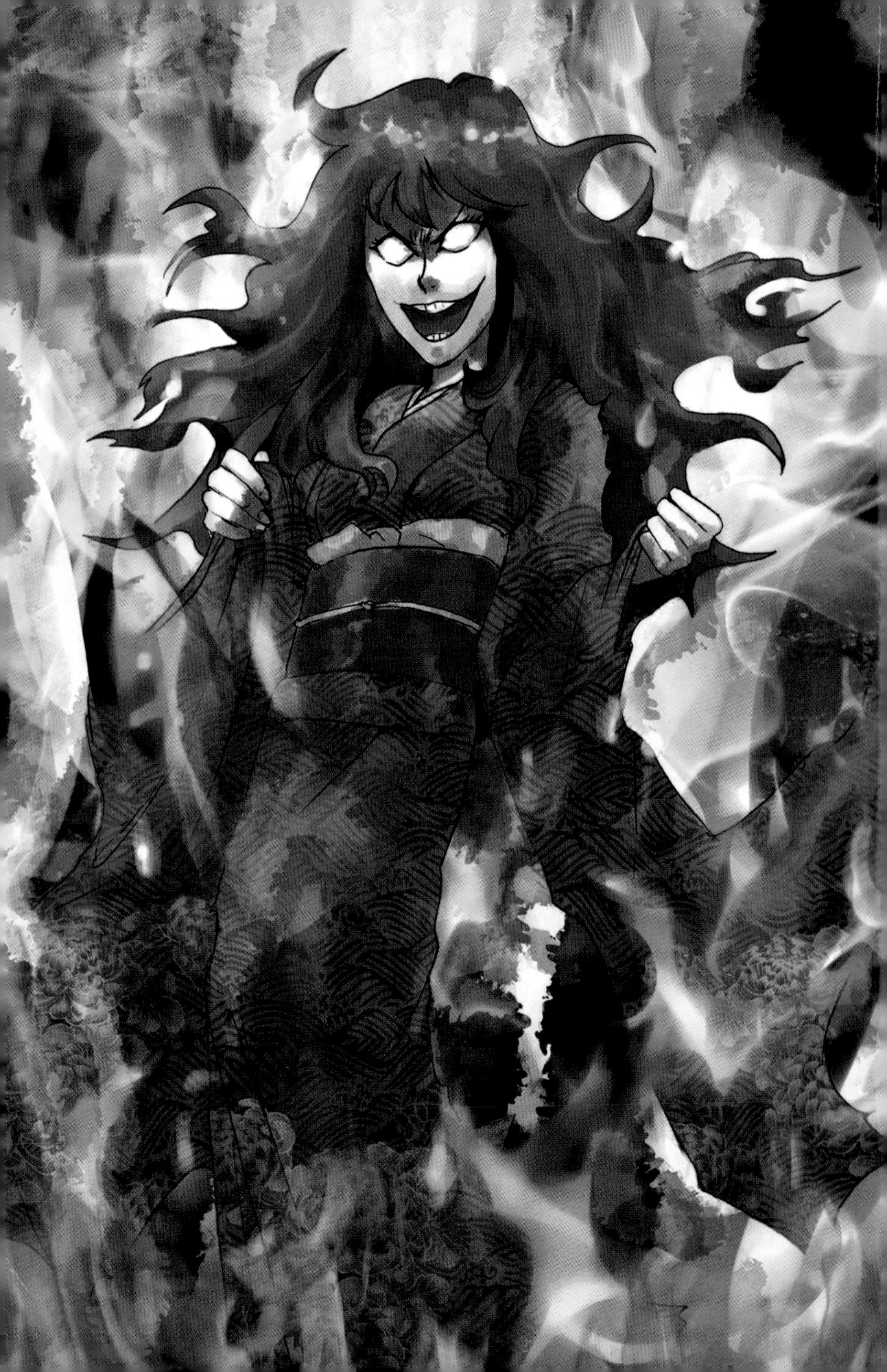

Yurei **Attack!**
The Japanese Ghost
Survival Guide

Hiroko Yoda and **Matt Alt**
Illustrations by **Shinkichi**

TUTTLE Publishing
Tokyo │ Rutland, Vermont │ Singapore

Yurei Attack! CONTENTS

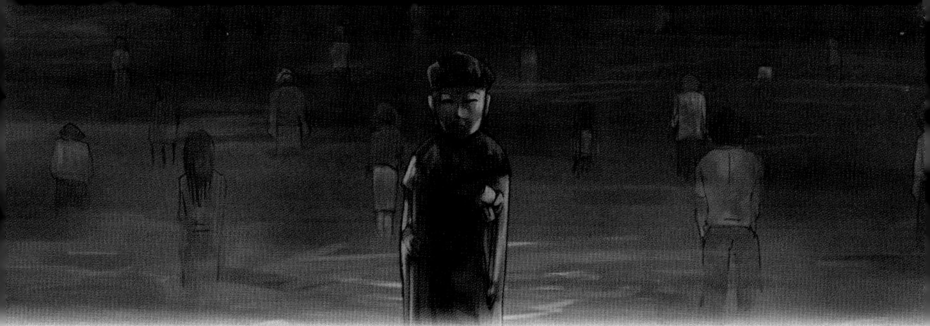

This book is dedicated to Tokyo's scariest resident, Oiwa-san, who's been putting the fear into Japan for close to two centuries and counting.

Published by Tuttle Publishing, an imprint of Periplus Editions (HK) Ltd.

www.tuttlepublishing.com

Copyright © 2012 Hiroko Yoda and Matt Alt
Illustrations © 2012 Satoko Tanaka

Library of Congress Cataloging-in-Publication Data

Yoda, Hiroko.
  Yurei attack! : the Japanese ghost survival guide / Hiroko Yoda and Matt Alt ; illustrations by Shinkichi. -- 1st ed.
    p. cm.
  Includes bibliographical references.
  ISBN 978-4-8053-1214-8 (pbk.)
  1. Ghosts--Japan. I. Alt, Matt. II. Title.
  BF1472.J3Y63 2012
  133.10952--dc23

2012001804

ISBN 978-4-8053-1214-8

Distributed by

North America, Latin America & Europe
Tuttle Publishing
364 Innovation Drive
North Clarendon, VT 05759-9436 U.S.A.
Tel: 1 (802) 773-8930
Fax: 1 (802) 773-6993
info@tuttlepublishing.com
www.tuttlepublishing.com

Japan
Tuttle Publishing
Yaekari Building, 3rd Floor
5-4-12 Osaki
Shinagawa-ku
Tokyo 141 0032
Tel: (81) 3 5437-0171
Fax: (81) 3 5437-0755
sales@tuttle.co.jp
www.tuttle.co.jp

Asia Pacific
Berkeley Books Pte. Ltd.
61 Tai Seng Avenue #02-12
Singapore 534167
Tel: (65) 6280-1330
Fax: (65) 6280-6290
inquiries@periplus.com.sg
www.periplus.com

First edition
16 15 14 13 12   6 5 4 3 2 1
1204CP

Printed in Singapore

TUTTLE PUBLISHING® is a registered trademark of Tuttle Publishing, a division of Periplus Editions (HK) Ltd.

INTRODUCTION

Do you believe in ghosts?

Generations upon generations of Japanese did. Many still do. This book is a collection of a nation's "conventional wisdom" on the topic. We didn't make up a single ghost or story that appears in the pages that follow. They're all completely "real" — real in the sense that they inhabit the historical and literary record. We scoured these for tales of terror from beyond the grave, pulling together as much background and context as we could. The sole embellishments are the the new illustrations that adorn each profile.

While this may be a survival guide, get any thoughts of playing junior exorcist out of your head right now. The best you can hope for in the event of an encounter is to make it out alive. And if generations of ghost stories are to be believed, there are plenty of opportunities for ghost encounters in the islands of Japan. They were, and some say still are, very much a part of daily life there.

Yurei

The Japanese word for ghost is *yurei*. They are the souls of dead people, unable — or unwilling — to shuffle off this mortal coil for whatever reason. The general concept is similar to that of ghosts in the Western world: an ethereal essence of a formerly living being that remains after death. Just as in the West, some yurei haunt a specific person or place; others tend to roam freely.

But the similarities with foreign ghosts end there.

In the West, spooks come out for Halloween. In Japan, spirits of all kinds are most active during the summer months, for that is the time of the Obon holiday — the festival of the dead, when the spirits of loved ones are welcomed home from the hereafter for their annual visit.

Abroad, ghosts come in all shapes and sizes. Some are terrifying, like the Headless Horseman in *The Legend of Sleepy Hollow*. Others are content merely to haunt, such as Banquo's quietly accusatory phantom in *Macbeth*. There's even *Casper, the Friendly Ghost*.

Japan's yurei are many things, but "friendly" isn't the first word that comes to mind. Not every yurei is dangerous, but they are all driven by emotions so uncontrollably powerful that they have taken on a life of their own: rage, sadness, devotion, a desire for revenge, or just a firm belief that they are still alive.

The most famous yurei by far are the angry ghosts. A great many of these are (or were) women. You don't have to be female to become a yurei, but it seems to help. There isn't any hard and fast answer as to why this is, other than tradition, but it's easy to make an educated guess. The most popular ghost stories are tales of betrayal and revenge. In times of old women occupied a lower rung of the social ladder than men in society, making them convenient targets for all sorts of nasty behavior: trickery, betrayal, even murder. The more dutiful and loyal the woman, the more powerful her ghost and the sweeter the inevitable revenge against her tormentor. Payback, as they say, is a bitch.

Yurei are all about payback.

The Power of Onnen

Nobody ever lives a long, happy life, dies peacefully in bed surrounded by family, and comes back as a yurei. The most dangerous yurei have an axe to grind — preferably against the neck of whoever it was that cut their lives short in the first place. They are fueled by a potent mix of fury, sadness, and a desire for revenge. What takes many words to describe in English takes only one in Japanese: *onnen*.

An onnen is a mix of grudge and anger so powerful that it takes on a literal life of its own, transforming into a force capable of exerting a malevolent influence on the physical world. This is the fuel that feeds an angry ghost.

The insidious thing about an onnen is that you don't have to have been the one who actually instigated the grudge to be affected. Like a virus, anyone who comes into contact is at risk. Even the totally innocent. That's what makes the prospect of a yurei encounter so terrifying. They are the paranormal equivalent of landmines, invisible and still dangerous long after they were first sown.

According to Japanese tradition, shaped by centuries and millennia of native Shinto and imported Buddhist beliefs, it is believed that the soul is eternal, passing from the body of the deceased into the world of the dead. But to do so it must remain in a purgatory of sorts among the living for a certain period of time. It is during this period that fierce emotion, whether positive or negative, can bind a soul to this world. The deeper the emotion, the higher the chance of a soul manifesting itself among the living again.

In the vast majority of cases, a yurei will remain trapped in our world until its onnen is soothed or appeased in some way. But there are exceptions. Some are so powerful that they remain in our world permanently. These represent the most dangerous sorts of spirits in Japanese folklore. A perfect example of this can be seen in Taira no Masakado (page 40), the samurai warrior whose furious spirit is believed to reside in downtown Tokyo even today, a millennium after his death on the battlefield. The perceived power of onnen is precisely why his shrine has remained untouched for centuries, even though it sits atop what is now some of the most expensive real estate on the planet.

Yurei vs Yokai

In times of old the inhabitants of Japan believed that they shared their country with all sorts of otherworldly inhabitants. These ranged from *kami* (gods), to *oni* (monstrously powerful ogres), to *bakemono* and *yokai* (shape-shifters and other supernatural creatures).

The yurei are often lumped together with the yokai, which we cover in great detail in the predecessor to this book, *Yokai Attack! The Japanese Monster Survival Guide*. In a nutshell, yokai are the things that go bump in Japan's night: mythical creatures from fairy tales and folklore. But make no bones about it yurei and yokai are very different sorts of things.

There's actually a handy rule of thumb for differentiating the two. A yurei is a someone. A yokai is a something. Yurei is a specific term. Yokai is quite general.

A yurei can cause all sorts of phenomena, from audible and visible manifestations to outright attacks. On the other hand, yokai tend to be personifications of phenomena themselves, attempts to put names and faces to inexplicable happenings. Yurei are human spirits, whereas many yokai are considered lesser gods of the natural world.

Another critical difference: yokai often come across as mischievous, in some cases borderline cute. Rotund *tanuki* (raccoon-dog) statues and glowering *tengu* (mountin goblin) masks are common sorts of decorations in Japan. But you will almost never find a yurei painting gracing a home or establishment. They have an unparalleled ability to put the fear into even modern-day Japanese.

Historical Portrayals Of Yurei

The undisputed originator of the distinctive appearance of a yurei, at least graphically, is the artist Maruyama Okyo. His 1750 painting Ghost of Oyuki featured many of the characteristics of a "stereotypical" yurei: long, unkempt hair, an ethereally pale pallor, a floating body that lacks clearly defined legs. Most importantly, it's a woman. And like all great ghost tales, it's even supposedly based on a true story: in this case, a vision of the artist's mistress, who died young and returned to him for a last visit in a dream.

But don't get the mistaken impression that Okyo was the first person to see a ghost in Japan.

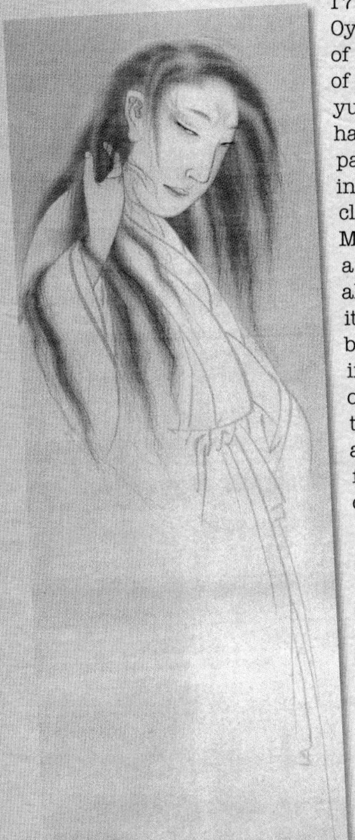

An 18th century painting by Okyo's student Nagasawa Rosetsu, in a style inspired by that of his master.

A haunting 18th century painting by a pair of brothers, Goshun (who did the ghost) and Keibun (who did the willows on the mounting.)

all sorts of mass entertainment. Elaborate kabuki stage productions complete with special effects rivaled modern-day Hollywood blockbusters for their ability to put people in seats. But feudal Japan wasn't a democracy, and strict regulations forbid playwrights from portraying anything that might be seen as critical of the Shogun or his government. Ghost tales came to the rescue. Stories of servants mistreated by their masters, loyal wives betrayed by their husbands, or innocent villagers killed for sport by aristocrats were framed not as social commentary but rather as "ghost-exploitation" stories, allowing artists free reign to wryly comment on contemporary issues without incurring the wrath of the authorities. (This wasn't idle paranoia; criticizing the status quo, even indirectly, landed many a writer in jail — or worse.)

Not by a long shot. His painting merely represented a longtime interest in the phenomenon that was clawing its way into the mainstream of popular culture. The "golden age" of the Japanese ghost story, when the conventions of the genre were clearly laid out, came in the early half of the 19th century.

Japan's booming middle class formed the perfect market for

Another popular way of letting off some steam, particularly during the sultry summer months, was a parlor game called Hyaku Monogatari — the "Night of a Hundred Tales." The idea was simple: gathering a group of friends and freaking each other out with ghost stories until the sun came up. Discussing weird happenings in the dead of night undoubtedly amplified the thrills and chills, as did rumors that a real ghost or creature would appear in the room after a successful session. It was interactive entertainment centuries before the advent of televisions, control pads, and keyboards.

Yurei culture

Some of the yurei tales portrayed in this book are based on the lives — and deaths — of people who actually existed. Others are obvious flights of fancy. More than a few are a little of both. But they form the bedrock of what could be called "yurei culture" in Japan.

Ghost stories represent some of Japan's greatest works of literature and entertainment. Nearly every Japanese has heard of Oiwa-san from the *Horror at Yotsuya* or Okiku, the Plate-Counting Ghost, for example. From the nearly thousand-year-old *Tale of Genji* to the 18th century chiller *Tales of Moonlight and Rain*, from Akira Kurosawa's *Rashomon* to "J-Horror" movies like *Ring* and *The Grudge*, it seems ghosts still have the power to terrify Japanese and non-Japanese alike.

Knowing what frightens someone is a wonderful window into their personality — which makes knowing what frightens an entire nation of people a powerful tool for understanding what makes them tick.

Using This Book

There are a lot of yurei and haunted spots out there, so we've organized things for easy under-standing — the better to help you make it through any close encounters.

Chapter 1 focuses on the most famous female ghosts. Chapter 2 collects stories of angry ghosts. Chapter 3 focuses on spirits driven by sadness or despair rather than fury. Chapter 4 covers Japan's

scariest haunted spots, including information about how to get to them. Chapter 5 details dangerous games that can bring people into contact with the spirit world. Chapter 6 showcases some of Japan's most famous encounters with the supernatural. And Chapter 7? Well, let's just say it's a vision of what lays in store for all of us. It explains what happens when things go "right" and your eternal soul passes into the afterlife without turning yurei.

So let us ask you again: do you believe in ghosts? Trust us, the yurei don't care. They're here, and they aren't letting you off the hook that easily. Fortunately for you, everything you need to know about them is contained right between the covers of this book. So what are you waiting for? You'd better get started. And if you have to sleep with the lights on for a while, just look on the bright side: you aren't alone.

—Hiroko Yoda & Matt Alt
Tokyo, Japan
2012

KNOW YOUR YUREI

Yurei come in many shapes and forms. Yet there are traits and accoutrements common to many of them. Very few if any yurei possess all of these features, but each is strongly indicative of things from beyond the grave. We created this composite illustration to help familiarize you with the basics. Think of it as a "generic Japanese ghost."

1. Triangular headdress.
This archaic Buddhist funerary headdress hasn't been used in actual funerals for generations, but it is a standard prop for yurei.

2. Long, stringy, unkempt hair.
Hair, particularly hair that grows out of control, is a common feature of Japanese ghost stories.

3. Crazed/aggrieved expression.
What, were you expecting a warm smile?

4. Dangling hands.
Don't let the limp wrists fool you. They aren't an indication of weakness, but rather a signal that you're dealing with the dead.

5. White kimono.
The kimono of the dead are folded in the opposite manner of that of living people. (For example, the usual left-over-right lapel style would be right-over-left for a body at a funeral.)

6. Hitodama.
Although literally translated as "human souls," these weird fireballs are generally considered manifestations of ghostly phenomena rather than actual spirits. They are commonly seen alongside yurei.

7. Lack of feet.
The absence of a physical connection to the ground is a hallmark yurei characteristic.

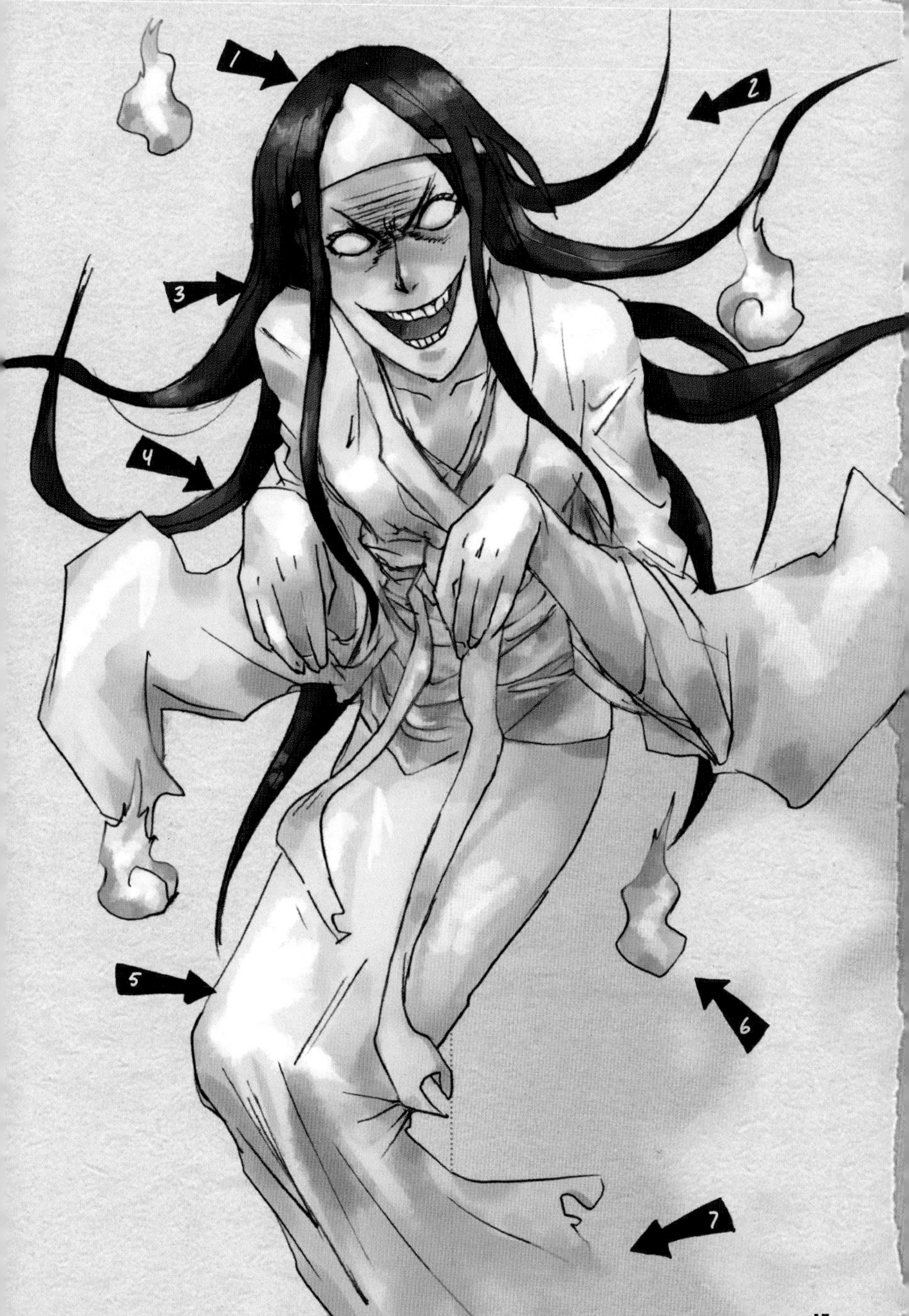
1
2
3
4
5
6
7

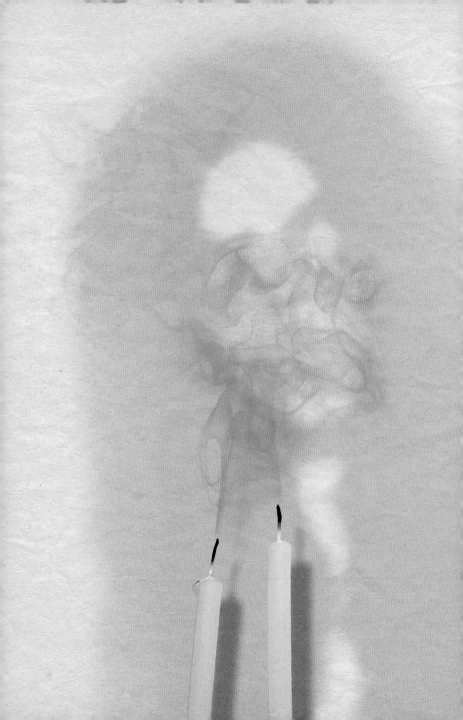

CHAPTER ONE
Sexy & Scary

Some of Japan's most famous ghosts are women. These ladies put the "fatale" in "femme fatale."

OIWA

Name in Japanese: 於岩
Origin: Yotsuya Kaidan ("The Horror of Yotsuya")
Gender: Female
Date of Death: 1636
Age at death: Early 20s (Estimated)
Cause of death: Suicide
Type of ghost: Onryo
Distinctive features: Right side of face horribly scarred; Bald spots, with hair falling out in clumps; Occasionally portrayed as having only one eye
Place of internment: Myogyo-ji Cemetery, Tokyo
Location of haunting: Tokyo
Form of Attack: Constant manifestations. Provocation of injuries similar to her own.
Existence: Based in part on a true story
Threat Level: Extremely High

Claim to Fame

Hands down the single most famous ghost chronicled in the pages of this book. A supernatural superstar for well over a century, she has inspired legions of imitators — most recently Sadako, from the hit J-Horror novel and film series "Ring." Without a doubt, her ragged tresses and ruined face are the first thing many Japanese think of when they hear the word "yurei."

The Story

Coherent English summaries of Oiwa's story are few and far between. Read on and you'll understand why. Her most famous turn, the 1825 kabuki "Tokaido Yotsuka Kaidan," packs more twists into a few hours than a modern TV miniseries does into an entire season.

Oiwa is married to Iyemon, a disgraced samurai. After the couple has yet another row, Oiwa's father takes her home. Iyemon sets up a private meeting to beg for forgiveness, but Oiwa's father reveals proof that Iyemon stole money from his former government job. Enraged, Iyemon stabs Oiwa's father to death.

Oiwa's sister Osode is happily married to a loyal man named Yomoshichi. But Naosuke, the neighborhood medicine peddler, carries a torch for her. In a coincidence of the sort that only happens in kabuki, Naosuke picks this very night to murder his rival. (Getting all this?)

When Oiwa and Osode stumble on the respective scenes, Iyemon and Naosuke convince the two that the victims were killed in robberies. They console the ladies by promising they'll get their revenge on whatever villains perpetrated these foul deeds. And so life goes on, with Iyemon and Oiwa reunited, and Osode and Naosuke able to court Osode.

But fickle, philandering Iyemon quickly loses interest in Oiwa after she gives birth to their child, and begins focusing his amorous attentions on Ume, the daughter of a high-ranking government official. Frustrated by his marital status, Iyemon bribes a masseuse to seduce his wife in an attempt to trump up grounds for divorce.

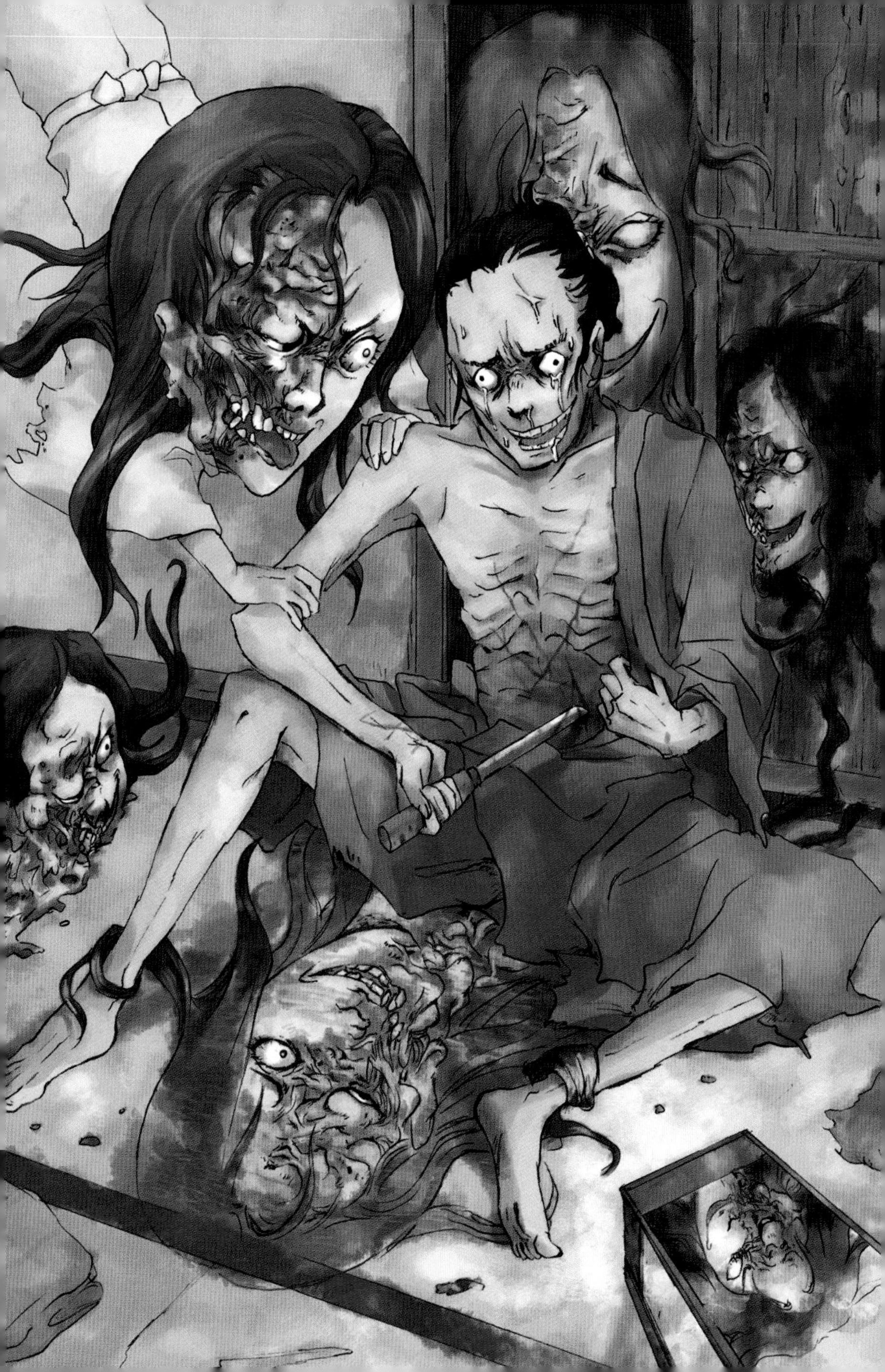

Iyemon doing his thing, on the cover of the program, from a 1925 Kabuki production of "Yotsuya Kaidan."

Meanwhile, Ume takes matters into her own hands by sending Oiwa a little baby-shower gift: a powerful poison disguised as a medicinal cream.

The poison does its job: the skin sloughs off Oiwa's face and her hair pulls out in clumps, leaving her horribly disfigured. The masseuse can't bring himself to carry out the deed, and blows the lid off of Ieymon's intrigue as Oiwa gazes upon her ruined face in a mirror.

She commits suicide while coldly proclaiming a curse on the soul of the man who'd wronged her. Iyemon responds by nailing her corpse and that of a lawman (who he also kills after the man comes sniffing around about a certain vial of missing poison) to a door, and hurls them into the Kanda River to make it seem as if the pair had died in a love-suicide.

The Attack

Things take a turn from "soap opera" to "spooky" on Iyemon and Ume's wedding night, when Oiwa's furious apparition manifests in the conjugal suite, causing Iyemon to lash out wildly and accidentally kill his bride. In the hallway another appearance causes him to mistakenly cut down her father. Pursued by the remainder of the household, he hurls Ume's mother and her servant into a canal, where both drown.

Meanwhile, Naosuke finally gets his wish when Osode agrees to sleep with him. But the minute the pair bed down, Yomoshichi's ghost appears in the room. Naosuke wrestles with the phantom intruder, accidentally killing Osode in the melee. And in yet another twist, it turns out that she was none other than his long-lost sister! Shocked (and presumably grossed out), Naosuke commits suicide.

Iyemon continues to be confronted by the deformed visage of his dead wife; she appears everywhere, even in the form of the paper lanterns swinging over his head. On the run and destitute, he attempts fishing for some food, only to hook the door he'd thrown in the river earlier, still festooned with the now horribly rotting corpses of his victims. Ghostly voices fill his ears as he runs far, far from the city to an isolated cottage on the ominously named Snake Mountain. Still he is unable to escape. Oiwa's face haunts him from the windows, walls, floor, even the trees and vines outside. He tries committing suicide, but her phantom hand stays his blade again and again.

Iyemon, by this point a total gibbering wreck, finally gets a lucky break when Yomoshichi pops up and puts him out of his misery. Making this one beautiful happy ending... If you're an angry ghost, anyway.

Surviving an Encounter

You're in big, big trouble if Oiwa is on your case. In spite of the fact that she is ostensibly a fictional character, she is believed to be as potent and dangerous a force today as when she first manifested. But you can content yourself with the fact that Oiwa doesn't want her victims dead — she just wants to make their lives a living hell.

Unconfirmed stories abound of those who become involved with her story being injured — often those who portray her in kabuki productions, but the cast and crews of television and film as well. For this reason, it is customary for anyone involved in a production of Yotsuya Kaidan to visit Oiwa's grave, at Myogyo-ji temple in the Sugamo district of Tokyo, to show their respects.

Want a little extra insurance? No problem. Visit the Tamiya Shrine, which is located on the site of Oiwa's family home in Yotsuya. For a fee, the priest there will perform a custom-tailored Shinto exorcism ceremony to cut any ties one might have to Oiwa's eternally furious spirit.

DONT WORRY: WE WENT AHEAD AND DID THIS. (REALLY!) - HIROKO AND MATT.

Analysis

In creating his portrayal of Oiwa for the 1825 kabuki production of Yotsuya Kaidan, the playwright Tsuruya Nanboku IV synthesized elements from several real-life murder cases (one of which really did involve a samurai nailing his wife and her lover to a door!)

Within the next few years, five people associated with the play would die under mysterious circumstances — including Nanboku. Curse or coincidence? You make the call.

Know Your Lantern

Oiwa's manifestation as a lantern is often mistaken for the very similar-looking yokai known as *bura-bura* or *baké-chochin* (see *Yokai Attack!*). The key to telling the difference: look for hair. Yokai lanterns tend not to have any.

Hokusai's famous rendering of Oiwa, is often mistaken for a Bura-Bura haunted lantern. 1831 woodblock print.

Sexy & Scary: 02

OKIKU

Name in Japanese: お菊
Origin: "Bancho Sara-yahsiki" (The Plate Mansion of Bancho), 1741
A.K.A. The Plate-Counting Ghost
Gender: Female
Date at death: Various. Early 1500s? Mid 1600s?
Age at death: Early 20s (Estimated)
Cause of death: Murder
Type of ghost: Onryo
Distinctive features: Apparently normal-looking young woman; Voice / apparition manifests from a well
Location of haunting: Various, including Himeji and Edo
Form of Attack: Incessant counting
Existence: Fictional. We think.
Threat Level: Low

Claim To Fame

Wells, particularly abandoned ones, are considered scary sorts of places all over the world—they're dark, they're dank, they're deep, they're potentially filled with who-only-knows-what sorts of creepy crawlies. But they enjoy a special sort of significance in Japanese tales of terror. Even modern-day fare such as Koji Suzuki's *Ring* or Haruki Murakami's *The Wind-Up Bird Chronicle* portray wells as channels of supernatural activity. While the story you are about to read certainly isn't the first example of a haunted well in Japanese folklore, it is undoubtedly the most well known.

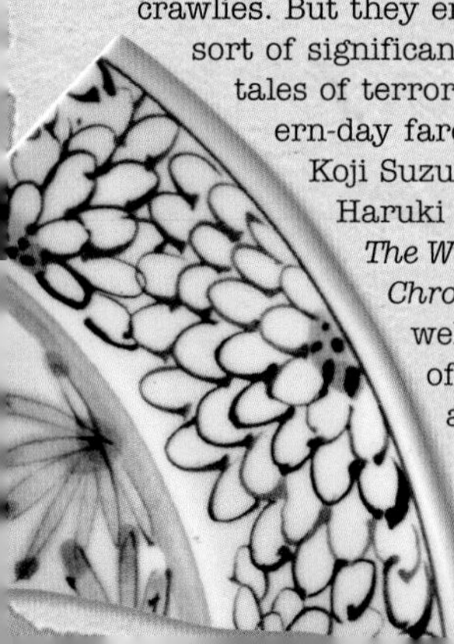

The Story

Long ago in the province of Harima, there was a beautiful woman by the name of Okiku. She worked as a maidservant for a samurai by the name of Aoyama Tessan, a vassal of the family that ruled the province from their seat of power in Himeji Castle. Tessan dreamed of ruling the province himself, and hatched a scheme to poison the lord of the castle at a party. But word of the plan leaked to its intended target, forcing Tessan to abandon the plot.

While nobody suspected Tessan's role, the lord knew there must be a traitor nearby. So he ordered his right-hand man, Danshiro, to uncover the mole. Danshiro quickly realized that Okiku was to blame, and this is where the plot thickens, for Danshiro had long carried an unrequited flame for the girl. Confronting her with the information, he offered to cover up her involvement if she would consent to being his lover. Okiku flat out refused. And so Danshiro hatched a plot of his own: he hid one of a set of ten priceless heirloom plates, then publicly blamed Okiku for losing it, essentially giving him carte blanche to deal with her as he wished. After killing the girl, he threw her bound body down a well.

From that point on, night after night, the voice of ghostly counting began to issue from the

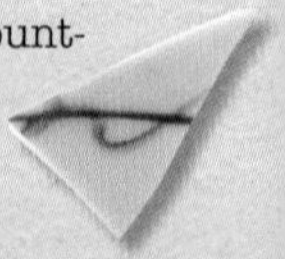

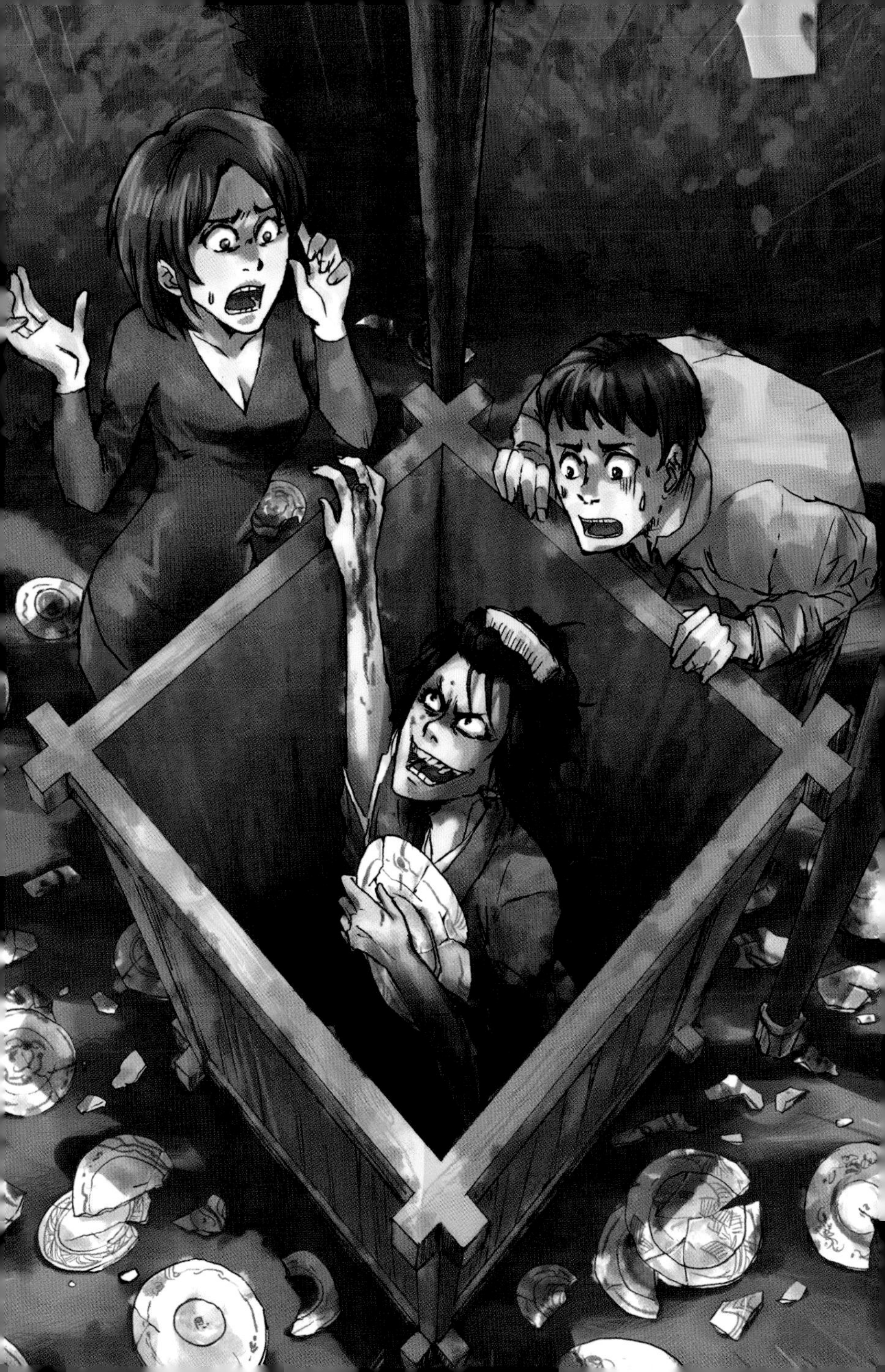

well, slowly reaching "nine" before breaking off and beginning again, over and over, night after night. Eventually, word of the entire sordid affair reached the ears of the lord of the castle, who ordered Tessan's suicide by disembowelment and dissolution of his family holdings.

There's another version of the story that takes place in Edo. In the quarter of the city that was home to higher-ranking servants of the Shogun stood a mansion owned by Lord Aoyama, the representative of the province of Harima. Aoyama had arrived in Edo with a precious family heirloom — a set of ten priceless Delftware plates from the Netherlands. When his kind but clumsy young maidservant Okiku carelessly dropped and shattered one of the treasures, the infuriated Aoyama responded by cutting off her middle finger as punishment for the lost plate and locking her in the mansion's dungeon. Somehow, Okiku managed to work her way out of her imprisonment, and flung herself to her death in the mansion's well to escape further abuse.

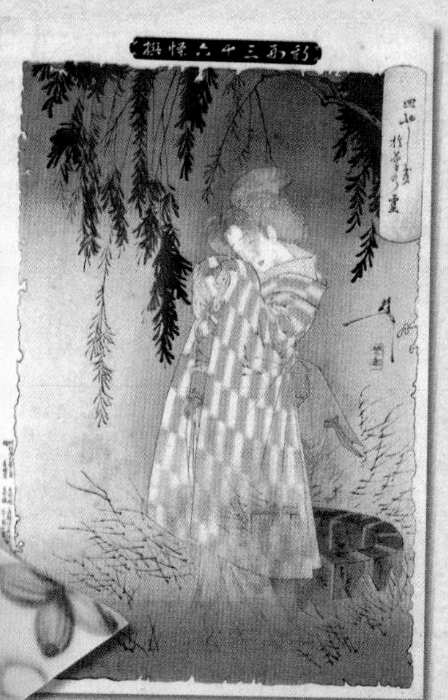

Yoshitoshi's classic portrayal of her weeping apparition materializing over the well. 1890 woodblock print.

The Attack

No matter the tale, Okiku's manifestations always follow the same pattern: night after night, an eerie voice issues from her well, counting slowly from one to nine again and again until dawn.

In the case of Lord Aoyama, things took on an even more sinister note when his first child was born missing a middle finger.

Surviving An Encounter

Realizing this was no normal haunting, Lord Aoyama called in the abbot of the local temple to read holy sutras over the well. But the relentless counting continued unabated. One night, perhaps out of sheer frustration, the abbot shouted "ten" at the end of yet another of Okiku's enumerations.

"Finally!" cried the voice from the well. And disappeared...

So there you have it. This is an easy one. Should a wailing, plate-counting ghost take up residence in your well, simply:

a) Grit your teeth and listen to her count.

b) At the proper moment, shout the digit that would logically come next in sequence.

c) Congratulate yourself on a spirit well appeased.

If the above doesn't work:

d) Consider moving.

Analysis

There appears to be no fear of bodily harm from a manifestation of this sort, but the real issue isn't the ghost. It's the way in which she died. Okiku is essentially a stand-in for every servant who's been mistreated by a master, and a warning to those with power to always treat those beneath them with respect. While shouting "ten" at the end of Okiku's count caused her to disappear, the mark she left on Aoyama's son can be seen as a symbol of the ripple effect violence has through the generations.

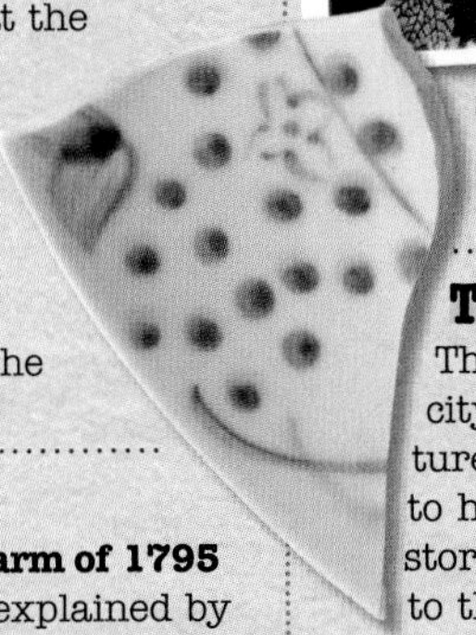

Trivia

Okiku-Mushi: The Swarm of 1795

For reasons yet to be explained by science, a species of black swallowtail butterfly known as *shako-ageha* hatched in massive numbers that year, with the resulting cocoons filling the walls of wells throughout the Harima area. Hanging in the darkness on filaments of web that resembled tiny ropes, the pupating insects evoked the torments poor young Okiku had suffered, and locals dubbed them Okiku-mushi — "Okiku bugs." The nickname remains even today.

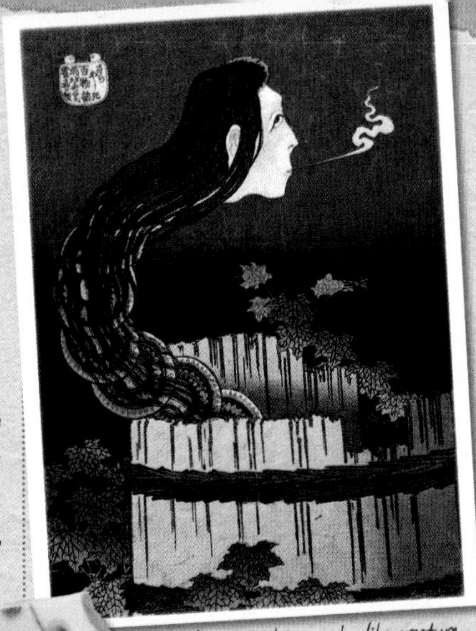

Hokusai's eerie take: a snake-like creature with a body made of plates, exhaling a ghostly breath. 1830 woodblock print.

The Real Deal

The temple of Chokyu-ji in the city of Hikone of Shiga prefecture owns a set of plates said to have belonged to Okiku. The story goes that they were given to the temple by her mother, so that the priests could perform a *kuyo* (funeral rite) over them and release her daughter's connection to them. Today only six of the original set remain.

An Okiku-Mushi takes wing.

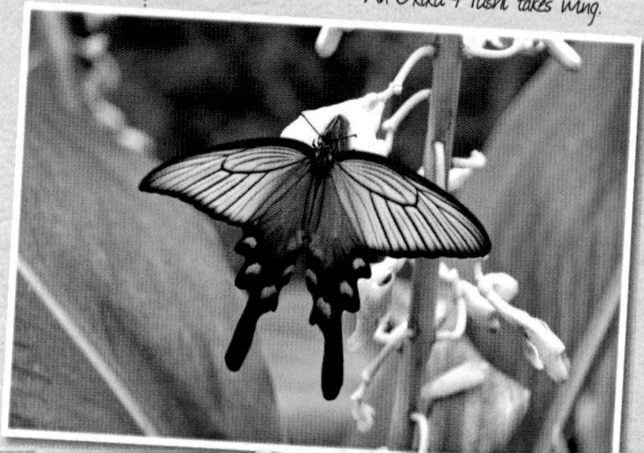

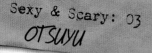

OTSUYU

Name in Japanese: お露
Origin: "Botan Doro" ("The Tale of the Peony Lantern")
Gender: Female
Translation of name: "Morning dew"
Age at death: 16 or 17 (estimated)
Cause of death: Heartbreak
Distinctive features: Superficially, a normal-seeming young woman carrying a peony lantern (see below). Often accompanied by servant, Oyone
Place of internment: Shin-Banzuin Cemetery, Tokyo
Location of haunting: Nezu, Tokyo
Form of Attack: Carnal pleasures
Existence: Believed to be fictional
Threat Level: Medium

Claim to Fame

Next to Oiwa (p.16) and Okiku (p.20) she is one of Japan's "big three" famous ghosts. But in contrast to Oiwa's furious retributions, Otsuyu's tale is one of grave affections.

The Story

The daughter of a *hatamoto*, a high-ranking samurai in the service of the Shogun, beautiful young Otsuyu's fate was sealed after a chance introduction to a masterless *ronin* named Hagiwara Shinzaburo. It was love at first sight for both sides, but a lowly ronin could never ask for the hand of a hatamoto's daughter in marriage — least of all from Otsuyu's father, a notoriously stern fellow with a nasty reputation for skewering those who displeased him.

For weeks and months, Shinzaburo begged the neighborhood physician who had introduced the pair to chaperone another visit to Otsuyu; but realizing that the smoldering fire he had inadvertently sparked could well erupt into a conflagration that would consume him as well, the wise but craven doctor hemmed and hawed and made excuses.

Pining for a true love she believed had abandoned her, Otsuyu began to waste away and died, followed shortly thereafter by her heartbroken maidservant Oyone.

Learning of Otsuyu's untimely death, Shinzaburo's misery knew no bounds. He inscribed her name on a memorial tablet and placed offerings before it daily. When Obon, the festival of the dead, rolled around that summer, he laid food and lanterns before the tablet as was the custom, and prepared for another night of lamenting love lost.

No sooner than Shinzaburo had lit the lanterns than he heard the clack-clack of wooden geta on the street outside his house. Sliding open a window, he caught sight of a pair of beautiful ladies. The younger of the two, apparently a servant, illuminated the way with a peony lantern. Shinzaburo rubbed his eyes. Could it be? There was no question about it: it was Otsuyu and her maid!

"I thought you were dead!" he cried.

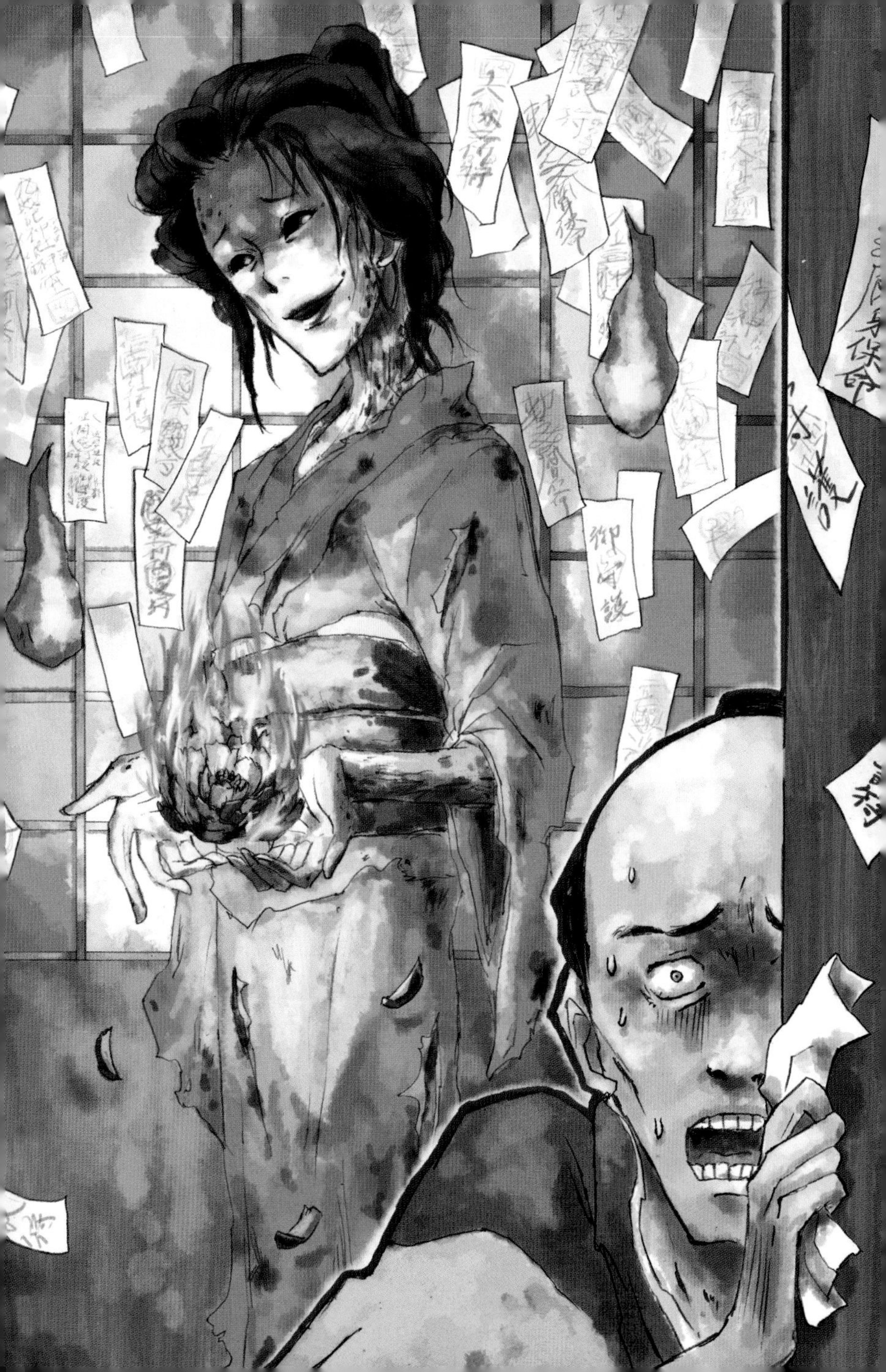
御守護

"And I you," replied Otsuyu in equal astonishment.

Shinzaburo quickly invited the pair into his home, where the trio pieced together how both sides had been deceived to keep them apart. They plotted through the night and separated at daybreak, with a promise that they would soon never part again. For seven nights — always at night — Otsuyu and her maidservant returned to cement their plans.

Shinzaburo's neighbor, a fortune-teller, overheard the regular mid-night chatter and grew suspicious. He peered into Shinzaburo's home through a crack in the wall. What he saw chilled him to the bone. For Shinzaburo was carrying on an animated conversation with a pair of desiccated corpses, their kimono stained and tattered, their eye sockets gaping holes.

The next day, the fortune-teller confronted Shinzaburo, who reluctantly confessed his plans to elope. But he refused to believe what the fortune-teller told him about Otsuyu's true form. After much back and forth, the fortune teller convinced Shinzaburo to pay a surprise visit to the neighborhood where Otsuyu claimed to live. Shinzaburo wandered from door to door asking after the pair; but the neighbors claimed no knowledge of any young women living there. On his way home, Shinzaburo took a short cut through the local cemetery at Shin-Banzuin temple, and that is when he spotted them: not the girls, but a pair of fresh grave-markers bearing the names "Otsuyu" and "Oyone."

Rushing back, the terrified Shinzaburo consulted the abbot of his local temple, who prescribed consecrated ofuda talisman slips to be pasted over his abode's every opening to keep the spirits at bay. In spite of his feelings for Otsuyu, Shinzaburo knew he had no choice but to oblige. Night after night, he desperately tried to ignore the heartbreaking wails of Otsuyu and Oyone, in turns angry and piteous, issuing from beyond his walls.

Desperate to help her mistress, the ghostly Oyone threatened Shinzaburo's servants, a married couple who had long served the ronin. With their own fates at stake, the husband and wife bargained with the ghost, demanding 100 ryo — an astounding sum — in return for betraying their master and livelihood.

The rest is history. It isn't known where or how Oyone obtained the money, but obtain it she did; and Shinzaburo's treacherous servants peeled just one ofuda from a crack in the wall of their master's residence.

The next morning, Shinzaburo was found dead in his bedchamber — his face a grimace of terror, and beside him the skeleton of a long-dead woman, its arms thrown around his neck in a final, eternal embrace. At the behest of the abbot with whom he had first consulted, Shinzaburo was buried alongside Otsuyu and Oyone.

The Attack

A product of a more genteel era, *The Tale of the Peony Lantern* is circumspect as to what precisely

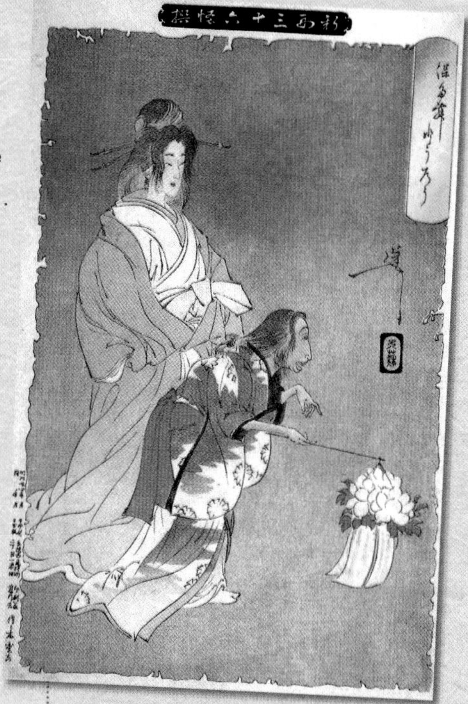

Yoshitoshi's interpretation of "Botan Doro" from his 36 Ghosts series, showning Otsuyu with Oyone carrying a peony lantern.

occurred within the walls (and more specifically, the bedroom) of Shinzaburo's mansion, but one can surmise the general details.

Surviving an Encounter

Otsuyu's fate was inextricably linked to that of her lover; his death effectively released her from her bondage to this Earthly plane. But while you'll never run into Otsuyu herself, unrequited love is no less powerful a force today than it was in medieval Japan. Should you find yourself in a similar situation, take a page from Otsuyu's tale and stock up on consecrated *ofuda* talismans (for convenience, we have included samples on p. 188). Pasting them on doorways, window frames, and over potential entrances is the time-honored method for keeping out all sorts of bogeymen — and women — out of one's home. You are safe as long as they are in place.

A word of warning for frustrated teens and/or adventurous sorts. Ghost-chronicler Lafcaido Hearn said: "the spirit of the living is positive, the other negative. He whose bride is a ghost cannot live." (Remember, Shinzaburo did not die with a smile on his face.)

The Literary History

The Tale of the Peony Lantern first appeared in *Otogiboko* ("A Child's Amulet"), a 1666 collection of short stories by the Buddhist monk and writer Asai Ryoi, which consisted of adaptations of old Chinese tales reworked for a (then) modern Japanese audience. Although well known, Otsuyu's story didn't truly take off until 1884, when it was expanded into a *rakugo* performance — a form of one-man verbal stage show. This led to an 1892 kabuki version, a performance of which happened to be seen by the one and only Hearn, who retitled the story "A Passional Karma" and included it in his 1899 book *In Ghostly Japan*.

Trivia Notes

Peony lanterns are an archaic form of illumination once used during the Obon festival. They were so named for the faux peony petals affixed to their tops.

THE LADY ROKUJO

Name in Japanese: 六条御息所
Origin: *The Tale of Genji, ca. 1001*
Gender: *Female*
Date of Death: *Not applicable*
Age at death: *N/A*
Cause of death: *N/A*
Type of ghost: *Ikiryo*
Distinctive features: *N/A*
Location of haunting:
The bedchamber of Lady Aoi
Form of Attack: *Causing of illness*
Existence: *Fictional*
Threat Level: *High*

Claim to Fame

Spirits don't always represent the souls of the dead. A textbook case in point concerns that of Lady Rokujo, a high-ranking courtesan in the Imperial court of the Heian era, a thousand years ago. She was the source of an extremely rare and quite dangerous phenomenon known as an *ikiryo* — a sense of resentment so powerful that it separates from the human body to stalk victims, often without the owner's awareness or consent.

The Story

Lady Rokujo's story is one of the most famous episodes in *The Tale of Genji*, an eleventh-century work of fiction considered by many scholars to represent the world's first modern novel.

In the Imperial courts of Heian Japan, discretion and control of one's emotions were paramount

to the nobility. This even extended to romantic affairs, which were conducted obliquely, with the pursuer and his prospective partner separated by screens, communicating at first almost exclusively by exchanging lines of poetry. Even the ends of relationships followed a proscribed trajectory, with a man expected to sooner or later move on to another conquest and the woman expected to quietly acquiesce to his departure. Human nature being what it is, however, things didn't always play out according to protocol.

Married to the Crown Prince, Rokujo was but a hair's breadth away from becoming Empress of Japan. But the untimely death of her husband stripped Lady Rokujo of her rarefied status and consigned her to social purgatory at the ripe age of twenty-seven (an old biddy by the standards of the day). Then she found herself involved in a quiet but torrid affair with a younger man: the legendarily frisky aristocrat-playboy Hikaru Genji.

Ladykiller though he was, Genji quickly found himself swept away by Rokujo's beauty, wit, and elegance, and they carried on discreetly, if not in exact secrecy, for some time. But Genji, a rising star in the Imperial court, found himself increasingly saddled with duties both official (attending ceremonies) and unofficial (attending to the ever-growing number of conquests he'd racked up among the court's various ladies-in-waiting). And to top it off, he reconciled with his legal wife, the Lady Aoi, now

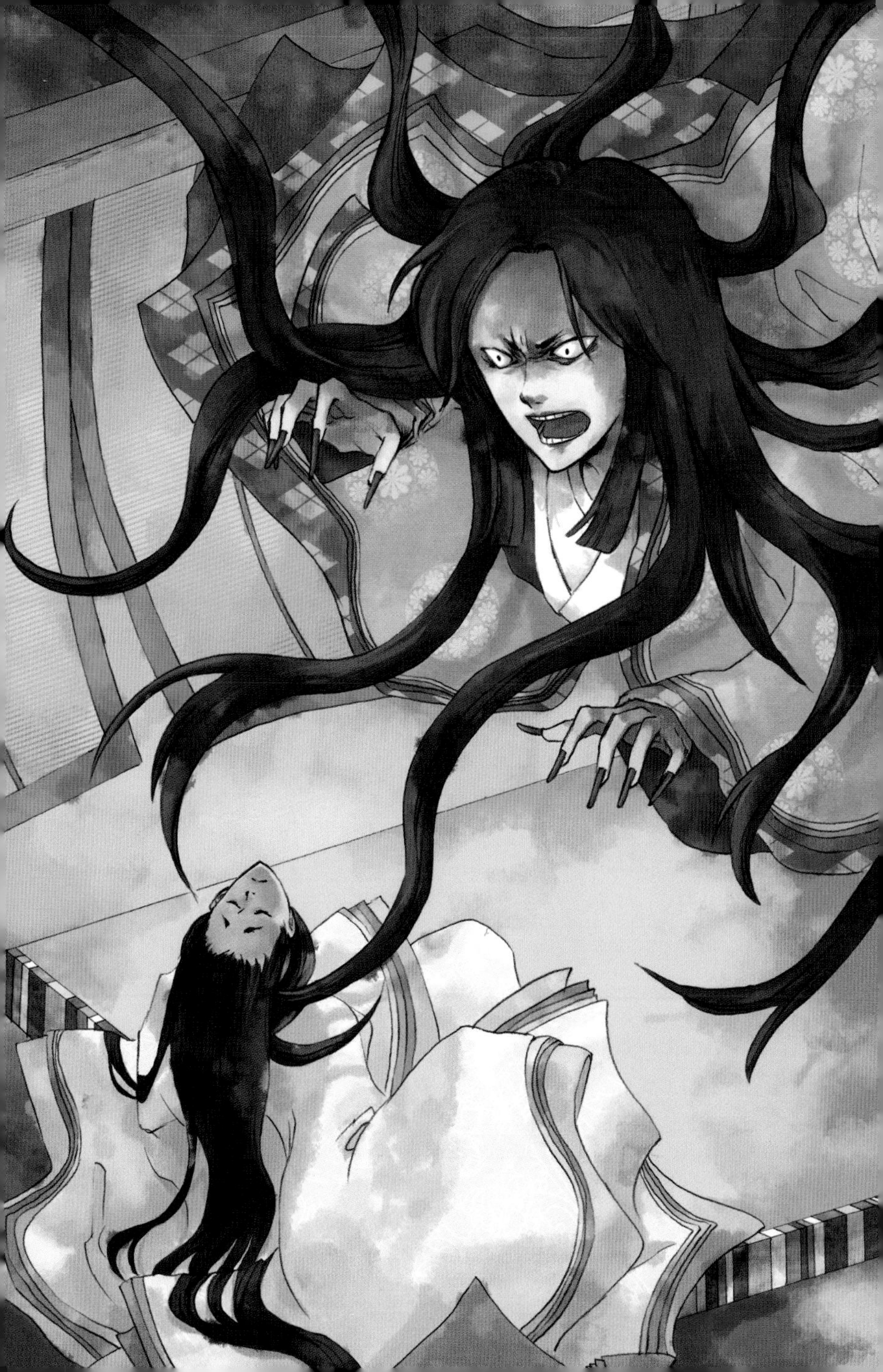

pregnant with his child. Sidelined from the one source of pleasure in her life, Lady Rokujo had already gone into a slow burn. But when a member of Aoi's retinue "dissed" her in public, Rokujo's resentment flared to life. Literally.

The Attack

Night after night, Lady Rokujo sank deep into dreams that dissolved into a repeating nightmare. In them, she found herself hovering over the sleeping Lady Aoi, whom she brutally snatched by the arm and proceeded to drag, strike, and whip against the walls of the bedchamber in fits of violence utterly alien to her reserved waking self.

These were no ordinary dreams. Aoi actually fell ill, taking to her sickbed for the remainder of her pregnancy, weeping inconsolably, and lapsing into choking fits. She wailed that "something alien" had entered into her. The best *onmyoji* exorcists money could buy divined that some tremendous accumulation of malice had erupted like a pox upon her soul, but were powerless to stop it; the best they could do was arrange a séance between Genji and the spirit inhabiting Aoi, in the hopes he could soothe its anger.

Surviving an Attack

The most insidious aspect of the ikiryo is that the individual generating it often remains completely unaware of the fatal effects their jealousy is having upon others. In this case, it is fortunate both that the Lady Rokujo connected her dreams with the sufferings of the Lady Aoi and that she was at heart a good woman. In spite of the humiliations she had suffered, Rokujo truly wished no physical harm upon Genji's wife or child. She focused her entire being on trying to banish her lover from her thoughts — no mean feat, as anyone who has deliberately tried to forget something will know. While Rokujo did not exactly succeed, the effort combined with the séance caused the ikiryo to release its hold. Unfortunately, though Aoi subsequently gave birth to a healthy baby boy, the combined strain of the pregnancy and psychic attack contributed to her death from natural causes several days later.

Fortunately, ikiryo attacks are extraordinarily uncommon. They cannot be generated at will, or by pure hate; in Lady Rokujo's case, it required the psychological "tinder" of abandonment and frustrated love, inflamed by an insult, to spark its existence. If you believe you or someone you love is suffering from an attack by an ikiryo, the best solution is to rack your brains to determine whom you may have wronged, and come up with a way to address

The English translation of "The Tale of Genji".

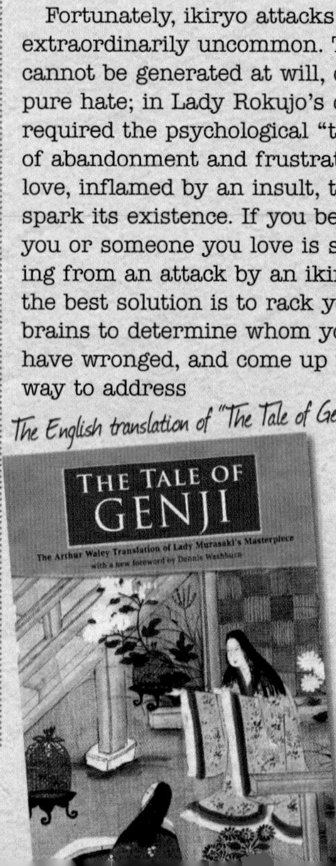
THE TALE OF GENJI
The Arthur Waley Translation of Lady Murasaki's Masterpiece
with a new foreword by Dennis Washburn

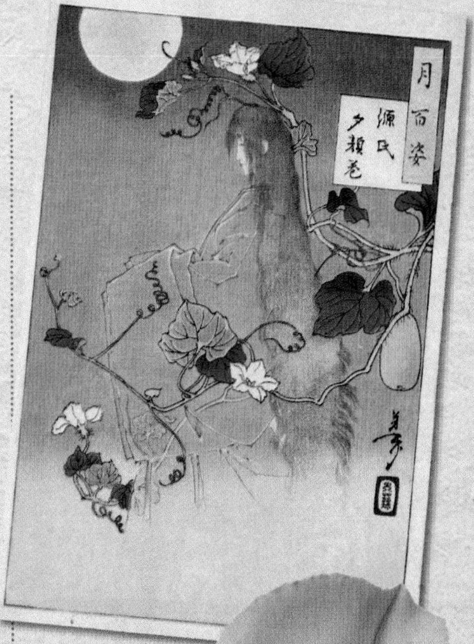
月百姿
源氏 夕顔巻

Aoi may not have been the only victim of Lady Rokujo's "living ghost." A girl named Yugao ("Moonflower"), another of Genji's girlfriends, died under mysterious circumstances as well. Print by Yoshitoshi, 1886.

the problem that does not involve shutting them out. In *The Tale of Genji*, the ikiryo is portrayed as much as the fault of Genji as that of the woman who unwittingly spawned it.

Trivia

Ikiryo are particularly problematic sorts of spooks — in many ways even more so than spirits of the dead. They are an extreme manifestation of that all too common human failing: holding a grudge. The negative energy and actions resulting from grudges are a powerful enough force even at levels below those needed to create a ferocious doppelganger. Addressing the hate and negativity that fuels an ikiryo is a far more difficult task than carrying out the measures needed to exorcize the spirits of the dead.

There is an intriguing potential connection between ikiryo and the yokai known as *nuke-kubi* (See *Yokai Attack!*). Nuke-kubi are female creatures whose heads separate from their bodies and take flight of their own accord. According to some theories, these yokai were once normal women who, through years of suppressing their feelings for another, have lost control of an important bit of their anatomy, which takes to the skies in search of their unrequited love. In these cases it is infatuation rather than hate that fuels the transformation.

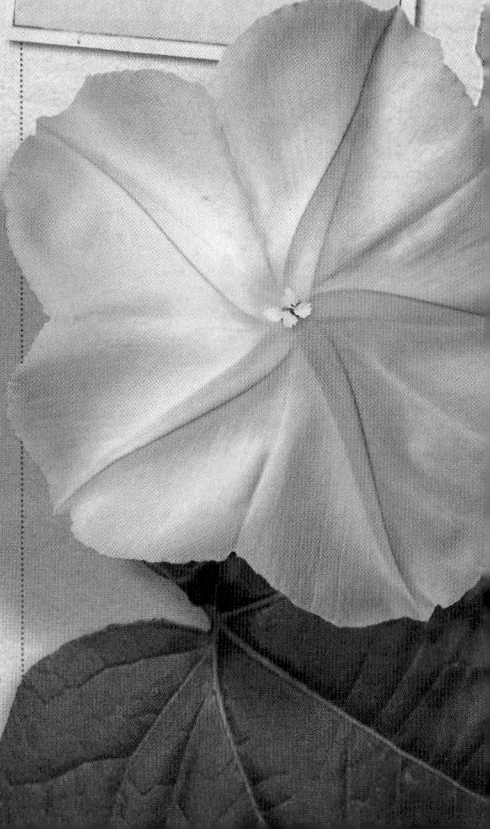

ISORA

Name in Japanese: 磯良
Origin: "The Kibitsu Cauldron" from Ugetsu Monogatari (Tales of Moonlight and Rain)
Gender: Female
Date of Death: ca. 1700s
Age at Death: 18?
Cause of Death: Heartbreak
Distinctive Features: A former beauty, rendered ghostly; Sunken eyes; Sallow skin; Wild hair
Place of internment: Okayama Prefecture
Location of haunting: Village of Arai (now Takasago), Hyogo Prefecture
Form of Attack: Manifestations; Brutal retaliation; Spiriting away of living humans; Forcible depilation (hair removal)
Existence: Fictional
Threat Level: High (if you happen to be married to her)

Claim to Fame:

Isora might not have the instant name recognition of other ghostly femme fatales like Okiku and Oiwa, but trust us, this is no spirit to be trifled with. Isora's is a caution- ary tale. Fooling around behind your spouse's back is one thing. But certain betrayals are so egre- gious that the only way to bury the hatchet is in the back of the offender's skull.

The Story

Long ago, in a far away village, lived a young man named Shotaro. He was the son of a farmer who worked very hard and built a small fortune, but he was not at all like his father. Instead of getting up early to till the fields, Shotaro stayed out late drinking sake and party- ing with the village girls. Finally, his parents got so fed up that they went and hired a matchmaker. They hoped that if they could just find the perfect wife for their son, he just might mend his wild ways. So they told the matchmaker to spare no cost in her search.

She looked long and hard before finally coming back with a match. Isora, the seventeen-year- old daughter of the head priest at a nearby shrine. When they heard about how wealthy Shotaro's family was, they were overjoyed. The fami- lies met and set a wedding day.

Because he was a priest, Isora's father decided to conduct a secret ceremony to determine the couple's fortune: the Kibitsu Cauldron Ritual. He assembled the shrine- maidens, made holy offerings to the gods, and boiled water in a sacred wooden cauldron. If Shotaro and Isora's future was bright, the boil- ing pot would make a deep sound, like a cow lowing. But the boiling pot made no sound at all. Even the insects outside stopped chirping.

It was a bad sign. But Isora's mother really wanted to see her married, and convinced her hus- band that the shrine-maidens had made some mistake. The wedding went ahead just as planned.

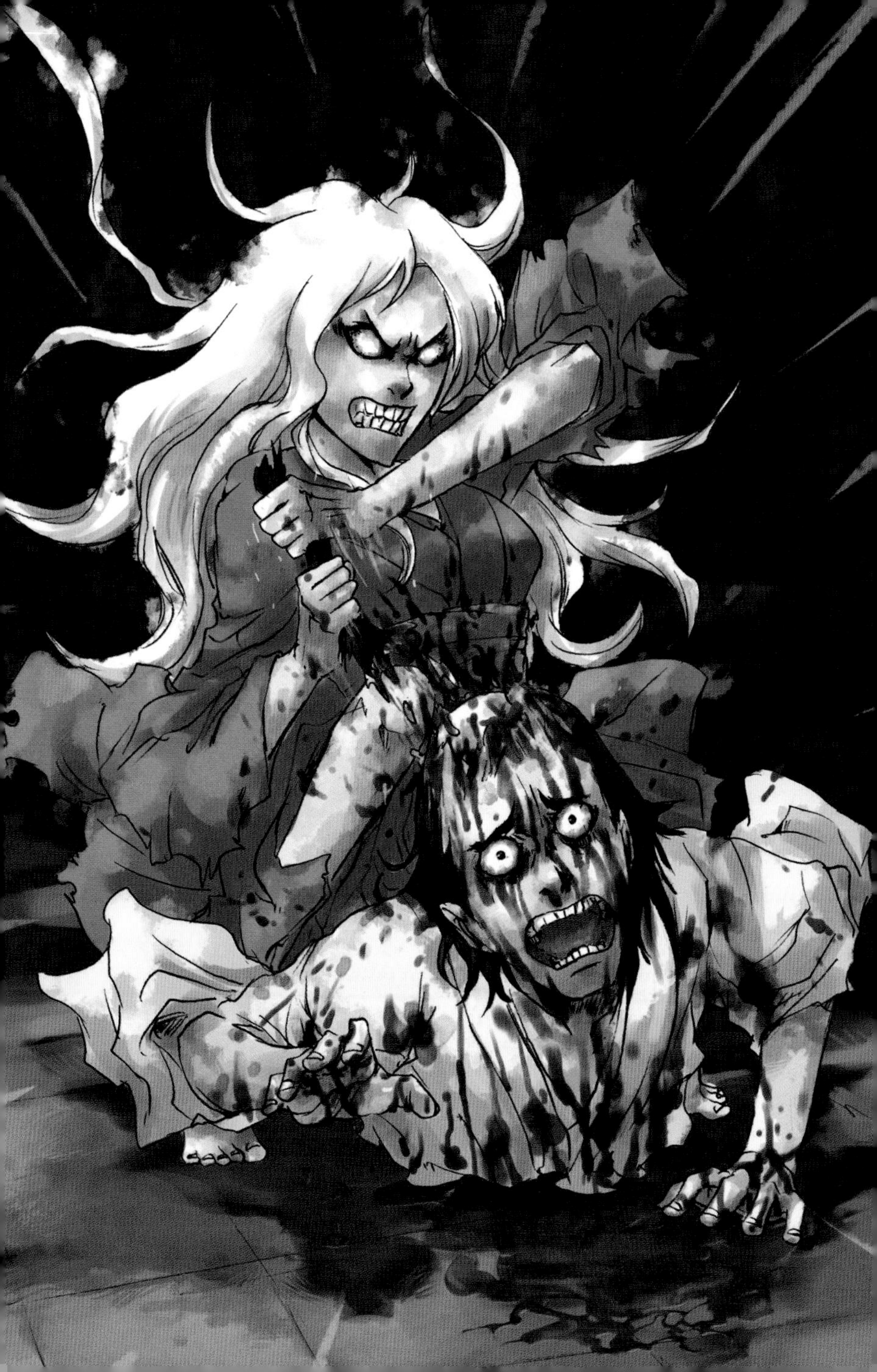

Shotaro and Isora settled into their new married life. At first, everything was great. Isora happened to be a crack koto floor-harp player and entertained the family with recitals. Even Shotaro seemed to have turned over a new leaf, staying home to listen to the poetry his devoted wife composed for him.

But you can't teach an old dog new tricks, and Shotaro was dog through and through. He launched into a poorly concealed affair with a lady of the night named Sodé, growing so infatuated that he actually bought out her contract and set her up in a private love nest. The more Isora told him to knock his sleazy antics off, the longer he stayed away from home. Shotaro's behavior even started embarrassing his own parents. They forbid him to leave the house until he pulled his act together.

After a week or so of being grounded, a chastened Shotaro emerged to plead for Isora's forgiveness. He promised to be faithful, and begged Isora for some money so that he could send Sodé away to begin life afresh in another city.

Isora saw the money as well spent if it meant having her husband back. She sold off her prized kimono and even asked her parents for a little extra money, just to make sure. Shotaro thanked her profusely... then ran off with Sodé, never to return.

Isora collapsed and took to her bed, unable to eat or sleep. In spite of the best medical care both families could buy, she slipped away soon after. She was gone; Shotaro had gotten away with it.

Or had he?

The Attack

Shotaro and Sodé settled into a new home in a distant village. She fell ill with what seemed to be a common flu, but quickly took a turn for the worse. She began hallucinating, then wailing of an "alien presence" in her chest, and a pain so fierce she could hardly stand it. After a week of agony, Sodé passed away.

Incidentally, her physical complaints are almost word for word those of Lady Aoi, the victim of Lady Rokujo's "living ghost" (p.28).

At the cemetery, a grief-stricken but incorrigible Shotaro wasted no time in chatting up a lovely lady tending the grave next to Sodé's. She offered to introduce Shotaro to her mistress, a beautiful woman who had only just lost her husband. Shotaro eagerly agreed to meet the widow and followed the servant to her house. For modesty's sake, the widow remained behind a screen — a common arrangement in times of old.

When Shotaro asked her name, the "widow" whipped the screen back, revealing herself to be none other than Isora! "Let me show you how I repay your cruelty!" she shrieked, her sunken eyes and ashen skin that of a yurei. Shotaro fainted from shock at the sight.

He regained consciousness in an empty field. It had all been an illusion woven by his dead wife's furious spirit! Terrified, Shotaro consulted an *onmyoji* (exorcist), who told him to paste consecrated ofuda slips on the openings of his house and — this was critical — to remain inside for forty-two days and nights.

But Isora's ghost was cunning; on the very last night, she made it appear as though dawn had broken early. When Shotaro ran out to greet the sun, he was confronted with the cold light of the moon, and realized with horror that he had stepped out too early.

Hearing a shriek, Shotaro's next-door neighbor came over to see what was wrong. But there was no trace of Shotaro ... except for blood-splattered walls and Shotaro's topknotted scalp, dangling from the eaves. His body was never found.

Surviving an Encounter

Simple. When the onmyoji tells you to stay in the house for forty-two days, stay in the house for forty-two days. C'mon, in the internet era this is hardly a stretch. Some useful tips:

1) Stock up on frozen foods, snacks, soft drinks, etc.

2) Don't forget the toilet paper, too.

3) When you get to forty-two days? Stay one more. At this point, how much worse could it be? (Rhetorical question; just go back and re-read a few paragraphs up to see how much worse it could be. You know how bad it hurts to peel a band-aid off of hairy skin? Imagine your whole head going that way.)

If holing up for weeks on end doesn't suit your style, you can always just wig out. Literally! Many Japanese variety shops carry faux "chonmage" wigs for use as party costumes. If you fear Isora may be breathing down your neck, donning one of these may give you the briefest of chances to escape when she gives your topnot a tug. Even better news: at just ¥600 (US $7) a pop, you can afford to stock up.

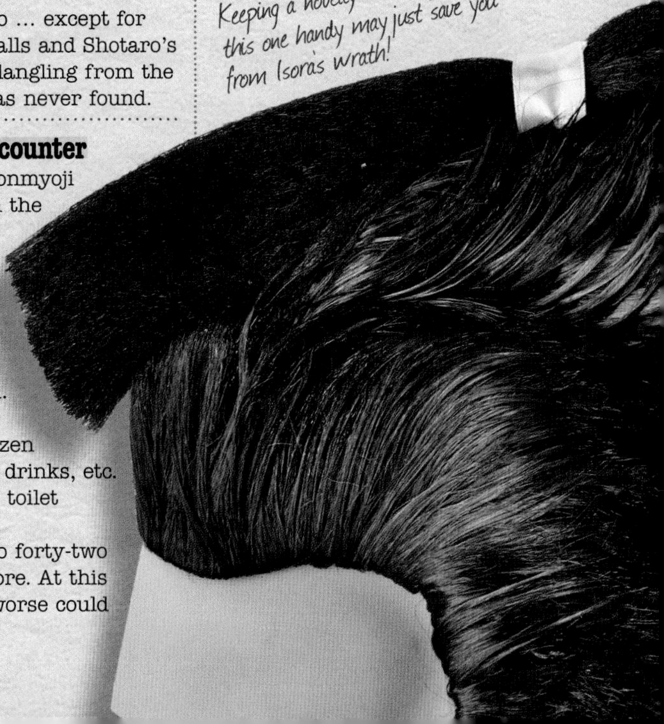

Keeping a novelty chonmage wig like this one handy may just save you from Isora's wrath!

ORUI

Name in Japanese: お累
Origin: A true story known as Kasane-ga-fuchi ("The Depths of Kasane")
Gender: Female
Date of death: 1647
Age of death: 32 (Estimated)
Cause of death: Murder by drowning
Distinctive features: Left side of face disfigured
Place of internment: Unknown
Location of haunting: Joso City (Ibaragi Prefecture)
Form of Attack: Haunting, causing of illness, possession
Existence: Based in part on a true story
Threat Level: High

Claim to Fame

This epic tale of murder and betrayal spanning sixty years and three generations is more "possession" than "haunting," but it is all the more chilling for being based on an actual crime. The tale of Kasane-ga-fuchi is considered a bookend to that of the Yotsuya Kaidan (p.16), as Orui's disfigurement is on the opposite side of the face as Oiwa's.

In fact, spoken or staged performances of Orui's story are traditionally never held on the same day as those of Yotsuya Kaidan. Although their origins are different (Orui's being natural, as you will see, while Oiwa's was caused by poison), the opposing disfigurements resemble each other so closely that bringing the two together creates a potentially dangerous symmetry for both performer and audience alike. Or so they say.

The Story

… begins in 1612, when a farmer by the name of Yoemon marries Sugi, a young widow with a little boy named Suké. Born with deformities from face to foot all down the left side of his body, Suké's presence grated on Yoemon, who was never really "father material" to begin with. So one fine spring morning after the snowmelt, he kicked the young boy into a raging stream. Yoemon swore it was an accident, a lie that those around him chose to believe. (In fact, some speculate that Sugi actually collaborated with Yoemon out of fear he would leave her.)

But you can't fool karma. When Yoemon and Sugi conceived their own child several years later, she was born with the exact same facial deformity and withered limbs as Suké. Although they named her Orui, villagers whispered of the evildoings that must have brought about such a strange fate. They began calling the child Kasane, an alternate reading of the same kanji-character, which means "double trouble."

Yoemon and Sugi died while Orui was still quite young, leaving her the home and their meager savings. Yet her handicaps made it difficult to find a husband, and she lived alone for many years. One day, a drifter by the name of Yagoro wound up on her doorstep, virtually collapsing into her arms from the many maladies that beset even young men in an era

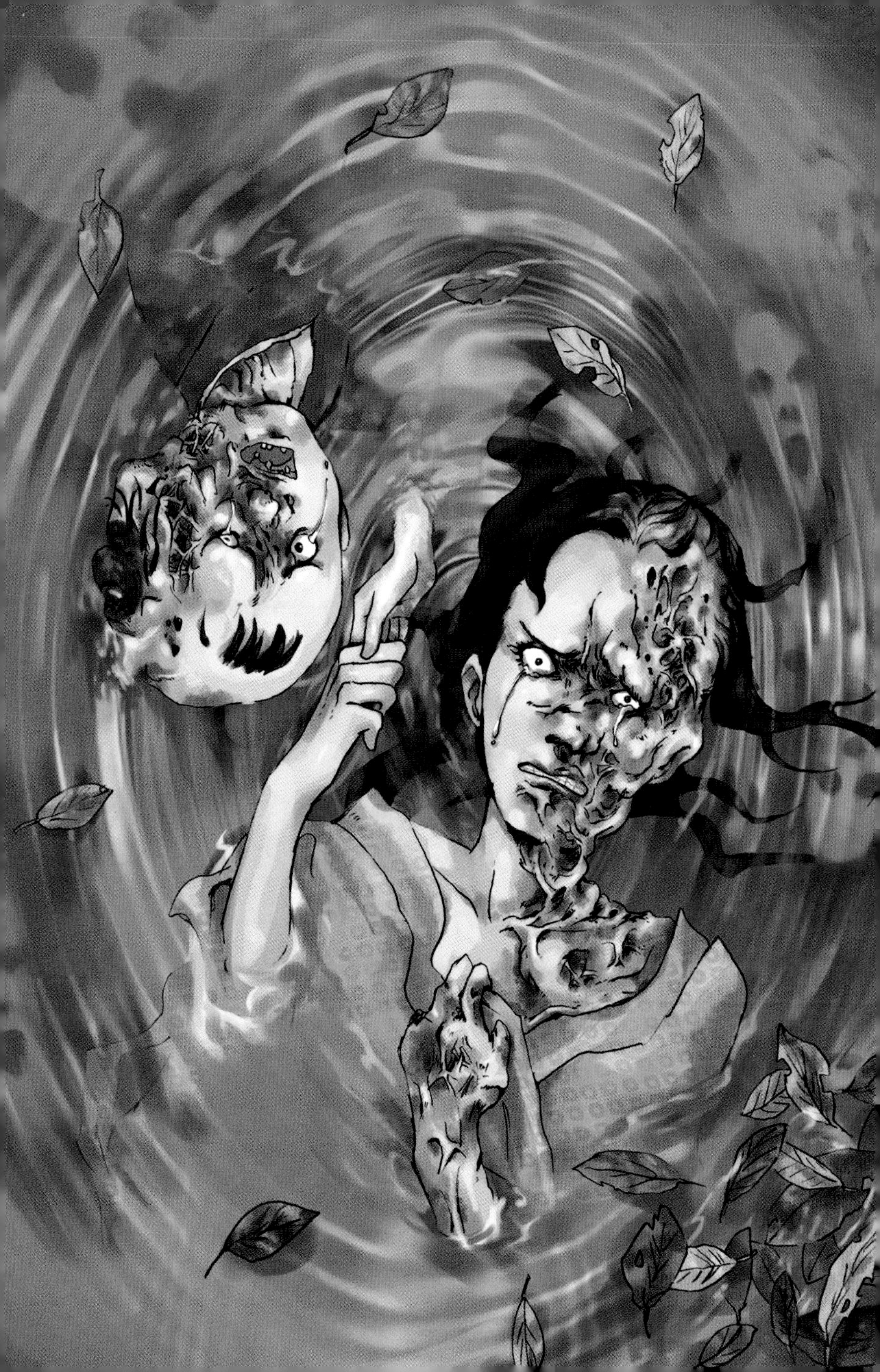

before hospitals or real medicines. Orui dutifully nursed him back to health, and the grateful Yagoro married her in thanks for her generosity. It must have seemed a dream come true for Orui.

But the good times wouldn't last. Yagoro quickly regretted his decision to marry and schemed with his mistress to get rid of Orui once and for all. Late in the summer of 1647, in a virtual replay of what had happened to her half-brother, Yagoro pushed Orui into a fast-moving river to drown.

Yagoro married his mistress, but soon after tying the knot she took to her sickbed and died. He met and married again, with the same result. And again. And again. Eventually, his final wife died in childbirth, leaving him a daughter, Kiku.

↰ Rivers are well-known haunts for spirits of various kinds.

The Attack

The problems began one December in 1672, when Kiku, now grown and married, fell ill and began speaking in a voice not her own. The voice claimed to be Orui, offering up a detailed account of how Yagoro had caused her death, and vowing to torment Kiku until given a proper funeral ceremony. A monk by the name of Yuten — a man we'll be reading more about in chapter six (p.164) — happened to hear of the story and arrived to perform the requested rites. But no sooner had he drawn the spirit from her body than she fell ill again. Yuten probed Kiku for information, and discovered that

she was inhabited by the restless soul of Suké as well. Connecting the dots between the two murders in a psychic version of a detective story, Yuten managed to guide the little boy's spirit to the afterlife.

Of what happened to Yagoro, no record remains — but given his evil deeds, one can assume the remainder of his life — and presumably afterlife — were anything but pleasant.

Surviving an Encounter

If you've gotten yourself involved in a sordid tale of betrayal like this, chances are you're beyond any help this book can give you. For the rest of us, the ghosts of Orui and Suké were content to make their own sad stories known and are no longer considered a threat. Rule of thumb for restless spirits: consult your local temple. And pray that an exorcist-monk as sharp as Yuten is on duty.

Trivia Notes

In 1957, director Nobuo Nakagawa filmed a version of Orui's story called Kaidan Kasane-ga-fuchi ("The Horror of Kasane Swamp"). It is based, however, on an old *rakugo* (spoken word) dramatization that bears little resemblance to the original story. In this version of the tale, the ghost of a blind masseuse killed by a samurai lures his murderer to his death in Kasane swamp, seemingly avenging himself. But when the masseuse's orphaned daughter Orui unwittingly falls in love with the samurai's son years later, the cycle of death begins anew.

CHAPTER TWO
Furious Phantoms

The "Onryō" are ghosts driven by righteous anger. Pray you don't chance into any of these fellows: they represent some of the most dangerous spirits to stalk the islands of Japan.

TAIRA NO MASAKADO

Name in Japanese: 平将門
Gender: Male
Date of Death March, 940
Age at death: Roughly 37
Cause of death: Killed in battle
Type of ghost: Onryo
Distinctive features:
Generally speaking, Masakado's ghost does not physically manifest
Place of internment: Tokyo
Location of haunting: Tokyo
Form of Attack: Death, disaster, and misfortune
Existence: Historical fact
Threat Level: Extremely High

Claim To Fame

One of Tokyo's most famous ghosts is that of a man many consider to be Japan's very first samurai. Decapitated on the battlefield, his disembodied head refused to die and took on a life of its own — something like a reverse Headless Horseman. In a testament to the power his name still holds over people, Masakado's shrine occupies some of the choicest real estate in the city today, surrounded by gleaming modern skyscrapers a five-minute walk from the Imperial Palace. Even now, none dare attempt to reclaim this land from Masakado. He is the prototypical *onryo* — angry spirit.

The Story

A minor but successful warlord, Masakado's ambitions put him at odds with the Imperial government of Kyoto. Establishing an independent kingdom in the Kanto region, he proclaimed himself the "new Emperor of all Japan." In response, the existing government — run, of course, by the "old" Emperor, who was none too thrilled by the prospect of sharing power — quickly placed a bounty on the warrior's head.

Within two months Masakado was dead, felled by an arrow between the eyes during a ferocious battle. The emperor's men decapitated the corpse and carried the head to Kyoto for a public showing.

Infuriated at the insult of being removed from its body, Masakado's head took to the skies over Kyoto and returned to the Kanto region in a frantic quest for its missing body. Desperate to make itself whole and fight another day, the head of the Japanese samurai searched far and wide to no avail.

Finally spent from the fruitless effort, the severed head crashed from the sky over a tiny fishing village called Edo (which would centuries later grow into the metropolis of Tokyo). It came to rest on a plot of land known forever after as Masakado no Kubizuka (The Hill of Masakado's Head). Terrified villagers washed the head, buried it and erected a memorial stone to appease its fury. Generations thereafter tended to it as a symbol of anti-authoritarian power.

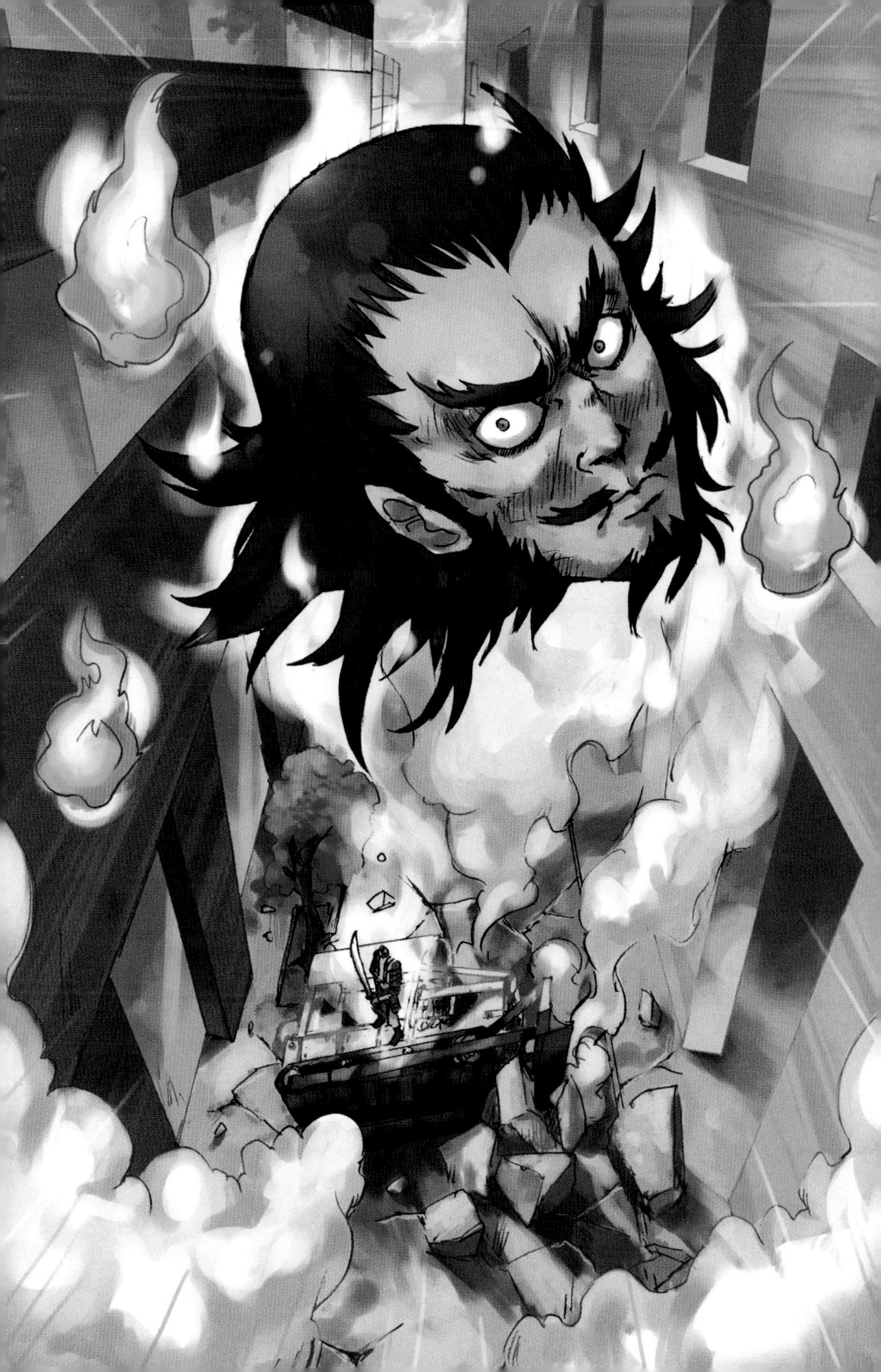

The Attack

Over the centuries, a great many calamities have been ascribed to Masakado's influence. Some of the most recent make up a "greatest hits" list of sorts.

When the Great Kanto Earthquake of 1923 destroyed much of the city, Tokyo's Ministry of Finance took the opportunity to level the Hill of Masakado's Head, filling in the pond where the Japanese samurai's head was supposedly washed and erecting a temporary office building on the spot. Within two years some 14 employees had died, felled by accidents, illnesses, and other misfortunes — including the Minister of Finance himself. In the meantime, a spate of inexplicable injuries broke out among the other employees, many to the feet and legs. Mounting fear of treading upon the cursed ground led officials to raze the building and rebuild the hill after holding a Shinto ritual to soothe the angry spirit. Thereafter, the government held a small service in its honor every year, until the outbreak of World War II, which drew the government's attention to other things, and the ceremonies eventually lapsed.

In 1940, the thousand-year anniversary of the warlord's death, lightning struck the Ministry of Finance, touching off a fire that destroyed much of the structure adjacent to Masakado's hill. In response, the latest Minister of Finance (undoubtedly moved by the fate of his predecessor) sponsored an extravagant ceremony to appease Masakado's angry soul

once again, erecting a stone memorial that stands on the site to this very day.

But the story doesn't end there. When the American forces took control of Japan after the war, they tried to raze the shrine to build a motor pool for military vehicles. During construction, a bulldozer inexplicably flipped over, killing the driver. A string of other accidents combined with pleas from local officials convinced the Americans to cancel the project, and Masakado once again enjoyed peace and quiet, and still does today.

Surviving an

It's a common misconception that all of the desks in the surrounding skyscrapers are arranged to face Masakado's shrine. While the burial plot is meticulously maintained, outside of its borders Tokyoites go about their daily business as usual.

Encounter

Masakado may be as potent a force today as he was on the battlefield a thousand years ago, but one thing is for sure: like a true samurai, he never launches an unprovoked attack. His fury is inevitably focused upon those who fail to pay proper respect to his final resting place. Bottom line: think twice before attempting to drive a bulldozer over it.

Perhaps because of his penchant for only lashing out at those who strike against his resting place, Masakado's presence certainly isn't viewed as a negative by locals. He is seen as a guardian of Tokyo — someone who might return one day to protect the city in times of danger.

Lone among the ghosts profiled in this book, Taira no Masakado actually has his own bank account. Opened at the nearby Mitsubishi Tokyo UFJ Bank, it's used by the volunteer organization that maintains the shrine.

All in the Family

Understandably upset, Masakado's daughter, the Princess Takiyasha, visited Kifune Shrine to place a curse upon those who had killed her father. The request was apparently a success, for one of Japan's most famous woodblock prints depicts her conjuring forth the skeletal yokai known as O-dokuro to terrorize the man responsible for her father's death. (For more about curses, see p.140).

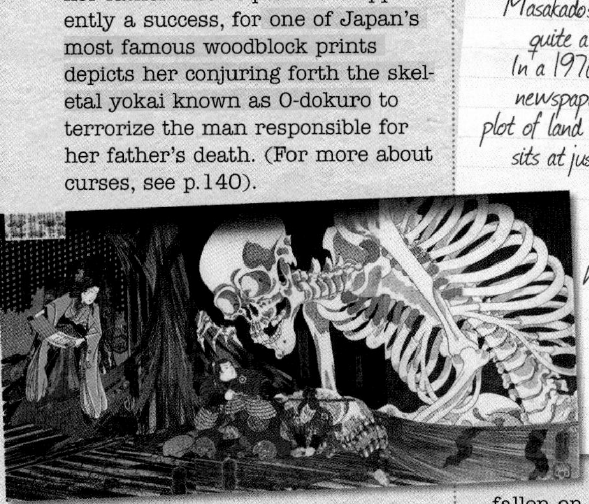

The skeleton conjoured up by Princess Takiyasha – Utagawa Kuniyoshi, (1798 – 1861)

Heading Home

With all of this talk about his head, whatever happened to Masakado's body? According to one legend, it went running around to look for its head!

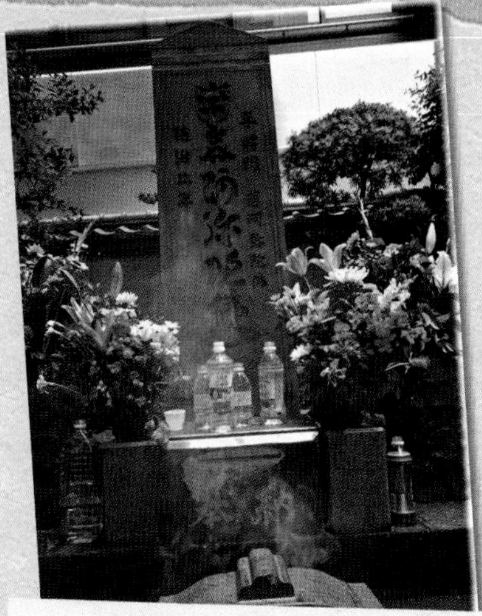

LOCATION, LOCATION, LOCATION

Masakado's head turns out to have been quite a shrewd real estate speculator. In a 1970 article, the Asahi Shimbun newspaper estimated the value of the plot of land upon which Masakado's grave sits at just under two hundred million yen, which is close to $2.5 million American dollars at the 2011 exchange rate. It hasn't been officially appraised in recent years, but given the prices in the surrounding area it must be many, many times that figure today.

It is believed to have fallen on the site of what is now Kanda Myojin Shrine, located in present-day Otemachi. Masakado may have been a traitor to Kyoto, but he was a hero to Tokyo. Every May, the Kanda-Myojin Matsuri festival is held in his honor. If you'd like to make the acquaintance of Japan's first samurai — or at least his body — feel free to drop by!

Furious Phantoms: 07

SUGAWARA NO MICHIZANE

Name in Japanese: 菅原道真

Gender: Male

a.k.a. Sugawara no Michizane; Tenman Daijizai Tenjin (after death); Kan Shojo

Date of Death: March 26, 903

Age at death: 57

Cause of death: Starvation

Type of ghost: Onryo

Distinctive features: Generally speaking, Michizane's ghost does not physically manifest itself.

Place of internment: Fukuoka, Kyushu

Location of haunting: Heiankyo (Kyoto)

Form of Attack: Causing plagues, droughts, other unpleasantness; Bolts from the blue

Existence: Historical

Threat Level: High

Claim to Fame:

A serious political operator turned angry ghost, hell-bent on avenging his mistreatment at the hands of the Imperial family.

In life, Michizane was a highly intelligent, artistically inclined scholar. (According to one account, he once wrote twenty complete poems on twenty entirely different subjects while eating supper.) Quickly rising through the ranks, he attracted the attention of then-Emperor Uda, giving his career a serious boost. Before long, he had climbed the ladder almost as far as a bureaucrat could climb, attaining influential positions including Udaijin ("Minister of the Right," essentially a Secretary of State), ambassador to T'ang era China, and Assistant Master of the Crown Prince's Household, among others. But while his future seemed assured, in reality storm clouds were brewing on the horizon.

The Michizane Incident

The imperial court burned many official records concerning Michizane in an attempt to obscure the connection to his furious spirit. The details of what came many years later to be known as the "Michizane Incident" must necessarily be pieced together from a variety of secondhand accounts.

Overwhelmed by his responsibilities, Uda abdicated the throne in 897, stripping Michizane of his former influence. Far less qualified people from families better connected to the new emperor were promoted, while the talented and loyal Michizane slid into undeserved irrelevance. Demoted, slandered, and accused of crimes he didn't commit, Michizane was banished to distant Kyushu in 901.

Michizane soldiered on and continued to compose poetry, but had been reduced to abject poverty. He succumbed to malnutrition in the early spring of 903. Upon hearing word of his demise, his rivals must have patted themselves on the back for a job well done. Only Michizane wasn't done. The attacks began that very year.

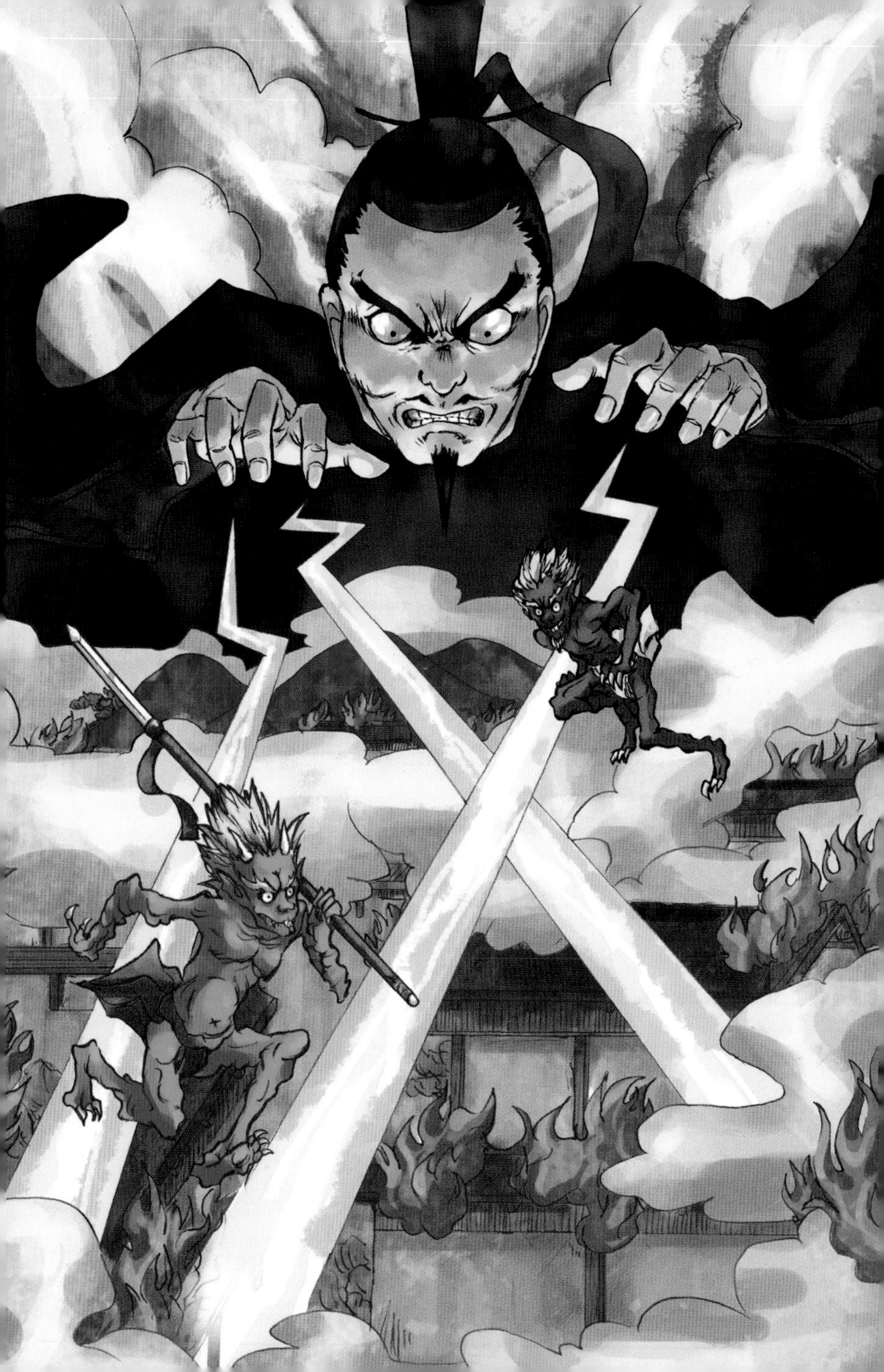

THE ATTACKS

A partial list of tatari (attacks) officially attributed to Michizane, by year

- 903 TORRENTIAL RAINS ALL YEAR LONG
- 905 DROUGHT
- 906 FLOODS
- 907 BAD FLOODS
- 910 TERRIBLE FLOODS
- 911 FLOODS OF THE SORT THAT SWALLOW ENTIRE VILLAGES
- 912 LARGE FIRE IN HEIANKYO
- 913 DEATH OF MICHIZANE'S RIVAL
- 914 MORE FIRES IN HEIANKYO
- 915 OUTBREAK OF CHICKEN POX
- 918 FLOODS SO HORRIFIC WE HAD BEST NOT SAY ANY MORE
- 922 WHOOPING COUGH OUTBREAK
- 923 UNTIMELY DEATH OF EMPEROR'S SON, THE CROWN PRINCE, AT AGE 21
- 925 UNTIMELY DEATH OF LATE CROWN PRINCE'S INFANT SON
- 930 BOLT OF LIGHTING FALLS WITHIN PALACE WALLS, KILLING NUMEROUS IMPERIAL OFFICIALS. EMPEROR DAIGO COLLAPSES FROM SHOCK. DIES THREE MONTHS LATER

Surviving An Encounter

Ever read the Bible? Remember the bit about the plagues Moses' God brought down upon the Egyptians? Similar thing here. You are in serious trouble. There is nothing the average individual can do to stem the mayhem, other than packing their bags and leaving town at the first hint of bad weather or outbreak of illness. Not exactly a realistic option.

If you happen to be the Emperor of Japan, on the other hand, it's another story. Appeasing a spirit of this magnitude requires major — almost infrastructural — measures. In this particular case, defusing the spirit's fury required the Imperial court not only to posthumously reinstate Michizane's former titles, but to underwrite the construction of an opulent memorial to his memory: the Dazaifu Tenmangu Shrine.

Note that this wasn't an exorcism — Michizane was far too powerful for that; remember the lightning bolts crashing down inside the palace walls? Rather, it was an extravagant show of respect, the closest thing to an official apology the Imperial court could muster. The successful effort formed the cornerstone of what could be called "onryo appeasement strategy" for centuries thereafter: venerating those the Emperor had wronged by elevating them to the status of gods.

Today, Michizane is better known as Tenjin, the Shinto deity of scholarship. So forget about surviving — a modern-day encounter with Michizane is all about passing. Passing your big test, that is. Millions visit his shrine annually for a leg up on their examinations. So stop worrying about ghost attacks and crack those books! Dazaifu Tenmangu Shrine is located just 30 minutes from the city of Fukuoka by train; the nearest station is "Nishitetsu Dazaifu."

Know Your Onryo

Michizane is the archetypical onryo in the most precise definition of

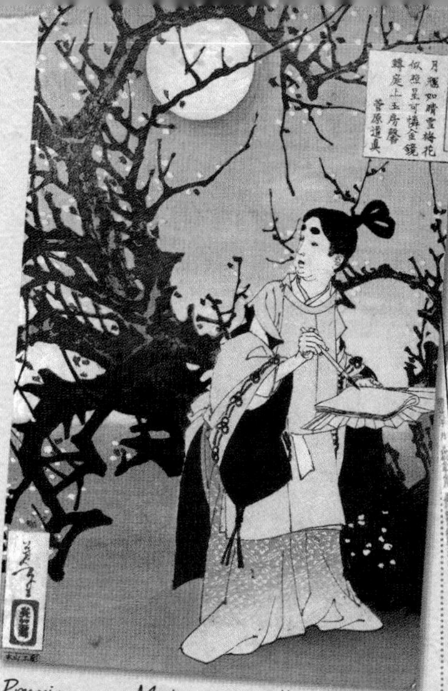
月耀如晴雪梅花
似照星可憐金鏡
轉庭上玉房馨
菅原道真

Precocious young Michizane at age 11, composing a poem with brush and ink. Print by Yoshitoshi.

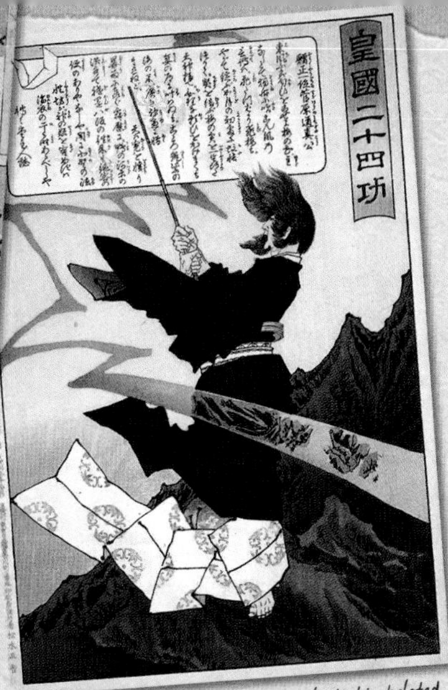
皇國二十四功

Michizane's spirit reacts triumphantly to his belated recognition by the Imperial Court. By Yoshitoshi.

the term. While the word is bandied about today to refer to all sorts of angry ghosts, originally and most correctly onryo applies only to those spirits bent on vengeance against the Imperial family.

We aren't exaggerating or overstating the case when we say that the Imperial government took the haunting seriously. A historical text from 1292 called *Gukansho* shows that the affair still remained a hot topic more than three centuries later. The thirteenth-century author theorizes that the gods orchestrated Michizane's posthumous reappearance as an example of the repercussions of false accusations, which can give an otherwise good man the necessary credentials, so to speak, to come back as an angry ghost.

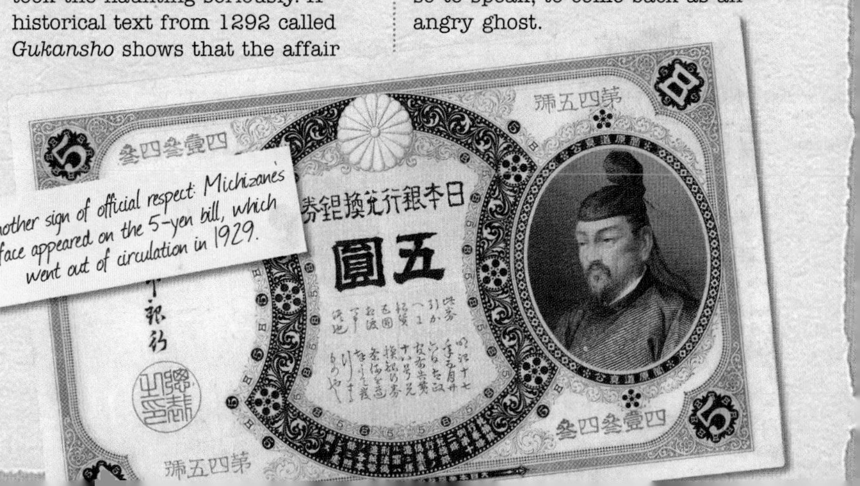
日本銀行兌換銀券
五圓

Another sign of official respect: Michizane's face appeared on the 5-yen bill, which went out of circulation in 1929.

Furious Phantoms: 09
EMPEROR SUTOKU

Name in Japanese: 崇徳天皇
Gender: Male
a.k.a. Sutoku Joko; Sanuki-in; Akihito
Born: 1119
Duration of Reign: 1123 - 1142
Date of Death September 14, 1164
Age at death: 45
Cause of death: Epic familial "dis"
Type of ghost: Onryo
Distinctive features: Generally speaking, Sutoku's ghost does not physically manifest itself.
Place of internment: Kagawa (island of Shikoku)
Location of haunting: Heiankyo (Kyoto)
Form of Attack: Deaths, droughts, bringing down entire regimes
Existence: Historical
Threat Level: High

Claim to Fame

Emperor Sutoku is another "traditional" onryo of the sort that specifically haunts the Imperial family. The product — and victim — of a complex web of political alliances and intrigues, his story is a fascinating reminder that even at the top of the "org chart," so to speak, life isn't any walk in the park.

Although well known as a historical figure, Sutoku is even better known for turning into one of Japan's single angriest ghosts. After reading his story, it isn't hard to understand why.

The Story

Sutoku was ostensibly the child of Emperor Toba and his official consort Fujiwara Shoshi, though a good deal of circumstantial evidence indicates he was actually the product of an affair between Shoshi and Toba's father, the former Emperor Shirakawa. Although Shirakawa had relinquished the reins of leadership to his son, he kept a stranglehold on power behind the scenes. Young Sutoku represented one of his prized pawns in this game of thrones.

Once Sutoku reached the ripe age of five, Shirakawa ordered Toba to abdicate. Normally, Toba would be named regent in this sort of situation. But in times of old, a father always "outranked" his son — particularly when said father was a former emperor himself. Toba seethed from the sidelines as Shirakawa manipulated the new child-emperor to his own ends. Even by the torrid standards of Heian politics, it was a bitter pill to swallow.

And so things remained until Shirakawa's death fifteen years later. Taking a page from dear old dad's playbook, Toba used his newfound parental seniority to force Sutoku to accept Toba's own four-year-old son Konoe as an adopted child. Sutoku readily agreed. (Adoptive parent or not, the rules of succession stated he would be named regent when Konoe eventually took power.) But Toba had another trick up his sleeve. When Konoe took the throne that

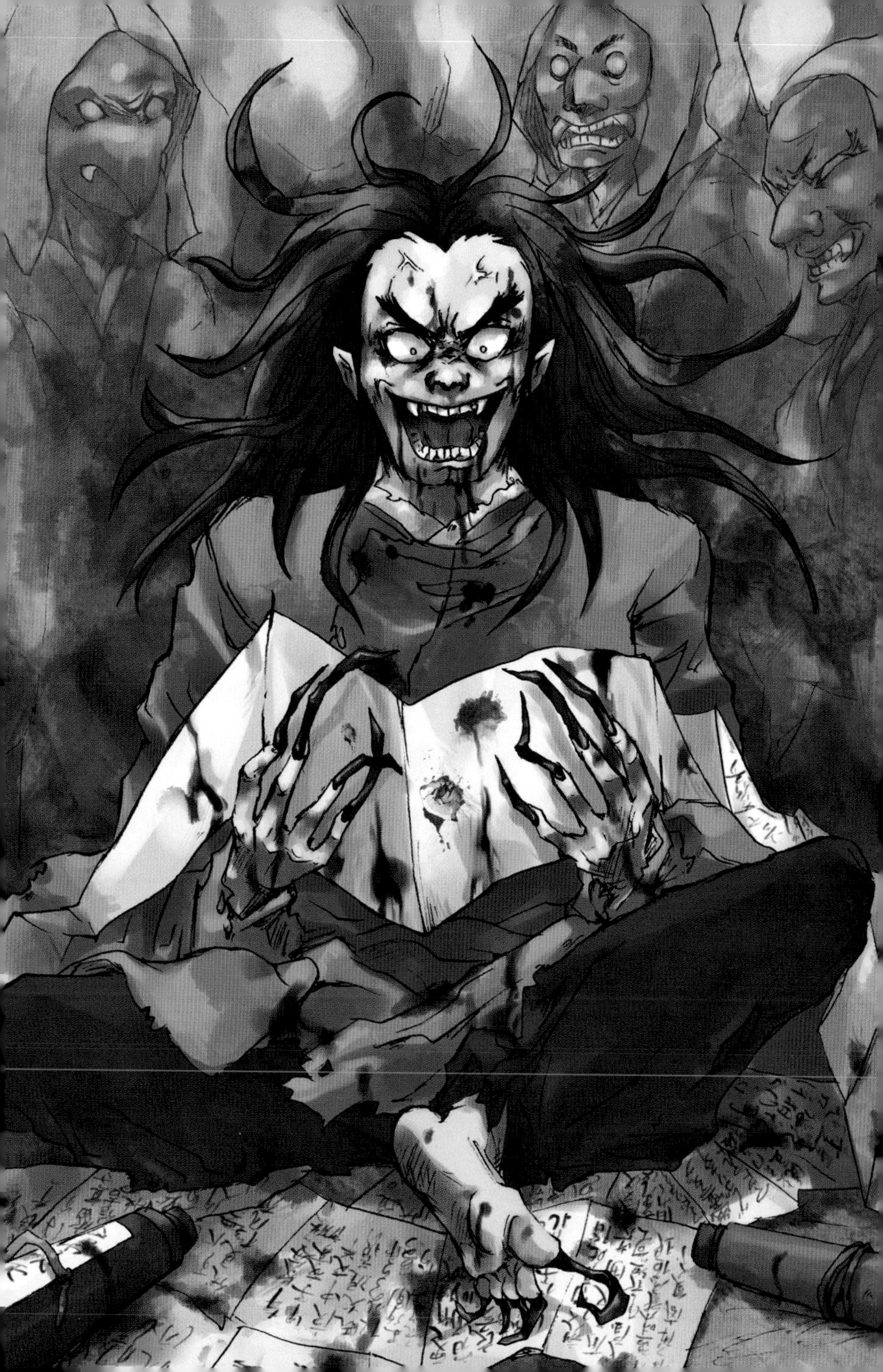

same year, Toba forced Sutoku to sign a wavier stating that Sutoku was actually Konoe's brother. Thus stripped of his parental authority, Sutoku could only watch helplessly as Toba took control of child-emperor Konoe from behind the scenes.

Alas, Konoe was a sickly child, plagued by illnesses and misfortune. He died at the age of 14, seemingly paving the way for Sutoku to get his own son on the throne. But it wasn't to be. Konoe's grieving mother swore that Sutoku had cursed her poor son to death. And so Toba blocked Sutoku yet again, installing his third son, Go Shirakawa, as emperor instead.

In a famous legend, his physical weakness was caused by a dangerous creature called a Nue — see Yokai Attack!

Saddled with a family tree that looked more like a football play diagram than a genealogical chart, Sutoku had had enough. He launched a coup d'etat against Emperor Go Shirakawa in an incident known today as the Hogen Rebellion. But Sutoku was quickly defeated, and the emperor banished him to the distant island of Shikoku as punishment.

Sutoku took his fall from grace surprisingly well. He entered a monastery, devoting himself to religious studies. Over the course of many years, he prepared a set of five key Buddhist sutras copied out in exquisite calligraphy. He sent the texts to Emperor Go-Shirakawa as an olive branch, begging that "at least the traces of my brush be allowed to enter the capital."

The emperor deeply mistrusted the scrolls, convinced that Sutoku had imbued the sutras with a curse of the sort that had felled Konoe years earlier. And so the he refused the gift, ordering them returned — in shreds, according to some accounts.

The Attack

Seeing the scrolls again, Sutoku sank into a cold fury. He swore that his eternal soul would haunt the Imperial family for all time, scrawling intricate curses in his own blood. Consumed body and soul by his hatred, his fingernails grew long and his hair longer. He spent the rest of his days vowing to bring the emperor and his lineage down to the level of commoners. He died in 1142.

In fact, the very next year the Imperial family began suffering all sorts of misfortunes. Go Shirakawa's son and successor, Emperor Nijo, died at just twenty-one, while massive fires raged through the city and insurrections broke out throughout the land. Famine followed.

Then things got worse. In an ironic twist, Sutoku's earlier defeat in battle had set up the entire Imperial court for its downfall. The rebellion sparked a rivalry between the Genji and Heike clans, with the samurai wresting control of the country from the aristocracy in the epic Battle of Dan-no-Ura in 1185. Within half a century the Imperial

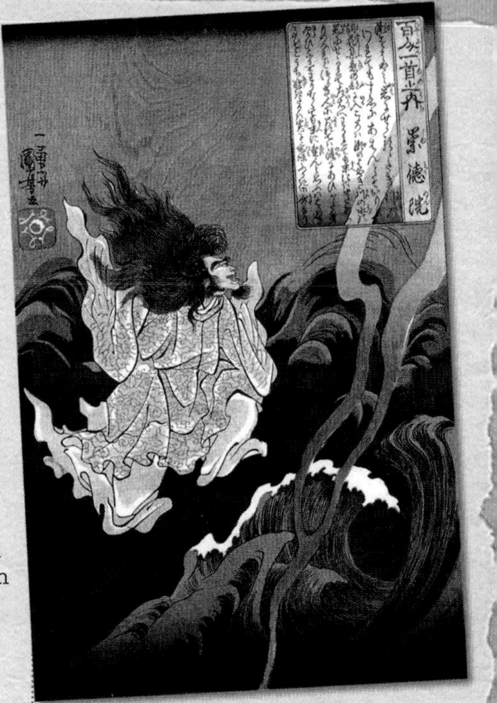

Sutoku unleashes a storm on the hapless citizens of Heiankyo in this 19th century woodblock print by Utagawa Kuniyoshi.

family had been reduced to mere figureheads.

How had it all gone so wrong, so quickly? Pundits of the day knowingly pointed to a single reason: Sutoku's furious spirit.

Surviving an Attack

There's nothing the average person can do to save themselves from the sorts of calamities that an angry spirit such as Sutoku causes. The only real way to achieve "release" is by venerating the angry spirit in question.

When the Shogunate finally collapsed and the Meiji Emperor took power once again centuries later in 1868, one of his first official acts was ordering the construction of a shrine to Sutoku in downtown Kyoto. Even 700 years after his death, Sutoku's onryo still struck fear into the hearts of powerful men.

Yokai Buddies

Sutoku's legend only continued to grow after his death. By the Edo period, some six centuries later, he was described as one of the top three most dangerous supernatural forces in Japan — the other two being a nine-tailed fox-yokai called "Tamamo-no-mae" and the legendarily hard-drinking demon-yokai "Shuten Doji." While he is most definitely considered to be an angry spirit and not a monster, Sutoku is a perfect example of the gray zone that exists between yurei and yokai in Japan.

Print showing Minamoto no Yorimitsu (Raiko) with four hand-picked warriors fighting the demon yokai Shuten Doji.

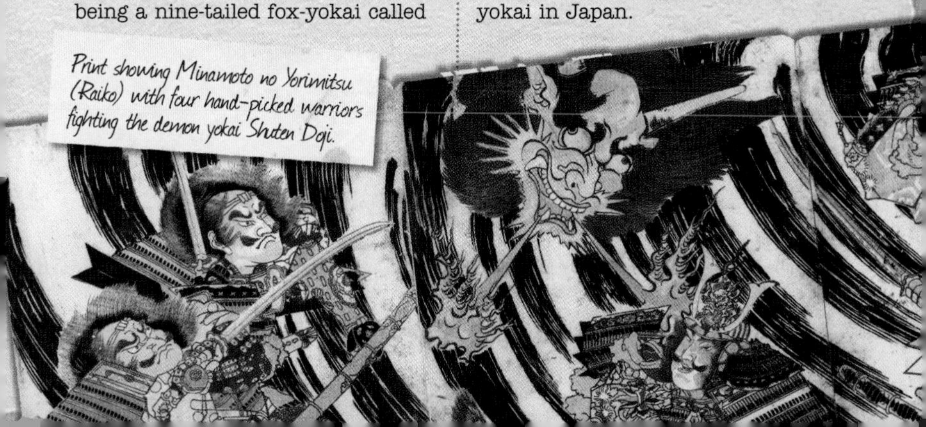

Furious Phantoms: 10

KOHADA KOHEIJ!

Name in Japanese: 小幡小平次
Gender: Male
Occupation: Kabuki Actor
Born: ca. early 1700s
Date of Death: ca. mid 1700s
Age at death: Unknown. Presumably 30–40.
Cause of death: Drowning
Type of ghost: Onryo
Distinctive features: A face only a ghost could love; Amputated right hand; Hand/fingers can operate independently
Place of internment: Asaka Swamp
Location of haunting: Edo
Form of Attack: Physical manifestations, illusions
Existence: Based (loosely) on a true story
Threat Level: Low (for the average person)

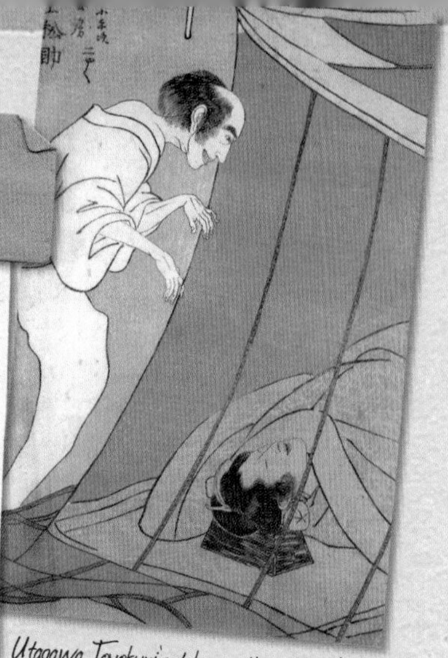

Utagawa Toyokuni's take on the ghost. 1820's woodblock print from the peak of Koheiji's fame.

Claim to fame

You'll be forgiven for not knowing his name, but you just happen to be looking at one of the most famous ghosts of a bygone era. In the early 1800s Koheiji was a superstar. In fact, kabuki actors believed he was such a force of nature that they shied away from even discussing him unnecessarily–a nineteenth century "He-who-must-not-be-named."

Kohada Koheiji is the protagonist of an 1803 book called *Fukushu kidan Asaka no Numa* ("Asaka Swamp: a Strange Tale of Revenge") by Santo Kyoden, a man some consider to be Japan's first modern novelist. Supposedly based on the life and violent murder of a real-life kabuki actor, it proved so popular that Santo penned a sequel several years later, called "Asaka Swamp: The Next Day's Vengeance." As you can probably tell from the titles, this was exploitation fare par excellence, custom-tailored to hook the reader with an outrageous betrayal and then satisfy with bloody revenge. The public ate them up, while the critics decried them as "mishmash" and "ludicrous."

These were the equivalent of modern-day bestsellers, and it wasn't long before famed playwright Tsuruya Nanboku IV penned an adaptation for the kabuki stage. His 1808 drama, disarmingly

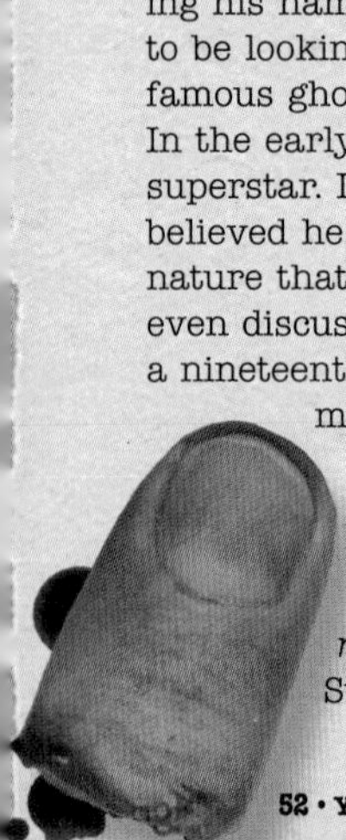

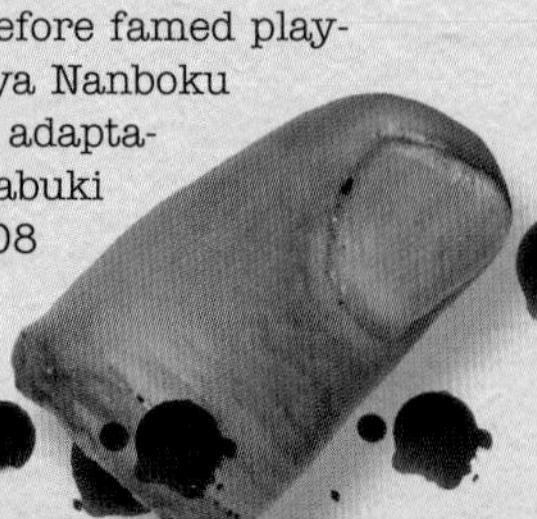

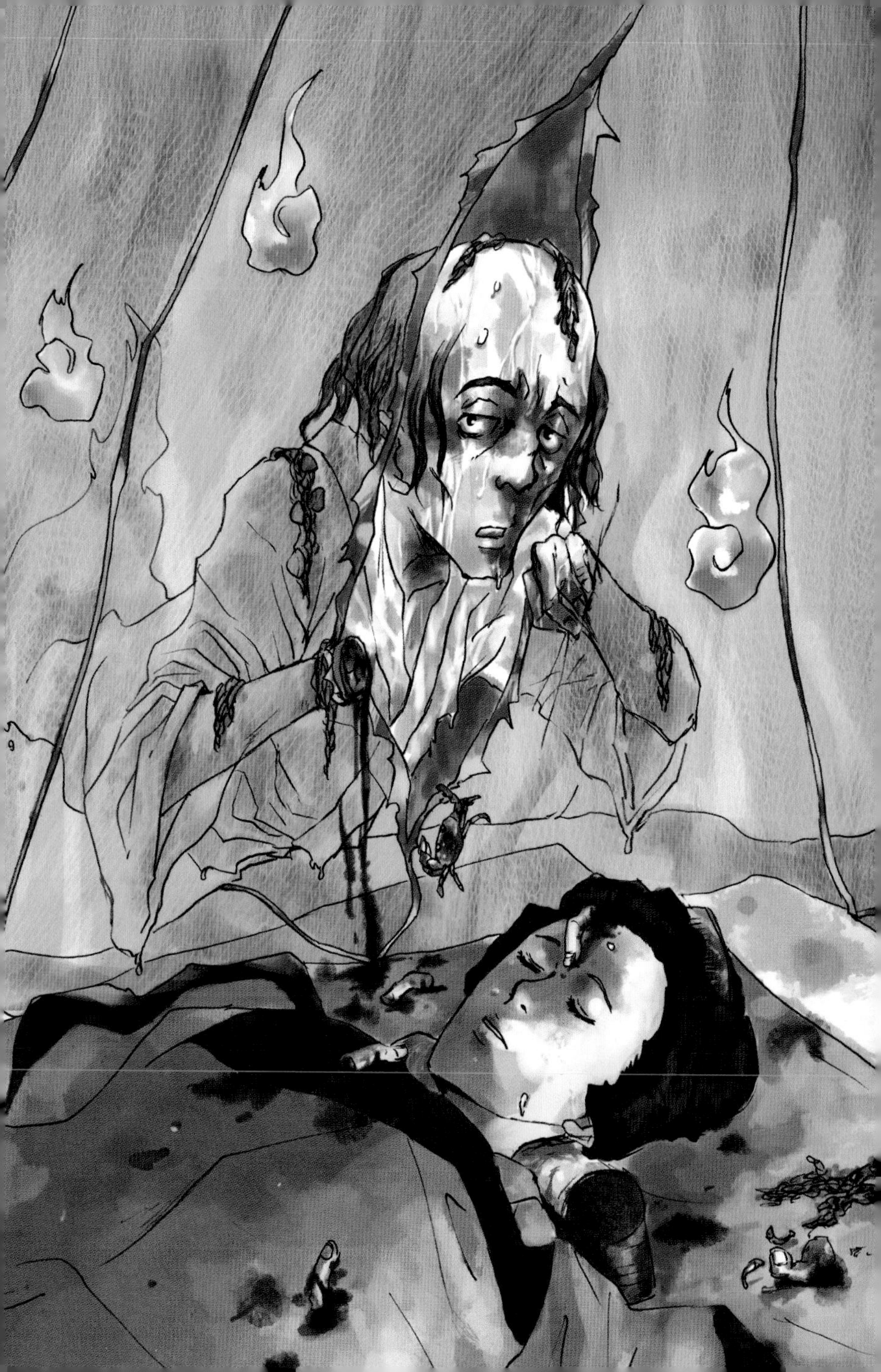

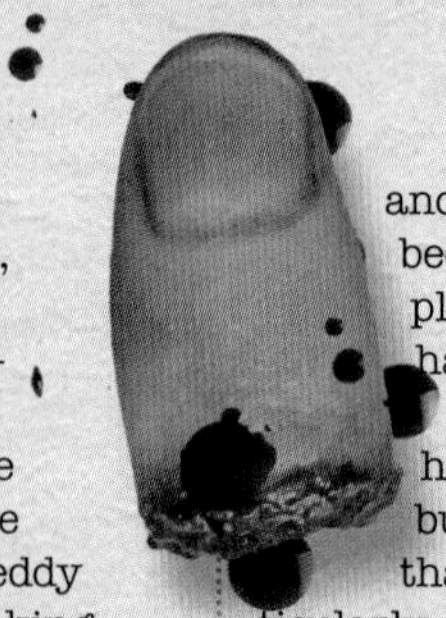

named *Iroiri Otogi-zoshi* ("The Colorful Storybook"), proved as popular as the books. Woodblock print artists one-upped each other with increasingly gruesome portrayals of the ghost. The Edo-era equivalent of a Freddy or Jason, Koheiji began making unofficial cameos in productions by other playwrights, giving rise to the term Koheiji-mono — basically, "the Koheiji-verse" — to describe the growing list of works in which he appeared.

The Story

Koheiji wants nothing more than to be a star of the Kabuki stage, but there's only one problem: he isn't very good. He practices constantly but simply can't land a part. His teacher resorts to bribing producers in an unsuccessful attempt to get the fledgling actor on stage.

But Koheiji's luck is finally about to change. One day, he's approached for a major role in an upcoming production.

"You've got the perfect face!" enthuses the director.

"For what?" asks Koheiji, hardly able to contain his excitement.

"A ghost!"

A backhanded compliment to be sure. And a ghost …! This was a superstitious era, and ghost roles were a double-edged sword, often believed to invite danger and misfortune for the actors who played them. But Koheiji was hardly in a position to say no.

As things turned out, Koheiji did so well that he landed another ghost role, and another, and another. Before long he'd become Edo's go-to guy for playing dead people. Koheiji had found his niche.

Koheiji may have earned his spot in the limelight, but it didn't change the fact that he'd never been a particularly sharp tack. He didn't even notice that his wife Otsuka was carrying on a torrid affair with his pal, a kabuki orchestra drummer named Sakuro. Wanting Otsuka for himself, Sakuro hatched a scheme to kill Koheiji on a fishing trip. When Koheiji cast his line, it was caught by one of Sakuro's confederates, who dragged the hapless actor from the boat to his death in the murky waters.

After fishing the body out of the river, Sakuro frisked it for money and valuables he could use to pay his accomplices. When he reached into Koheiji's sopping kimono, the dead man's right hand streaked out and griped his wrist. Sakuro screamed. One of the accomplices lashed out with his sword, severing the corpse's limb mid-forearm.

Shaken but resolved, Sakuro headed back home to tell Otsuka the good news.

"I killed Koheiji."

"Are you drunk?" she laughed. "Koheiji got home a little while ago. He's in the other room."

The Attack

An apprehensive Sakuro finds the sliding fusuma door into the adjoining room stuck. Unbeknownst to him, a rotting hand is clamping it shut from behind. He forces the fusuma open with a shove, sending

the hand's fingers flying and filling the house with an atrocious
stink. This convinces Otsuka that
her husband really is dead, but she
tells Sakuro to suck it up — "after
all, he's just a ghost."

Bad move. Things only get
stranger. A man materializes in bed
between Sakuro and Otsuka as they
sleep one night. Later, a waterlogged corpse peers in through the
mosquito netting. The pair start
seeing Koheji everywhere, even
during the day. Returning from the
local tavern one night, Sakuro spies
a man running into the bedroom.
Infuriated, he rushes after with
sword drawn. But there is no man;
the woman had been sound asleep.
Shocked awake by the commotion,
she instinctively reaches out to
block the blade — losing the
fingers on her hand in the
process. (Are you sensing a
motif here?)

Gangrene sets in. As
Otsuka wastes away, Sakuro
casts about desperately for
help in ridding his home of
Koheiji's unforgiving spirit.
He hears a scream from the
bedroom; when he rushes
in to check, he finds Otsuka
missing, the walls and ceil-
ing splattered with blood and
chunks of scalp. Eventually
Sakuro loses everything,
laying in bed dreaming of
swamp-water filling his lungs
— a nightmare from which he
never awakes.

How to Survive

Koheiji is a classic example of
a ghost hell-bent on revenge.

Unlike his counterpart and spiritual successor Oiwa-san, however,
he isn't known to stalk victims in
the modern day.

That is, unless, you happen to
be a kabuki actor. That's a different story. At the peak of Koheiji's
popularity, rumors of accidents,
illnesses, and other troubles befall-
ing those actors who portrayed him
swirled through the kabuki scene.
As such, actors kept discussions
of him to a minimum. Perhaps following suit wouldn't be a bad idea.
In fact, maybe you should just go
ahead and turn the page now.

Hokusai's wonderfully ghastly portrayal of a waterlogged and decaying Koheiji pushed the envelope of acceptability in woodblock prints. From 1830.

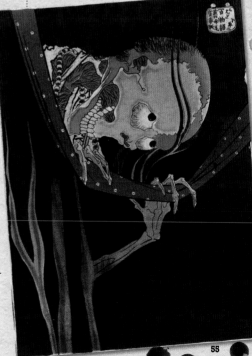

SAKURA SOGORO

Name in Japanese: 佐倉惣五郎
Gender: Male
a.k.a. Kiuchi Sogo (actual name)
Date of Death: Sept. 24, 1653
Age at death: 48
Cause of death: Crucifixion
Type of ghost: Onryo
Distinctive features: Battered and bloody; Bound to wooden cross; Often seen alongside his wife, who is in similar condition
Place of internment: Narita
Location of haunting: Narita
Form of Attack: Incessant manifestations
Existence: Historical
Threat Level: Extremely dangerous (if you're a hatamoto) – see below

Claim To Fame

In times of old, conventional wisdom held that anyone who lost their lives in an unsuccessful bid for justice would return as a spirit hell-bent on vengeance from their oppressors. Perhaps nowhere is the phenomenon more clearly illustrated than in the brutal tale of "peasant martyr" Sakura Sogoro.

There is scant evidence that he actually existed, but the story is all too plausible. This was an era when those above could treat those below them with total impunity — at least from the justice of man. Justice beyond the grave, however, was a different matter.

The Story

The *hatamoto*, nobility with titles and land-holdings bestowed directly by decree of the Shogun, had virtually free reign over the inhabitants of the lands they owned. Lord Hotta, the hatamoto of Sogoro's village of Kozu (in the vicinity of what is now the city of Narita) happened to be greedier than most, squeezing the peasants below him of every last grain of rice — the currency of the day — to fill his already swelling coffers.

In spite of their fertile lands, the farmers of Kozu found themselves driven to the brink of poverty and starvation while their landlord lived high on the hog, ignoring their repeated pleas for reductions and deferments. A few pooled money and attempted a bribe, which Hotta happily accepted, and then ignored. Driven to the brink, many villagers were forced to sell heirlooms and even their own homes to make ends meet; others fled in the night, praying for greener pastures elsewhere.

Sogoro, head of the village, wasn't the sort of man to take this sort of treatment lying down. He organized his fellow farmers together and prepared a petition to take to the Shogun himself — a daring move in an era when going over the heads of those above you could mean losing your own. With the help of the villagers, he hid under a bridge where he knew the Shogun's retinue would soon pass

Tying the document to the end of a bamboo pole, he thrust it into the window of the palanquin as it was

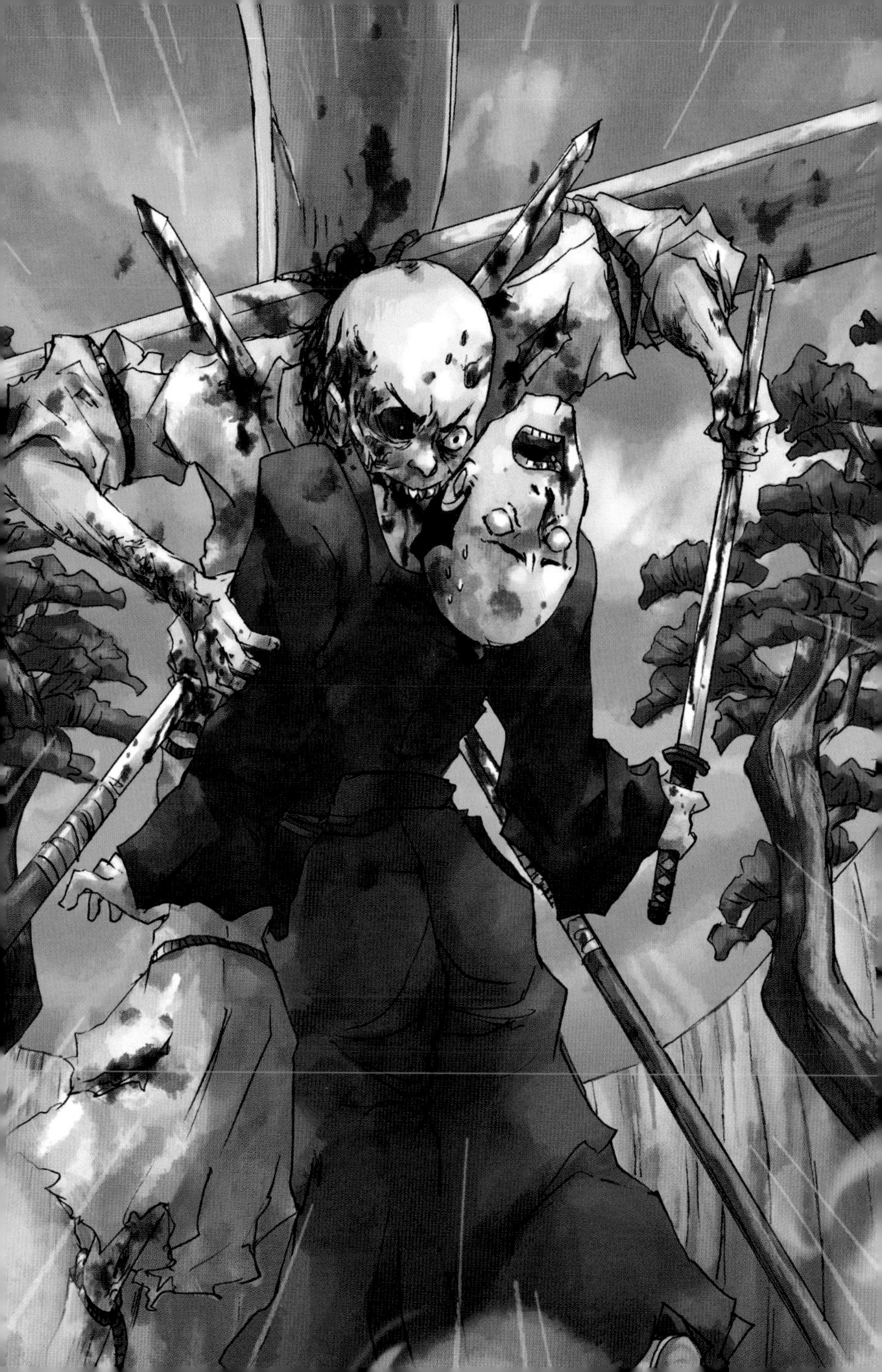

carried past, begging for the Shogun to grace it with his attention.

As luck would have it, the effort intrigued the Shogun, who ordered Hotta to consider the villagers' request. Word of the petition and Hotta's avarice spread through the chain of command like wildfire. Hotta had been humiliated in front of his superiors by a bunch of peasants.

Of course, Hotta felt no responsibility or remorse for the taxes he was forcing on his subjects — just a simmering rage at having been publically embarrassed. He had Sogoro's entire family rounded up, informing them that he was happy to accept the petition on the Shogun's behalf and would henceforth reduce the burden upon the village. But according to law, Sogoro still must pay for having gone over Hotta's head.

The peasant leader had steeled himself for this very possibility, but none could have predicted the brutality of the sentence. Hotta

crucified Sogoro and his wife and forced them to watch as their four young sons, just eleven, nine, six, and three, were decapitated; then he left Sogoro and his wife hanging in tortured anguish for another three days before killing them. As the executioners prepared their spears for the death-strikes, Sogoro cursed Hotta and swore he would return for revenge. Wickedly sharp blades were thrust into his bowels again and again. Yet as he died, his head lolled to the side, its now sightless eyes fixed firmly on the castle in which the hatamoto of Kozu made his home.

The Attack

The haunting began almost from the moment of Sogoro's death. In the castle, strange lights illuminated the bedchamber of Hotta's pregnant wife as eerie, disembodied cackles rang throughout its corridors. Before long the phantoms had coalesced into actual form; apparitions of Sogoro and his wife, still bound to their crosses, appeared in her ladyship's room, vigorously shaking the poor woman and swearing to make her last days a hell on earth. Night after night Hotta burst into his wife's chambers, swinging his sword wildly in a futile attempt to drive the ghosts away. As the wife sickened and died, depriving Hotta of his child to be, the ghosts moved to the chambers of Hotta's only son.

Woodblock print master Utagawa Kuniyoshi's rendition of "Asakura Togo," as Sakura Sogoro was re-named to avoid inflaming the authorities when his story was dramatized as a kabuki play in 1851.

A Kuniyoshi tryptich portraying Sakura Sogoro's torment of the hatamoto. Note how his presence warps perceptions so that Hotta believes his own retainers are demons rather than humans. This ability to bend minds is key to Sakura Sogoro's haunting.

The incessant attacks led to sleepless nights and increasingly erratic behavior. One night Hotta mistook his maidservant for a phantom, killing her with a crazed swing of his sword. But the final straw came on a visit to the Shogun's castle in Edo. Thoroughly out of his mind by this point, Hotta mistook a fellow nobleman for Sogoro, cutting him down in cold blood. This sort of thing was a social faux pas of the highest order, and the furious Shogun ordered Hotta stripped of his title and holdings.

Surviving an Encounter

This is yet another one of those situations where "you made your bed, now lie in it!" Vengeful spirits such as that of Sakura Sogoro aren't interested in haunting for haunting's sake — they're interested in making the individuals responsible for their deaths pay. If you aren't involved, you're safe; if you are, heaven help you, because we sure can't.

There are many variations as to how the tale ends. In one, Lord Hotta, belatedly realizing that his own depravity was to blame for his troubles, swore to see Sogoro venerated as a god if his spirit would relent its campaign of terror. The hauntings began to taper off, and the Shogun took pity and restored Hotta's holdings. The chastened Hotta, true to his word, spent a vast sum dedicating a shrine to Sogoro that was "as beautiful as a gem." So it came to pass that Sogoro became a patron saint of the peasantry, while the hatamoto himself is all but forgotten today.

Trivia

As you might expect, stories such as Sogoro's made great fodder for thinly veiled criticism of the status quo. In 1808, the Edo government actually passed legislation forbidding the public telling of tales involving vengeful ghosts. (That the law was ineffectual is putting it mildly, as the sheer number of woodblock prints, books, and kabuki plays featuring ghosts over the following decades will attest.)

MORINAGA SHINOH

Name in Japanese: 護良親王
Gender: Male
a.k.a. Moriyoshi Shinoh (alternate reading of name); Prince Morinaga / Moriyoshi; Daito-no-miya; Ooto-no-miya
Date of Death: August 12, 1335
Age at death: 27
Cause of death: Execution
Type of ghost: Onryo
Distinctive features: Known to manifest in the form of a Tengu (see below)
Venerated at: Kamakura-gu Shrine
Location of Haunting: Kamakura
Form of Attack: Curses
Strategic rebirths?
Existence: Historical
Threat Level: High (Historically),
Low (Currently)

Claim to Fame

Morinaga Shinoh is the angriest spirit in the city of Kamakura, a historic city (and former capital) located just over an hour from Tokyo.

He is a typical onryo akin to Sugawara no Michizane or Emperor Sutoku, who you read about earlier. Like them, Morinaga's unjust death at the hands of political rivals fueled his transformation into an angry ghost hellbent on bringing down the Imperial family.

Although not as well known today as the onryo of Sugawara or Sutoku, Morinaga's ghost remained enough of a threat that the Meiji Emperor felt compelled to build a shrine to his memory in 1869, more than five hundred years after Morinaga's death.

The Story

... Begins in the 14th century. A clan of warlords known as the Hojo ruled Japan from the city of Kamakura in a military dictatorship known as a Shogunate, relegating the Emperor Go-Daigo to a figurehead sequestered in the city of Kyoto.

The ambitious Go-Daigo wasn't content to be a puppet. During his reign, he launched several plots — it's hard to call them coup d'états when it's the emperor behind them — against the Hojo clan. (Incidentally, the first failed attempt gave rise to one of Japan's most famous ninja tales. Go-Daigo's loyal right-hand man Hino Suketomo took the fall for the plot, accepting a death-sentence so that his master could remain in the clear. After Hino's death, his son Kumawaka-Maru took revenge against the executioner in a cunning ambush chronicled in chapter 1 of *Ninja Attack!*)

Go-Daigo's second plot kicked off a civil war called the Genko-no-ran, in which Morinaga Shinno played a key part. Go-Daigo's forces attacked Kamakura, but were finally vanquished a year later. The Hojo exiled Go-Daigo to a distant island.

Enter Go-Daigo's son, Prince Morinaga Shinoh. He may have been born with a silver spoon in his mouth, but he was no pushover.

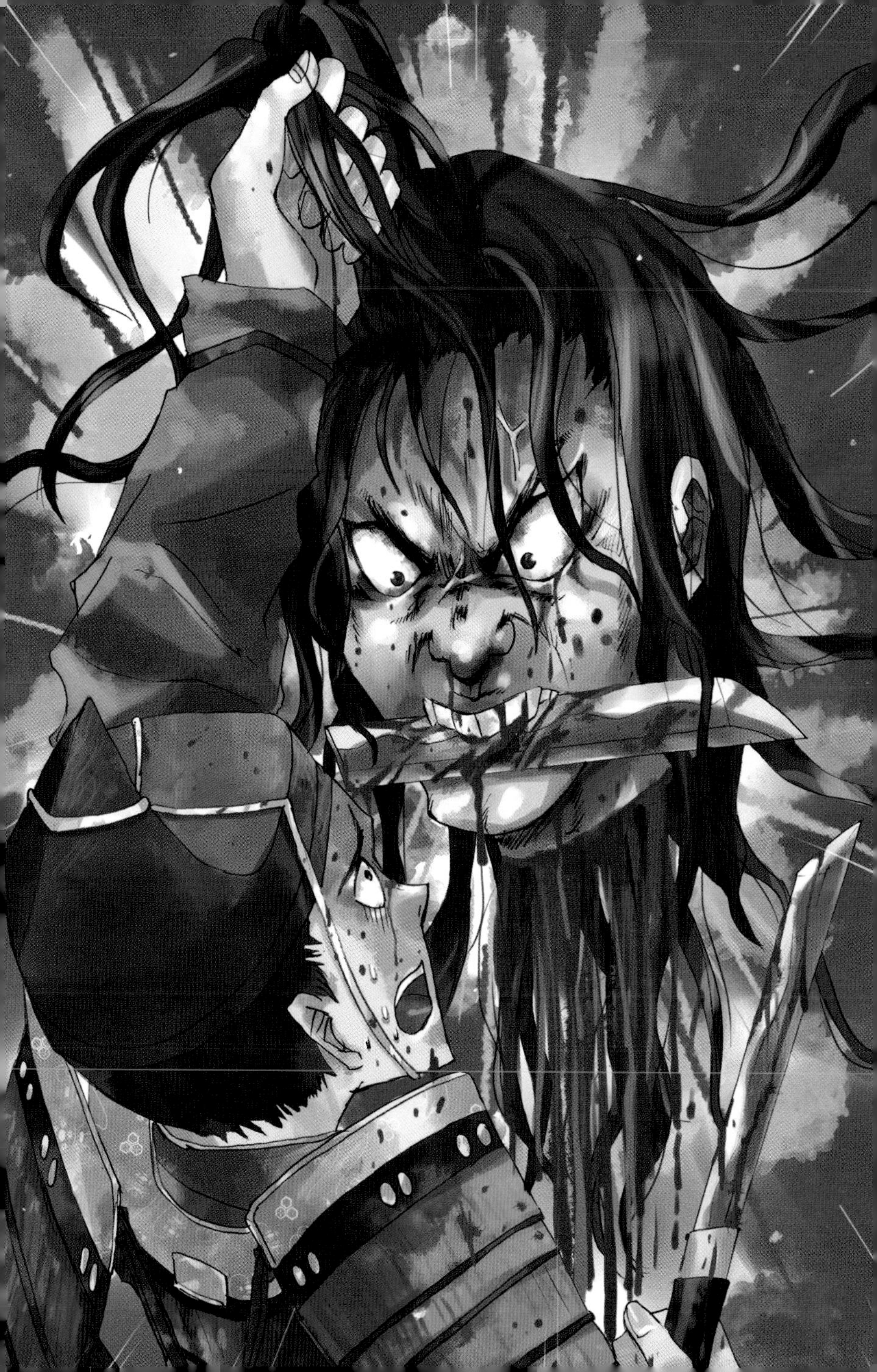

Trained in the martial arts since childhood, he was a talented and fearless warrior. Taking up the battle cry in his father's name, Morinaga joined forces with other Hojo rivals to successfully topple the Shogunate. Once the smoke cleared and the Emperor Go-Daigo was restored to his rightful place in Kyoto, he rewarded Morinaga with the title of Shogun himself.

Happy ending, right? Wrong. Unfortunately for Morinaga, the story doesn't end here.

One of the key generals in the fight against the Hojo, a man named Ashikaga Takauji, demanded the Emperor bestow the title of Shogun upon him instead of Morinaga. Rebuffed, Takauji launched his own coup. Making a long story short, Takauji's forces quickly overwhelmed Morinaga's, delivering both the city of Kamakura and the new Shogun into Takauji's hands.

As the undisputed victor, Takauji could re-write history. He defended his actions by falsely charging Morinaga with plotting against Emperor Go-Daigo. Takauji imprisoned the Prince/Shogun in a dank cave in the hills of Kamakura.

The successful coup rendered Go-Daigo powerless yet again, forcing him both to recognize Ashikaga Takauji as Shogun — and to leave his loyal son to rot in a hole.

The victory was short-lived. When remnants of the Hojo clan regrouped and launched another coup against the new Ashikaga Shogunate, a rebel like Morinaga became a potentially dangerous political symbol. So Takauji's

brother quietly ordered a henchman to get rid of the former Shogun once and for all.

The Attack

The task fell to a samurai by the name of Fuchinobe Yoshihiro, a seasoned veteran of the prior decades of political violence.

Fuchinobe bound and dragged Morinaga out of his cell. He forced the man to kneel, and raised his long tachi blade. But Morinaga did not cower before the killing stroke. In fact he moved to intercept it with his mouth, biting down with such ferocity that he not only stopped the blade between his teeth, but broke it clean from its pommel. Fuchinobe was forced to switch to his tanto short-sword to complete the task.

Even in death, Morinaga's decapitated head refused to give up the blade. In fact the expression of rage on its face was so unrelenting, so palpable, that it gave even an unflappable battle-veteran like Fuchinobe the willies. Breaking into a terrified sprint, he dropped the head he was supposed to bring back to his master.

Morinaga had done everything right. He had trained. He had stood by his father. He had taken back the throne for him. Yet he ended his life in a filthy cave, released only for the purposes of an unceremonious execution. He was the perfect material for an onryo.

The ancient chronicle of Japan *Taiheiki* ascribes a variety of misfortunes that befell the Imperial Family and Shogunate due to Morinaga's angry ghost, and claims

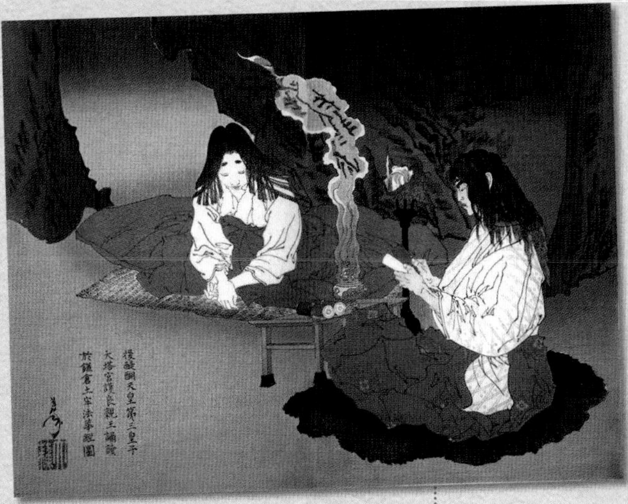
後醍醐天皇第三皇子
大塔宮護良親王
於鎌倉土牢法華経圖

Morinaga receives a conjugal visit in this woodblock print by Yoshitoshi. Legend has it Morinaga conceived a son with her while imprisoned, and that she spirited away his head after Fuchinobe dropped it. Believe it or not, the head is still around. Now mummified, it is displayed every January 15 at Ishifune Shrine (town of Asahibaba, Yamanashi Prefecture).

he re-appeared on at least one occasion as a ferocious Tengu (a creature chronicled in chapter 1 of *Yokai Attack!*)

It also records an intriguing episode — by what means this information was gathered we'll never know — where a group of fellow angry ghosts convened to discuss how best Morinaga could avenge himself. In a devious twist they decided that the best way to throw a monkey-wrench into the works was for Morinaga to be reborn as the son of the man who had ordered his death — Takauji's brother! Talk about "sins of the father."

Surviving an Encounter

Fortunately for you, this particular spirit seems to have been successfully appeased. But it can't hurt to pay your respects.

In 1869, the Emperor Meiji sponsored the construction of an elaborate shrine on the site of Morinaga's cell and execution. Kamakura-gu stands to this very day; you can see both the cave and the place where Fuchinobe dropped Morinaga's head there. It's a thirty-minute walk from the east exit of JR Kamakura station.

The shrine is considered to be a "Yurei Spot," and some visitors claim to experience strange sensations and phenomena such as camera malfunctions. But even if you aren't a believer, it's more than a little chilling to know you're standing precisely where Morinaga lost his life.

Morinaga's cell at Kamakura-gu Shrine.

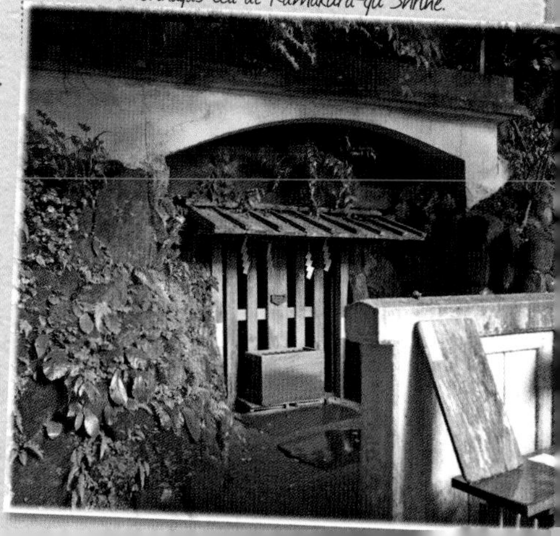

HIIMI-SAMA

Name in Japanese: 日忌様
Gender: *Male*
a.k.a. *Kainan Hoshi;*
Kannan Boshi (local Izu dialect)
Born: *Various*
Date of Death: *1628*
Age at death: *Various*
Cause of death: *Drowning*
Type of ghost: *Onryo*
Distinctive features: *None who've seen them have lived to tell the tale.*
Place of internment: *Sea in vicinity of Izu islands*
Location of haunting: *Izu Oshima and other Izu islands*
Form of Attack: *Various (see below)*
Existence: *Historical*
Threat Level: *High*

Claim to Fame

Yurei that haunt the islands of Izu. They are the souls of twenty-five local men who took it upon themselves to free the islands from an oppressor, yet were turned away by their fellow islanders when they sought refuge. Known collectively as "Hiimi-sama" (honored souls to be mourned) and "Kainan Hoshi" (holy men lost at sea), their spirits collectively haunt the islands to this very day. When they

return — which they do once a year, without fail — no islander in their right mind even thinks about setting foot out of their homes.

The Story

The setting is Izu Oshima, the largest of a chain of volcanic islands that extend into the Pacific south of the Izu peninsula. Although today the islands are treated as part of Tokyo for administrative purposes, travelling to them still demands calm seas. So one can imagine how difficult it must have been to reach them on wooden boats in times of old.

The time is the mid-17th Century. The governor has arrived to collect his yearly taxes — which on the islands are paid in salt rather than rice, as on the mainland. But it has been a difficult year. Forest fires have devastated local industry; food of any kind is scarce, let alone refined salt. Yet the governor will not take no for an answer. The tax must be paid. He forces the islanders to forage through their own larders for potatoes, their only source of food until the next spring. This was bad enough, but when he began demanding the services of the village's young women, a group of twenty-five young men made the fateful decision to confront him.

Undoubtedly realizing that things wouldn't end well, the group split up to warn their neighbors. "Don't leave your homes. Don't look

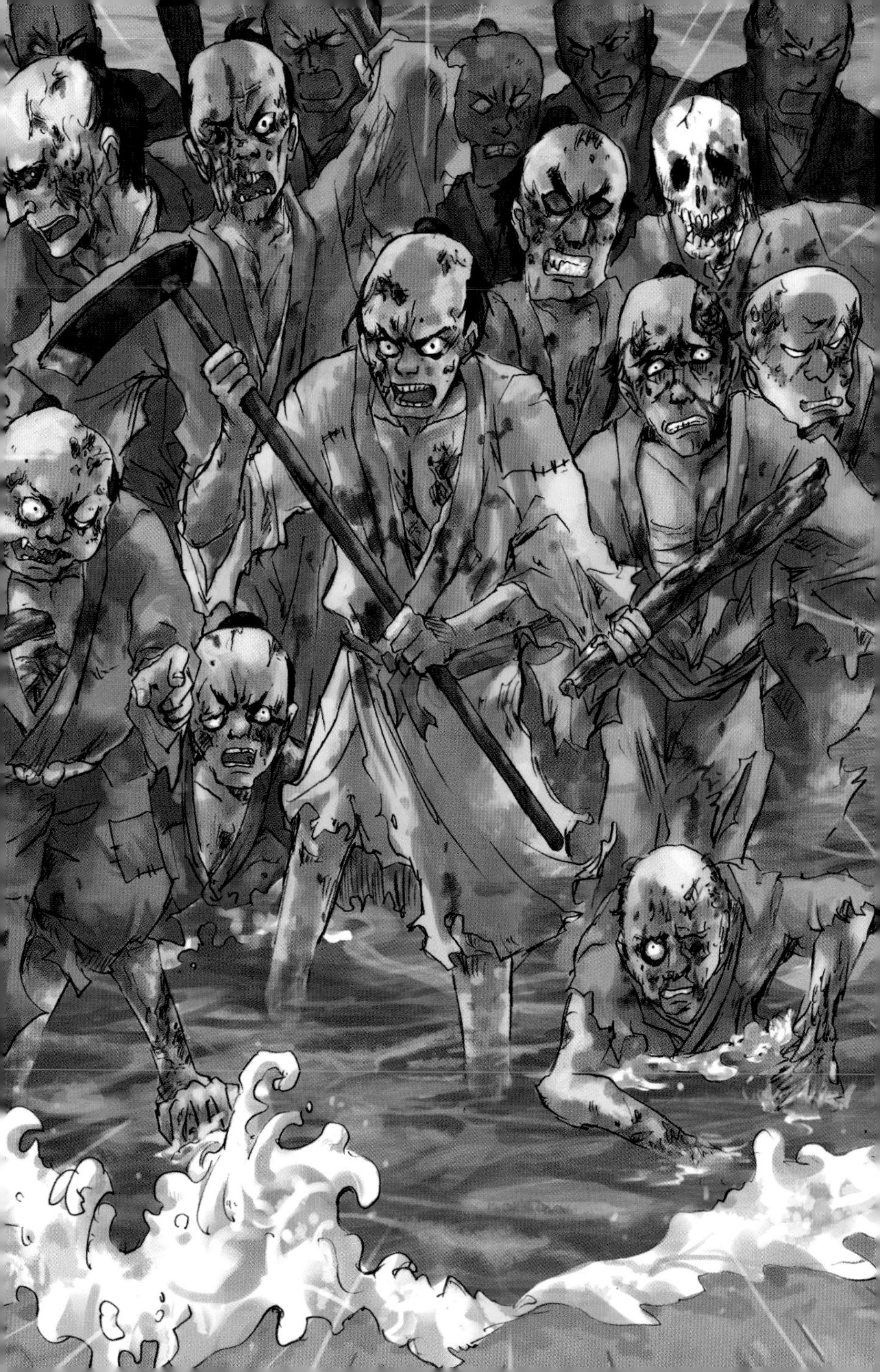

outside or make any noise. And whatever you do, don't look at the sea."

That night, the men gathered once again. Tracking down the governor (an easy task, given how loudly he was carrying on with yet another local girl), they dragged him outside, punching, kicking, and beating the life out of his body.

Now that the deed was done, they knew they had to escape. Staying would bring the wrath of the Shogun down upon the entire island. Not wanting to involve any of their neighbors as accomplices, they chose to hastily build a boat rather than commandeering one. Retreating to Hachikama shrine, they felled one of its holy cedars and quickly fashioned it into a large dugout canoe. With twenty-five men, a job that would normally take days was finished in mere hours, and the group set out before the morning light, seeking refuge on one of the neighboring islands.

They made landfall as dawn broke, marching into the nearest village to beg for shelter, even if only for a night. But upon hearing what the men had done, the locals quickly turned them away. Again and again, the men were sent back to the ocean by timid villagers too fearful of the consequences to give them sanctuary. And so they made one final voyage into the sea — one from which they would never return. The day was January 24th.

The Attack

Every year on January 24th, the angry souls of the dead men return to haunt the ports and beaches of the Izu islands and Izu Oshima in particular. Generations of locals making penance for their ancestor's failure to offer the Hiimi-sama shelter lock their doors, close their shutters, avoid looking at the sea, and don't leave for any reason. (And we mean ANY reason. In times of old before indoor plumbing was invented, this even meant relieving oneself in a bucket inside rather than heading out to use the privy.)

Those foolish enough to venture outside over the years are reported to have returned doused in blood, blinded, or driven insane by the sight of the Hiimi-sama. And that's a best-case scenario. Others have wound up dead… or never returned at all.

How to Survive

Haven't you been reading? Check the calendar. Is it January 24th? Do you happen to be on Izu Oshima? Stay inside! And quit making such a racket!

Yokai Connection

The Hiimi-sama superficially resembles a similar yokai called, somewhat confusingly, "Funa Yurei," ("Ghost Mariners" or "Sea Ghouls" — see *Yokai Attack!*). The key difference between the two is that the Hiimi-sama are the souls of a group of specific individuals lost in a certain incident, while the Funa Yurei aren't connected to any person in particular; rather, they symbolize the general concept of dying at sea. Remember: yurei tend to be a "someone," while yokai tend to be a "something."

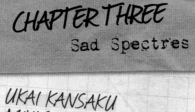

CHAPTER THREE
Sad Spectres

Not every yurei is fueled by anger or hatred. A sense of loss can be a powerful catalyst as well. These ghosts are driven by romance, family ties, and motherly love.

Sad Spectres: 14

UKAI KANSAKU

Name in Japanese: 鵜飼勘作
Gender: Male
a.k.a. Taira Tokitada
Born: 1130
Date of Death: 1189
Age at death: 58
Cause of death: Drowning
Type of ghost: Jibakurei
Distinctive features: Dressed in traditional fishing clothing
Place of internment: Isawa River
Location of haunting: Isawa River
Form of Attack: Incessant Manifestations
Existence: Historical
Threat Level: Low

Claim to Fame

Ukai means "cormorant fishing": the art of catching fish using trained waterfowl. Ukai Kansaku was one of these intrepid watermen, but his unfortunate choice of fishing waters led to his untimely demise — and return as a ghost.

The Story

Nichiren knew something was wrong the moment he set foot into the tiny hamlet.

The Buddhist monk had travelled far and wide through the countryside, ministering to those in need. On his various stops he had confronted illness, violence, even death, many times before. But he'd never seen anything quite like this. At the peak of the afternoon, the village paths were deserted, its shabby little homes shut tight, the nearby Isawa River quiet when it should be filled with the sounds of children, washer-women, and fishermen going about their daily lives.

Puzzled, the monk wandered from home to home and down to the riverbank. Fishing skiffs of the sort used to carry ukai fishermen and their birds sat on the banks, empty and disused, their nets in desperate need of repair. Had plague come to the area? Or was some villain threatening them with harm? Returning to the village, he caught sight of wary eyes peeking from cracks between boards, heard faint whispers inside the homes. So people did live here. What on earth had put the fear into them? Nichiren was determined to find out.

Explaining his calling, he asked why they shut themselves in at the height of the day. He learned that what struck terror into their hearts wasn't weather, plague, or war. It was a ghost. A ghost that refused to leave.

The Attack

According to the village elder, the ghost would rise from the water, prowl the vicinity, gurgling and moaning, its horribly waterlogged countenance terrifying anyone who caught sight of it. Nobody likes coming face to face with a ghost, but in a country filled with far more terrifying creatures, the villagers' desperate attempts to shut the spectre out seemed like overkill to the curious monk.

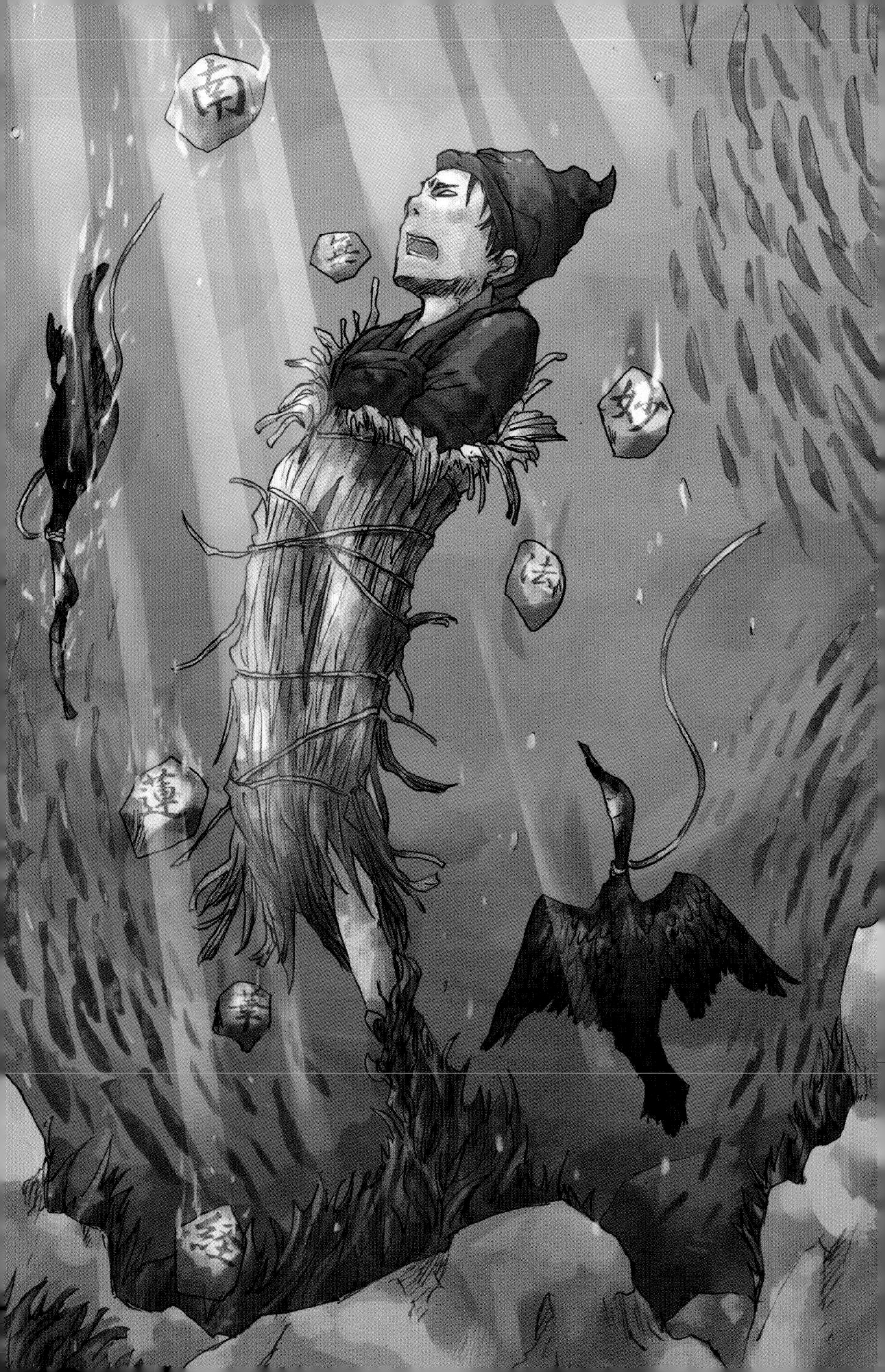
南
妙
法
蓮
経

Yoshitoshi's portrayal of the drama unfolding on the riverbank. 1885 woodblock print.

Nichiren made a beeline for the tributary where the ghost most often appeared. He sat upon the banks and meditated, waiting for it to show itself. He didn't wait long.

Nichiren addressed the ghost directly. What he learned from the spirit was the village's darkest secret — the story of a brutal murder.

The ghost's true name was Taira Tokidata, born an aristocrat and raised a warrior. His family line had long ruled all of Japan. But a bitter struggle erupted between the Taira and a rival clan called the Genji.

The Taira maintained a precarious grip on the throne until the 1185 Battle of Dan-no-Ura. The brutal confrontation all but wiped the Taira off the face of the map. Tokitada numbered among a handful of survivors.

It was often customary for new rulers to dispatch the followers of the old. Yet luck was with Tokitada yet again. During the battle, he had been charged with protecting a sacred mirror, one of three pieces of Imperial regalia used to confer legitimacy upon the emperor. Rather than flinging himself and the mirror into the sea, he quietly handed it over to the victors. In return, Yoritomo, leader of the Genji and soon to be Shogun, spared Tokitada's life, sentencing him to banishment rather than death.

Once a member of the upper crust, Tokitada was now reduced to eking out a life of poverty. Fortunately, as a boy he had learned the ways of ukai — how to select, catch, and train cormorants to fish for him. Now the vaguely remembered childhood pastime would prove to be his lifeline.

Taking a new name, Kansaku, he began wandering the countryside in search of a new life. After many days, he spotted a particularly promising tributary and loosed his birds. Almost at once a posse of locals appeared. They were furious that the interloper had violated their village's greatest taboo: fishing in a holy stretch of river where the taking of any life, even that of an insect, was forbidden.

Kansaku pled ignorance and begged forgiveness. But the mob would not be swayed. They viciously beat him, wrapped him tightly in a straw mat, and threw him into the chilly waters of the river, whereupon he sank like a stone. It hadn't been a pleasant death, or a just one, and that is why he now found his soul compelled to stay.

Upon hearing the sad tale, Nichiren could only shake his head, unsurprised at yet another example of man's cruelty to his fellow man. However little the villagers deserved relief, the least he could do was devise a way to release Kansaku from his bondage to the physical world.

Nichiren was a fervent believer in the power of the Lotus Sutra (and in fact would go on, later in life, to establish an influential sect of Buddhism based around it.) He began gathering rocks from the riverbank. One by one, he painted each with a single character from the sutra and tossed them into the waters that marked Kansaku's watery grave, some seventy thousand characters in all.

Nichiren neither ate nor rested for the three days and three nights it took him to complete the sutra. When he had finished, Tokitada/Kansaku appeared one final time, proffered his thanks, and departed to the spirit realm.

Surviving An Encounter

This is a ghost that needs your help. Situations like this aren't about personal safety, but rather in guiding a lost soul to a better place. Remain calm. Sit and listen. At the very least, you might hear an interesting story. And who knows — you just might unravel the problem that's been binding a spirit to the material world.

LEGACY OF A HAUNTING
Several of the actual stones Nichiren pitched into the river are on public display in an ornate container at Ukaisan Onmyo Temple (left). It is located in Yamanashi Prefecture, an hour and a half west of Tokyo by train. Both the temple and the river where Kansaku met his demise are a short walk from Isawa Onsen station, accessible via the JR Kaiji express from Shinjuku station.

MIYAGI

Name in Japanese: 宮木

Origin: "The Weed-Choked House" from Ugetsu Monogatari (Tales of Moonlight and Rain)

Gender: Female

Date of death: ca. 1456

Cause of death: Heartbreak

Distinctive features: Soot-darkened skin, unkempt hair, exhausted, sunken eyes. Otherwise, no indication of ghostly features

Place of internment: Unknown

Location of haunting: Mama Village (Currently Ishikawa, Sakura City, Chiba Prefecture)

Form of Attack: None (see below)

Existence: Believed to be fictional

Threat Level: Low

Claim to Fame

The tragic tale of the peasant Katsushiro and his faithful wife Miyagi isn't the first example in Japanese literature of a conjugal visit from the hereafter. But it is the most well-known.

The Story

Katsushiro's family had long eked out a living from the paddies in their village, but the backbreaking labor of rice-farming never quite suited the restless young dreamer. After inheriting the fields from his long-suffering parents, Katsushiro slept late, ignored his crops, and generally managed to drive his remaining family to the brink of ruin before hitting upon a scheme to revive his fortunes. Enchanted by the romance and potential riches of a wandering life, Katsushiro sold off the family's rice plots one spring, purchased a quantity of plain silk, and made preparations to leave for the far-flung capital of Kyoto.

In spite of his lackadaisical ways and sagging fortunes, Katsushiro had prospered in marriage: his wife Miyagi was a woman of uncommon beauty and intelligence. Unconvinced of the wisdom of selling off the fields — an asset with a humble but virtually guaranteed return — she begged and pleaded with her husband to abandon his plan. But this was medieval Japan, and a man's home was his castle. The stubbornly determined Katsushiro dismissed his wife's concerns with a promise to return before the autumn leaves fell.

In the capital, Katsushiro was able to sell all of his cloth for a tidy profit. Perhaps he had found his calling after all! But then came a development Katsushiro couldn't possibly have anticipated: a fracas broke out between rival warlords, with the losing side's forces retreating into the very province in which his village stood. Before long, civil war raged across the country, cutting off travel to vast swaths of the countryside.

Back in the village, Miyagi anxiously awaited the return of her husband, but autumn came and went with no sign of Katsushiro. The following year proved even worse for traveling, as marauding gangs swarmed into the region's now-lawless towns and cities. Besieged by a mix of

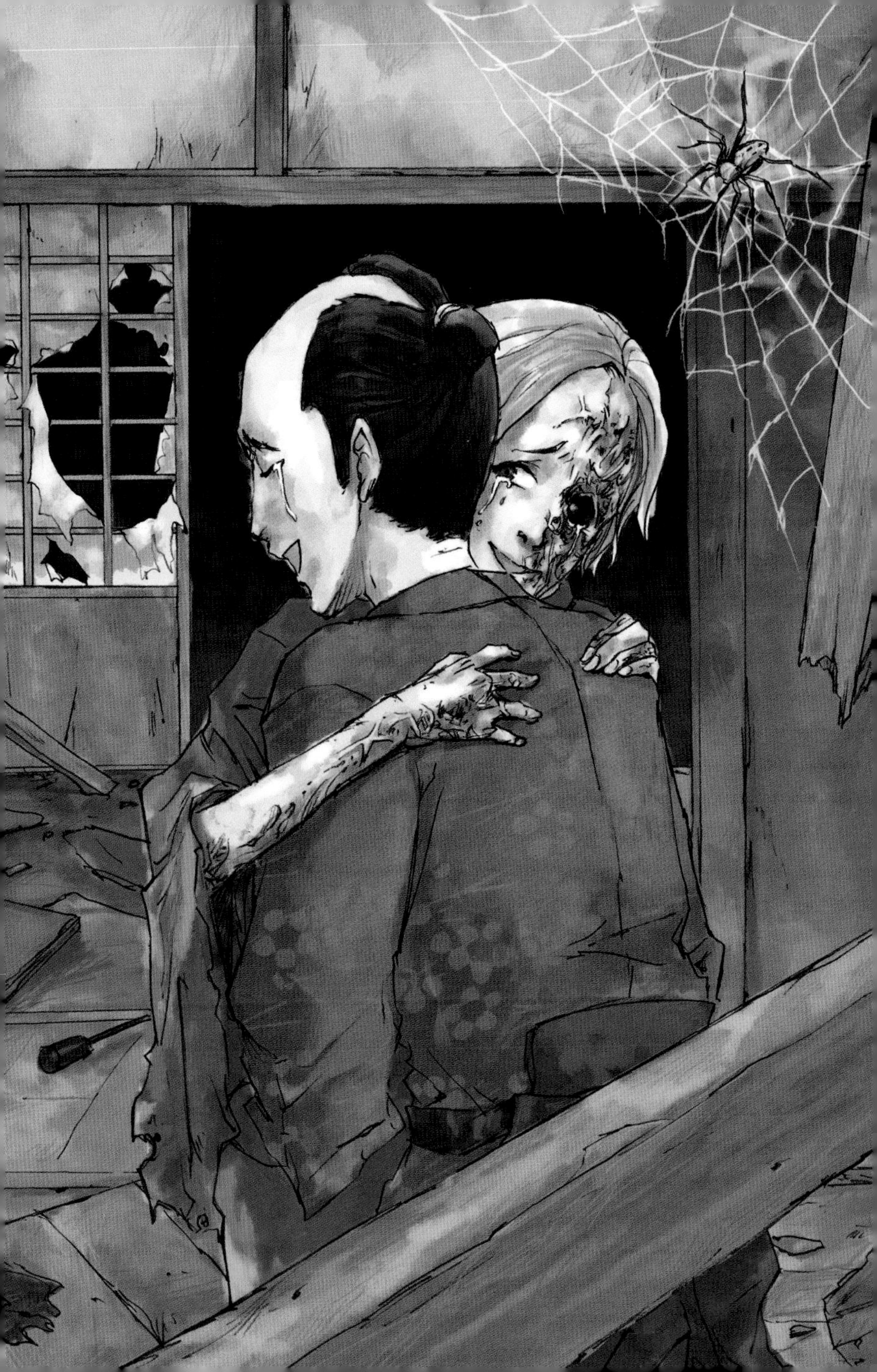

smooth-talking suitors, soldiers, and bandits eager to make the acquaintance of an apparently single woman, faithful young Miyagi barricaded herself in her home with rapidly dwindling supplies to wait… and wait… and wait. It would be seven long years before the conflict eased and Katsushiro was finally able to make his return.

Even knowing of the battles that had raged throughout his homeland, Katsushiro regarded the devastation that now surrounded him with a mix of awe and horror. The village's bridge had collapsed into the river. Once well-trod footpaths were obscured by high weeds. The handful of ramshackle dwellings still standing looked nothing like those he remembered, and bore family names he'd never heard. He was only able to identify his own by the sight of a large pine tree that stood on his property, though it had been ominously riven in two by a lightning strike. Yet his heart leapt to see his old house, standing beside the tree as always, apparently undamaged. There was even a flickering light in one window — his wife Miyagi was home! Katsushiro's heart began to pound as he approached the door.

It slid open before Katsushiro even managed to compose his thoughts. Miyagi stood before him, still beautiful in spite of bedraggled hair, worn clothes, and grimy skin. Wordlessly the pair embraced, the still air punctuated only by the sounds of their sobs. Inside, Katsushiro explained what had taken him so long. He had attempted to return years earlier, but had been robbed of his money and possessions by bandits along the way. He had no choice but to return to Kyoto, where he lived as a beggar, scrimping and saving the money he needed to make the long journey home. The couple talked through the night. And when the hour grew late, Katsushiro and Miyagi laid down together as husband and wife for the first time in seven years.

The Attack

Early the next morning, after the soundest sleep he'd enjoyed in years, the gentle drip of water on his face awakened Katsushiro. Through the clouds, he made out the waning moon shining beautifully overhead. Wait a second … where on earth was the roof? Katsushiro sat bolt upright on what had been a thick futon when he slept. Now he found himself in a decrepit room, its roof torn clean away to reveal the elements. Weeds poked through the crevices of shattered plaster walls and emerged from between the sodden seams of the rotting tatami mats. Hurrying to a window, he threw aside the skeleton of a shoji screen, its paper long since turned to dust. The house garden, once filled with carefully tended rows of herbs, was a labyrinth of twisting vines.

Forget the roof. Where was his wife? Plunging into the remains of his home, Katsushiro called out for Miyagi again and again. Back in the bedroom they had shared, he noticed the floorboards in one corner had been pulled up. Peering into the space, he saw what appeared to be a tiny burial mound sitting atop the earthen foundation. And before it, speared upon a sharpened stick, was a tiny scrap of stained paper with faded lettering. Plucking off the note, Katsushiro found a poem in the unmistakable handwriting of his wife:

Believing he would soon return
deceived by my own heart,
I lived on, until today.

Later Katsushiro learned that Miyagi had died many years previously.

Surviving an Encounter

Your life isn't in any danger from a yurei such as Miyagi's. But you certainly can't discount the emotional shock of realizing just how badly you screwed up by leaving your wonderful wife behind and galavanting off in search of riches. What were you thinking, man?

Really, this tale is more of a moral allegory than a horror story. The bottom line: always remember the consequences of your actions upon your loved ones here — or prepare to face them in the hereafter.

Trivia

Director Kenji Mizoguchi chose this episode as the focus for his theatrical version of *Ugetsu Monogatari*, which debuted in 1953. It is widely considered one of the classics of Japanese film. It won the Silver Lion Award for Best Direction at the Venice Film Festival that year, and continues to top best-of lists even today. The film's title was shortened to just *Ugetsu* for foreign markets.

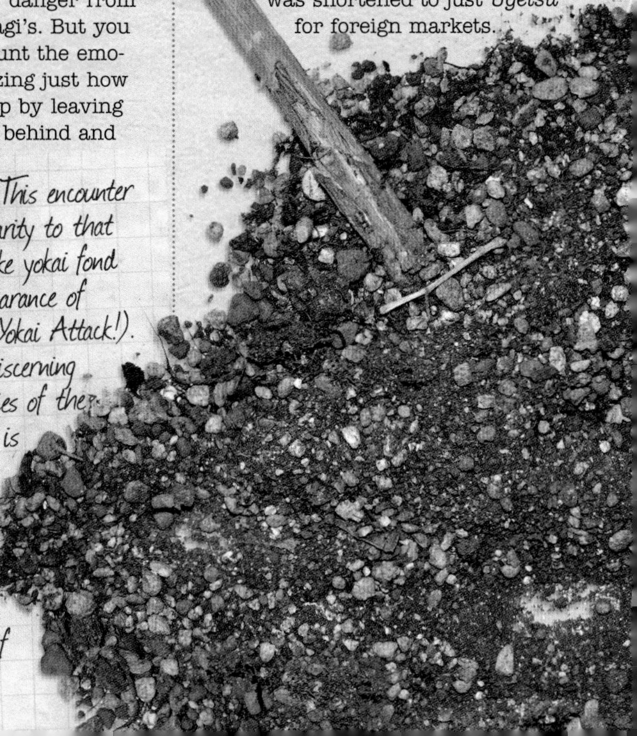

FOXY PHANTOMS: This encounter bears a deceptive similarity to that of a kitsune, the fox-like yokai fond of mimicking the appearance of beautiful women. (See Yokai Attack!). The best method for discerning between phantom ladies of the yokai and yurei variety is to follow Katsushiro's example and look for a burial mound nearby: the presence of human remains is a strong indicator of a yurei.

AME-KAI YUREI

Name in Japanese: 飴買い幽霊
Gender: Female
a.k.a.: The Candy-Buying Ghost (literal translation), Kosodate Yurei ("The Child-Rearing Ghost")
Occupation: Mother
Born: Unknown. Probably Late 16th century.
Date of Death: 1599?
Age at Death: Teens — early twenties (estimated)
Cause of Death: Poverty
Type of Ghost: Kosodate Yurei
Distinctive Features: Apparently normal, if impoverished young woman
Place of Internment: Daioji Temple, others
Location of haunting: Matsue, Kyoto, others
Form of Attack: N/A
Existence: Fictional??
Threat Level: Low

Claim to Fame

The Candy-Buying Ghost is one of Japan's most famous ghost tales. The single most well known version hails from the city of Matsue, as related by the legendary folklorist Lafcadio Hearn.

While there isn't any particular date associated with the Candy-Buying Ghost, it isn't set in modern times. The bare bones of the story — pun intended — are believed to hearken back to "Records of Yi Jian," a thirteenth-century Chinese text that's something like a *Grimm's Fairy Tales* for Song-era China. It contained a story about a "Rice Cake Buying Ghost" that bears many similarities to the later Japanese tale.

The Story

Late one evening, a certain candy shop had long since closed its shutters for the day when a knock came at the door. The shopkeeper, an elderly man who had served the community for years, was surprised to have a caller at such a hour — normally, the shop's young customers would all be tucked in bed with their families by this hour.

He was even more surprised when he opened the door. Standing before him wasn't a child but a grown woman, and a beautiful one at that. Even stranger was her outfit: white from head to toe, a color usually reserved for funeral ceremonies.

Apologizing for bothering him after hours, the woman begged the shopkeeper to sell her some candy. All she could afford was one *sen* worth — a trifling sum even by medieval standards, but the shopkeeper for his part was happy to oblige and wrapped up a single rock-sugar candy for her. Thanking him profusely, the mysterious woman turned and disappeared into the night. For the following five days, the same scene played out like clockwork. The late-night knock on the door. The woman in white. The single sen exchanged for a piece of cheap candy. The departure into the darkness.

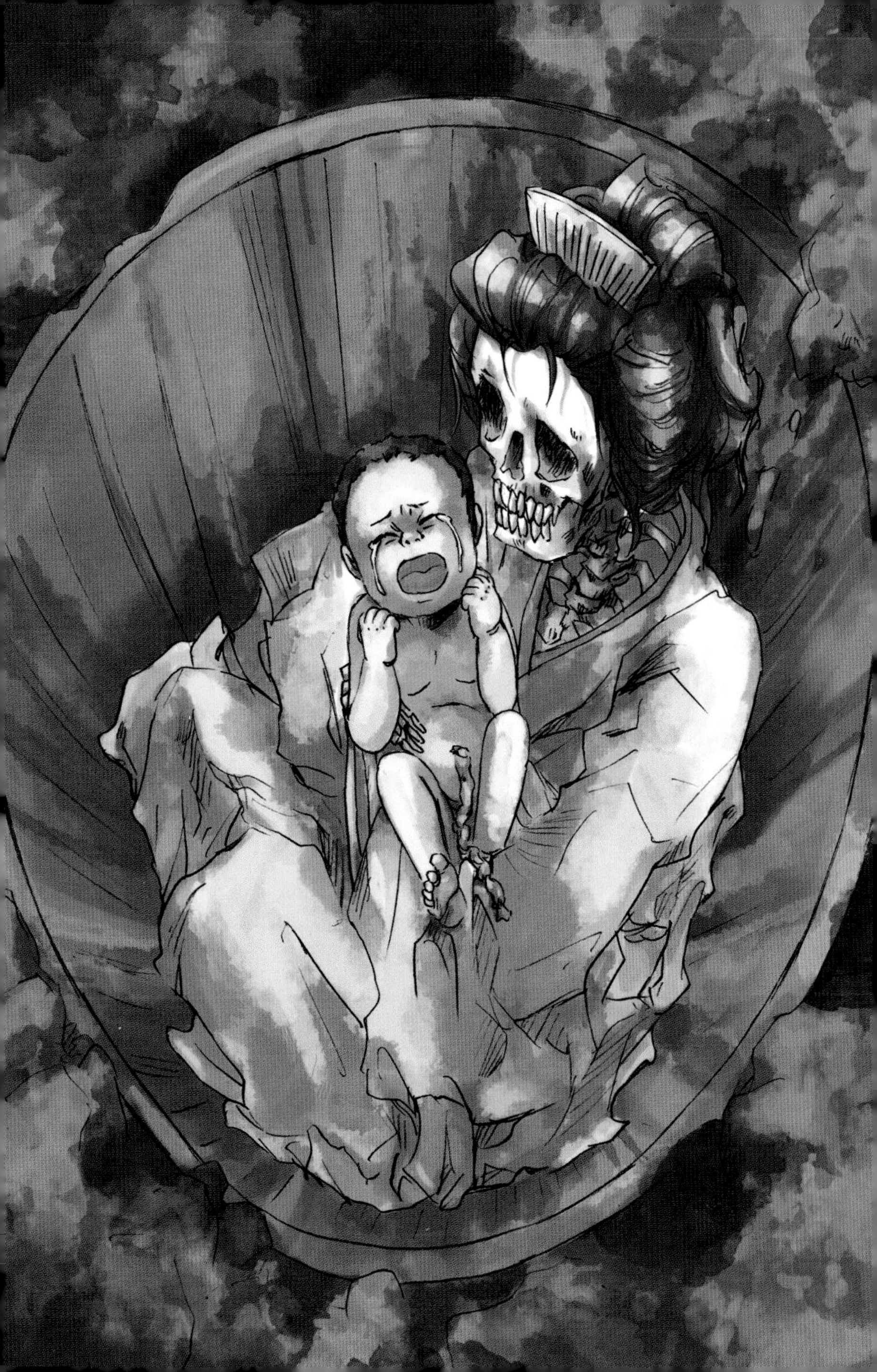

The shopkeeper's interest was piqued by this strange after-hours activity, but he wasn't sure what to do. The woman dressed strangely, but she seemed polite enough. And she certainly wasn't doing anything wrong; she was even paying him for his product. But something was definitely up. The only question was what.

His answer came on the seventh day. By then the shopkeeper had come to anticipate the nightly knock on his door. But things were different this time; that much was obvious from the downcast expression on her face. She had spent her last sen, she said, but desperately needed another candy. Could he spare just one more for her? "It will be the last time I bother you," she sobbed. Fortunately for her, the shopkeeper was a kindly sort. He didn't even think twice before handing over a piece of candy, gratis. And once again, the woman turned heel and began receding into the twilight.

Kind he may have been, but incurious he wasn't. Letting a few moments pass to build up enough distance between them, the shopkeeper slipped out and began to follow the strange woman.

Down the road he followed her, and around a corner. The path took her away from the residential area. In fact, it seemed to be leading into the local temple. Sure enough, the woman in white ducked through the side-entrance at the temple's gate. The shopkeeper scurried ahead and slipped through after her. She wasn't headed for the temple proper, but straight for the cemetery. In the dead of night. With candy. Why on earth?

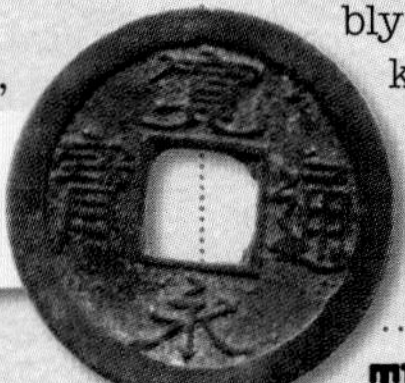
寛永通寳

A vintage sen coin. Six of these buys you passage to the underworld.

The shopkeeper wasn't exactly the sort who enjoyed prancing through a dark graveyard, but he'd come too far to turn back now. Peering from around a headstone, he caught sight of the woman again, pausing by a certain grave. Was she leaving the candy as an offering? Just then, she inexplicably turned to look at the shopkeeper, fixing him with her gaze. But he'd been quiet as a mouse! The old man went white as a sheet, his body frozen in terror.

The Attack

Just as the candy-seller tried to will himself into action, the woman glowed for a moment as if lit by some inner flame and promptly vanished from sight, her eyes never leaving his face the while.

The graveyard was dark and quiet once again. Coming to his senses, the shopkeeper made his way to the grave at which she had last been standing. It was a fresh one, he could tell. But there was no sign of the woman, or even the candy.

He heard sound, familiar yet utterly out of place. Straining to listen, the shopkeeper picked up the distinct yet muffled strains of a baby's wail. It couldn't be.... The shopkeeper dropped and pressed an ear to the ground. Now there was no mistaking it. The crying seemed to issue from the very grave itself!

Rushing to the temple, the shopkeeper returned with the monks — and a shovel. Hurriedly they excavated the grave, pulling the coffin from the ground, the baby's wails growing louder all the while. And prying off the lid, they found a perfectly healthy newborn, candy gripped in his tiny hand, held lovingly in the arms of a dead woman dressed entirely in white.

It was her.

Upon hearing the candy-seller's strange story, the monks surmised that the woman, who had been pregnant when she died, had somehow managed to give birth to her child in the grave. In Japanese funerals of the day, bodies were traditionally provided with six sen to pay the ferryman at the River Sanzu (Japan's River Styx); and these very coins were the ones she had used to purchase the candy that kept her child alive within the confines of their coffin. How fortunate that the candy-seller had chosen to follow her on that final night!

Surviving an Encounter:
Lucky for you, a certain candy store in Kyoto produces hard candies for just this sort of occasion: the Yurei Kosodate Ame ("Ghost Child-Rearing Candies"). The shop is called Minatoya and is located in Kyoto's Higashiyama ward, just a stone's throw from Rokudo Chinnoji Temple. It certainly can't hurt to stock up for those times you run into phantom mothers ... or their children. Where else can you buy this kind of "insurance" for just 500 yen?

For those not able to visit Kyoto, the Shinjuku branch of Tokyo's Isetan department store carries the candies as well.

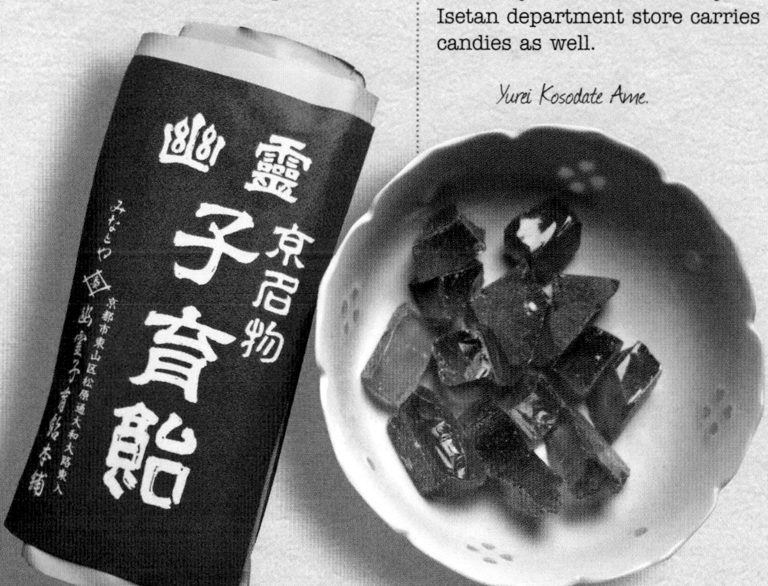
幽霊子育飴
京名物
みなとや
京都市東山区松原通大和大路東入
幽霊子育飴本舗

Yurei Kosodate Ame.

Sad Spectres: 17
THE OKIKU DOLL

Name in Japanese: お菊人形
Gender: *Female*
Occupation: *Being a doll*
Created: *ca. 1918*
Height: *Roughly 16 in (40cm)*
Type of Ghost: *Haunted doll*
Distinctive Features:
Standard Japanese doll; Dressed in kimono; Long, jet-black hair
Place of Internment:
Mannenji Temple, Hokkaido
Form of Attack: *Freaking people out with endlessly growing hair*
Existence: *Real*
Threat Level: *Low*

Claim to Fame

A surprising number of Japanese claim to be scared of dolls — not Barbie dolls or plush toys, but traditional Japanese dolls of a certain style. Those searching for the roots of this terror need look no further than the Okiku doll. It is the prototypical, stereotypical haunted doll of folklore. The Okiku doll occupies much the same spot in the Japanese heart as "Chucky" does in that of Americans, with one major twist: the story isn't fiction, and the doll resides in a certain temple to this very day.

The Story

The tale of the Okiku doll is of relatively recent vintage. It begins on Friday, August 15, 1919, when an eighteen-year-old by the name of Eikichi Suzuki took a trip to see the Semi-Centennial Exposition. The event, held in downtown Sapporo, commemorated the fiftieth anniversary of the island of Hokkaido's opening to settlement. The largest exposition ever held outside of a major city at the time, it featured dozens upon dozens of exhibits dedicated to local industries such as mining, logging, agriculture, and marine biology. Representatives from as far away as Sakhalin, Korea, and Taiwan sponsored pavilions. Close to 1.5 million people visited over the month-long course of the expo. It was a grand affair, the grandest Hokkaido had ever seen, and Eikichi must have been eagerly anticipating it, for he went soon after it opened.

Eikichi's younger sister, Kikuko, was just three years old, too small to accompany him on his trip. But the little girl must have been in his thoughts, for on the way back home he stopped by Sapporo's Tanuki Street, the city's largest shopping arcade, to pick up a gift for her. It was a beautiful Japanese doll, clad in a tiny silk kimono, its ivory-colored face topped by short tresses in a style known as a "bowl-cut" in English and okappa in Japanese.

A classic kid hairstyle, named after the yokai. (See Yokai Attack!) ⇨

It was an instant hit. Kikuko carried her new doll with her everywhere, and even took it to bed with her at night. But that winter, just after the new year, Kikuko fell ill. The Spanish

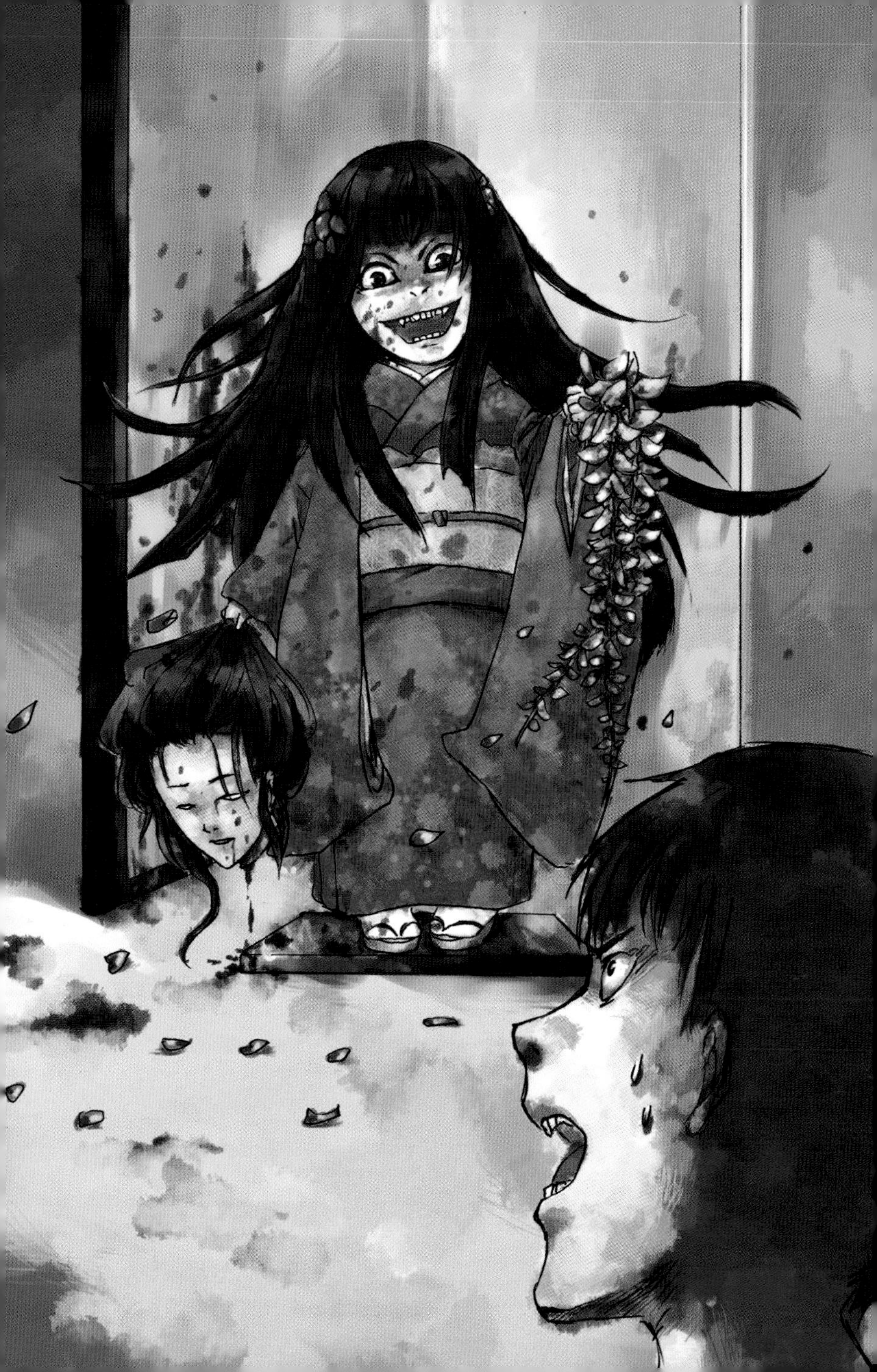

Flu pandemic was raging across the globe, and the government had severely restricted travel to and from the islands in an attempt to halt its spread. While the quarantine efforts helped, they weren't fully effective. Eventually, a quarter-million Japanese would succumb to the killer virus. Kikuko, who passed away on January 24, 1920, was one of them.

The loss devastated the family. In keeping with tradition, they placed the urn with Kikuko's ashes in their Buddhist altar. Eikichi put her favorite doll right alongside it. The family prayed before the altar daily, as is custom. And one day, Eikichi noticed something strange.

The Attack

The doll's hair seemed to be growing. Before long, the former bowl-cut had reached the doll's tiny shoulders.

The family didn't react to this discovery with fear. For their part, they came to believe that the soul of their beloved daughter had come to inhabit the doll, and continued to tend the altar daily.

Fast-forward twenty years to 1938. Eikichi's parents had long since passed away. War was on the horizon, and Eikichi had been drafted into the Imperial Army. When he received orders to deploy to Sakhalin with his regiment, he knew he wouldn't be able to look after Kikuko's ashes and her doll properly. He left both with his local Buddhist temple, Mannenji, for safekeeping.

We don't know what sorts of horrors Eikichi witnessed on the battlefields of the far north, but it is obvious that Kikuko was never far from his thoughts. When he returned after the war — narrowly avoiding being taken prisoner when the Russians overran Japanese defenses — he headed straight from the train station to Mannenji temple. What he saw there shocked him: now the doll's hair extended almost down to its feet. Word of the doll and its strange ability spread throughout Japan.

Well-loved dolls being prepared for their send-off in a "ningyo kuyo" (doll funeral) ceremony.

Some claimed the "Okiku doll" phenomenon, as it came to be called, was the result of a young girl's anger at having departed this world so quickly; others believed it was driven by sadness at having to part from her beloved brother and a wish to stay with her favorite possession.

We tend to embrace the latter theory, ourselves, as there is no question a deep connection existed between the two siblings. Of the rest of Eikichi's life, little is known. But the Okiku doll remains in the possession of Mannenji, where its locks continue to grow, slowly but surely, to this very day.

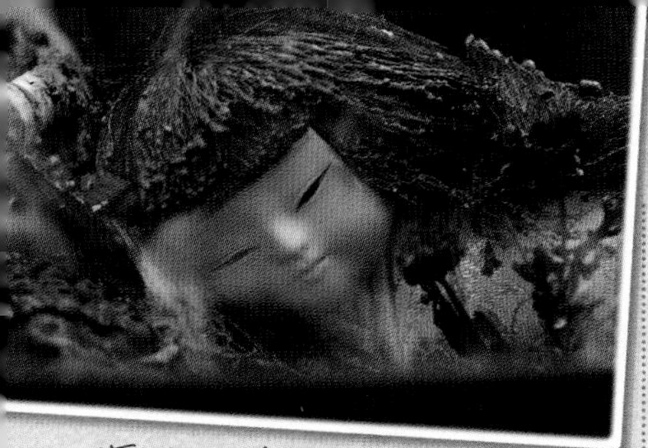

The climax of the ceremony.

Surviving an Encounter

There's nothing to fear except fear itself as far as the Okiku doll is concerned. That said, Okiku is but a representative of a phenomenon that is believed to occur throughout Japan. The concept of a wayward soul coming to inhabit a doll, whether sad or angry, is the stuff of nightmares in Japan.

Perhaps that's why *ningyo kuyo* — the practice of bringing dolls to a temple for consecration and cremation — remain common even in thoroughly modernized contemporary Japan. While this treatment is most common for disposing of "classic" figures, such as the *ohina* dolls that are traditionally displayed in homes during the Hinamatsuri doll festival, it isn't uncommon to see other toys that have spent a long time in the presence of people to be given the treatment as well.

In the vast majority of cases, individuals who bring dolls to ningyo kuyo ceremonies do so as a simple sign of respect; even if you aren't Japanese, it's easy to sympathize with not wanting to throw something once treasured by a child out with the garbage. But it's certainly a viable option for dealing with dolls inhabited by a spirit of some kind. (That said, do you really need to? Note that Mannenji hasn't burned the Okiku doll. Unlike "Chucky," there aren't any known cases of Japanese dolls — possessed or not — actually injuring their owners, save perhaps by gravity if they happen to fall off a high shelf.)

Hairy Science

In times of old, dollmakers often used real human hair for their dolls. In one method of attachment, a long (roughly 1-inch (25cm)) strand of hair would be folded over and attached at the midpoint to fully "flock" the head. Over time, the threads used to attach the strands can deteriorate while the hair itself remains strong, allowing the hair strands to gradually flop out to their full lengths. That said, critics feel this doesn't explain the very regular pace of growth of the Okiku doll's hair.

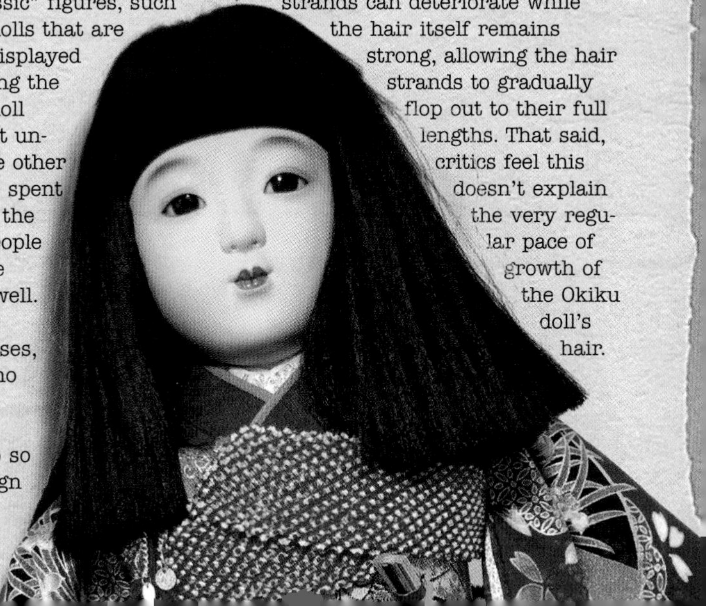

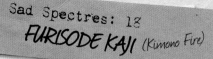

Sad Spectres: 18
FURISODE KAJI (Kimono Fire)

Name in Japanese: 振り袖火事
Name of Subject: Umeno
A.K.A.: Osame (in Lafcadio Hearn's retelling)
Gender: Female
Occupation: Dutiful daughter
Born: 1638
Date of Death: January 16, 1655
Age at Death: 17
Cause of Death: Heartbreak
Type of Phenomenon: Possession
Distinctive Features: No physical manifestation
Place of Internment: Honmyoji Temple
Location of Haunting: Edo (Tokyo) Area
Form of Attack: Sickness, death, fire
Existence: Unknown
Threat Level: Extremely High

Claim to Fame

Although Edo — as Tokyo was called prior to 1868 — ranked as one of the world's largest cities, its buildings were constructed almost entirely out of wood and paper. Fires easily spread from home to home and escalated to epic proportions, often devastating entire neighborhoods.

← For this reason, arson was one of a handful of crimes that warranted an instant death penalty.

Over the course of the seventeenth through nineteenth centuries, some one hundred major conflagrations swept the city. The largest of them broke out in 1657 and raged for nearly a week, wiping out more than half of the city and killing some 100,000 people — a disaster on par with the Great Kanto Earthquake of 1923 or the firebombing of Tokyo in 1945. Officially, it was called the Meireki Conflagration. But the survivors knew it by another name: the Furisode Kaji, or "Kimono Fire."

The Story

Sometimes tragedy begins with love at first sight.

On a fine spring morning two years before the conflagration, a young woman by the name of Umeno was out for a walk with her mother after attending services at Honmyoji Temple. Strolling the streets of Ueno, they happened to pass a beautifully-dressed young squire to a samurai hurrying along on an errand.

He vanished into the crowd in the blink of an eye, but something about the boy had lit a fire within Umeno. She dreamed of him by night and pined for him by day. First her parents indulged her, then scolded, then began to worry. As wealthy pawnbrokers they had the money to launch a search for the mysterious boy, but with little more than a hazy, half-glimpsed memory to go by it proved fruitless.

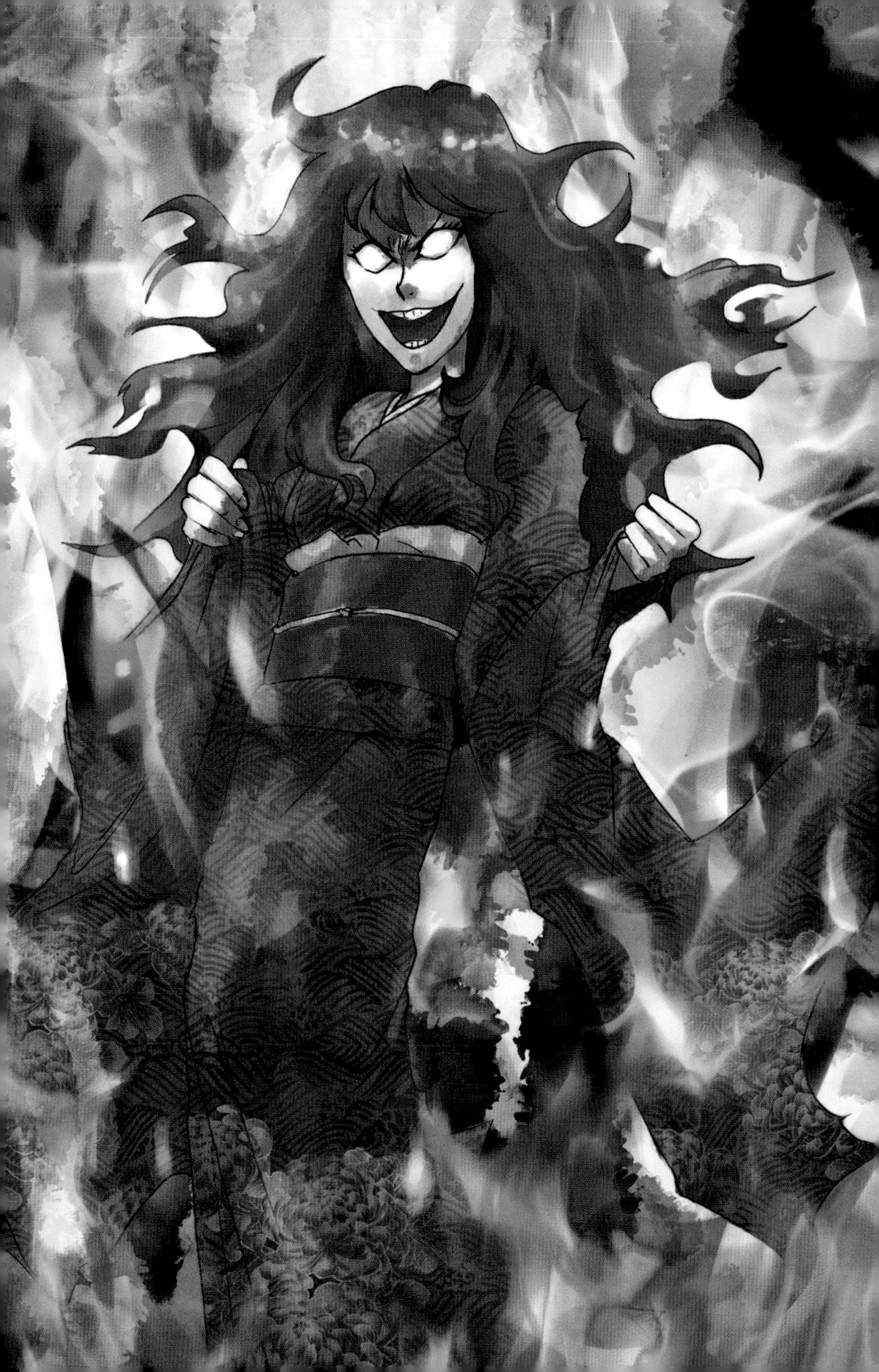

Umeno was inconsolable. She stopped eating and sleeping. Before long the formerly healthy young woman was a shadow of her former self. In a desperate attempt to forge some connection to her would-be lover, she begged her parents to make her a kimono as beautiful as the one the boy had been wearing. They reluctantly agreed, commissioning a beautiful silk garment adorned with chrysanthemum, bellflower, and waves, identical to the squire's in every way, save for being a long-sleeved cut of the sort worn by a woman.

The kimono served to lift her spirits somewhat, but the damage to her health had been done. Early the next year, Umeno passed away at the tender age of 17. Her distraught parents used the kimono to cover her coffin as it was transported to the cemetery, and then bequeathed it to Honmyoji Temple.

In keeping with custom of the time, the abbot of the temple sold the garment to a used-clothing dealer. The striking kimono quickly sold to another family, whose daughter wore it for only a short time before succumbing herself to illness at the age of 17. The kimono again made its way back to Honmyoji, whereupon it was re-sold to the clothing dealer. Another family purchased it for their daughter, and she too soon passed on at just 17 years old.

By now, the abbot knew he had more than just a kimono with a sad story on his hands. He called the parents of the deceased together. After discussing the situation, all parties agreed that it would be best to burn the kimono rather than see it cause further harm. And so the abbot prepared a *kuyo* ceremony to give the garment a proper send-off.

The Attack

The monks of the temple built a pyre to cremate the kimono according to Buddhist tradition. But in spite of performing the appropriate rituals, the spirit within was apparently unwilling to go quietly into the night.

The moment the kimono was laid atop the pyre, a sudden and powerful wind fanned the flames to frightening proportions. According to one account, a pillar of fire reached more than thirty-three feet (ten meters) into the air.

The monks, ill-equipped to deal with a blaze of these proportions, watched helplessly as the flames engulfed the temple, then leapt from rooftop to rooftop. Spreading first through the neighborhood and then into the district, the fire raged out of control through the streets of the city, apparently driven by the sheer power of a young girl denied her love and her life. Within hours, hurricane-force winds driven by the rising heat fanned the flames far beyond the abilities of even the fire brigades to deal with them. By the time the conflagration burned itself out some six days later, the Shogun's castle lay in ruins and the remains of the city were swathed in smoke so thick that it would be days before the victims' bodies could be located and buried.

Individual funerals were out of the question as entire families had been immolated in the blazes.

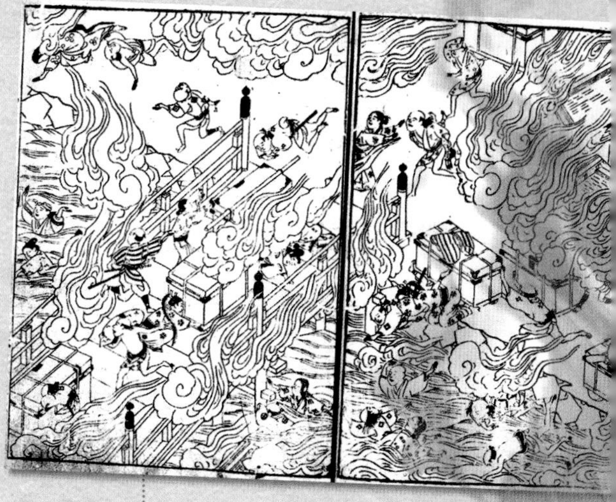

Scenes of the terror, chronicled in the 1661 book Musashi Abumi, by Asai Ryoi.

As such the Shogun ordered the construction of a memorial, "The Mound of a Million Souls," at what is now Ekoin Temple in Ryogoku district of Tokyo. Today it offers a final resting place for the souls of those who pass away without relatives or friends to care for them.

Of what happened to Umeno's family, or the mysterious samurai boy whose handsome looks kindled a metaphoric and literal fire, no record remains. But had he any foreshadowing of what his simple appearance and disappearance would have wrought, undoubtedly the young man would have made time to stop and chat with a lonely girl on that fine spring day.

How to Survive

The kimono in question is long since gone, but you're in serious trouble if you ever encounter a similarly possessed garment. If you choose to burn it, do so only under extremely controlled conditions.

Yokai Connection

The yokai called Kosode-no-te (see *Yokai Attack!*) is a kimono with phantom arms that enjoys frightening the individual who unwittingly puts it on. This rather playful behavior is a sharp contrast to the devastation wrought by the possessed garment that caused the Kimono Fire. It's also a good example of the general difference in modus operandi between yokai (who tend to be satisfied with scaring people) and yurei (who prefer to torment and kill them).

A Fiery Conspiracy?

The fire resulted in wide-ranging changes to Edo. In the two years it took to rebuild the city, large numbers of residents "immigrated" to outer suburbs, reducing the load on the city's jam-packed, overburdened downtown area. Meanwhile, in an effort to create firebreaks that would halt the spread of future conflagrations, the Shogunate expanded many of the city's narrow roads into boulevards called *hirokoji* — an innovation that can be seen today in Tokyo station names such as Ueno-Hirokoji. In fact, the changes were so sweeping and beneficial, rumors swirled that the government had set the fires on purpose in order to speed the process of change along.

THE FUTON OF TOTTORI

Name in Japanese: 鳥取の布団
Ghosts' Names: Unknown; two young brothers
Gender: Male
Born: Unknown
Age at Death: 6 and 8, respectively
Cause of Death: Hypothermia
Type of Phenomena: Possession
Distinctive Features: Vocalization only
Place of Internment: Kannon Temple
Location of Haunting: Tottori Pref.
Form of Attack: Pitiful crying
Existence: Unknown
Threat Level: Low

Claim to Fame

This oldie but goodie is one of the first *kaidan* (ghost stories) to reach the Western world, courtesy of translations by the great early-twentieth century Japanophiles Lafcadio Hearn and Frederick Hadland Davis.

Remote Tottori, located in Western Honshu, is the source of a great deal of folklore; even today, it retains an exotic, otherworldly sort of image as the country's least-populated prefecture. It also happens to be the birthplace of a famed contributor to yokai lore: Mizuki Shigeru, the manga artist who created the hit "Ge Ge Ge no Kitaro" series. (The connection runs so deep, in fact, that in 2010 Tottori's Yonago Airport officially changed its name to "Yonago Kitaro Airport.")

The story "Futon of Tottori" is the region's single most famous tale of terror. Ironically, most Japanese know it through the translation of Hearn's English retelling, the first time that the story was ever put down in writing.

The Attack

Long ago one winter, a small Tottori inn opened its doors to receive its first guest. The inn was a new establishment with a none-too-wealthy proprietor, and it was furnished entirely with items purchased from the local pawnbroker. Everything from the pillows to the utensils customers used to eat their meals had once been owned by someone else. While this may sound shocking to those raised in a more wealthy (not to mention hygienic) era, it was far from uncommon in those days.

The first guest, a travelling merchant, arrived to much fanfare, pampering, and of course, plenty of warm saké. After the guest had had his fill, the proprietor saw him off to his room and bade the man good night.

No sooner had the weary merchant laid his head down to rest than the sound of children's voices filled his ears. Faint but distinct, the refrain was repeated over and over again: "Are you cold, ani-san?" (the last bit being the way a younger addresses an older brother in Japanese.) "No, but you are, right?" came the reply. Again and again.

The merchant assumed the inn-keeper had kids, and put up with the racket for a while before finally

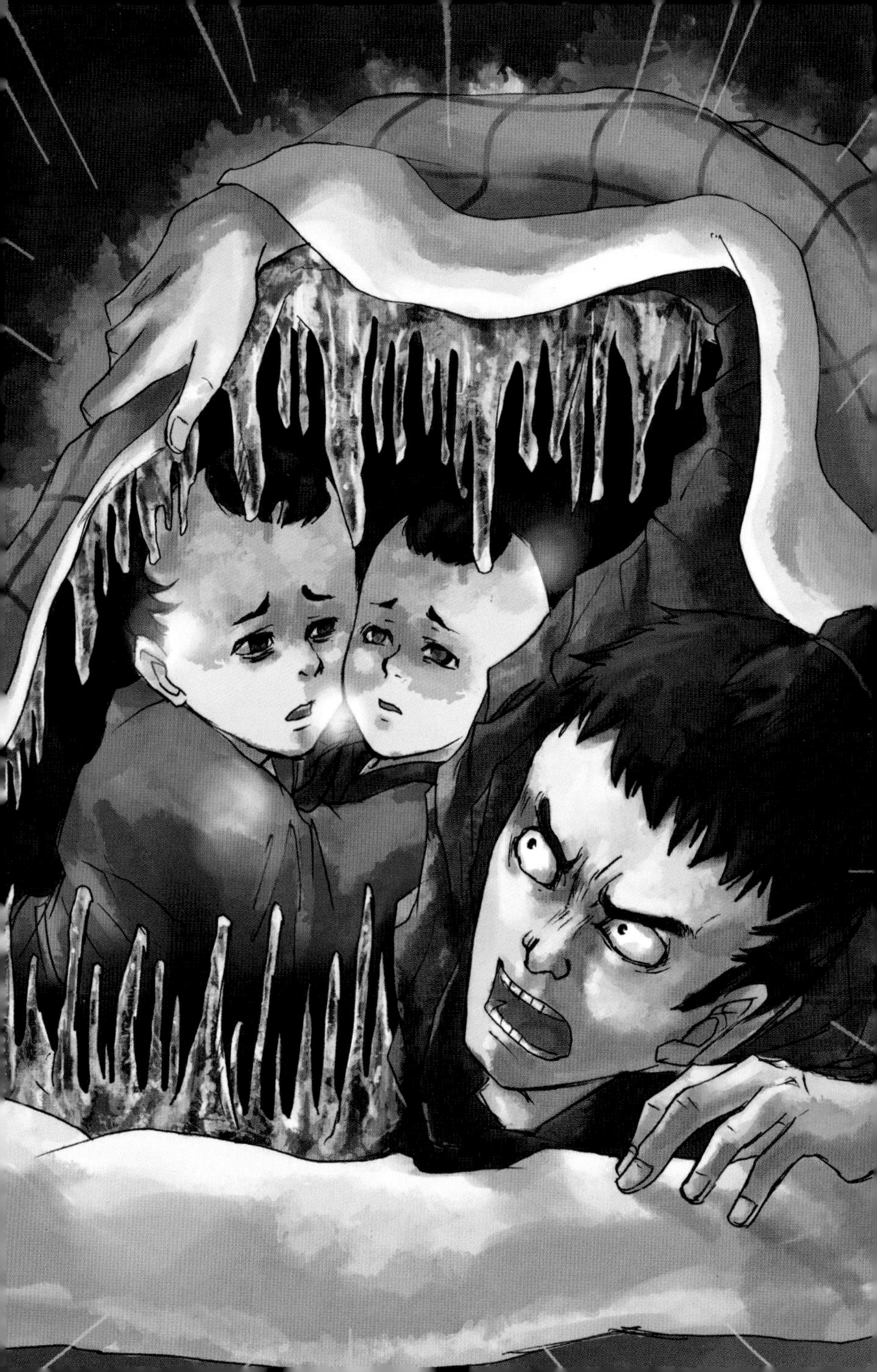

shouting for the tykes to pipe down. But just as he began drifting off to his long-awaited sleep …

"Are you cold, ani-san?" "No, but you are, right?" Again and again.

The funny thing was, the more he scrunched under the pillows and covers, the louder the plaintive voices grew. In fact, they seemed to be coming from the very futon-quilt itself! His hair practically standing on end, the man hurriedly gathered his things and headed for the innkeeper's chambers, demanding to check out. The innkeeper, incensed at being awakened at such a late hour, not to mention having his first customer run out on him, tried to persuade the merchant that the voices were nothing but saké-fueled dreams. But the merchant paid his tab in full and disappeared into the chilly night. The innkeeper scratched his head, went back to bed, and promptly forgot about the incident.

Until the next night, when the inn's second guest rushed out of his room, pounded on the innkeeper's door, and announced he was checking out. In the middle of the night. In a snowstorm. And this guy hadn't even touched the saké.

Now the innkeeper knew he had to investigate this for himself. Wrapping himself in the seemingly innocuous bedclothes that night, he lay and waited. Then it came. Quietly at first, almost too quiet to make out, then louder until unmistakable: "Are you cold, ani-san?" "No, but you are, right?"

The next morning, the innkeeper rushed to the pawnbroker from whom he'd bought the bedding. The pawnbroker said he'd purchased it from yet another. The innkeeper followed the trail to a tiny pawnshop in a ramshackle part of town, where he finally learned the sad story behind the haunted futon.

A young couple had arrived in the city that winter looking for work with their two young boys, just six and eight. The father died suddenly, followed quickly by the mother, leaving the two orphans on their own in a strange town. Remembering how their parents had made ends meet, the two began pawning their meager possessions for a day's food here and there, but eventually ran out of everything save a lone futon-quilt. Their landlord was a brutal man who tossed them out on their ears when they couldn't pay their rent. With nowhere to turn and a snowstorm blowing, the pair huddled together outside their former home, the falling snow providing a blanket for their final rest.

Surviving an Encounter

Suck it up or change rooms. Ghosts of this sort aren't particularly common, and when they do appear you're better off just rolling with it rather than getting upset. After all, the ghosts themselves had a pretty rough time to get where they are. C'mon, let 'em snuggle for a while. It's the least you can do.

In the case of the Futon from Tottori, the innkeeper gave the bedding to the monks at the temple at which the two young boys had been buried. They prayed for the souls of the children, whereupon the cries ceased and were never heard again.

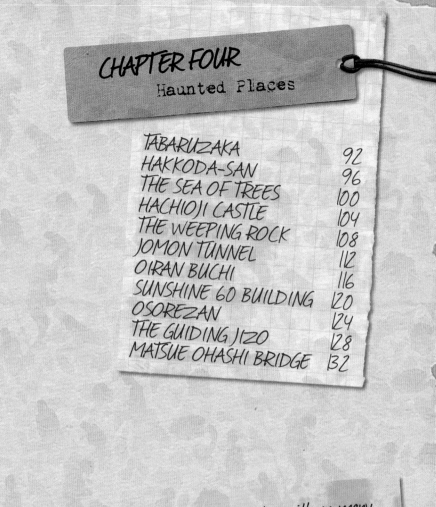

CHAPTER FOUR
Haunted Places

In a country with as many ghosts as Japan, is it any surprise there are so many haunted spots? Here's an overview of some of the most famous.

TABARUZAKA

Name in Japanese: 田原坂
a.k.a: Tabaru Hill; Tabaru Slope; "The Last Samurai Battlefield"
Location: Kyushu, Japan
Nearest Station: JR Tabaruzaka (Kagoshima Main Line)
Length of path: 1 mile (1.5km)
Altitude: 197 feet (60m)
Key Figure: Saigo Takamori (1828 – 1877)
Event that Caused Haunting: The Battle of Tabaruzaka, March 4, 1877
Type of Spot: Yurei-zaka ("Haunted hill")
Type of Phenomenon: Manifestations of fallen soldiers; Strange sounds; Strange odors
Threat Level: Variable

Claim to Fame

In a country as mountainous as Japan, perhaps it shouldn't be surprising that a great many hills and slopes are believed to be haunted for one reason or another. But the great-granddaddy of haunted hills is Tabaruzaka, just outside of the city of Kumamoto on the island of Kyushu. It paid for its reputation the old-fashioned way: with plenty of blood and guts. Tabaruzaka is the hill upon which Saigo Takamori, the real-life "Last Samurai," made an epic stand against the Japanese military during an attempted coup d'etat called the Satsuma Rebellion.

The Story

Saigo lived in turbulent times. For centuries, the samurai made their livings through fiefdoms called *han*. A han was ruled by a feudal lord called a daimyo, whose entire fortune rested upon taxes paid in rice by the many peasants who farmed the han's land. The Meiji Restoration of 1868 put an end to all of that.

In a successful attempt to modernize the country, the Emperor established a centralized government that confiscated all of the han from the daimyo. This was easier said than done, and often required a great deal of negotiating. Sometimes it required the threat of force.

As you might expect, being stripped of their ancestral holdings didn't sit well with this legendarily well-armed group of warriors. Tensions ran high, and less than a decade later, they flared into the Satsuma Rebellion of 1877, led by a former government bureaucrat turned revolutionary, Saigo Takamori.

Ironically, Saigo had played a key role in convincing (and on occasion forcing) key daimyo to hand over their domains. But he had a falling out with his fellow bureaucrats. He resigned his post and moved back south to his hometown of Kagoshima, where he founded a series of training academies. His only intention had been to give disaffected young samurai who had been stripped of their raison d'etre a place to go. But in traditional fashion his schools focused on martial as well as scholarly arts, and before long he had assembled what amounted to a

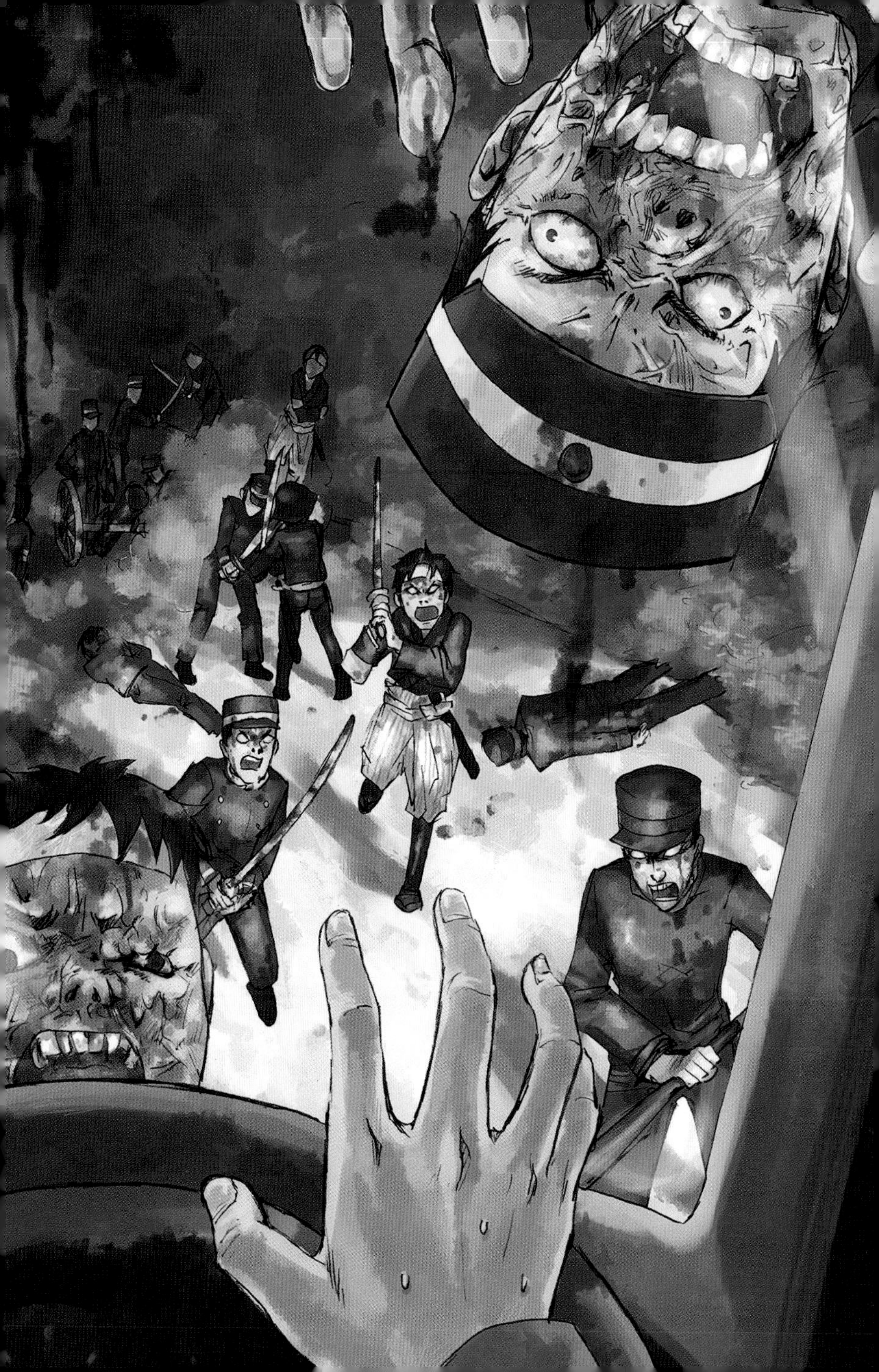

highly trained private army.

The passage of a controversial law in 1876 that banned both the wearing of swords and topknot hairstyles further inflamed the former samurai. When rumors of a government plan to assassinate Saigo surfaced, he could no longer reign in his troops and led them on a long march to the capital. The Satsuma Rebellion was on.

Yoshitoshi's woodblock print capturing the fighting around Kumamoto Castle (in the background).

The Battle of Tabaruzaka (Tabaru Hill) was one of four major skirmishes during the rebellion. The narrow road leading up the hill was a key supply route for Kumamoto Castle, which Saigo's men had surrounded, trapping a contingent of Imperial Army troops inside. Saigo placed a great number of his men on Tabaruzaka in an effort to block the reinforcements he knew would attempt to retake the castle. Imperial troops arrived on March 4, 1877, fully armed with modern rifles and cannon; many of Saigo's troops carried only swords or spears, but had the advantage of having occupied the hilly terrain first.

The going proved rough for both sides. Temperatures hovered near freezing, while an incessant cold rain turned the steep terrain into a morass of mud and rock. For seventeen days and nights the Imperial Army and the Satsuma rebels traded fire and engaged in hand-to-hand combat. By the end of it the slopes ran red with the blood of the fallen from both sides. Some two thousand men lay dead with an equal number wounded, and neither side able to declare victory. Even today the name Tabaruzaka carries connotations of a drawn-out war of attrition, similar to the American Civil War's Battle of Antietam.

Although neither side truly "lost," the stalemate signaled the beginning of the end for Saigo's revolution. Choosing to retreat, Saigo led several other major skirmishes but was felled by enemy gunfire in the Battle of Shiroyama, just outside of Kagoshima, on September 24, 1877. And the Satsuma Rebellion died with him.

Although the samurai never regained their former place in society, Saigo's fighting spirit and refusal to compromise his ideals made him a folk hero. Public sentiment forced the government to issue a posthumous pardon in 1889.

The Attack

Tabaruzaka's hills remain a popular place for local youth to test their mettle in midnight visits to the former battlegrounds. The most "active" spots are said to be the area around a life-sized bronze statue of a mounted soldier, around which the spectres of foot-soldiers are said to rally, and the Nanamoto Military Cemetery, home to the remains of 300 soldiers from both sides. Strange smells and ominous phantoms have been reported in the area, particularly around the graves.

How to Survive

Tabaruzaka's ghosts have never been implicated in any deaths. But if you're the sort who doesn't want a close encounter, try to visit on a sunny day. According to local lore, ghosts are far more likely to appear on Tabaruzaka when it rains. And whatever you do, stay out of the phone booth in front of the visitor's center at night. You've been warned.

Getting There

Tabaruzaka is located just out-side of the city of Kumamoto in Kyushu. The park is a twenty-minute drive from JR Tabaruzaka Station on the Kagoshima Main Line. The park itself is open 24 hours; the visitor's center is open from 9am-5pm daily (closed Mondays).

THE SLIPPERY SLOPE OF HAUNTED HILLS

Tabaruzaka is but the most famous of a wide variety of "yurei zaka" (haunted hills) throughout Japan. But it's important to make a distinction among those truly believed to be haunted, those where weird phenomena take place, and those that are essentially place names.

A good example of the latter is the "Yurei Zaka" located in the Mita ward of Tokyo. Found amidst a great number of Buddhist temples and graveyards and clearly marked as a haunted slope, a pedestrian there might be forgiven for worrying about chance encounters with the undead. But in reality, the name is just a play on words; it was formerly written with characters that are a homonym for ghost: 有礼坂. There are actually nine "Yurei Zaka" in Tokyo, the vast majority so called because they are dark sorts of places that aren't particularly fun to walk at night.

The second type of supposedly haunted slope is the sort of place called a "magnetic hill" or "gravity hill" in English. These are places where the topography and an obscured horizon conspire to create the illusion that a slight downward slope is actually an uphill one. A ball, or car left in neutral, will thus appear to roll up rather than down. Hills of this sort include the "Yurei Zaka" of Fukuoka, the "Obake Zaka" of Gunma, and the "Mystery Zaka" of Iwate Prefecture.

And that brings us to our third and final category: haunted slopes that are what their name implies. Tabaruzaka is the most famous of this type, but there are many others as well. Our personal favorite is the Kiinokuni Zaka (Kii Slope) in downtown Tokyo, upon which faceless yokai called the Nopperabo were once believed to dwell. (See Yokai Attack!)

Haunted Places: 21

HAKKODA-SAN

Name in Japanese: 八甲田山
a.k.a. *Mount Hakkoda: The Hakkoda Mountains*
Location: *Aomori, Japan*
Terrain: *Volcanic (dormant)*
Nearest Station: *Aomori*
Highest Peak: *Mt Odake: 5,200 ft (1,585 m)*
Cataloged in: *100 Famous Japanese Mountains*
Key Figures: *Japan's Imperial Army Fifth Infantry Group*
Event that Caused Haunting: *"The Hakkoda Exercise" of January 23, 1902*
Type of Location: *"Yurei spot" (Haunted area)*
Type of Phenomenon: *Visible/Audible manifestations*
Threat Level: *Variable*

Claim to Fame

You're caught in a blizzard. Wearing nothing but thin cotton clothes. With no food. No way to start a fire. No one to turn to for help. Zero visibility. Zero idea how to get back home. All you can do is walk in circles as the relentless cold slowly eats away your limbs and your sanity.

Sounds like a nightmare — only it's reality. This was the harsh fate awaiting the Imperial Army's 5th Infantry Group on a winter day in 1902. 210 healthy young men climbed Mount Hakkoda on a routine training mission. Within a few days, one hundred and ninety-nine of them would be dead. And that is why Hakkoda is widely considered to be Japan's single most haunted natural spot.

Although it's actually a range and not a single peak, the area is commonly referred to as "Mount Hakkoda" in Japanese and English.

The Story

The Hakkoda range has long been renowned for its treacherous weather. Paths disappear in sudden white-outs that last for days, while temperatures regularly plunge to some of the lowest in the country.

After the 1868 Meiji Restoration (see p.92) Japan modernized at a breakneck pace. Within just two decades, it had transformed from an isolated feudal backwater into an aggressive regional power with designs on creating an empire in East Asia. Their chief rival in this enterprise was Russia, which had even managed to establish a naval base just north of the Korean peninsula.

In the event of a war between the two powers, the Japanese military theorized that the Russians might attack from the north, shelling rail lines and roadways in an attempt to launch an invasion from the port city of Aomori. If the Russians succeeded, the only way to get troops to the hot zone would be through the mountain passes of Hakkoda. During the warmer months, this

One really did break out a few years later: the Russo-Japanese War (1904–05) ⇨

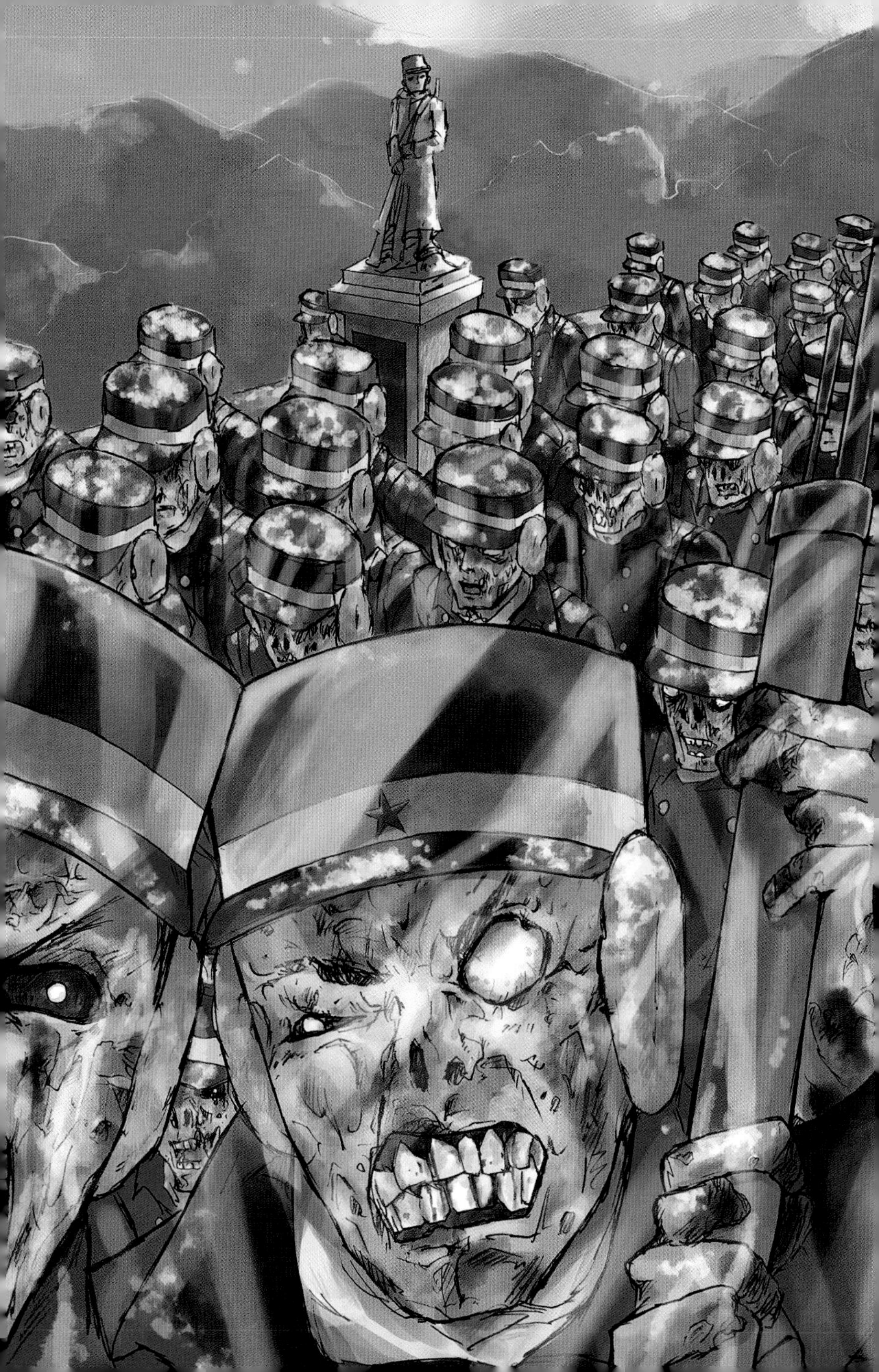

would merely be a pain in the neck. But what if the attack came in mid-winter?

The commanding officers of the Imperial Japanese Army's 8th Division decided to settle the question by conducting a "test-run."

The objective of the mission was to gather data about dealing with extreme conditions. But none of the commanders had any experience living or working in extreme cold. The soldiers were issued standard gear and rations, and given no training in mountaineering or survival techniques. Even worse was the muddled command structure. Although the group's Captain had planned out the entire mission, his superior officer, the Major, made a last-minute decision to tag along as well. While the Captain had some sense of just how arduous of a trek this would be, his Major firmly believed that Imperial Fighting Spirit would trump the effects of snow and ice.

The expeditionary force left on January 23, 1902. As the 5th made its way into the mountains, the weather showed obvious signs of storm and local villagers attempted to talk them out of making the climb. But the Major's arrogance prevailed, and the company pushed on without even bothering to hire a local guide. The next day a blizzard descended, the likes of which had never been seen in Japan then or since. The path disappeared in white out conditions as the temperature plunged to the lowest ever recorded in Japan.

The weather trapped the soldiers on the mountain. They struggled through waist-deep snow in cotton uniforms that soaked with the sweat of exertion and then turned to ice. Their rations froze so solid that it took a hit from a bayonet to shatter them. They couldn't even manage to start a fire. The Captain ordered the troops to dig trenches in an effort to wait out the gale, but at two in the morning the Major had had enough and ordered a perilous night descent. The Captain led the way for several hours, only to be relieved midway by the Major, who took the company in the completely wrong direction. By morning more than forty men were missing and presumed dead in the wind-whipped snow.

Frostbite and exhaustion set in. The men of the company began losing their minds. Stands of trees

PEE PERIL

The devastating cold rendered even the most mundane of tasks impossible. The simple act of urination proved deadly for the men; stricken by frostbite, many were unable to re-button their pants after relieving themselves, hastening heat loss and thus their demise. Those who saw this and chose to wet themselves instead wound up with frozen pants and an equally fast death.

⟵ Literally. Nearby Asahikawa registered -41° during the storm, a record that has stood for more than 100 years.

were mistaken for rescue teams. Some removed their clothes and attempted to "swim" back through the chest-deep drifts. On day three, command totally disintegrated.

By the time a rescue team made its way into the area on January 27, some 199 of the original 210 were missing, including the Captain. Only eleven horrifically frostbitten soldiers eventually survived, many of them as multiple amputees. It would take until May to recover the bodies of their comrades.

The Attack

Today, a statue of Fusanosuke Goto, the first survivor found, stands on Mount Hakkoda as a memorial to the men who lost their lives in the incident. The statue represents how he was actually discovered, frozen upright in mid-stride.

This entire area in the vicinity of the statue is treated as a highly active "yurei spot" and reports of apparitions both audible and visual abound; footage of purported specters has even been broadcast on Japanese TV. Common reports include strange lights, the sound of men calling out, and even the appearance of rows of soldiers in period clothing.

How to Survive

Don't want to run into any ghosts? Don't go to the memorial on Mount Hakkoda, especially in the dead of night, and even more especially in the dead of winter. The conditions atop Mount Hakkoda in a snowstorm can be far more dangerous than any ghost (though that said, there's actually a ski resort up there now).

Getting There

The Snow March Memorial Museum is a roughly 45 minute drive from JR Aomori Station. It's open from 9am to 6pm daily (closed Tuesdays). It houses a variety of items carried by the victims and survivors. A trail from the museum leads into the mountains themselves, where the statue of Fusanosuke Goto stands.

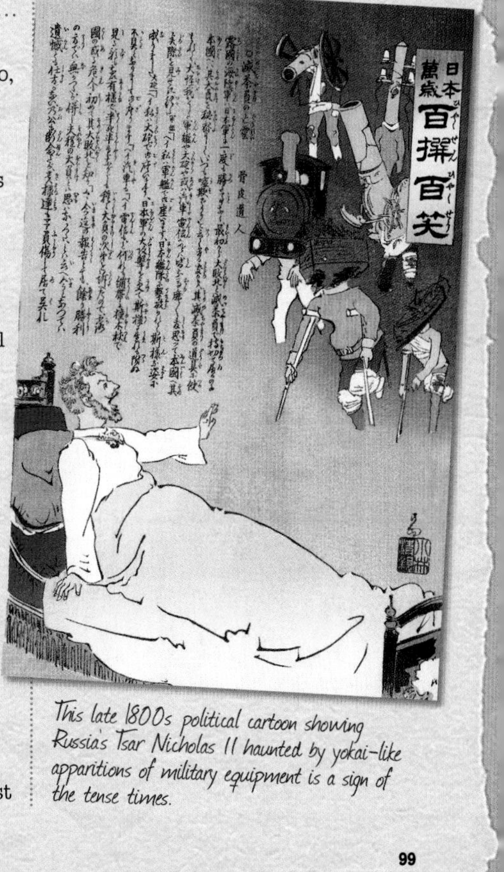
日本萬歳
百撰百笑
骨皮道人

This late 1800s political cartoon showing Russia's Tsar Nicholas II haunted by yokai-like apparitions of military equipment is a sign of the tense times.

THE SEA OF TREES

Name in Japanese: 樹海
a.k.a. Jukai ("Sea of Trees" in Japanese);
Suicide Forest; Aokigahara (official place name)
Type of Forest: Primeval (old-growth)
Location: Shizuoka and Yamanashi Prefecture
(Base of Mount Fuji)
Nearest Station: JR Kawaguchiko
Part of: Fuji-Hakone-Izu National Park
Altitude: 3000-4250 feet (920 – 1300m)
above sea level
Foliage: Mixed coniferous/deciduous
(Mainly hemlock and cypress)
Area: Roughly 7,500 acres (30 km2)
Event that Caused Haunting: Many, many
suicides (Or are they just a symptom?)
Type of Location: Suicide Spot
Type of Phenomenon:
Once you go in, you don't get out
Threat Level: Depends on your frame of mind

Claim to Fame

At the foot of iconic Mount Fuji lies the Jukai (Sea of Trees), Japan's single most famous spot for suicides. So named for its seemingly endless expanse as seen from the mountain's peak, this is a stretch of wilderness so dense and untamed that the Japan Self-Defense Forces uses it to conduct survival training exercises.

Some say that those wanting to end their lives here are attracted by a combination of the site's notorious reputation and its remote location. Others hold that there is something very wrong with the forest itself, and that it traps innocent victims along with those who choose to end their lives here.

The Story

Mount Fuji has long been venerated by the Japanese, both because it truly is an awe-inspiring volcanic peak and for its exquisite symmetry. Its existence is so singular that it is considered a *reizan*, a hard-to-translate term that is usually rendered as "sacred mountain." But note that rei — it's the exact same one as used in the word yurei. The general idea is that this isn't a peak to be taken lightly. It has a soul. There are powerful energies at work here. It's the type of place that gets angry from time to time and isn't afraid to show it.

The Sea of Trees covers a vast expanse of terrain in the foothills of this holy peak. True to its name, it really was once a massive body of water. Although Fuji is dormant today, a 9th century eruption filled the former lake with a thick, mineral-rich deposit of debris and ash that in turn gave rise to the dense forest that blankets the area now.

Today it's officially known as Aokigahara, which means something like "Green Fields." Sounds like a great place for a picnic, right? Yet these fields are more black than green, as the dense foliage strains out most of the

Potential suicides often mark their trail through the foliage with colored vinyl tape marking a way back out of the forest should they change their minds.

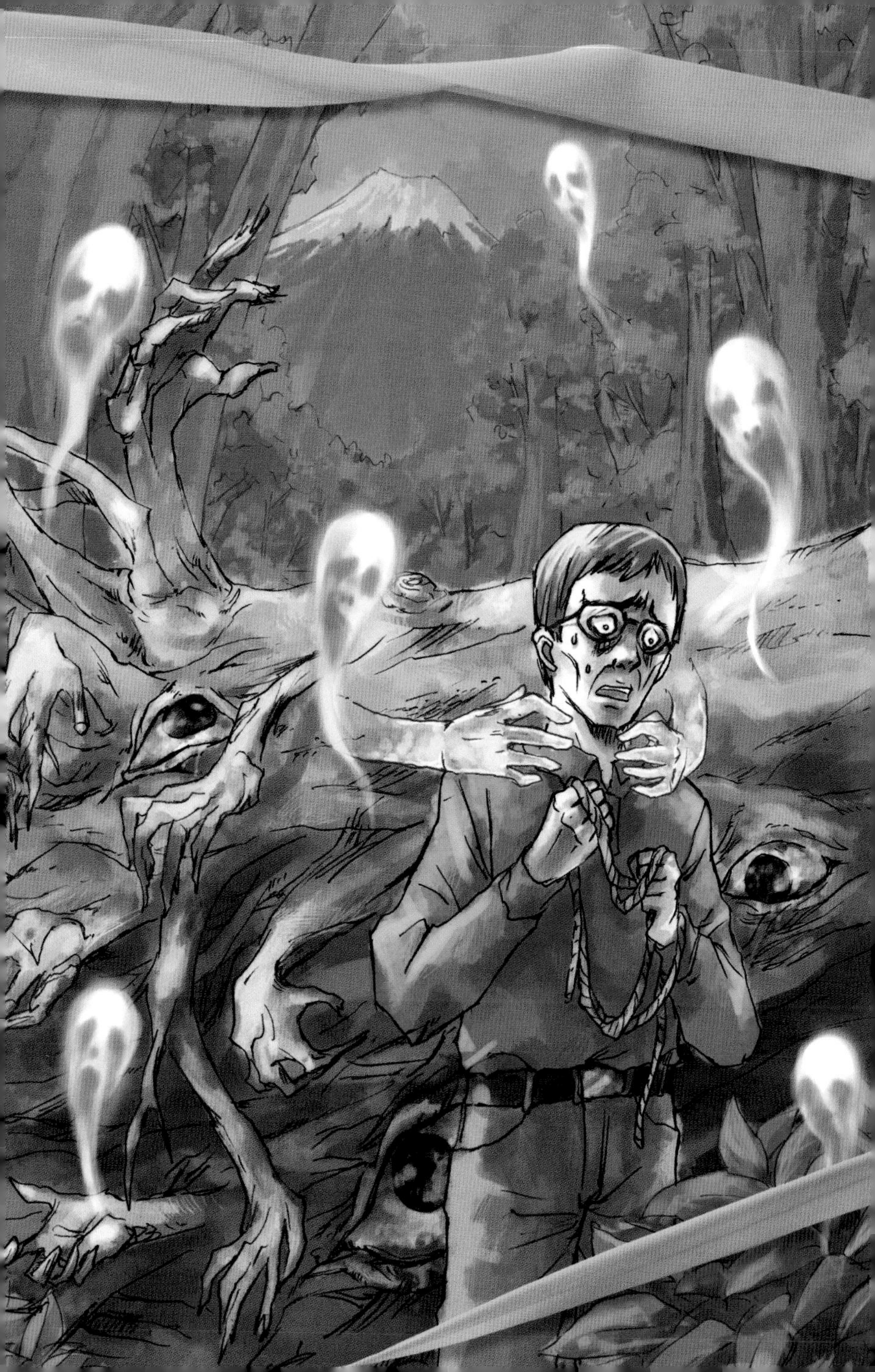

sunlight before it has a chance to reach the forest floor. And strange forces are at work in the area — some that can be explained by science, and some that cannot.

The Attack

The Sea of Trees claims its victims in one of two ways.

The first is simply losing one's way in the dark forest. Low light levels make it easy to misjudge the time of day. The thick tree cover and underbrush absorb sounds, making it easy to become separated from others. And while scientists refute the claim, many swear that their compasses only work sporadically here — supposedly thrown out of whack because of magnetic ore in the magma deposits that form the base layer of the forest. Whatever the case, it's a fact that it's easy to get lost here — and occasionally never make it out again at all, even if that was your original intention.

But the Sea of Trees didn't earn its notoriety from navigational issues. It's infamous for suicides. People come from all over Japan to end their lives here. The police conduct annual sweeps for bodies of missing people here, but the terrain is vast and rugged. Some of the victims are found in advanced stages of decomposition, or ripped to pieces by the animals of the forest. Many are never found at all, their skeletons quietly moldering away amidst the trees. Some feel that more is at work here than mere media sensationalism — that the dead are calling the living to join them.

Whatever is calling them, there's no question the dead are here. Annual suicide rates climbed throughout the Eighties and Nineties; in 2003 alone, one hundred bodies were recovered from the forest. As such the trailheads are marked with large signs imploring the desperate to reconsider: "your parents gave you life; think about them, your friends, and your children one more time, and call us at the number below." A box filled with pamphlets for a crisis hotline is even blunter: "Before you go to the underworld, read this."

Surviving an Encounter

1) Forget about the ghosts. Focus on the living. If you encounter someone who seems out of sorts in an area known for suicides, you have an obligation to approach them and see if there is anything you can do to help. Sometimes even the slightest human contact can be enough to turn a desperate soul away from the edge.

2) Follow the lines. Those still struggling with their inner demons often mark their trail through the foliage with vinyl tape or rope, leaving them a "lifeline" to return should they change their minds. In a best-case scenario, these trails can lead to someone in need of serious help. But you also need to steel yourself for the worst-case scenario, which is arriving too late.

3) Take solace in the fact that while the number of people who attempt to kill themselves in the Sea of Trees increases every year, so too do the number of people rescued by local outreach efforts. In

2010, 193 people were persuaded to seek help rather than ending their lives in the Sea of Trees.

Why, Jukai?

The Sea of Trees is but the most recent in a series of famed suicide spots. In the prewar era, Japan's most well-known suicide spot was another active volcano: Mount Mihara on Izu-Oshima Island.

After the sensationalized report of a young girl's suicide on the volcano's peak dominated newspaper headlines in 1933, young men and women began making pilgrimages to the island with the aim of ending their lives in the volcanic caldera. Driven by crushing poverty, illness, and other personal problems, close to a thousand of them threw themselves into its bubbling cauldron that year. All told, some 3,000 young Japanese chose to end their lives on Mount Mihara in the decade leading up to the end of World War II. It even inspired a grotesque tourist industry in which local ferry lines played up the tragedies to attract desperate souls and rubberneckers alike.

The shift in attention to the Sea of Trees seems to be due in at least part to celebrated Japanese novelist Seicho Matsumoto, who used it as a setting in his best-selling 1959 novel *Tower of Waves*. The romantic thriller climaxed with an unfaithful woman ending her life in the Sea of Trees. Matsumoto had undoubtedly been inspired by earlier reports of sporadic suicides in the area, but the popularity of his book and the subsequent movie adaptation cemented the connection in the mind of the public. Even today, a half-century later, the Sea of Trees remains virtually synonymous with suicide in Japan.

Getting There

In spite of its macabre reputation, the Sea of Trees represents a thriving patch of Japan's dwindling virgin wilderness. Crisscrossed by clearly marked hiking trails, it's a treat for those who enjoy the outdoors. Just don't forget to bring an extra compass or two along, just to be safe. From JR Kawaguchiko Station, it's a 35 minute ride on the Saiko Retro Bus to the trailhead.

Dare you follow the path into the Sea of Trees?

HACHIOJI CASTLE

Name in Japanese: 八王子城
a.k.a. Hachioji-jo
Location: Hachioji City, Tokyo
Nearest Station: JR Takao
Completed: 1587
Height: 1450 feet (445 meters) above sea level
Ranking: Top 100 Castles of Japan
Key Figure: Warlord Hojo Ujiteru
Event that Caused Haunting: Siege of July 23, 1590
Type of Spot: Yurei Spot
Type of Phenomenon: Manifestations of fallen warriors and family; Strange sounds
Threat Level: Variable

Claim to Fame

In a country with a martial tradition as strong as Japan's, it should come as no surprise that certain of its battlefields and castles are considered haunted. One of the most famous of these is Hachioji Castle. Even today, it is said to be haunted by the specters of the Hojo Clan, a powerful samurai family who died here, quite horribly, on an early summer day in 1590.

The city of Hachioji — literally, "Eight Princes," so named for a Buddhist parable set here — is a sprawling suburb of the Tokyo metropolitan area, just an hour from downtown by express train. Today more than a half a million people make their homes here, and the roads are dotted with the same sorts of shopping centers and coffee shops and restaurants as anywhere else in Japan. But no matter how much the landscape changes, one key feature remains the same: Shiroyama ("Castle Mountain"), the tallest peak in the area. This strategic high ground is where the Hojo clan built their fortress, Hachioji Castle, some five centuries ago.

Today, Shiroyama is home to a quiet, leafy park. It's an ideal sort of place for a summer stroll, with shaded footpaths, excellent vistas, and wide-open spaces, all of it narrated by chatter of birds and even the occasional monkey in the treetops. It's perfect for a picnic.

But as you savor your tea and sandwiches, you may notice the vestiges of what was once a great castle: a stone staircase here, a wall there. A closer look reveals scorching and damage from what must have been an epic battle. And come to think of it, the forest and footpaths here happened to be dotted with stone memorials of the sort use to quiet the spirits of the restless dead. You've finished dessert and it's starting to get dark when you start thinking: perhaps this wasn't the best place for a picnic after all.

For right where you're sitting, not so very long ago, the slopes of Mount Shiroyama ran red with blood of man, woman, and child alike. And come nightfall, they say, the long-dead former inhabitants of Hachioji Castle rise to stalk its ruins yet again.

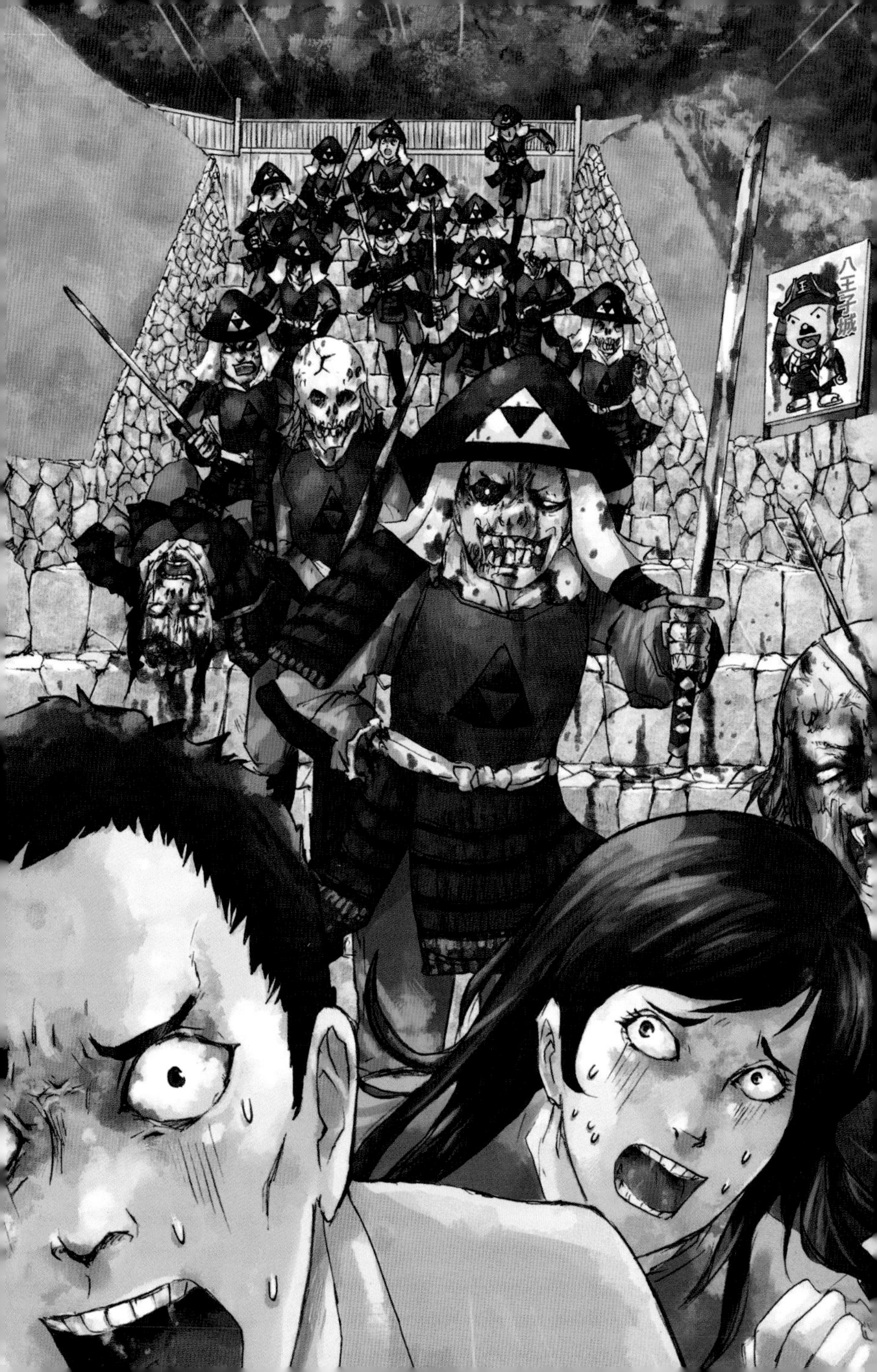
八王子城

The Story

The 16th century was an era of civil war so protracted that it came to be known as *Sengoku Jidai* — the Era of Warring States. This generally involved more powerful warlords turning weaker rivals to their cause... or simply crushing them. After generations of fighting, a few key players had consolidated enough power by the end of the 1500s to make a run at taking over the entire country for themselves.

One of them was a brutal warlord by the name of Toyotomi Hideyoshi. By early 1590 he had steamrolled the opposition, all but solidifying the control of Japan under his iron fist. Only one major obstacle remained: the Hojo clan.

They couldn't be turned. No, Hideyoshi knew he would have to destroy them. And that meant taking their "home base": Odawara Castle. Ever wily, however, he eschewed a direct attack in favor of smashing their outposts one after another, leaving the biggest prize for last. Hachioji Castle represented the Hojo's greatest stronghold outside of Odawara, and Hideyoshi's two top generals launched an early-morning pincer attack on it in July of 1590. Although the castle had been designed as an impregnable fortress, it was manned by young warriors who were quickly overwhelmed by Hideyoshi's battle-seasoned commanders. Some one thousand died in the initial assault, mostly on the defending side. But the Hojo forces put up enough of a fight to temporarily halt the generals in their tracks.

Meet Ujiteru-kun, the mascot of the Ruins of Hachioji Castle! One wonders what the ill-fated Ujiteru would have made of this cuddly effigy.

The defenders, led by Hojo Ujiteru, son of the clan leader, knew that the reprieve was only temporary. While they might hold the fortress for some time, its fall was virtually a certainty. Hideyoshi's troops had never been known for their sense of mercy. So the families of the men defending the castle took advantage of the lull in the fighting to ensure that they would never fall into enemy hands. The women and children assembled atop a waterfall on the castle grounds to determine their fates. Some cast themselves off the edge to the jumble of sharp rocks below; others committed suicide by slicing their jugular veins with short swords or knives.

The castle fell later that same day. Toyotomi's men killed every last defender and burned the castle to the ground. The waterfall ran red with blood for three days and three nights. In fact the castle and its inhabitants were so thoroughly wiped from the face of the earth that within a few generations many forgot that a castle had even stood on the spot.

The Attack

Ujiteru's wife was one of the few survivors of the battle. She spent the remainder of her days wandering the forest in tattered clothing, playing the flute as had been her hobby in happier times. Undoubtedly these weird strains of out-of-context music did much to encourage locals in their belief that the site was haunted. Rumors spread of the phantom sounds echoing through the hills: of horses braying, of gunfire and swords crossing, of the shouts of footsoldiers killing and being killed. The more extreme claimed the ghosts would attack any who dared violate their resting grounds — or worse yet, follow one home to rain misfortune upon one's family and friends. For generations the entire area was treated as unholy ground, taboo, never to be entered, the forest covering the hills believed to be filled with as many yurei as trees.

And so it remained until well into the 20th century, when an archaeological team finally pushed through the dense foliage overgrowing the site and excavated the long-buried remains of Hachioji Castle. In 1990, the area was officially reopened as a national park.

Surviving an Encounter

These days, few believe that the area poses any real physical threat, but reports of sightings and strange phenomena abound. If you don't want to run into any ghosts, simply visit during the day. Manifestations occur mainly at night, with chances of encounters increasing greatly during

a full moon. Misty or rainy conditions, as existed during the siege itself, are considered another precursor as well.

The vast majority of encounters are said to occur in the vicinity of the waterfall and surrounding stream, where the women and children killed themselves; apparitions of women sitting on the rocks contemplating their jumps are a common theme. The anniversary of the castle's fall, July 24th by the reckoning of the modern calendar, is said to be particularly "active."

If you do go at these times, don't be surprised if you aren't alone — as a famed "yurei spot," the ruins are a popular place for local youths and ghost hunters to test their mettle.

Getting There

From Tokyo's Shinjuku Station, take the JR Chuo Line to Takao Station. Take the #1 Bus from the North Exit. Disembark at the Reienmae (霊園前) stop and follow the signs for the Ruins of Hachioji Castle.

Below: A modern reconstruction of the entrance to the castle grounds.

THE WEEPING ROCK

Name in Japanese: 夜泣き石
a.k.a. *Yonaki ishi (transliteration)*
The Nightly Weeping Rock (literal translation)
Location: *Sayo no Nakayama (Shizuoka Prefecture)*
Cataloged in: *The Seven Wonders of Enshu*
Height of Rock: *Roughly 3 feet (1 meter)*
Weight: *Estimated 2,480 pounds (1125 kg)*
Key Figure: *Oishi ("Ms. Stone")*
Date of Incident: *Unknown.*
Early 17th century?
Event that Caused Haunting:
Murder of innocent woman
Type of Spot: *"Mystery Spot"*
(place where strange things happen)
Type of Phenomenon:
Audible manifestations
Threat Level: *Low*

Claim to Fame

"Weeping rocks" are a surprisingly common phenomenon in
Japan. The vast majority are
stones that supposedly emit a wailing, keening, or crying sound as a
direct result of having once been
drenched in the blood of the victim
of a crime. These include weeping
rocks in Nagano prefecture, the
city of Kyoto, and the suburbs of
Osaka. The single most famous
of these strange stones, however,
is the weeping rock of Sayo no
Nakayama, which is considered one
of the Seven Wonders of Enshu.

The Story

Long ago, a very pregnant
woman by the name of Oishi
(a family name meaning
"Stone") was making the long
journey back home through
the mountains. She had
reached Sayo no Nakayama
mountain pass when her water
broke unexpectedly early.
Wracked by contractions, she
collapsed, unable to go any
further. A passer-by, a ronin
named Todoroki Goemon, happened upon her. But when she
offered to pay him to help her
back to town, the greedy man
unsheathed his sword, cut her
down, took the purse, and ran.

Although the sword had
pierced her belly, in his haste
Todoroki had clipped a large
stone when he swung, causing him to just miss the fetus
within. After his retreat, the
baby emerged through the wound
in the dying woman's stomach.
Having been born in such an
unconventional manner, the infant
hung on the cusp of life himself,
unable even to muster the strength
to cry. As she died, the woman's
spirit transferred into the stone
that had stopped the blade. And
astonishingly, inexplicably, the stone
began to wail in an attempt to alert
someone to the child's presence.

Fortunately, a monk returning
to nearby Kyuenji Temple heard
the cries. He discovered the crime
scene, and found the rapidly fading
baby. Lacking any milk or food, he
gave the newborn a hard sugar-
candy to suck on as he rushed
back to the temple. (Similar to

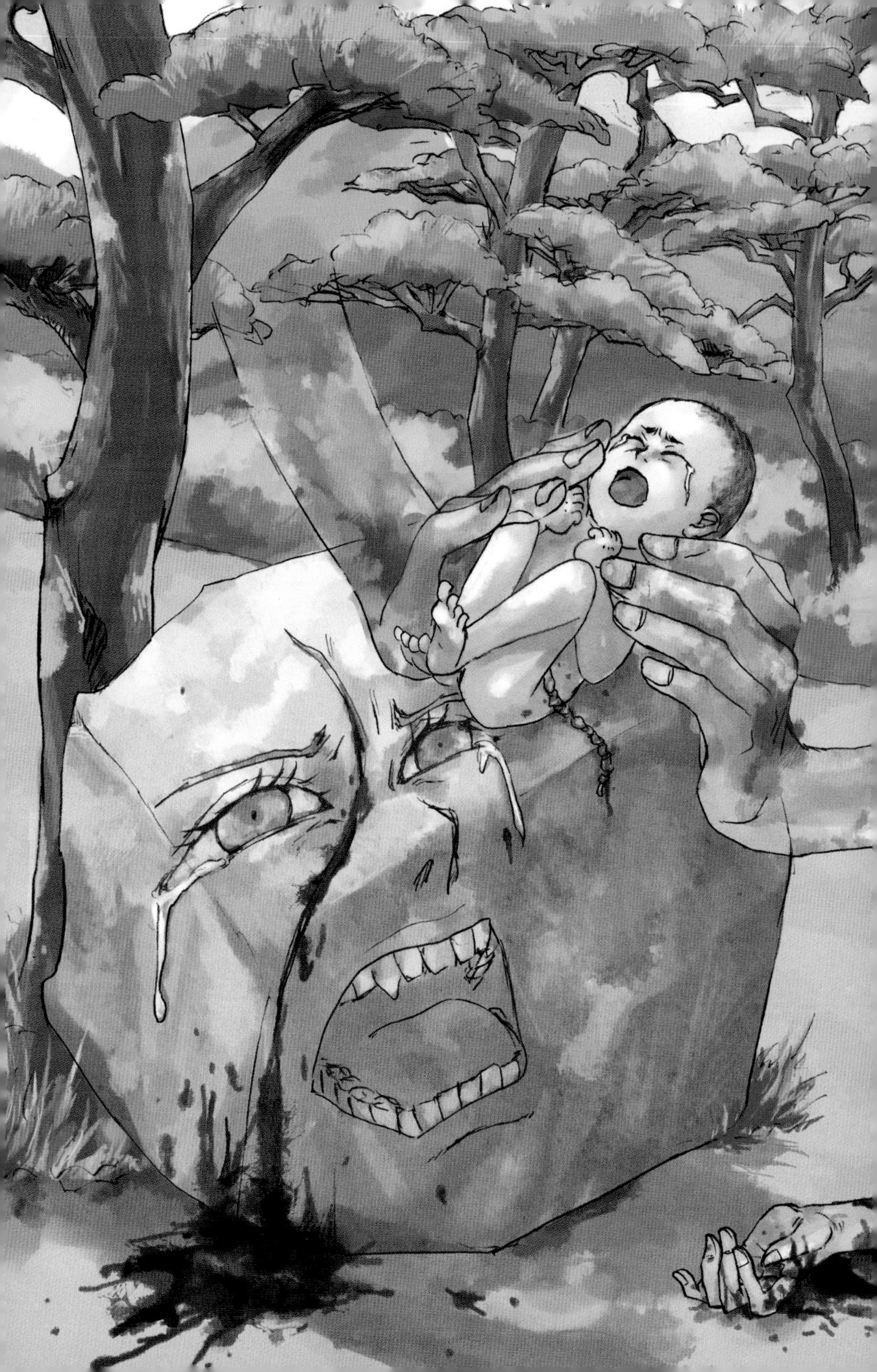

the Candy-Buying Ghost on p.76!)

As it so happened, the baby boy eventually grew into a healthy teenager named Otohachi. Although surprisingly well adjusted, avenging the crime that had robbed him of his mother always remained at the back of his mind, for the rock upon which he had been found continued to weep nightly.

One day while praying to Kannon (the Goddess of Mercy), Otohachi saw a vision telling him to become a sword-polisher. He left the temple, travelled the countryside, and eventually found a master with whom to apprentice. After many years of hard work, he became a master sword polisher himself and opened his own business.

His very first customer arrived not long after he hung out his sign: an old ronin with a chipped blade. When Otohachi asked how it had been damaged, the ronin told him that he had chipped it close to twenty years earlier on a stone on the Sayo no Nakayama Pass. His eyes widening, Otohachi realized why he had seen the vision so many years before. Still holding the blade in his hands, he told the ronin just who he was.

They say Todoroki didn't even try to run when Otohachi cut him down with a single stroke of his own blade.

The rock really exists. It is on display at Kyuenji Temple in Shizuoka Prefecture,

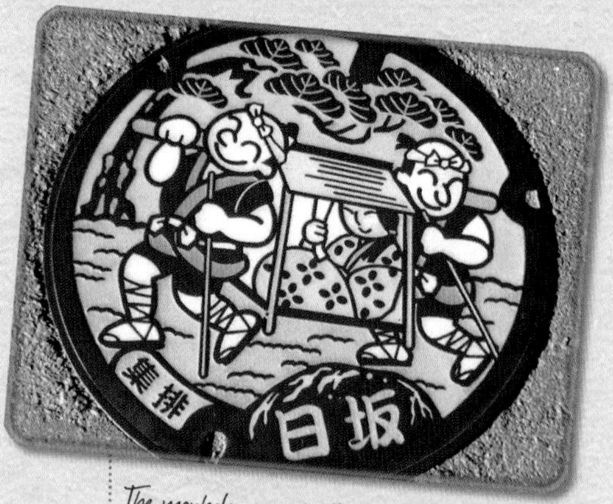
日坂

The manhole covers in the nearby town of Nissaka feature a rather upbeat portrayal of the famous stone.

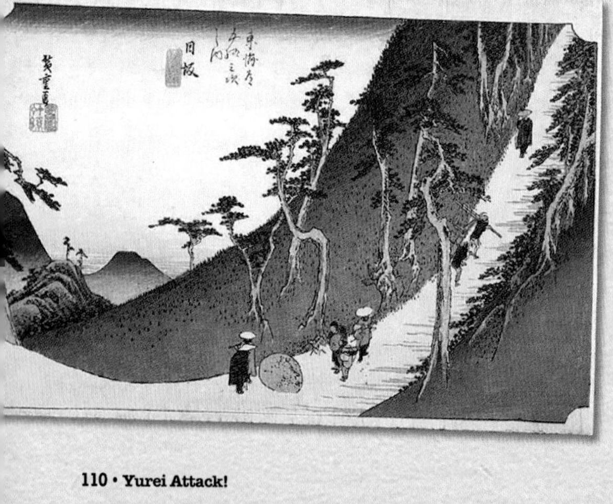

The Weeping Rock proved popular enough for master woodblock print artist Utagawa Kuniyoshi to create his own portrayal of the spooky stone. In his take on the legend, the woman's spirit managed to attract the attention of her husband, and remains with him until he tracks her murderer down and avenges her death.

a short bus ride from Kakegawa Station on the JR Tokaido Line.

Surviving an Encounter

Invest in earplugs? You don't have anything to worry about from weeping rocks, save the uncomfortable feeling of hair standing on end if you're the sort who frightens easily.

Rock Stars

In Japan, strange rocks come in all shapes and sizes. In addition to the ones described above, these include:

- Okayama's Kosokoso-Iwa, or "Whisper Rock," which whispers unintelligibly.
- Kagawa's Omanno-Iwa, or "O-man's Rock," which projects a phantom image of an elderly lady that claims "I'm O-man's mother."
- Nagano's Mono-Iwa, "The Rock," which shouts "You'll be killed!" to passer-by whose lives are in danger;
- And our personal favorite, Okayama's Shakushi-Iwa, or "Rice-Scoop Rock," which extends a phantom rice-scoop and audibly demands miso paste from passer-by.

These sorts of rocks are better described as exhibiting strange phenomena rather than being haunted per se, and as such are generally categorized as "yokai" rather than "yurei."

THE SEVEN WONDERS OF ENSHU: Similar to "urban legends" – although given the era and location, "rural legends" is more accurate – these supposedly true stories all hail from the Province of Enshu, an area that corresponds to part of modern-day Shizuoka Prefecture. In addition to the Weeping Rock, these include "The Great Serpent of Sakura-ga-ike," "The Phantom Lake of Ike-no-daira," "The Tengu-Fire of Omaezaki City," and eight others. (Yes, that's twelve in total. In Japanese, "seven" is often used in conjunction with the powerful and mysterious.)

A Weeping Rock from the city of Takachiho, Kyushu. This particular one is said to have the ability to quiet any crying baby brought into contact with it!

JOMON TUNNEL

Name in Japanese: 常紋トンネル
a.k.a. Hitobashira Tunnel
(Human Sacrifice Tunnel)
Location: Hokkaido
Type of Tunnel: Railway
Originally Opened: 1914
Length: 1,660 feet (507m)
Max depth: 980 feet (300m)
Duration of construction: 3 years
Event that Caused Haunting:
Human sacrifice
Type of Spot: "Yurei Spot"
Type of Phenomena: Audible
manifestations; Visible manifestations;
Psychic trauma / illness for regular users
Threat Level: Varies

Claim to Fame

Tunnels are classic sorts of places to run into yurei. Part of this is undoubtedly because they aren't particularly pleasant places. They're dark, they're stuffy, they're damp, they're deep under the ground — kind of like a grave, when you think about it. But whatever trepidation you might feel in travelling through a tunnel is nothing in comparison to that of the people who actually have to make them.

Japan's mountainous terrain is a veritable Swiss cheese of tunnels, many of them dating back to ancient times. Even with modern techniques and powerful mechanical equipment, digging tunnels can

be dangerous work. But conditions today pale in comparison to times of old, when tunnels had to be dug entirely by hand.

More often than not, this involved forced labor of one sort or another — either prisoners, or people who for whatever reason had no better choice of work. In addition to long hours, low-to-absent pay, and generally appalling working conditions, these workers had another worry hanging over their heads: being turned into *hitobashira* — "human pillars."

Human pillars are human sacrifices, buried alive in the foundations of structures as offerings to the gods. They're more frequently associated with castles and bridges (which we explore in more depth on p.132) But in at least one case, they seem to have been used in a tunnel as well: Jomon Tunnel in Hokkaido. Welcome to Japan's single most haunted hole in the ground.

Jomon Tunnel stretches just over a half kilometer — hardly long by the standards of tunnels. Yet it extends through some of the hardest, remotest terrain the far-flung island of Hokkaido had to offer. It is a region of dense forests and plunging valleys, a place where temperatures regularly hit thirty below during the winter.

The Story

At the turn of the Twentieth century, Japan raced to extend its railways to every corner of its country. The demand for laborers far outstripped supply. Few skilled

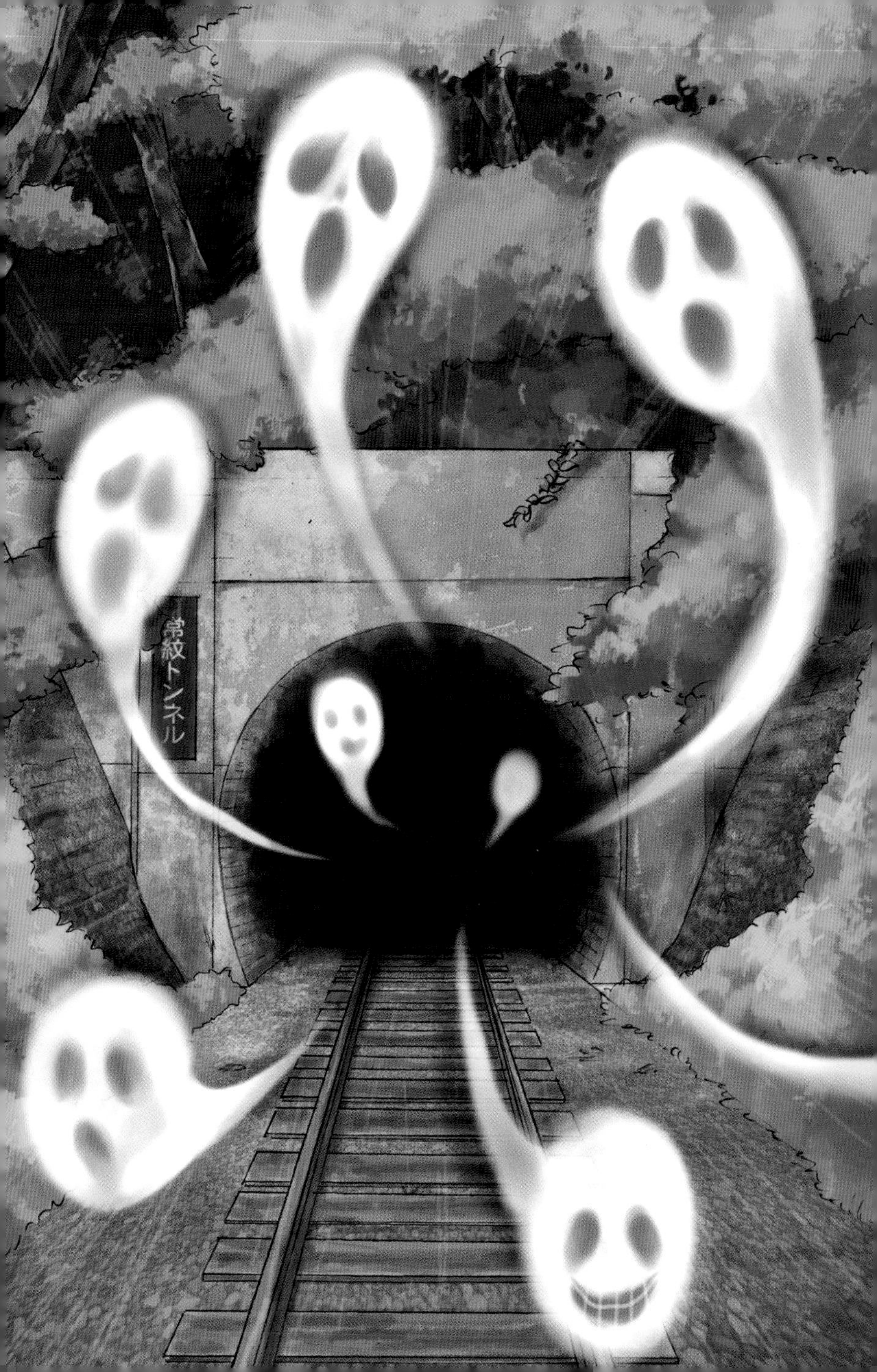
常紋トンネル

tradesmen wanted to work in the harsh environment of Hokkaido, Japan's furthest, coldest frontier. So the government made up the difference with a captive labor pool: prisoners.

The convicts worked in a chain gang style that came to be known as *takobeya rodo*: "octopus jar labor." The name came from the traps laid by fishermen, designed so that once an octopus slithered in it would never get out. By day, the men worked constantly; by night, they suffered through sub-zero conditions in uninsulated huts, the entire gang shackled to a giant wooden bed-platform with a single log extending down one side as a "pillow." (In lieu of an alarm clock, come morning the warden would give the log a couple of whacks with a hammer to set the prison-ers' heads ringing.)

It took a mixed force of pris-oners and laborers conscripted from other parts of Japan three years to build the tunnel, one of several along an isolated rail line that pushed the Hokkaido frontier even further north. Rumors of hauntings swirled from almost the moment Jomon Tunnel opened. Even though trains passed through it at high speed, conductors and riders reported all sorts of strange phenomena inside and just outside its openings.

The stories claimed that the ghosts were those of the men who had built the tunnel. The condi-tions had been unbelievably harsh, more like gulags than work-camps. The captive labor pool consisted of everything from murderers to political criminals to simple debt-ors. Whatever they had been before arriving here, they were essentially human machines now, subject in equal parts to the brutality of nature and the brutality of the men who watched over them, worked until they could work no more — then discarded.

Even if the wardens and guards had cared about the well-being of their prisoners, the nearest doc-tor was many, many miles away. Malnutrition was a fact of daily life for workers. Diseases such as beri-beri (a chronic vitamin deficiency that is fatal if untreated) swept through the ranks. When guards encountered fallen prisoners, they would simply pile the bodies atop hand-trolleys for onsite burial in side-shafts and work-tunnels. And if they found someone still barely clinging to life? Too bad. No medicine anyway. Into the pit. *The bodies are still there today!* locals whispered. *That's why it's haunted!*

For years, officials dismissed both the rumors of the prisoners' treatment and the sightings as speculation and exaggeration. But in 1970, a repair crew entered the tunnel to patch a crack in the wall from an earthquake. Behind crumbling brick, the workers dis-covered several skeletons that had apparently been bricked up behind the wall in a standing position. Human sacrifice? None who had worked on the project were alive to tell the tale, but further excava-tions revealed a burial pit near the entrance filled with dozens and dozens of human bodies — some say hundreds.

The stories were true.

The Attack

Reports from those passing through the tunnel included:

- A general sense of unease
- Unexplained sighing and moaning sounds
- A voice calling "I'm hungry... Mama, feed me," on several occasions
- A higher than normal instance of illness, physical and mental, among those who worked on the train line and their families
- In one case, the appearance of a blood-splattered individual staggering through the tunnel caused a conductor to apply emergency brakes, but when the area was searched no sign of a trespasser or body was found.

Surviving an Encounter

Hold on to your seat and make it through the tunnel. There have been no reports of injuries or fatalities to those who simply pass through. This is one of Japan's more isolated train lines, so avoiding it shouldn't be hard. But if you're the thrill-seeking type, it's the Sekihoku Main Line, which connects the cities of Asahikawa and Abashiri. The tunnel itself is near Kinka Station.

Locals have played it safe by erecting a memorial to the fallen workers, just outside of the station, but reports of manifestations continue to this day.

GREETINGS FROM ABASHIRI PRISON

You can explore actual "octopus jar" work camps for yourself at the Abashiri Prison Museum, located in the city of the same name in northern Hokkaido. Once a source of labor for the taming of Hokkaido's wild frontier, it was closed in the Sixties and re-opened as an educational facility in the Eighties.
http://www.kangoku.jp/

A Japanese-style chain gang, from the turn of the 20th century, recreated at the Abashiri Prison Museum.

OIRAN BUCHI

Name in Japanese: おいらん淵
a.k.a. The Courtesans' Abyss (Literal translation); Gojugonin Buchi ("The Abyss of the Fifty-Five"); Choshi-no-taki (Choshi Falls; official name);
Terrain: Waterfall (river valley)
Location: Yamanashi Prefecture
Origin of Haunting: Mid-1570s
Type of Spot: "Yurei Spot"
Type of Phenomena: Audible Manifestations; Curses
Existence: Historical Fact?
Threat Level: Varies

Claim to Fame:

Waterfalls are commonplace in Japan. Many of them are venerated as holy spots and places of spiritual purification. Reciting sutras beneath the ceaseless hammer of a frigid waterfall is a classic sort of training in the religions of Buddhism and Shugendo.

Other waterfalls have darker stories. At first glance, this particular waterfall seems like a little slice of heaven on earth. But on a summer day some five hundred years ago, fifty-five courtesans were unwittingly led to their deaths here. Now known as the Courtesans' Abyss, it is considered one of the country's most haunted spots.

The Story:

Many centuries ago, in the Era of Warring States, the warlords of Japan clashed for supremacy in an attempt to take control of the country for themselves. Just as with modern military campaigns, these affairs required vast sums of money. Intelligence needed to be procured, alliances with potential allies forged, and of course soldiers trained, housed, and fed. This was all on top of the usual operating costs of running a fiefdom.

There were many ways to get these funds. You could invade a rival's territory and plunder their assets. You could find financial backing by partnering with the enemies of a common enemy. Or you could make it yourself.

One particular clan of warlords, the Takeda, funded their exploits with gold excavated from a secret mine in the foothills of Mount Kurokawa Kinzan. This was a huge operation, involving many overseers, workers, and assorted other types of individuals, including a stable of female entertainers who kept the men occupied in the off-hours.

This funding wasn't used purely for making war. Quantities of it were cached in buried vaults of sorts. Still more was buried in the hills and mountains as offerings to the gods in religious rituals intended to give the Takeda an edge in battle. Some believe that the buried treasure lies in the hills and mountains of Yamanashi Prefecture even today. We don't recommend going on a treasure hunt, though. While the gold stashed for savings purposes would be a literal treasure trove, the gold used as offerings was buried as part of arcane religious rites. Any who disturb the

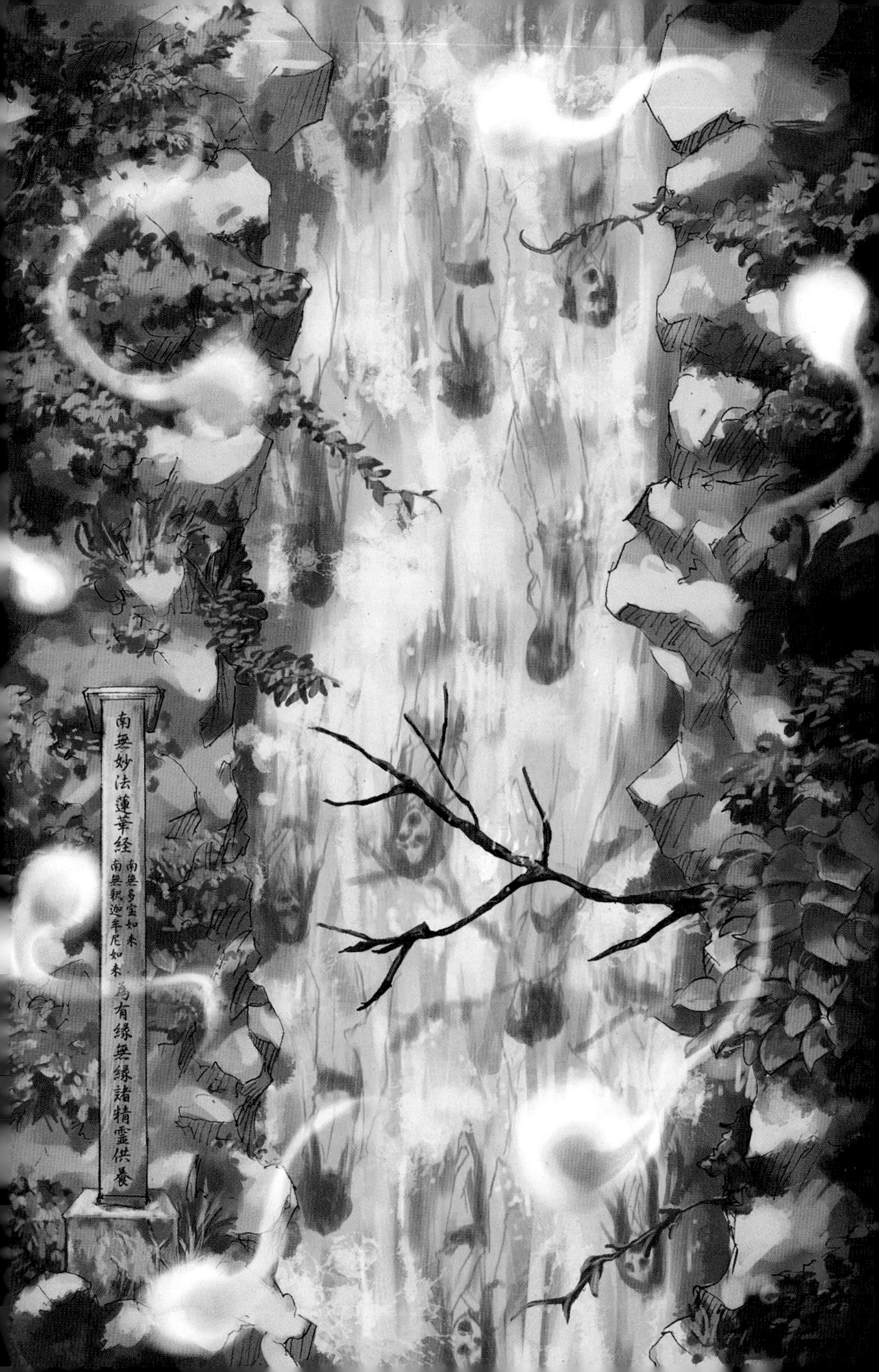
南無妙法蓮華経
南無多宝如来
南無釈迦牟尼如来
為有縁無縁諸精霊供養

carefully chosen resting places of these hoards risks breaking the elaborate spells incanted by the Takeda and bringing curse and ruin upon themselves. Or so they say.

Ladies Night

Partly because of declining yields and partly because the clan was rapidly losing ground to other warlords, the Takedas were forced to close the mining operation. In an effort to prevent information about the mine's existence and location falling into enemy hands, clan leaders made a decision to dispose of what they saw as a key potential intelligence leak: the women who had entertained the miners. The Takedas knew well the power of pillow talk; many of the workers could have let slip the location of gold caches or other important information during a fit of passion. And while the men would remain as labor for other future projects, the women would need to be set free. Or would they?

The Takedas constructed a massive platform suspended over a river gorge near the mine. The fifty-five courtesans were led to this makeshift stage and ordered to perform, ostensibly as practice for a lavish "thank you" party to be held later that night. But just when the ladies' song and dance routine reached full swing, Takeda men hacked away at the rope supports with their swords, sending the screaming women plunging to the sharp rocks far below. The few who survived the fall into the gorge were swept off a waterfall to certain death.

A Ninja Nightmare

The above represents the conventional wisdom as to what happened at Courtesans' Abyss. But it leaves two big questions unanswered. Why go to all the effort of protecting a played-out gold mine? And if the warlords had simply wanted the women dead, why the need for such an elaborate trick? In that day and age, women were essentially second-class citizens, all but owned by men.

But we have a theory. What if neither the courtesans nor the story about protecting the secrecy of the mine were what they seemed to be?

The Takeda's gold mining — and influence — peaked under the leadership of warlord Takeda Shingen, a strategic genius who also used the funds to establish an elaborate spy organization. He is particularly known for his adept use of female spies — known euphemistically as "walking maidens," but essentially ninja — to gather intelligence. Posing as everything from holy women to servants to prostitutes, they used feminine wiles to strip secrets from Takeda's rivals. (For more info, see *Ninja Attack!*) After Shingen died in 1573, his rivals wasted no time in eating away at his holdings — and his son Katsuyori wasn't able to stop them.

What if the beleaguered Katsuyori decided to use the rapidly failing mine as a cover story to silence his father's spy network? The "walking maidens" knew many of the Takeda clan's secrets, and Katsuyori was undoubtedly getting paranoid as he lost his grip on his father's legacy. The performance at the mine would have made a convenient ruse to lure the women, who were expert entertainers as well as spies, to the site. These highly trained female ninja were well capable of defending themselves. Suddenly, the overly elaborate plan to get rid of fifty-five "courtesans" in one fell swoop starts to make a lot more sense.

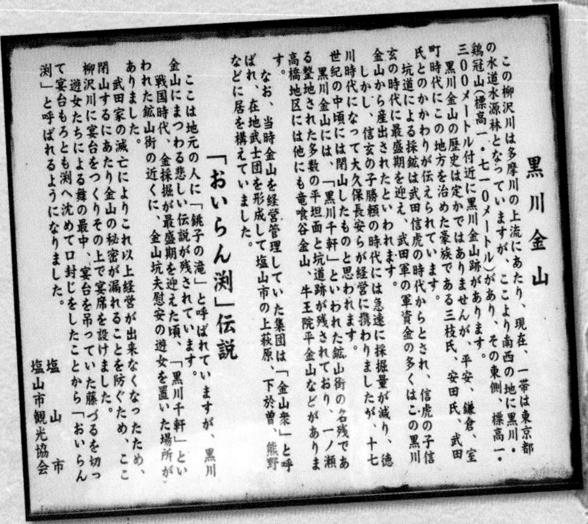
黒川金山
この柳沢川は多摩川の上流にあたり、現在、一帯は東京都の水道水源林となっていますが、ここより南西の地に黒川・鶏冠山(標高一・七一0メートル)があり、その東側、標高一・三00メートル付近に黒川金山跡があります。
黒川金山の歴史は定かではありませんが、平安、鎌倉、室町時代にこの地方を治めた豪族である三枝氏、安田氏、武田氏とのかかわりが伝えられています。
坑道による採鉱は武田信虎の時代からとされ、信虎の子信玄の時代に最盛期を迎え、武田軍の軍資金の多くはこの黒川金山から産出されたといわれます。
しかし、信玄の子勝頼の時代には急速に採掘量が減り、徳川時代になって大久保長安らが経営に携わりましたが、十七世紀の中頃には閉山したものと思われます。
黒川金山には、「黒川千軒」といわれた鉱山街の名残である整地された多数の平坦面と坑道跡が残されており、一ノ瀬高橋地区には他にも竜喰谷金山、牛王院平金山などがあります。
なお、当時金山を経営管理していた集団は「金山衆」と呼ばれ、在地武士団を形成して塩山市の上萩原、下於曽、熊野などに居を構えていました。
「おいらん渕」伝説
ここは地元の人に「銚子の滝」と呼ばれていますが、黒川金山にまつわる悲しい伝説が残されています。
戦国時代、金採掘が最盛期を迎えた頃、「黒川千軒」といわれた鉱山街の近くに、金山坑夫慰安の遊女を置いた場所がありました。
武田家の滅亡によりこれ以上経営が出来なくなったため、閉山するにあたり金山の秘密が漏れることを防ぐため、ここ柳沢川に宴台をつくりその上で宴席を設けました。
遊女たちによる舞の最中、宴台を吊っていた藤づるを切って宴台もろとも渕へ沈めて口封じをしたことから「おいらん渕」と呼ばれるようになりました。
塩山市
塩山市観光協会

The cursed sign of the Courtesans' Abyss. Dare you read it all the way through?

The Attack

Similar to Hachioji Castle and Tabaruzaka, Oiran Buchi is a popular place to test one's courage at night. It's isolated, with no residences or buildings nearby. It's dark. It's quiet. Cell phones don't work.

Reports of strange phenomena at the site include:

- The sounds of women crying out in pain, presumably those of the courtesans after the fall.
- Singing voices — old songs of the sort that a courtesan might have known.
- Today, a metal sign describing the fate of the courtesans marks the spot. Rumor says that those who read it from start to finish will be cursed.

Surviving an Encounter:

Many "ghost hunters" dismiss reports of phenomena at this location as flights of fancy, pointing out that it only represents the bend in the gorge from which the victims' bodies were eventually recovered. The truly haunted spot is the one from which the unfortunate women were actually dropped — a place called Shin no Oiran Buchi ("the True Oiran Buchi"). We suppose the general idea behind this theory is that the shock and trauma of being so suddenly dropped, rather than that of dying, is what "imprinted" on the area.

For better or worse, however, the location of the True Oiran Buchi isn't readily accessible or publicized. Marked by a handful of makeshift wooden grave-markers, it sits atop a precipice that is as treacherous today as it was four hundred years ago. The very real danger of slipping and falling far outweighs any potential danger from the courtesans' spirits. If by some way you do manage to make it there, we strongly suggest watching your feet instead of looking for ghosts.

SUNSHINE 60 BUILDING

Name in Japanese: サンシャイン60
a.k.a. Sunshine Rokujuu (as pronounced in Japanese)
Type of Structure: Skyscraper (Mixed-use high-rise)
Construction: Steel and reinforced concrete
Stories: Sixty
Location: Ikebukuro, Tokyo
Ground broken: 1973
Opened: 1978
Height: 786 feet (239.7 m)
Elevators: 41
Type of Spot: "Mystery spot"
Type of Phenomena: Manifestations of various types; Fireballs; Strange happenings; A generally "bad vibe"
Threat Level: Varies

Claim to Fame

For a brief time in the 1980s, this was Asia's tallest skyscraper. It may have lost the height title, but it still reigns supreme in another, less publicized category. Sunshine 60 is considered by many to be the world's most haunted high-rise. But as you'll see, its reputation has less to do with ghosts than it does with the sheer number of bad things that have happened on this other- wise unassuming patch of Tokyo real estate over the years.

The Story

Urban legend has long treated Higashi Ikebukuro, the Tokyo neighborhood in which Sunshine 60 stands, as volatile ground. Call it fate, call it karma, call it what you will, but it's a fact that nasty stuff just seems to keep happening here. Don't believe us? Just take a quick look at a timeline of the area.

1721: Ikebukuro is at this time a sleepy suburb of mansions, temples, and farms. A mysteri- ous individual (or individuals) begin ambushing passer-by in a series of incidents euphemisti- cally described as *tsuji-giri*, or "sword testing." They claim some sixty-four victims in total — at one point, killing seventeen in a single night. The perpetrator is never identified.

1895: The convicts of Ishikawa- jima Prison, established by legend- ary lawman Hasegawa Heizo (see *Ninja Attack!*, p. 144) are moved to a new facility in Ikebukuro. Now called Sugamo Keimusho (prison), it is based on then-modern European prison designs.

1920s: As Japan descends into totalitarianism, Sugamo Prison's mandate shifts from rehabilitat- ing criminals to housing political prisoners, those guilty of "thought crimes," and others seen by the government as undesirable influ- ences. Their stays are undoubtedly less than pleasant.

1930s-40s: During the war years, Sugamo Prison's inmates are joined by assorted spies and prisoners of war, all of whom are brutally

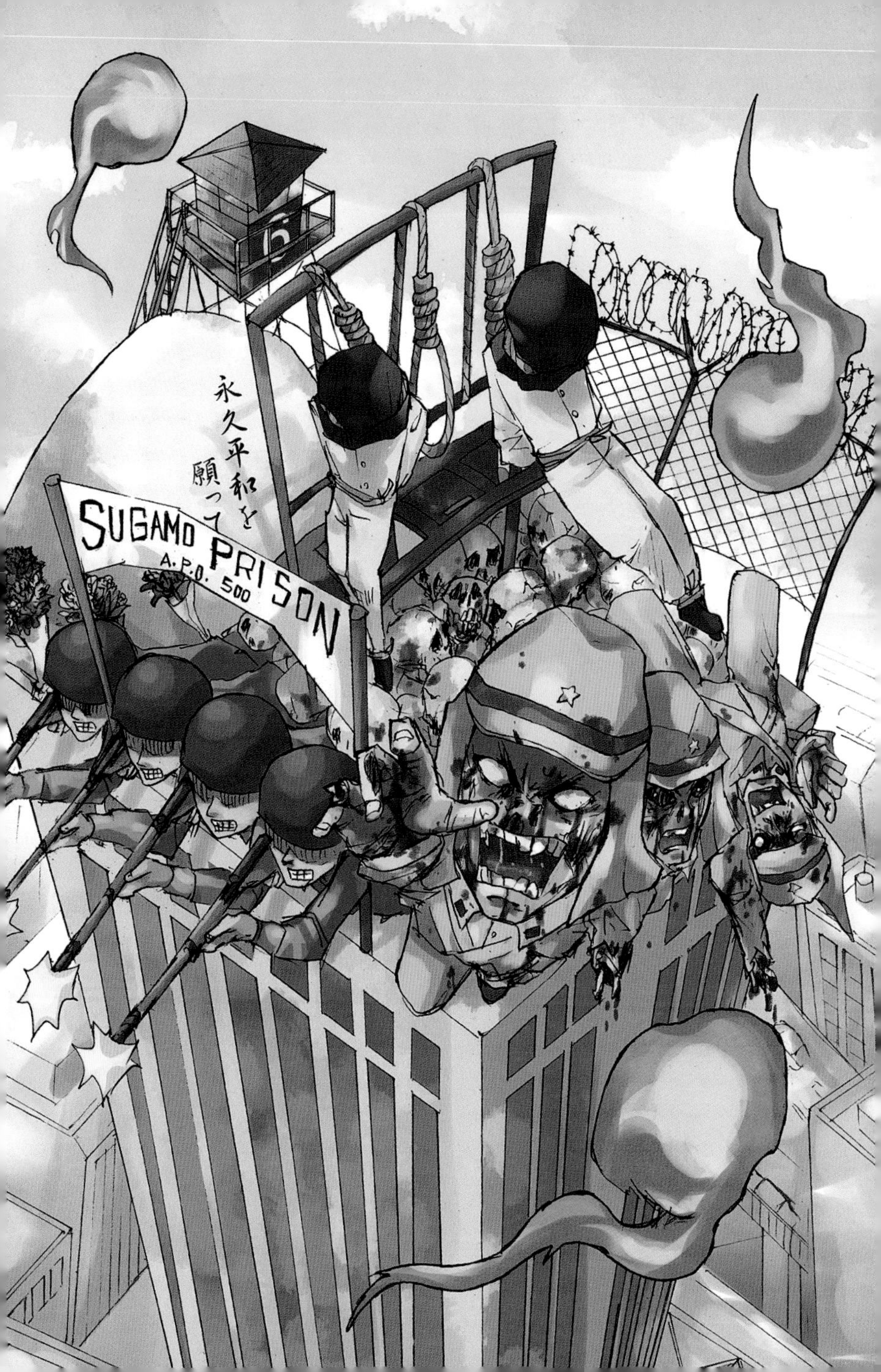
永久平和を願って
SUGAMO PRISON
A.P.O. 500

interrogated and many of whom are executed.

1945 (April): Bombing raids devastate the entire city, Ikebukuro included. The huge number of casualties overwhelms mortuaries; the 731 Ikebukuro residents killed in the raids must be cremated in a mass pyre in a local park.

1945 (August): Sugamo Prison is seized by American forces, cleared out, and used to house individuals accused of war crimes.

1948: Seven men convicted in the Tokyo War Crimes Tribunal are executed at Sugamo Prison. Rather than using the standard Japanese method, the American forces build their own Western-style scaffold to hang the men.

1958: The remainder of the war criminals not sentenced to execution are released after serving their sentences. Sugamo Prison is officially closed.

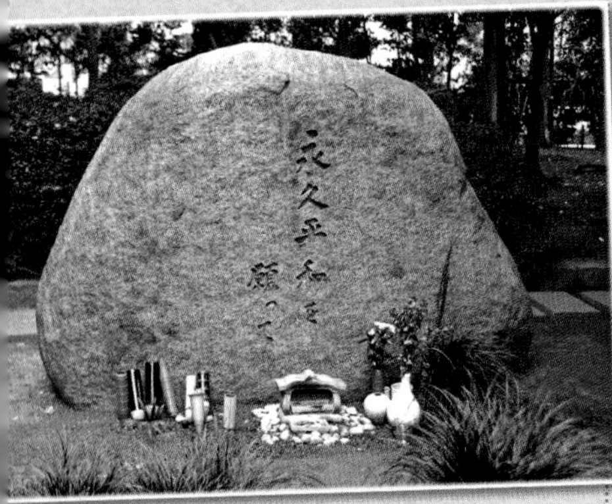
永久平和を願って

The stone memorial erected on the spot of the hangman's gallows, in the shadow of the Sunshine 60 tower.

1966: The area is officially renamed "Higashi Ikebukuro" (East Ikebukuro).

1971: The abandoned remains of Sugamo Prison are dismantled.

1973: Ground is broken for the Sunshine 60 building. The skyscraper goes up atop the same ground once occupied by Sugamo Prison. Construction workers report a variety of strange happenings, including a strange moaning sound emitted during the groundbreaking, the unearthing of a large amount of mysterious rotting cloth, a higher than usual number of injuries, and unexplained equipment malfunctions.

1978: Sunshine 60 opens to great fanfare. It breaks the record both for tallest building in Asia and the fastest elevators in the world.

1980: A stone tablet is quietly installed on a corner of the property as a memorial to the individuals who died at Sugamo Prison. It actually sits atop the site of the scaffold where the prisoners were hung. It's still there today.

1999: In an eerie echo of the unprovoked attacks 278 years earlier, a deranged man armed with a knife and a hammer kills two pedestrians and seriously wounds six others. He is caught and sentenced to death.

The Attack

By day, Sunshine 60 is a clean, bright, and bustling commercial, center. It's filled with shops, restaurants, theaters, stages, and tourist attractions including an observation deck and an aquarium. There's even a nod to the darker side of the building's history. "Namja Town," a popular date spot for Tokyo teens, is an indoor theme park with a haunted house and other carnival fare. Like many urban commercial complexes, however, it all but empties at night. And that's when things get strange.

Witnesses have reported all sorts of odd phenomena in and around the building after hours. These include:

- Phantom footsteps echoing through the halls.
- Inexplicable music issuing from empty stages and orchestral areas.
- Mysterious reflections of human faces in the glass doors and windows of the entrance area, ostensibly of those once imprisoned there.

But the most famous incident took place on August 8, 1979, the 39th anniversary of the end of World War II, when a trio of high school students spotted mysterious fireballs hovering over the building that night. Like the "will o' wisp" and "foxfire" of European folklore, lights of this sort have long been associated with ghostly phenomena in Japan. When reports of the incident appeared in newspapers the next

day, many other locals stepped forward to claim similar sightings.

Surviving an Encounter

For all the strange behavior, there haven't been any reports of injuries caused by anyone other than human beings. But if you're the sort who scares easily, let us lay it out for you. Avoid Higashi Ikebukuro at night!

Trivia

Urban legend has it that the staircase to the gallows was left intact and incorporated into the structure of the building's basement. The alleged staircase is supposedly deep within the building's lower levels and not accessible by casual visitors.

And undoubtedly inspired by its otherworldly reputation, the manga collective CLAMP incorporated the Sunshine 60 building into two of their works, "X" and "Tokyo Babylon," as the source of occult-magical powers.

A shrine erected to commemorate the lives lost in the 1721 stabbings. Today the area is home to many homeless people.

OSOREZAN

Name in Japanese: 恐山
a.k.a. Mount Fear (literal translation)
Terrain: Volcanic
Location: Tohoku, Japan
Altitude: 2,880 feet (278 meters)
Nearest temple: Bodai-ji Temple
Type of Spot: "Reijo" (Hallowed ground – a gathering place for souls)
Type of Phenomena: Encounters with the dead
Threat Level: Low

True Story

It's hell up on Mount Fear. Literally. Feet scramble for purchase on volcanic scree. The rotten-egg stink of sulfur hangs thick in the air. Boiling steam rises from deep rents in the earth. Murky liquids stained otherworldly hues percolate drowsily in natural stone cauldrons. The only sign of life are the cairns of stones left by previous visitors, the only sound the drone of countless spinning pinwheels left as offerings. Low clouds descend like the lid of a coffin, shutting out the sun and turning the waters of Lake Usoriko a bilious yellow hue. No ripples break its surface. Its sulfur-infused waters are as barren as the landscape that surrounds it.

A couple surveys the wasteland.

"Can you remind me," asks Matt, "why you wanted to come here for our wedding anniversary? There's nothing living here."

"That's okay," answers Hiroko. "People don't come to Mount Fear to meet the living."

Claim to Fame

Over a thousand years ago, a monk by the name of Ennin was studying Buddhism in China when he dreamed a vision. "You will walk thirty days to find the mountain of the dead, carve a bodhisattva there, and promote the Way of Buddha." He returned home immediately and set off on a pilgrimage. The place at which he found himself exactly one month later was called Osorezan — Mount Fear. His tiny religious retreat eventually grew into the temple now known as Bodai-ji.

Mount Fear isn't actually a mountain but rather sits within a broad volcanic caldera. Locals have long believed that the souls of their loved ones linger here for a time before going to the underworld proper.

As such it isn't exactly "haunted" in the traditional sense of the term. More precisely it is known as a reijo, which is often translated as "sacred" or "hallowed ground," but literally means a place where souls dwell. In fact, Mount Fear is classified as one of the "Three Great Reijo of Japan." (The other two are Mount Hiei in Shiga Prefecture and Mount Koya in Wakayama Prefecture.)

It is a purgatory-like area, deliberately sought out by those looking to make contact with the recently deceased. The desolate landscape, steaming vents, and all-around eerie atmosphere are also considered a sort of "image training" for one's own eventual visit to the underworld. (For an in-depth look

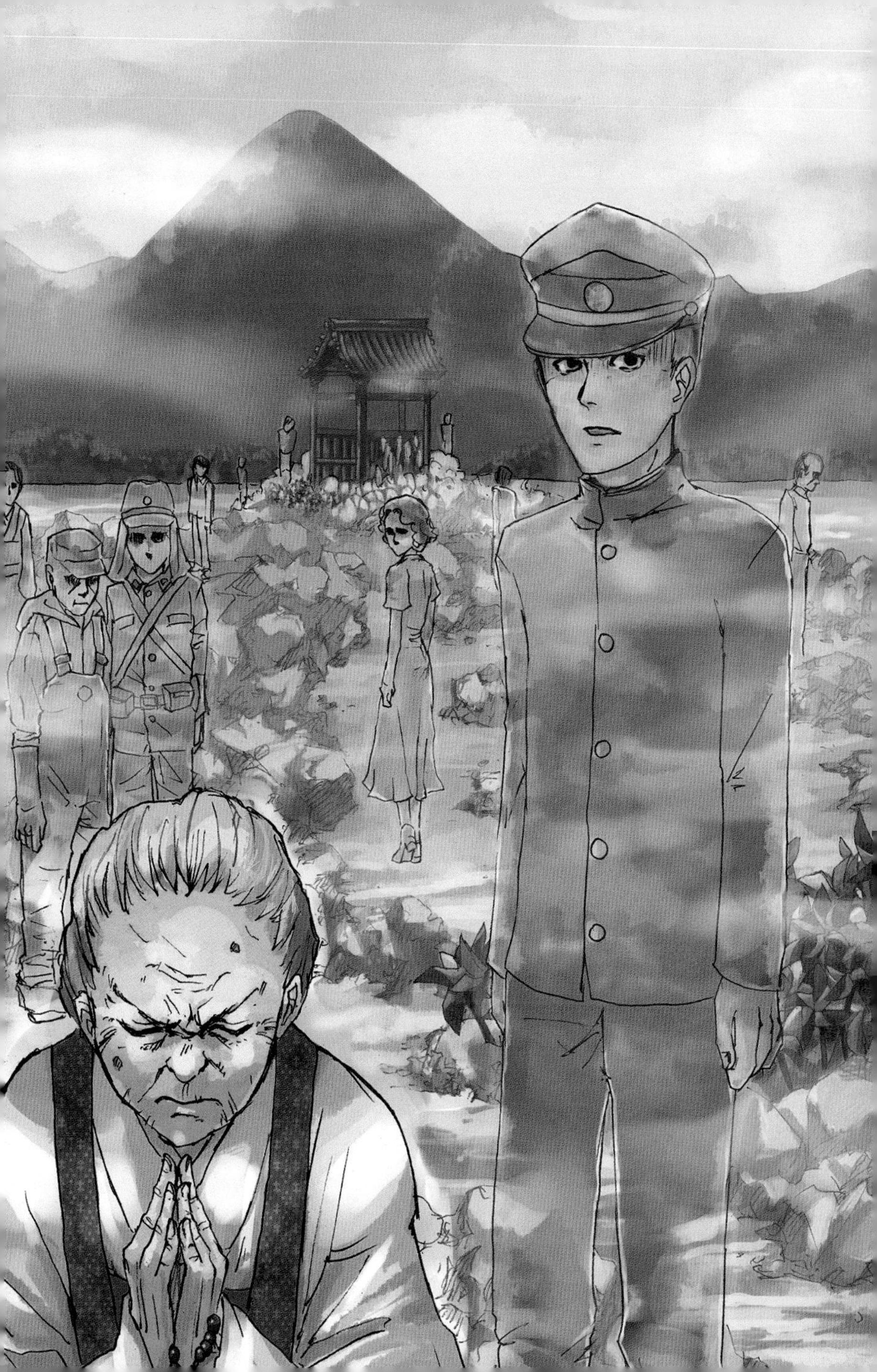

at what awaits, see chapter 7).
In fact, the stream that one must cross to enter the Bodai-ji temple area is called Sanzu-no-kawa — The River Styx. The living can cross back over and return home. The souls of the dead cannot.

The Medium is the Message

Twice yearly, Bodai-ji temple holds weeklong festivals in which local *itako* — spirit mediums — gather to hold sessions for visitors.

Itako is the name for a shaman of the Tohoku region (the northernmost part of Japan's main island of Honshu). They are almost always female, and many are blind as well. They are famed for their ability to locate and channel the souls of the dead in a technique that is known as *kuchiyose*. For a set fee — usually in the ¥4,500 (US $50) range — an itako will contact a deceased loved one and channel their voice through her body. The only trick: the spirits inevitably speak in the itako's natural voice regardless of gender or nationality. That means a thick Tohoku accent, impenetrable even to many native Japanese speakers. Good luck trying to figure out where Grandma left that long-lost family egg salad recipe.

Itako employ a variety of methods for contacting the dead. The use of ritual chanting over a Buddhist rosary is most common. In times of old many hundreds of young women trained and worked as itako; today, theirs is largely a dying art (no pun intended), with numbers dwindling to just over a dozen.

Whether you believe in the supernatural abilities of the itako or not, there is no question that they perform a positive community service. In times of old, this was one of the few ways a sight-impaired woman could earn a living. And their presence is often of great comfort to the bereaved. The coastal areas surrounding Mount Fear were home to many fishing villages, and over the years no small number of men who headed out to sea failed to return. The itako still perform an important role in easing the pain of grieving family members. In fact, their ability to help surviving families come to grips with suicide is currently the subject of a 1.1 million yen study by the Aomori University of Health and Welfare.

The Attack

People come here to meet the dead. Remember that ¥4,500 you just paid to the itako? There is no attack. If you make contact with a loved one, consider yourself lucky.

That said, we heard an interesting story from the driver of the bus that took us to the mountain several years ago. One day, he was seized by a whim to purchase one of the shiny foil pinwheels from Mount Fear, but rather than leaving it in the "underworld" as is custom, he brought it home as a present for his daughter. She happened to fall sick with a fever several hours later, and when his wife learned from where the pinwheel had come, she blew her stack. He was forced to drive back to the mountain, climb a fence, and plant the pinwheel

— in the dead of night. When he returned, his daughter's mysterious fever had broken.

Surviving an Encounter

"Survive?" Come on, quit worrying! The whole point of coming here is contact. Try to ignore the sulfur fumes, and focus on those who are in the process of moving from this realm to the next. Mount Fear is pretty much the last, best chance you'll get to make contact with them.

It's standard to make offerings, both out of respect and out of a desire to make the spirits' time here more comfortable. These include:

- Coins (particularly five-yen coins, as their Japanese name ("go-en") is a homonym for good fortune
- Pinwheels (commonly left behind as playthings for the souls of children)
- Canned drinks, snacks, and other refreshments
- Objects of personal significance to the recently deceased (we've seen everything from toys and items of clothing to jars filled with pachinko balls, so feel free to leave whatever you think they'd like to have with them.)

Welcome to Hells

In Japan, the word *jigoku*, literally "hell," generally refers to the underworld as a whole rather than as a place of punishment per se. In addition to the "hell" atop Mount Fear, there are other hells as well. These places earned their names because of their sulfurous, volcanic landscape rather than any association with the supernatural. These include Unzen-Jigoku of Unzen-Amakusa Park in Kyushu, and Jigokudani ("Hell Valley") of Nagano, whose natural hotsprings are populated not with the souls of the dead but rather snow monkeys.

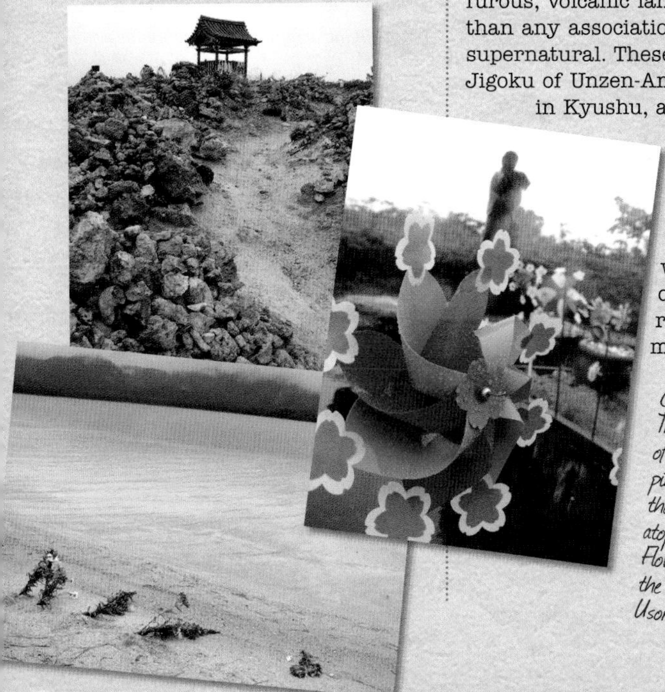

Clockwise from top: The volcanic landscape of Mount Fear; A pinwheel spins amidst the mist and gloom atop Mount Fear; Flowers left along the shoreline of Lake Usoriko.

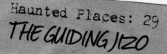

THE GUIDING JIZO

Name in Japanese: 導き地蔵
Location: Kesennuma-Oshima
Terrain: Island
Size: Roughly 3.5 square miles (9km2)
Access: Ferry from Kesennuma Port
Origin: Folktale
Date of Event: 1770s?
Cause of Haunting: Natural Disaster
Type of Spot: Holy Ground
Type of Phenomena: Doppelgänger
(Death Omen)
Threat Level: Low (for observer);
high (for those affected)

Claim to Fame

This spooky tale hails from the
local folklore of Kesennuma, one of
the areas hardest hit by the 2011
tsunami. The setting of the story
isn't explicitly clear, but appears to
be set in or around the 1770s.

The island of Kesennuma Oshima
is located twenty-five minutes from
the mainland by ferry. After the
2011 tsunami, it was almost completely cut off from the mainland
for weeks, save for periodic visits
by American naval ships.

But this tale is set in the 17th
century. Even at the calmest of
times it must have been a very
isolated place back then. Yet it was
fertile ground, home to a small village of people who made their lives
by farming and fishing the waters
between island and mainland.

The Story

A certain forest on
Kesennuma Oshima was once
home to a statue called the
michibiki jizo — the guiding
bodhisattva.

In and of itself, this is hardly
noteworthy. Virtually the entirety
of Japan is dotted with statues
of the diminutive Buddhist deity.
Roughly knee-high, they are
often found alongside trails and
roadways. Jizo are effigies of the
patron saint both of travelers and
of children who pass away before
their parents. (The soul of a child
who passes before its parents cannot cross the River Sanzu into
the afterlife proper, according to
Buddhist tradition, spending its
existence instead building towers
of stones on its shores that are
endlessly kicked over by the denizens of hell. Jizo cares for these
little souls by giving them refuge
amidst his flowing robes. In appre-
ciation for his efforts, passer-by
leave stones before Jizo statues in
a symbolic effort to ease the children's burden.)

The guiding jizo of Kesennuma
Oshima was different. According to
local legend, the soul of someone
who is about to die, unbeknownst
to them, appears before this particular jizo the day before their
fated date. (This resembles "doppelgänger" legends of Europe, in
which phantom doubles of victims
of misfortune are seen in far-flung
locations just before or after the
victim's death.)

One evening, just before twilight,
the wife and young son of a fisher-
man were returning home from a

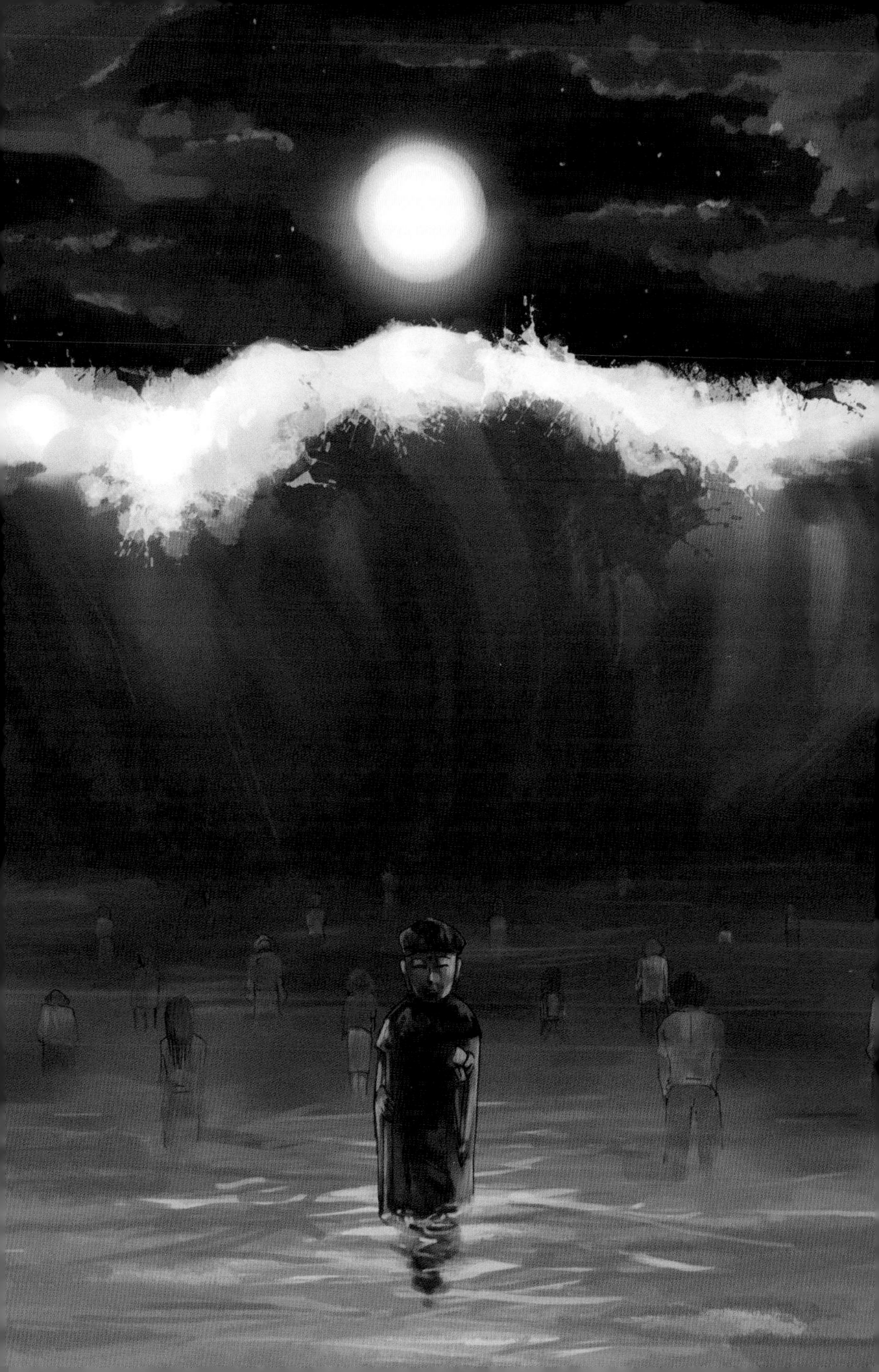

Jizo statues are a common sight throughout Japan. Hats and bibs are common accouterments, left as offerings to clothe the little souls in the afterlife.

long day of hard labor spent helping a neighbor plant a rice field in exchange for food. As their path brought them near the Guiding Jizo, the mother sensed a presence nearby. Cautiously peering around a tree, she spotted the statue — and a whole host of spirits materializing before it. One would be shock enough. But this was a veritable parade of ethereal men, women, and children. And even stranger, the vast majority seemed to be in the prime of their lives.

After hearing the story later that evening, the father laughed it off as a figment of their imaginations. But the very next day, when the family was gathering seaweed along the coastline at low tide, something strange happened. The tide pulled out and didn't return. Before long an ominous shadow appeared on the horizon. Spooked, the mother, father, and son rushed to higher ground.

Minutes later, a tsunami plowed into the coast, wiping out the entire fishing village as the three watched helplessly from a hilltop. They were the only survivors.

That's when it dawned on them. The phantoms the mother and boy had seen were none other than those of their fellow villagers, paying their final respects to the jizo as their bodies went about their lives, blissfully unaware of the fate they would suffer just twenty-four hours hence. If only the mother had realized, if only the people had known…! But it was far too late for that.

Tohoku and Tsunami

Given the fact that Kesennuma made headlines for the very same reason in 2011, there is no doubt that this "fairy tale" is based at least in part on a true story.

Foreign media outlets rushed to describe the scale of the 2011 tsunami disaster as "unprecedented," which is true as far as the nuclear meltdowns are concerned. But the term is sadly far from accurate when it comes to earthquakes and tsunami. Similar catastrophes occurred in 1933, 1896, 1611, 869, and undoubtedly many times unrecorded by history as well.

In fact, stone markers dot the Japanese coastline warning of

There are other Guiding Jizo, although with different legends surrounding them. One is located near Gokuraku-ji Temple in Kamakura, just an hour from Tokyo by train. Parents pray to this particular Guiding Jizo to ensure the healthy growth and development of their children.

tsunami from times of old, a literal message to future generations from ancestors long since shuffled off this mortal coil. Some date back centuries. One of the more recent, in nearby Aneyoshi City, was erected in 1933. It reads: "High dwellings mean peace for your descendants. Remember the disaster of the great tsunami. Do not build houses below here."

In every case, the 2011 tsunami waters broke before reaching these markers. Aneyoshi was one of the few locales where residents actually followed the markers' warnings. In many other places, the stones were treated as ancient history or all but forgotten.

Surviving an Encounter

Although many locals understandably relocated to higher ground after earlier tsunami, new residents who lacked a visceral memory of the dangers slowly repopulated low-lying areas once again, leading to tragic repetitions of history.

The true horror of tsunami is the fickleness of human memory. Occurring just once or twice a century, very large tsunami arrive just beyond the limits at which personal experience can guide us rather than history. Both stone markers and folktales are ways in which the victims of previous tragedies attempt to reach out to future generations.

The bottom line: in this era of science and technology it is tempting to brush off myth and legend as superstition. Sometimes, however, they're more than just stories. Listen to them.

Yokai Connection

In spite of their name, Funa-yurei (see *Yokai Attack!*) are treated as yokai rather than yurei because they represent the concept of drowning at sea rather than any single individual. They have a nasty habit of preying upon unwary fishermen, particularly in the twilight hours.

Unfortunately, a belief in these creatures may have caused the deaths of many victims pulled out to sea by the 1896 tsunami, which hit roughly the same area as the 2011 tsunami. The following is from a report made many years later.

"In one village (in Iwate prefecture)... 40 fishermen in five or six boats went out the evening of the tsunami." Returning unaware of what had happened while they were at sea, the "fishermen heard voices calling out for help in the dark as they returned. Local lore regarded voices in the water as those of ghosts. Moreover, answering the calls of such ghosts would result in their pulling the responder into the water. This situation resulted in delays in the fishing boats mounting rescue operations."

MATSUE OHASHI BRIDGE

Name in Japanese: 松江大橋
Location: Matsue, Japan (Western Honshu)
Type of Bridge: Stone (in original form) Concrete and steel (in current form)
First Built: Around 1608
Length: Roughly 426 feet (130 meters)
Date of Haunting: Around 1608
Cause of Haunting: Human sacrifice
Name of Sacrifice: Gensuke
Type of Spot: "Yurei Spot"
Type of Phenomena: Visible manifestations
Threat Level: Low

Claim to Fame

Matsue Ohashi Bridge has been feared as a spooky spot for more than four hundred years. The story concerns an infamous phenomenon from times of old called a *hitobashira* — literally a "human pillar" but more colloquially a "foundation sacrifice."

Hitobashira are one or more human beings deliberately entombed in the base of a structure in a superstitious effort to ensure its safety and durability. Rumors of foundation sacrifices swirl around all sorts of medieval construction projects, including levees, canals, and tunnels (see p.112). But they are particularly associated with castles and bridges. The Matsue Ohashi Bridge is the most famous of the latter.

The Story

Matsue is one of Japan's most storied cities — literally. Folklorist Lafcadio Hearn, who penned a series of collections of Japanese ghost tales at the turn of the 20th century, heard most of them in and around Matsue.

Matsue is a remote sort of place, a "castle town" divided into southern and northern halves by the Ohashi-gawa River. In the early 17th century, the daimyo who ruled Matsue commissioned the construction of a series of new bridges across the waters in order to hasten the completion of his home and fortress.

Time and time again, foundation stones were laid in the Ohashi-gawa. But the area happens to be an estuary, a channel for waters flowing between Lake Shinji and the sea. Currents swirled wickedly with every ebb and flow of the tides. Bridge foundations — and on more than one occasion, half-completed bridges — were swept away one after the other, as though the river-gods were taunting the audacity of man for attempting such a thing.

This wouldn't do. And so the powers that be conceived a plan. They would quiet the rumblings of the river gods with an offering. A sacrifice: A human sacrifice.

But who to pick? They decided to select the victim — we mean, honored offering — randomly. Really randomly: they decided to nab the next man who happened to walk by the construction site without pleats in his hakama (the traditional article of clothing worn by men at the time). That unfortunate man just happened to be Gensuke.

The workers grabbed him, bound him to a foundation stone, and

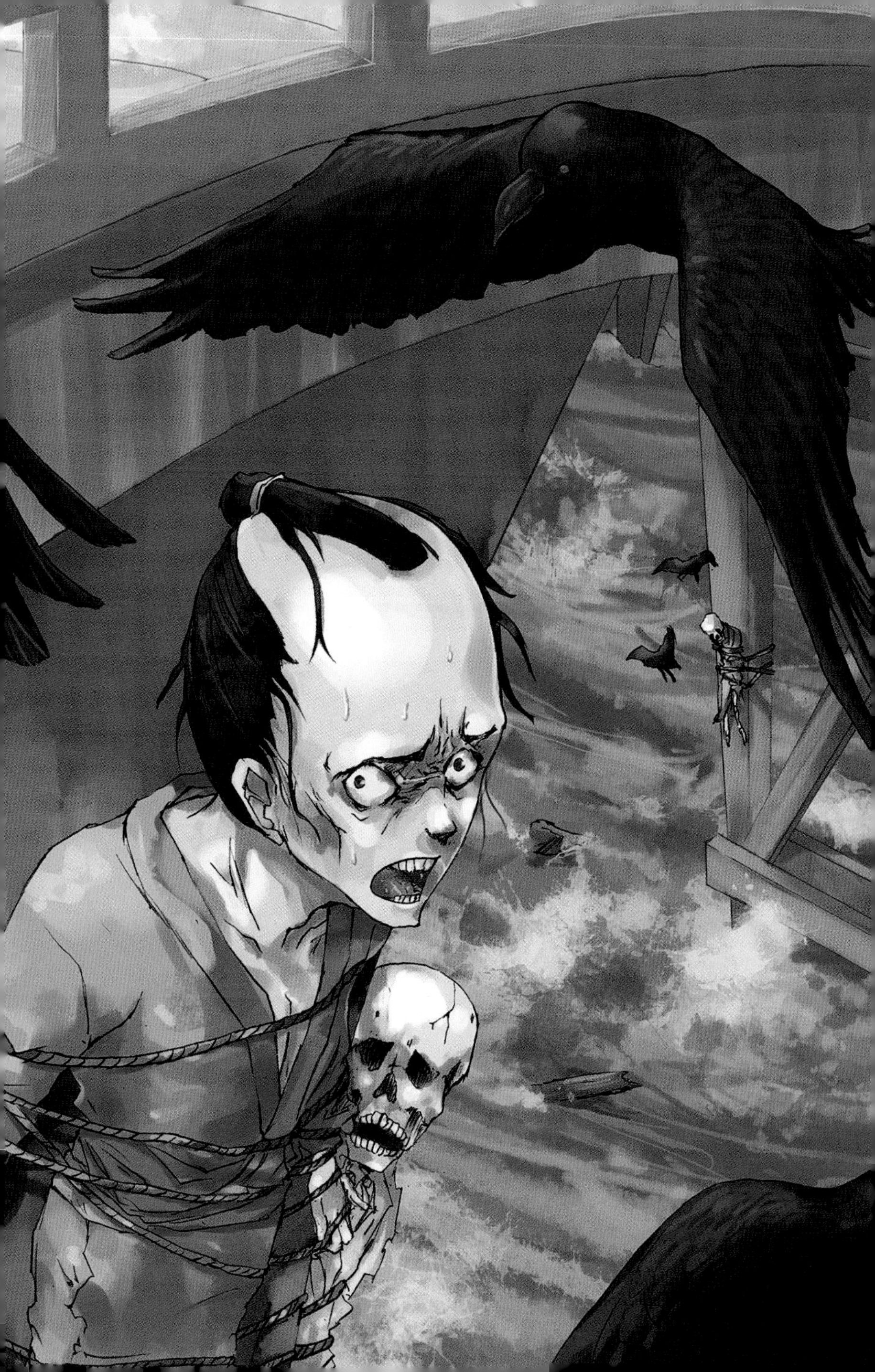

sunk the (presumably screaming) man precisely at the spot where the waters were at their most turbulent. That was the last anyone saw of poor Gensuke alive.

The hitobashira apparently did the trick. No longer did the tides sweep away the foundation-stones and the bridge quickly went up without a single hitch. The people of Matsue hailed "Gensuke's Pillar" for its stabilizing influence on the project. Although it has been rebuilt many times in the intervening centuries, an incarnation of Matsue Ohashi Bridge stands on the spot to this very day, more than four hundred years later.

The Attack

Allow us to quote Hearn, from his 1894 classic *Glimpses of Unfamiliar Japan:*

> Upon moonless nights... a ghostly fire flits about [Gensuke's] pillar — always in the dead watch hour between two and three; and the colour of the light was red, though I am assured in Japan, as in other lands, the fires of the dead are most often blue.

In addition to the visible manifestation, there is at least one fatality associated with the bridge (other than Gensuke's, of course). When Matsue Ohashi was overhauled and rebuilt into its current form in 1936, a worker by the name of Kiyoshi Fukada died when a heavy metal bucket slipped off the bridge and fell on his head. Contemporary news reports placed the cause of his death squarely at the foot of Gensuke's Pillar, upon which the man had been working when the incident occurred. Gensuke's curse? Unfortunate coincidence? You make the call.

Surviving an Encounter

So long as you don't plan to monkey around on the pillar itself, there's no need to worry about physical harm — Gensuke's pillar is mainly known for its ghostly late-night glow. You can also take solace in the fact that regardless of how barbaric we may find the custom today, hitobashira were introduced specifically to make dangerous places safer for the living. For that reason, if anything you should offer thanks for his (literal) sacrifice rather than turning heel and running.

In fact, the city of Matsue does precisely that every year. The Gensuke Matsuri Festival, held in late October, begins in Gensuke Park at the foot of the bridge. After a thirty-minute Buddhist kuyo (purification) ritual to appease the souls of those who gave their lives to build the bridge, the festivities segue into more upbeat workshops, lectures, and performances.

Yokai Connection

Gensuke isn't the only spook to haunt a bridge in Japan. The Hashi-Hime (see *Yokai Attack!*) is a yokai that actively preys upon travelers. It takes the form of a beautiful man or woman who enchants a passer-by, then reveals her hideous true form to scare them to death. While Gensuke's yurei haunts the bridge under which he is buried, Hashi-Hime seems free to roam across bridges throughout Japan.

CHAPTER FIVE
Dangerous Games

Read on for an overview of everything from parlor tricks to methods for contacting the "spirit plane" – Japanese style.

HYAKU MONOGATARI

Name in Japanese: 百物語
a.k.a. One Hundred Stories
(literal translation); One Hundred Candles
Type of Game: Parlor game
Origin: Unknown
Peak of Interest: Late Edo Era
(early 19th century)
Things You'll Need: 100 candle-lit
paper lanterns or candles (slow burning
type); 100 scary stories; A space with
two or three distinct rooms; Blue robes
for participants; A low table; A mirror;
A long summer evening with nothing else
on the schedule
Type of Phenomena: Horrifying
manifestations of various sorts (both yurei
and yokai)
Threat Level: Depends on who you
scare up!

The 1666 story collection
"Otogiboko" describes a terrifying
winter session of Hyaku Monogatari.
Five men gathered and completed the
game; suddenly, amidst the snow swirling
outside their window countless tiny lights
began to glow like fireflies. The strange
phosphorescent particles entered the room
and began to converge in a corner, forming
a sphere whose surface turned smooth
like that of a mirror. Almost as soon as
it manifested, the sphere shattered with
a sound so unsettling to human ears that
it knocked the men senseless. They were
revived by family members, but there
was no sign of lights or fragments. The
event remains unexplained.

Claim to Fame

Traditionally played during the
summer months, when ghosts and
other spooks are believed to be at
their most active in Japan, Hyaku
Monogatari is a parlor game from
a bygone era. It involves telling
one hundred scary stories over
the course of a very long evening,
extinguishing a candle after each.
The ostensible reason for this is
that once the hundredth tale
has been told, a vaguely-defined
mysterious happening will, uh,
happen.

How many participants actually believed a ghost would

appear once the final tale was told,
we'll never know. But undoubtedly
more than a few people joined in
the fun for a decidedly down-to-
earth reason: long before the advent
of air conditioning, listening to
scary stories was a quick and easy
way of getting a shiver and cooling
down in the doldrums of summer!

Nobody is quite sure where the
game originated. Judging by the
name, it may have been inspired
by tales of the Hyakki Yagyo ("The
Hundred Demons' Night Parade"),
a supposedly true story of an 11th
century invasion of Kyoto by supernatural forces. (For more about this
terrifying tale, see *Yokai Attack!*)

Although records
of Hyaku Monogatari
sessions date
back to at least the
mid-1600s, it was
undoubtedly played
far before that. It

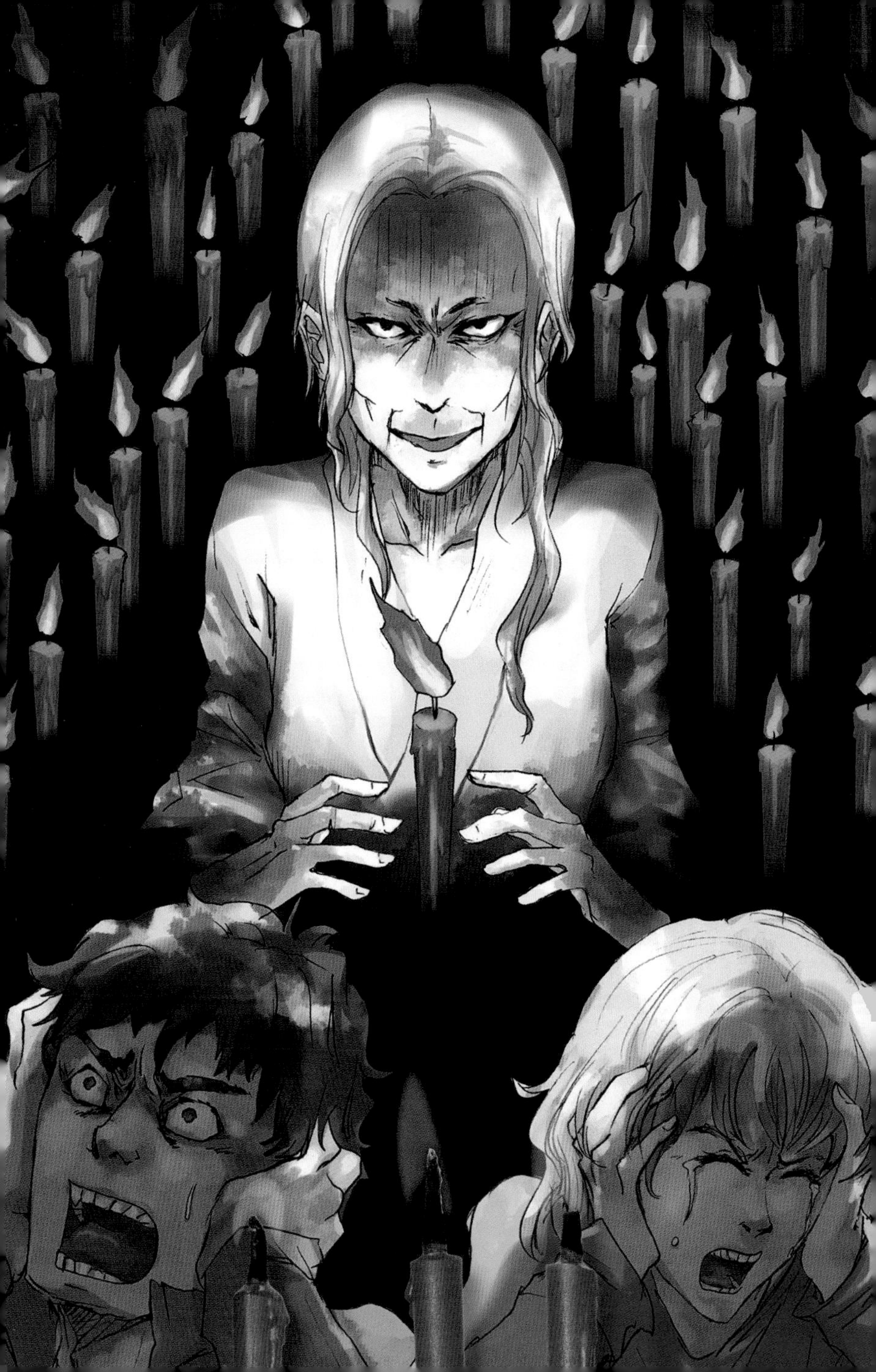

seems to have originally been a way for aristocrats to pass a summer evening, but soon spread like wildfire through society at large. Its popularity coincided with an emerging mass popular culture and dovetailed perfectly with the worldwide phenomenon of Spiritualism in the mid-to-late 1800s. A popular summer pastime for two and a half centuries, the concept of Hyaku Monogatari inspired a great deal of literature and art, including spooky series by some of Japan's masters (such as Katsushika Hokusai, pictured below). The long hours and preparation required has made sessions few and far between in our faster-paced modern era, but even today, the phrase remains synonymous with tales of terror.

How to Play

While the game itself existed long before, the 17th Century story collection *Otogiboko* details the traditional method of playing.

1) Gather a group of at least 3 and preferably more (you're going to be telling a lot of stories here).

2) Wait for a night of the full moon.

3) Assemble at the home of one of the participants.

4) Prepare a space consisting of at least two rooms, though three are preferable, and an L-shape more preferable still.

5) Darken the rooms. In the one furthest from the room in which the group is assembled, arrange 100 lanterns lit by candles. Lanterns should preferably use blue tissue-paper rather than the standard white. In the center place the table, and atop the table the mirror.

↫ As gathering a hundred paper lanterns is quite a task, candles alone are permissible as well.

6) Participants should wear blue clothing and leave their swords at the door (remember, this was written in the 17th century; this was standard tea-house etiquette of the day. Modern-day participants should follow suit by leaving stunguns, pepper sprays, Tasers, Glocks, etc. at the door.) Remove all potentially dangerous items from the room.

↫ This is the oldest known version of the game; later generations dropped the requirement for blue clothing, so this can be considered optional.

7) Pick your tales ahead of time. Traditionally, the stories told at Hyaku Monogatari sessions involved not ghost stories but tales of strange or odd happenings. But really, any form of spooky tale intended to set the listener's hair on end will do.

Choose stories of a reasonable length. Each participant will only have an average of just five minutes to tell a tale. Think about it: five minutes times one hundred equals more than eight hours. This sort of entertainment hails from a slower era and demands serious concentration and endurance.

8) After each tale is told, the teller rises and goes into the room with the lanterns. After extinguishing a lantern, they must gaze at themselves in the mirror and return to the storytelling room. (The group may talk amongst themselves during this time.)

The Attack

The room gets progressively darker and gloomier as the candles are blown out. Once the hundredth is extinguished and the rooms are plunged into total darkness, something is supposed to happen.

Here's the catch: the "something" isn't clearly defined. Nearly any strange phenomenon is possible. Perhaps someone will be seized by a spirit, or a yokai or yurei will appear in the room. Details vary from account to account, but a late 18th century portrayal of a session illustrated by legendary woodblock artist Katsushika Hokusai shows participants sprinting in terror from a home that is literally overflowing with strange creatures. This is undoubtedly an exaggeration, but caution is advised. Some sources claim that once invoked by a successful Hyaku Monogatari, strange phenomena will continue unabated for thirty days.

Hyaku Monogatari don't have to be spoken aloud; reading one hundred scary stories under the right conditions can have the same effect. Wait a second — how many stories are between these covers, again?

Surviving an Encounter

Simple: tell less than 100 stories! At the peak of Hyaku Monogatari's popularity in the mid-Nineteenth century, participants customarily stopped at 99 stories, spending whatever remained of the night hours chatting and waiting for sunrise. This was in large part an attempt to make the game more appealing for those who liked scary stories but didn't want to run into any actual spooks.

Hokusai's portryal of a Hyakumonogatari session gone horribly wrong... Or right? (Woodblock print, circa 1780.)

Dangerous Games: 32

JAPANESE CURSES

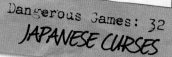

Name in Japanese: 丑の刻参り

a.k.a. *Ushinokoku-mairi (transliteration) "A Shrine-Visit at the Hour of the Ox" (translation); "Japanese voodoo doll"; "Japanese poppet"*

Type of Activity: *Curse*

First Described: *Wooden dolls with nail marks have been dated to at least A.D. 700s*

Peak of Interest: *Still going strong, among a certain set*

Things You'll Need: *A straw doll; White robes; Seven "gosun-kugi" (large iron nails); Three candles; A "gotoku" (iron brazier); White facial powder or paint; A tree; A full moon; A heart full of anger*

Result of Playing: *Horrible things happening to target*

Threat Level: *Just how angry are you?*

Claim to Fame

Cultures and religions around the world describe methods of targeting individuals for harm or misfortune. Some of the most famous in the Western world include so-called voodoo dolls and "jinxes" from African-American folk religion, the "evil eye" curses of some African, European, and Mediterranean cultures, and the "hexes" of the Pennsylvania Dutch.

The Japanese have the Ushinokoku-mairi. The term literally means "Visiting the Shrine at the Hour of the Ox," the latter being an archaic measure of time that corresponds to the period from 1 to 3 in the morning. Synonymous with curses in Japan, it is perfect for those who want to bring the wrath of the supernatural down on a cheating mate, perceived enemy, duplicitous friend, etc., etc., without all the hassle of dying and becoming a yurei themselves.

The ritual is complicated. Its origins date back well over a millennium. The very first individual to carry it out was a woman infuriated at her philandering husband, guided by a Shinto priest who divined its particulars in a strange dream. (Incidentally, this woman was so successful at her task that she transformed into a yokai. She is known as "Hashi-Hime," the Bridge Princess, for her penchant of ambushing victims on bridges. (For more information about her, see *Yokai Attack!*))

Here's how it works.

First! Make Your Own Curse-Doll!

1) Divide straw into two bundles, one slightly thinner than the other.

2) Thread the thinner bundle through the other to form a cross shape.

3) Use thread to tie off the ends of the thinner bundle to form "hands."

4) Separate the thicker bundle into two parts and tie each off to form "feet."

5) You're ready for action.

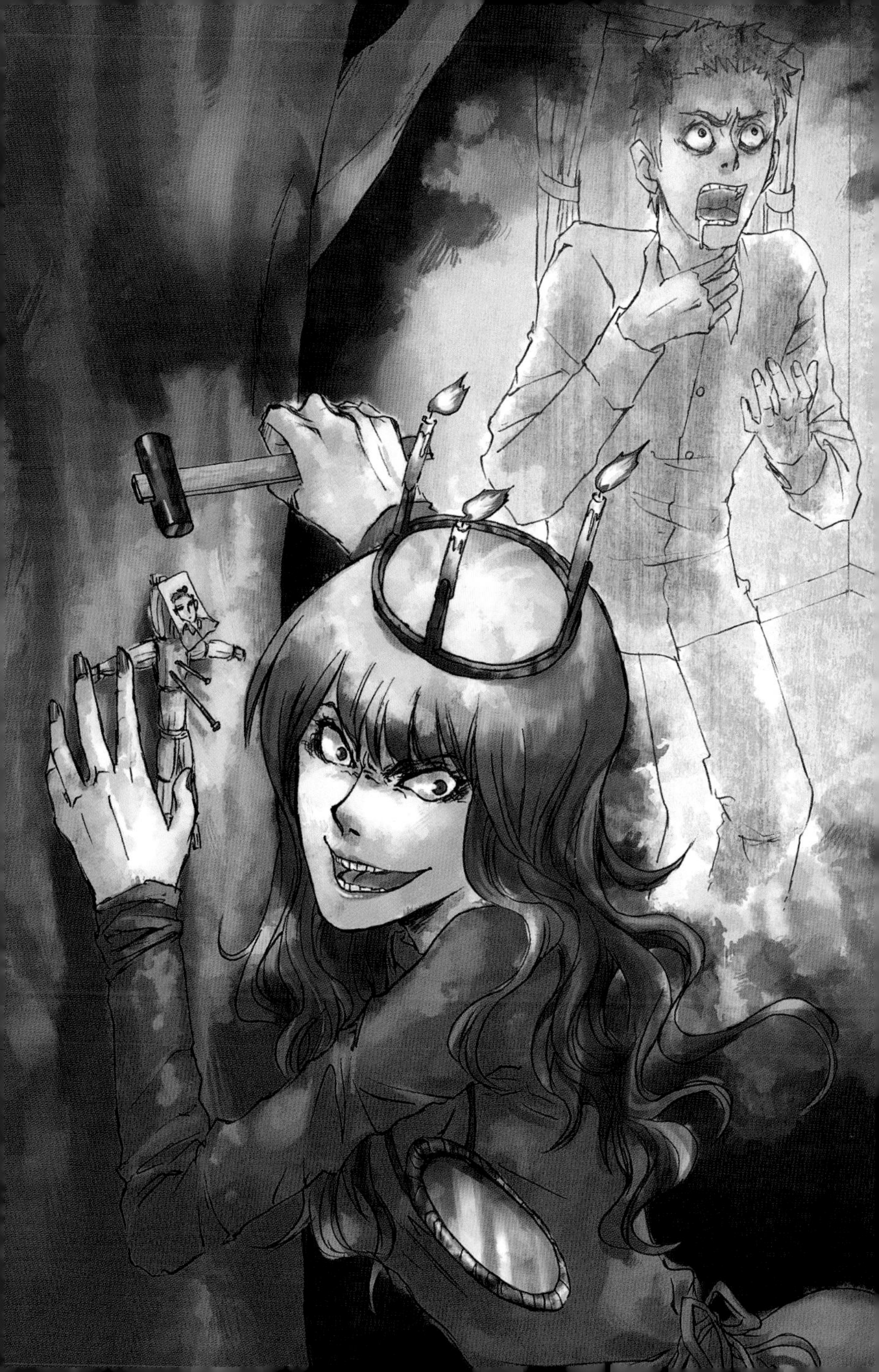

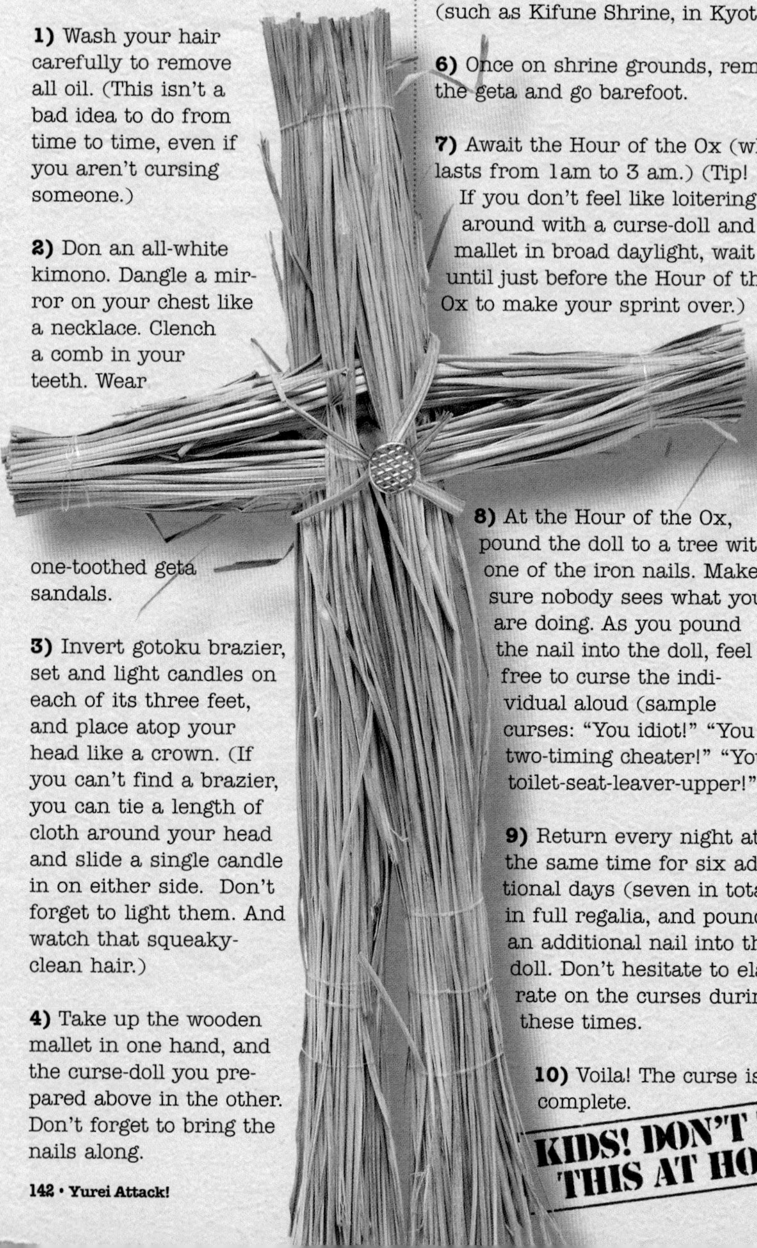

Next! Preparing a Curse the Old-Fashioned Way

1) Wash your hair carefully to remove all oil. (This isn't a bad idea to do from time to time, even if you aren't cursing someone.)

2) Don an all-white kimono. Dangle a mirror on your chest like a necklace. Clench a comb in your teeth. Wear one-toothed geta sandals.

3) Invert gotoku brazier, set and light candles on each of its three feet, and place atop your head like a crown. (If you can't find a brazier, you can tie a length of cloth around your head and slide a single candle in on either side. Don't forget to light them. And watch that squeaky-clean hair.)

4) Take up the wooden mallet in one hand, and the curse-doll you prepared above in the other. Don't forget to bring the nails along.

5) Run like heck to the nearest shrine known for accepting curses (such as Kifune Shrine, in Kyoto).

6) Once on shrine grounds, remove the geta and go barefoot.

7) Await the Hour of the Ox (which lasts from 1am to 3 am.) (Tip! If you don't feel like loitering around with a curse-doll and mallet in broad daylight, wait until just before the Hour of the Ox to make your sprint over.)

8) At the Hour of the Ox, pound the doll to a tree with one of the iron nails. Make sure nobody sees what you are doing. As you pound the nail into the doll, feel free to curse the individual aloud (sample curses: "You idiot!" "You two-timing cheater!" "You toilet-seat-leaver-upper!")

9) Return every night at the same time for six additional days (seven in total), in full regalia, and pound an additional nail into the doll. Don't hesitate to elaborate on the curses during these times.

10) Voila! The curse is complete.

KIDS! DON'T TRY THIS AT HOME.

Tips

Pounding nails into various parts of the doll will affect the corresponding body parts of the curse-ee. (Is that a word?) For example, nailing the leg will cause leg problems; the chest, heart problems; the crotch, uh, crotch problems... Avoid driving a spike into the doll's head unless you truly want the individual dead.

Another rule of thumb: try to avoid hitting spots on the doll that correspond to the chakras of the human body. Hitting the doll's shoulder chakra, for example, could well have the effect of curing the victim's stiff neck.

Trivia

Kyoto's Jishu Jinja, located in the shadow of world-famous Kiyomizu-dera Temple, is famed for making — and breaking — ties between lovers. Today, it's mainly visited by singles in search of a husband or wife. But in times of old, a certain large tree behind the main shrine building was one of the city's most popular ushinokoku-mairi spots. You most probably won't see any dolls there, but you can see the holes left in the tree's trunk from countless curse-ceremonies conducted over the ages.

Compu-Curses

For those too busy to actually weave their own curse-dolls and gather the necessary items, a variety of websites offer convenient pre-prepared curse kits containing all of the basic implements one needs to carry out their dirty deed. Some sites even helpfully offer to conduct the curse themselves, complete with video so that you can gloat over the proceedings at your leisure. Prices start at around ¥10,000 (US $115) for a starter kit.

Note: sending said DVD to the intended victim can potentially get you in serious trouble with the law. While few in the modern era truly believe preparing a curse-doll can actually cause physical harm, the psychological effects on the target are another matter altogether. In certain cases, cursing someone can be seen as a criminal threat, as you can see below.

Surviving a Curse

Let's take a look at a real-life criminal case involving a curse.

> prospect is extremely gloomy.
>
> **AKITA PREFECTURE, 1954.**
> When young Yoshie Tanaka collapsed from sudden chest pains, her boyfriend Tetsuya Yamamoto filed a report with his local police department. Claiming that she was the victim of a curse, he explained that his former girlfriend, a woman by the name of Kiyoko Hotta, was taking out her frustrations on Tanaka to repay Yamamoto for having dumped Hotta several months prior. The police duly conducted an investigation. Discovering a nail-studded straw doll in her possession, they arrested Hotta for suspicion of making threats. Upon her arrest, Tanaka's physical complaints completely disappeared and she returned to perfect health. Doctors believe she merely suffered from believing in the curse — in other words, the placebo effect. But the actual truth may never be known.
>
> • • •
>
> LOCAL HERO MISSING

KOKKURI SAN

Name in Japanese: 狐狗狸さん

a.k.a. Japanese Table-Turning;
Japanese Ouija; Japanese Séances

Type of Game: Parlor game

Origin: 1884

Peaks of Interest: Meiji era (Late 1800s)
Showa era (Mid-1970s)

Things You'll Need: (Meiji era version)
3 bamboo or wooden sticks roughly 16 inches
(40cm) each; Round rice-pot lid; Cloth
(preferably white);
(Showa era version) White paper; Ten-yen coin

Type of Phenomena: Spirit communication;
Spirit possession

Threat Level: Depends on who you contact

Claim to Fame

A form of spiritual divination that
enjoyed two booms of popularity in
Japan, once in the late 1800s and
again in the 1970s. In its earliest
form, it involved a makeshift device
used in a manner similar to 19th
century table-tilting séances; in its
later incarnation, it reappeared in
a form reminiscent of the Western-
style Ouija board.

Before we get into the nitty-gritty
of Kokkuri-san, we have to discuss
its roots in Spiritualism, an occult-
religious movement that swept
the world in the late 19th century
and still exists today, albeit much
reduced in scope.

The story begins in March of
1848, when a series of strange
occurrences in the town
of Hydesville, New York
captivated the United

States. A pair of teenage
sisters, Maggie and Kate
Fox, managed to convince their
family, friends, and a growing
circle of strangers that they had
the ability to contact the spirit
world. Simply via the expedient
of snapping their fingers, the girls
seemed to be able to compel an
invisible spirit to respond to their
questions by rapping — not of
the MC-and-DJ variety, but rather
by making a knocking sound.
Conjuring up one-if-for-yes and
two-if-for-no style responses to
questions from their neighbors,
the girls claimed the spirit was
that of a man who had been
murdered decades earlier by the
home's prior owner.

Before long, their older sister
stepped in as their manager,
arranging sensational (and lucrative) public séances that swept
the mass media. Within a few
years, the idea that nearly anyone
could initiate direct contact with
the spirits of the departed gave
rise to a new religious movement
dubbed Spiritualism. At its peak
in 1897, some eight million people
subscribed to Spiritualist beliefs; a
séance was even held in the White
House, attended by no less than
Abraham Lincoln.

Chief among Spiritualism's
tools for contacting the world
beyond was a parlor game called
"Table-Turning," also known as
"Table-Tipping" or "Table-Rapping."
This involves a group of people
sitting around a table with their
fingers resting along the top
edge. The leader of the séance
verbally asks for spirits to make

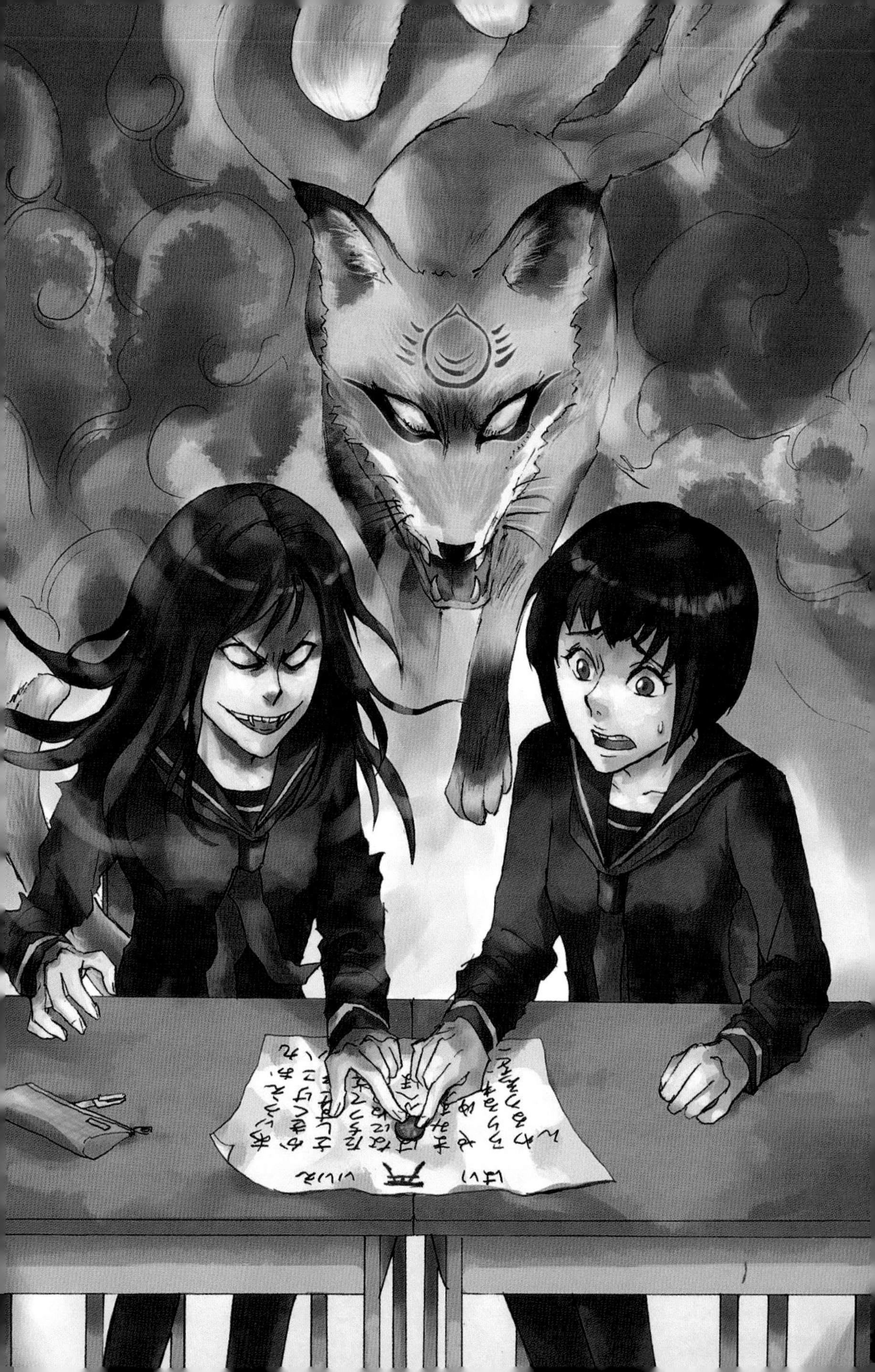

contact. In response, the table may vibrate, pivot, or rise and drop. Traditionally, the "spirits" communicated answers to questions by shaking or dropping the table as letters of the alphabet were called out. The practice originated in the United States and eventually spread to other countries.

Table-turning reached Japanese shores in 1884. That is the date famed paranormal researcher Inoue Enryo theorized that it was introduced via the port of Shimoda by a group of foreign sailors, who played the game to while away the hours as their ship was repaired from storm damage. Unable to understand or even pronounce the words "Table Turning," locals dubbed the game "Kokkuri," perhaps taken from the onomatopoeia for a nodding motion.

Kokkuri-san (as it came to be affectionately known) spread like wildfire throughout Japan. Before long, fans of the game re-christened the word with three characters: fox (*ko* = 狐), dog (*ku* = 狗), and tanuki (*ri* = 狸), animals believed to possesses a host of spooky supernatural powers. (See *Yokai Attack!* for a detailed run-down of the tricks these wily rascals like to play on humans.)

← Foxes.... Fox sisters. Coincidence? Or sign of strange powers at play?

Within a few years, Kokkuri-san exploded into a full-fledged pop-cultural phenomenon. Kokkuri literature attempted to explain the "science" behind the game by using theories such as "human electricity." Specialty shops stocked and sold the necessary equipment.

There were even Kokkuri schools, which purported to teach novices how to play. The craze peaked in the late 1880s, but never disappeared from the collective consciousness.

Nearly a century later, a new version of Kokkuri-san would sweep the nation once again. The 1970s saw a worldwide resurgence of interest in things supernatural, and Japan was no exception. Horror films such as "The Exorcist," "The Omen," and "The Shining" drew sellout crowds. Paranormally-themed manga and magazines filled bookstore shelves. Psychics such as Uri Geller captivated audiences in live and televised performances. Against this backdrop, perhaps it shouldn't be any surprise that Kokkuri-san re-emerged to enchant legions of schoolchildren (and undoubtedly more than a few adults) throughout Japan. It is the quintessential late-night slumber party activity, a modern version of parlor games like the Hyaku Monogatari (see p.136).

How to Play

There are two different ways of playing Kokkuri-san. See the list of materials at top.

1) Original method (Meiji era: 1880s).
This version of the game is considered archaic and is not widely practiced anymore.

The three bamboo sticks are arranged in a free-standing tripod. The rice-pot lid is balanced atop them and covered with the sheet of cloth.

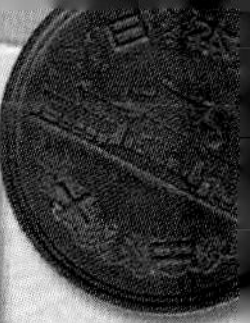

There is a totally unfounded rumor that warlord Oda Nobunaga engaged in a version of Kokkuri-san, but given that he died in 1581, this is undoubtedly wishful thinking.

The participants kneel on the floor facing the device with the fingers of one hand gently resting along its edge. A leader asks questions of the spirits; if one is contacted, it is addressed with simple yes-or-no questions to which it responds by causing vibrations, clattering, or lifting of one of the legs. Traditionally, questions proceeded along the lines of whether any of the participants or their friends might suffer misfortunes, changes in the weather ("raise a leg if it will rain tomorrow"), and the like.

2) Modern method (Showa era: 1970s). You will need to prepare a Kokkuri-san sheet. This is a piece of paper marked with a Torii gate symbol at top, flanked by the Japanese words for "yes" and "no," with the letters of the Japanese alphabet in columns beneath. (You can write it out by hand yourself.) This is placed atop a table, and a ten-yen coin is placed atop the torii symbol. The participants — usually no more than three — each place a finger lightly atop the coin.

The leader initiates contact by saying "Kokkuri-san, kokkuri-san, if you are here please indicate 'yes.'" Success results in the coin moving from the torii mark to the "yes" mark, at which point it can be queried to spell out a response. (The system is generally identical to that of a Ouija board and its accompanying planchette pointer.)

The Attack

The alleged danger of activities such as these is that the spirits one encounters may not be willing to go gentle into that good night, either forcing the participants to continue playing against their will or (worst-case scenario here) possessing them body and soul.

Surviving an Encounter

The conventional wisdom on avoiding problems with Kokkuri-san is as follows.

1) Never abandon a Kokkuri-san session in the middle. See rule 5.
2) Participants must remain in contact with the coin no matter how fast it moves.
3) The Kokkuri sheet must be shredded and discarded at the end of a session.
4) The ten-yen coin must be spent within the day.
5) Sessions must be ended with a proper show of respect: "Thank you for coming. Please return now." If the coin does not move back to the torii mark, repeat the request until it does. See rule 1.

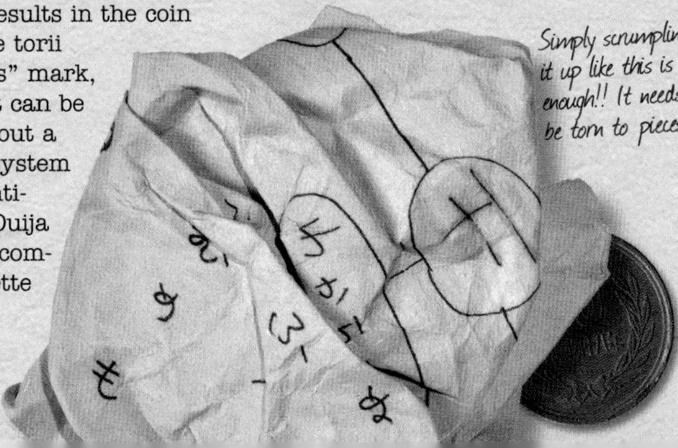

Simply scrumpling it up like this is not enough!! It needs to be torn to pieces!!

HANGONKO

Name in Japanese: 返魂香
a.k.a. Soul-summoning incense
(Transliteration); Hangon Incense;
Hankonko (alternate reading of kanji);
Hankon Incense; Fan Hung Hsiang (in Chinese);
Wizard-incense (Lafcadio Hearn's interpretation)
Used for: Summoning of the dead
First Described: 16th century
Peak of Interest: Unknown, but really,
it's a timeless sort of desire
Things You'll Need: Hangon Incense
an incense burner, a specific dead person you
want to contact
Result of Use: The ability to see a
deceased loved one
Threat Level: Low physically;
potentially quite high psychologically

> Although the power of making visible
> the forms of the dead has been claimed
> for one sort of incense only, the burning
> of any kind of incense is supposed to
> summon viewless spirits in multitude.
> – Lafcadio Hearn, *In Ghostly Japan*, 1899

Claim to Fame

Hangonko is a legendary form of
incense supposedly hailing from the
distant borders of Western China,
capable of summoning a dead soul
back to the world of the living for a
brief time when burned.

Incense plays a key role in
religious ceremonies throughout the world, chief among them
Buddhism, which makes copious
use of it in a wide variety of rites

and rituals. But in Japan,
incense has always been as
much about entertainment
as enlightenment. For more
than a millennium the rich
and powerful collected rare
varieties of the stuff, both
as a personal luxury and to
impress visitors. Knowing
one's incense — what varieties suited which occasions
— was a hallmark of being
a cultivated soul, akin to the
Western obsession of wine
pairings with food. Incense
parties — *kokai* — rose
to popularity in the 14th
century, parlor games in
which groups of aristocrats
would pass around censers
of incense and attempt to
correctly identify and list
the specific types burning
within. Although not widely
played anymore, at their
peak of popularity incense
parties were considered
every bit as prestigious as the
tea ceremony and ikebana flower
arrangement, giving rise to an art
called *kodo* (the way of incense).

Incense remains a part of the
fabric of daily life in Japan. It is
burned in home Buddhist altars
as offerings to one's ancestors and
the gods. Visitors to many Buddhist
temples encounter a large cauldron
of burning incense, the smoke of
which is scooped over one's body to
purify it before proceeding inward.

But we digress. The topic at hand
is not incense in general, but a very
specific type, used for a very specific purpose, rarer than rare, and
priceless beyond measure. Although

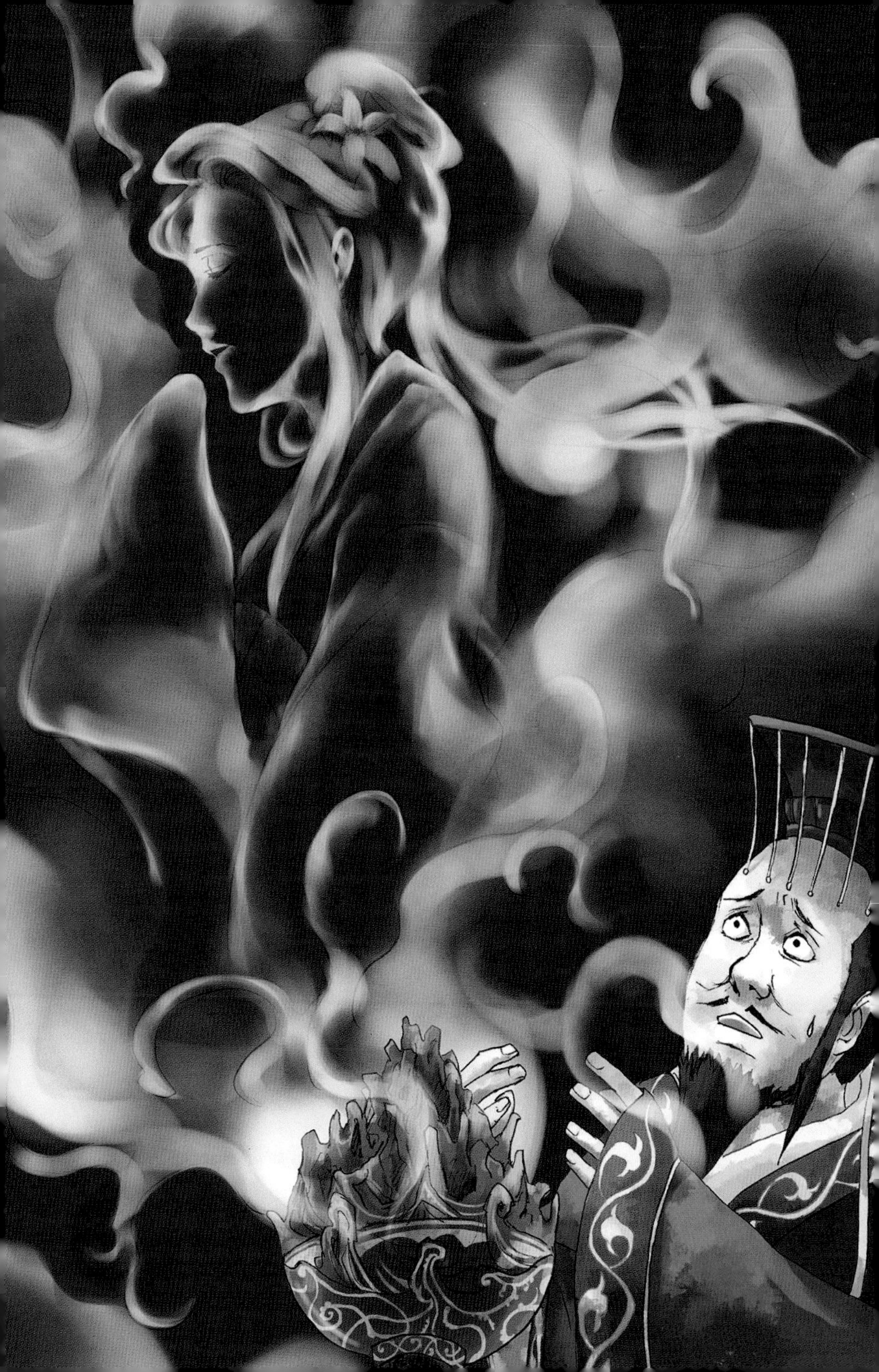

the concept of Hangon Incense seems to have originated in Chinese lore, it is well known throughout Japan and referenced or used as a plot device in a variety of traditional entertainments such as Kabuki dramas. Its literal translation is "soul-returning incense."

A variety of properties have been ascribed to Hangon Incense. Lesser grades are said to restore even the mortally ill to perfect health; the most potent varieties can actually resurrect the dead — so long as no more than three days have passed. But these two details are secondary lore. The vast majority of sources speak only to its ability to conjure forth imagery of the dead within the contours of its smoke. In our modern era of widespread home photography and video, this sort of imaging system may not seem like a very big deal. But in times of old, the images of those we lost remained locked within the fragile confines of human memory.

The original Hangon Incense legend is set in the ancient Chinese capital of Xi'an during the Han Dynasty, ruled by Emperor Wu (157 – 87 BC). The emperor's favorite consort perishes in the prime of her life, stolen from him by illness. Days upon weeks upon months are consumed by unceasing sorrow; his vassals and servants begin to seriously worry about his health. Desperate to see his beloved one more time, the emperor finally demands the kingdom's entire store of priceless Hangon Incense, which numbers just three grains. He kindles it while focusing on the image of his consort. Lo and behold, the outlines of her beautiful form begin to coalesce within the smoke, hazy at first and then almost blindingly bright. Overcome with emotion, he calls out to her again and again. But there is no response. In anguish he reaches out to touch her — but the moment his fingers make contact, she evaporates like the mirage she merely was. The priceless incense is gone, and the emperor is plunged even deeper into grief at this renewed loss. This is the double-edged sword of Hangon Incense.

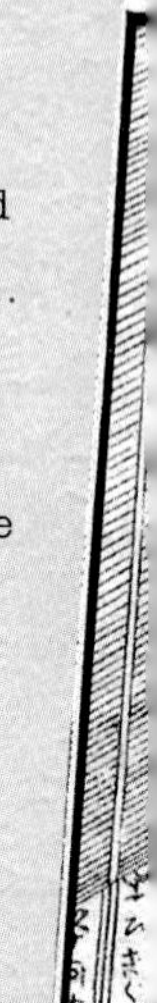

How to Use:

All one needs is to kindle the incense, pronounce certain words, and keep one's mind fixed upon the memory of the person one wishes to contact.

But here's the trick. Before you use Hangon Incense, you have to find Hangon Incense. Not an easy task.

According to the 1712 *Wakan Sansaizue*, an illustrated encyclopedia of Chinese medicine and lore for Japanese readers, Hangonko is "a phantom incense created from the mysterious Hangon Tree, the leaves of which resemble a sweetgum or oak, and whose intoxicating aroma is said to waft for some one hundred ri (50 km)." Its roots are boiled to a pulp that is then formed into pellets and dried.

Emperor Wu's stash supposedly came as tribute from the Yuezhi tribe, harvested in their lands beyond what was then the far Western border of China. That the powerful emperor of a vast land had but three tiny pieces of the stuff in his treasure hoard should give you a sense of how tough it is to find.

But let's say you do find it. What about those "certain words"? Of that, the historical record is silent. If you manage to get your hands on the incense, perhaps you can ask whoever you're buying it from for advice.

返魂香
Toriyama Sekien's portrayal of hangonko in action (1776).

Surviving an Encounter:

There is no physical danger associated with using Hangon Incense. However, as the tale of Emperor Wu shows, its use quite often leads to only deeper sorrow, for the image of the dead is just that: an image, not reality. The very emotion that allows one to conjure forth the spirit is what cuts them all the deeper when they are unable to make real contact.

Trivia:

The Hangon Tree makes a guest appearance in the video game "Final Fantasy 11," translated into English as "Revival Tree Root."

YOKAI CONNECTION:

Although not directly related to Hangonko, the yokai known as Enen-ra (see Yokai Attack!) is another mysterious phenomenon associated with smoke, including that from incense. Enen-ra are creatures that manifest from smoke; they are particularly associated with the eaves of Buddhist temples, which are filled with more than the usual amount of incense smoke. There is no particular danger from these apparitions, but they can startle.

SPIRIT PHOTOGRAPHS

Name in Japanese: 心霊写真
a.k.a. Shinrei shashin (Japanese); Ghost Photography; Spirit Photography
Used for: Freaking out friends; Content on Japanese variety shows, etc, etc.
First Described: 1861 (U.S.) 1879 (Japan)
Peak of Interest: Some things never go out of style.
Things You'll Need: A camera. (If you're a traditionalist, film, not digital.) A vivid imagination.
Threat Level: Low physically; potentially quite high psychologically

Claim to Fame:

Spirit photography has been with us since the advent of photography in the mid-1800s. The very first photo purporting to show a ghost was taken in 1861 by a Boston engraver named William Mumler. Shocked to discover a phantom person standing behind him in a self-portrait taken in an empty studio, he switched gears and launched a new career as a full-time spirit photographer. The concept dovetailed perfectly with the nation's growing interest in Spiritualism, a lay religious movement centered on a belief that nearly anyone could establish direct contact with the spirits of the dead.

Haunting though they may be, today it's obvious at a glance that Mumler's photos are staged double-exposures. But at the time, he was able to leverage the public's naïveté about the photographic process into a lucrative (if macabre) business in supplying "spirit photos" of Civil War dead to their grieving families.

For a while, Mumler was the nation's undisputed top spirit photographer, with customers including prominent socialites, journalists, and even a First Lady. But by the end of the decade, Mumler's critics caught up with him. Embroiled in a costly fraud case of which he was eventually acquitted, his reputation never recovered and he died penniless in 1884.

Japan's very first spirit photograph appears to have been taken in 1878. Alas, no copies survive today. Famed 19th century paranormal researcher Inoue "Dr. Yokai" Enryo reported that it showed a victim of the Satsuma Rebellion (see p. 92).

The first widely seen spirit photo emerged the following year, taken in a Yokohama studio by a photographer named Yaichi Mita. Unlike Mumler's case, Mita's seems to have been an honest accident. Ostensibly a portrait of the head monk of a local Buddhist temple, the developed image revealed what appeared to be an ethereal female presence standing behind the subject. When a local newspaper ran the photograph, it kicked off a craze for spirit photography in Japan that has lasted for well over a century.

Today, spirit photography — known as *shinrei shashin* in Japanese — is as popular as ever

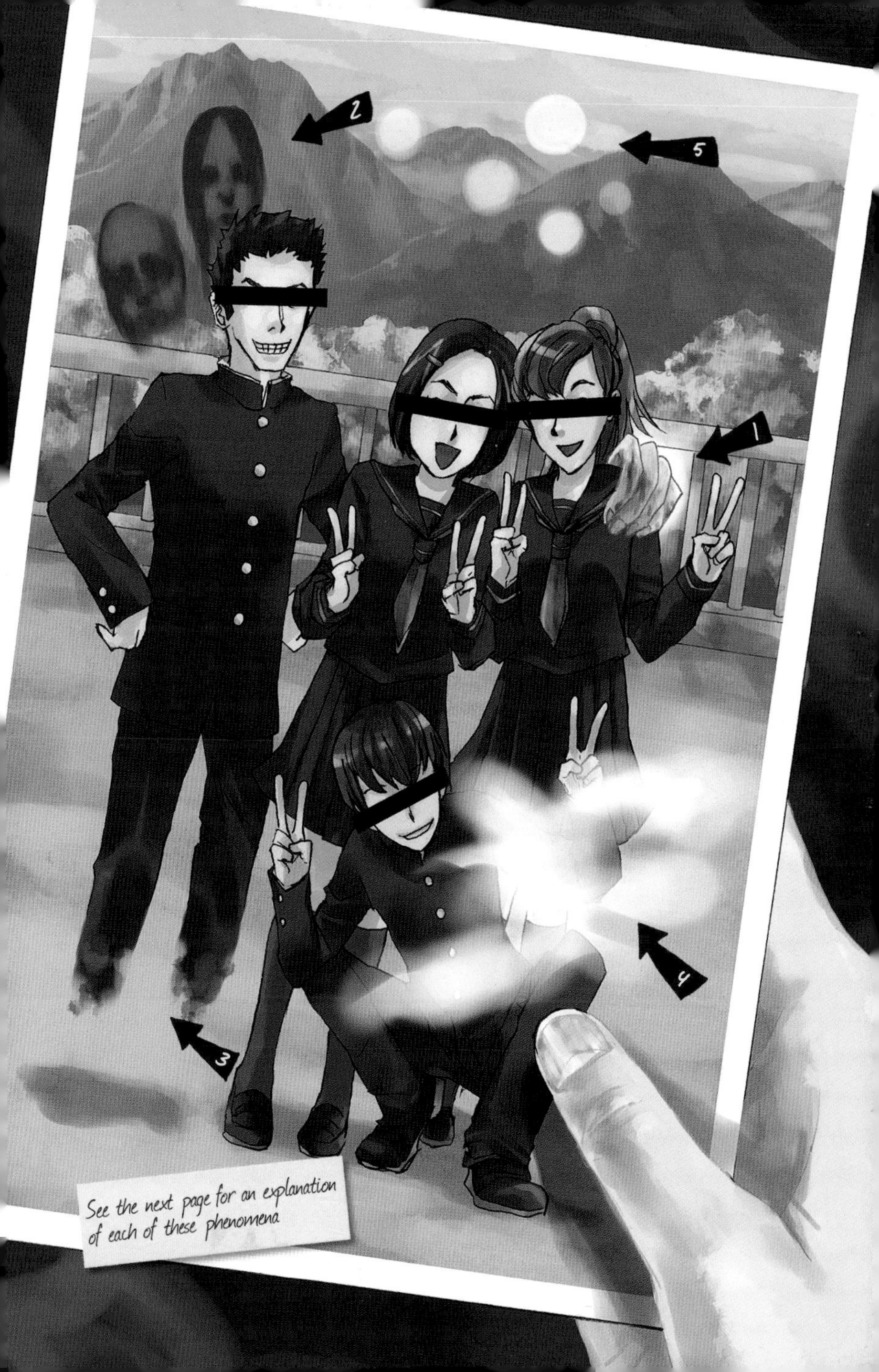
2
5
1
4
3
See the next page for an explanation of each of these phenomena

among a certain set. Modern-day spirit photos differ from their 19th century counterparts in critical ways. This is driven largely by technology: as digital cameras have eclipsed film-based models in popularity, the double-exposures and shutter effects that that caused "spirit photographs" with film cameras have largely been replaced by phenomena specific to digital cameras. And then there's always Photoshop, which lets even relative amateurs doctor photographs in ways unheard of even a decade ago, let alone a century or more.

A phantom figure captured in front of a row of Jizo statues... a dead priest perhaps?

Spirit photos continue to pop up again and again on Japanese television shows, with entire (and occasionally multi-hour) specials dedicated to deciphering spooky submissions sent in by viewers, complete with "psychic experts" weighing in with interpretations of the doom about to befall those captured in the images. The times may change, but one thing is for sure: spirit photography will never die. No pun intended.

NENSHA: PSYCHIC PHOTOGRAPHY

An offshoot of spirit photography, "psychic photography" involves projecting an image in one's mind directly onto a camera's film without actually triggering the shutter. Called nensha in Japanese, the phenomenon peaked in the Seventies and isn't widely practiced or studied today. Also known as "Thoughtography," it was used as a plot point in the horror film "Ringu."

Common Elements of Shinrei Shashin

1) Extra Limbs
Often seen in group photos, these are extra hands, legs, or feet that can't possibly belong to anyone in the shot.

2) Phantom figures
Actual imagery of what appears to be an individual who was not present when the photo was taken. Sometimes hazy; sometimes quite distinct. Often spotted in photographs of accident scenes or other areas where victims perished.

3) Missing Limbs
Subjects of photographs with mysteriously "deleted" limbs, usually legs or arms. Said to represent misfortune affecting the limb in question.

4) Strange streaks or discolorations

Abstract shapes that can be interpreted in all sorts of ways, depending on the color (red is often said to be worse than white) and the individuals or parts of the body that are affected.

5) Orbs

By far the most commonly encountered phenomena. Critics claim these floating spheres are nothing more than reflections from dust motes or water droplets in the air. Proponents fervently believe they represent tiny souls, or simply denote supernaturally active areas. (Note: these photographic manifestations should not be confused for "hitodama" or "oni-bi," fireballs that appear over graveyards and the like.)

Sorry, photographs of ghost paintings don't count as shinrei shashin.

HIROKO'S STORY

Shinrei shashin were hugely popular when I was in middle school in the early 1980s. My school library even carried three different collections of spirit photographs, which we'd pore over in our spare time. It goes to show how big of a phenomenon they were back then.

One day when I was in the tenth grade, my home economics teacher announced to the class that she had taken a "wonderful photograph" when visiting her family grave that weekend. (It's common for families here to make an afternoon of tidying up their family plots from time to time.) She was a soft-spoken older woman without, so far as we could tell, any particular interest in the occult. She went on to describe it for us, even illustrating it on the blackboard. She drew the grave, her family members posed around it, and the leaves of a tree forming a canopy over it all. This was the kicker: in the photo, each leaf supposedly revealed a tiny, smiling human face. Hundreds of faces, floating over a grave! The class sat in total silence when she was done. She offered to bring it in so that we could see it. But we were all too terrified to take her up on it — both of the photo and her strangely upbeat reaction!

Dangerous Games: 36

HOUSES WITH HISTORIES

Name in Japanese: 訳あり物件
a.k.a. *Wake-ari Bukken; Haunted homes; Real estate with a checkered past; The scourge of a real-estate agent's existence*
First Described: *Undoubtedly around the time the concept of "real estate" was invented*
Peak of Interest: *As long as people keep dying, there'll be houses with histories*
Main Types: *Roughly 7, legally speaking (see below)*
Result of Use: *Potentially seeing a ghost; Potentially taking severe emotional shock; Potentially getting a really great real estate deal*
Threat Level: *Depends on location and specifics... And your state of mind!*

Claim to Fame

You know the old saw about how the three most important things in real estate are "location, location, location?" That's true in Japan, too, but it's inevitably followed by another three: "history, history, history."

The Japanese call the problem children of the real estate world *wake-ari bukken*: literally, "real estate listings with reasons" for being cheaper than they normally should. This is a catch-all term. Some of these reasons are patently obvious, such as small or oddly shaped lots, basement apartments that don't get a lot of direct sunlight, or a location whose only view is that of a graveyard.

But there is a subset of wake-ari bukken that concerns listings with flaws that are darkly referred to as "psychologically harmful." In other words, homes that have the potential to hurt you. Forget walls that have ears; these are walls that have seen some pretty terrible stuff.

The Attack

According to law, a listing is considered "psychologically harmful" to residents if it meets any of the following seven criteria. Some are universal sorts of things — nobody wants to live near a dump or a hotbed of crime. Others are less so, like proximity to wells (which, as we saw in chapter 1, can be pretty frightening places in Japan.) Let's take a look at the criteria, which are:

- Located near criminal organizations (many Yakuza syndicates operate from clearly-marked office buildings.)
- Built by, or on ground once owned by, a religious cult
- Built atop a well, whether open or filled in
- Located near a waste-treatment facility or crematorium.
- Legal entanglements (such as questions of ownership).
- A history of fires or flooding that caused death or injury
- A suicide, murder, or "lonely death" having occurred on the premises.

The last two in particular are considered particularly bad and are sub-classified as *jiko bukken* — "accident listings" that have been

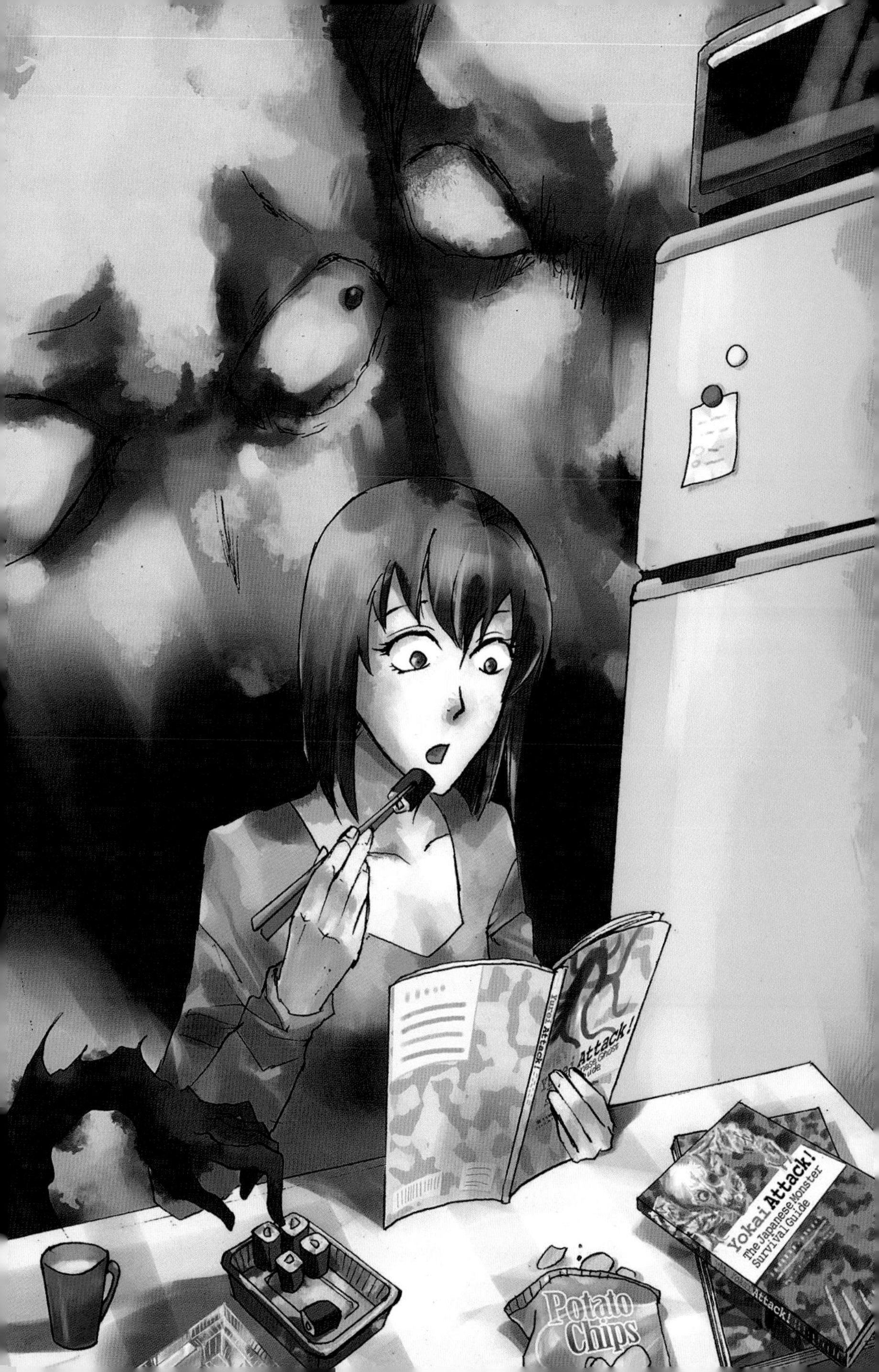
Yurei Attack!
Attack!
Yokai Attack!
The Japanese Monster
Survival Guide
Attack!
Potato
Chips

tainted by death. Mind you, this can't be just any death. A ninety-year old woman dying of natural causes surrounded by family is sad but doesn't exactly qualify as a tragedy; if things like that counted, nearly every real estate listing in Japan would have a "history."

The deaths that most concern potential buyers and tenants are "bad" ones. The death of a family in a housefire. The suicide of a former occupant. A murder having occured on the property. A lonely death, such as a shut-in passing away and their body remaining untouched for months... or years.

Surviving an Encounter

There are two ways to approach this sort of thing:

1) Avoid "homes with histories" altogether. This is at once simple and tricky. Those selling or renting property are legally obligated to disclose the history of a listing if it meets any of the conditions listed above, even if a potential buyer or renter doesn't specifically ask about them.

But there are several loopholes. One is that they are only required to disclose this information a single time, to the buyer or renter immediately following the incident. Once another person has lived in and left the property, they are no longer required to make the disclosure. But they are still obligated to truthfully answer any direct questions about the history of a property. If this sort of thing bothers you, make sure to ask.

Another loophole: unscrupulous realtors will often attempt to hide a death on the property by claiming that the person was discovered there, but actually died at the hospital, or (in the case of someone who leaps out a window) actually died on the ground, not in the room itself. Because of this, a variety of privately-run websites have emerged that cross-reference police reports with housing listings, allowing potential renters and buyers to double-check. (One is Oshimaland, http://www.oshimaland.co.jp/, which conveniently highlights them on Google Maps.)

2) There's an entirely different approach as well: taking it in stride. Because of the law requiring disclosure to the next renter or buyer, there is actually a thriving market for houses and apartments with histories. By openly explaining what happened and offering steep discounts (in some cases, more than half) on rent, landlords are able to target clients who value saving money more than potential loss of peace of mind.

These sorts of places are almost shockingly candid about the histories of their properties; the clipped, businesslike descriptions of what happened to former occupants are like a porthole into the depths of the human soul. One site uses colorful icons to denote the assorted types of mayhem that occurred within the walls of their listings. Another even plays up the fear factor, asking renters to consider "sharing a room with a ghost!"

Who knows? You could well make some fearsome new friends.

CHAPTER SIX
Close Encounters

Only a handful of individuals have had run-ins with the dead and lived to tell the tale. These are their stories.

HOICHI THE EARLESS

Name in Japanese: 耳なし芳一
Gender: Male
Occupation: Biwa-hoshi (lute player)
a.k.a. Mimi Nashi Hoichi (Japanese pronunciation)
Born/Died: Unknown. 14th or 15th century?
Lived in: Shimonoseki (Westernmost city of Japan's main island of Honshu)
Description: Bald head. Blind from birth. Usually seen carrying a biwa lute
Method of contact with spirits: Accidental
Existence: Fictional

Claim to Fame

This gentle and talented monk's painful encounter with the angry dead ranks as a classic — some would say the classic — Japanese ghost story.

In order to appreciate Hoichi's tale, you need to understand a key point of Japanese history: the rivalry between the Genji clan and the Heike (also known as Taira) clan. In 1180, the Genji launched a coup d'etat against the Heike, who controlled the nation through their child-emperor. The civil war ended five years later at the brutal Battle of Dan-no-Ura. Driven to desperation by the relentless Genji forces, the Heike launched a small armada of boats in a last-ditch attempt to retake the initiative by sea. But a hail of Genji arrows pounded the Heike fleet. Knowing their ambitions had come to an end, the entire Heike clan, including the young emperor, leapt to their deaths in the murky, turbulent waters rather than suffer the humiliation of surrender.

One of the few survivors on the Heike side was Ukai Kansaku, who you read about in chapter 3.

The Story

Late one summer evening, Hoichi whiled away the hours waiting for the heat to fade by playing tunes on the Japanese lute known as the biwa. Blind from birth, he had been trained in the instrument from childhood. Now a young man, Hoichi was an expert strummer. His skills had earned him both local renown and room and board at the Buddhist temple in which he currently lived.

The abbot had stepped out to perform a funeral service, leaving Hoichi alone save for the chirping of crickets and the strains of the lute. But late that night, as he played yet another classic song, Hoichi heard the sound of determined footsteps approaching. Even without sight Hoichi knew at once they were not those of the head priest.

A voice boomed out. The man introduced himself as a samurai. His lord had heard of Hoichi's skill, and requested that the lute-player recite the tale of Dan-no-Ura for him as he gazed out over

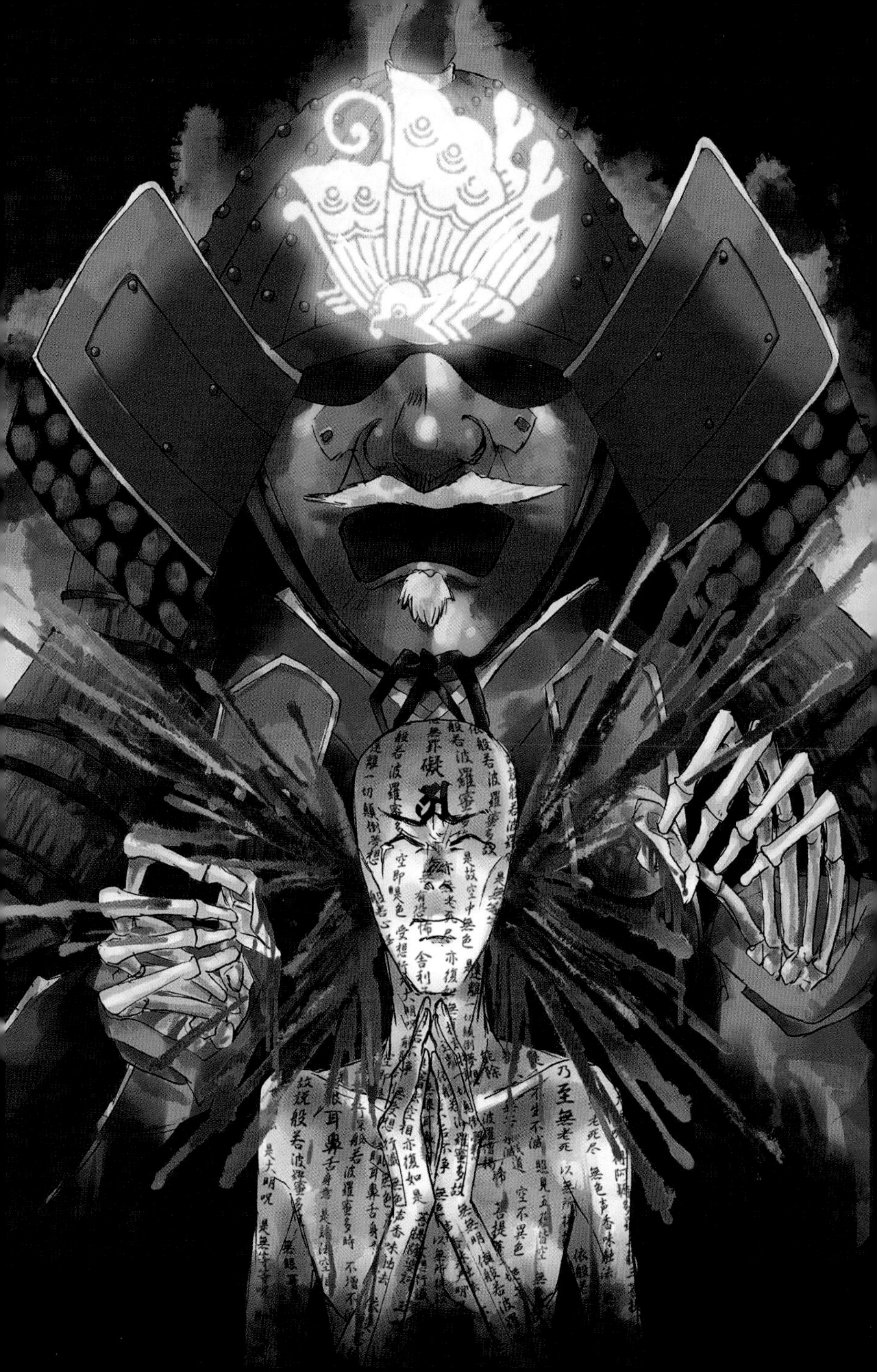

the straits where the tragic battle had unfolded. Hoichi could hardly refuse the direct request of such an eminent man, and allowed himself to be led to his residence.

Settling himself on the stage, Hoichi began to play for an assembled crowd. He could hear the sound of silks rustling and a great many voices speaking in the exalted language of the Imperial court. He was among royalty.

His fingers flew across the strings of the lute, mimicking the sounds of flying arrows and ships cutting through the surf as accompaniment to the epic battle-poem. At its climax the assembled let loose a cry of anguish at the bitter suffering of the Heike clan. They entreated Hoichi to come back again for the remainder of the week — six more nights.

The next morning, the worried abbot asked where Hoichi had been.

The Heike Gani crabs found off the coast of Shimonoseki have a distinctive shell pattern reminiscent of a samurai's facemask. Legend has it these crabs are the souls of the Heike, reborn deep in the ocean depths.

Unusually reticent, Hoichi mumbled something about a private engagement. Concerned about the young man, the abbot quietly asked two of his monks to shadow the lute-player on his next excursion. It took them five nights to find him, and what they saw chilled them to the bone: Hoichi sitting alone in midst of the Heike clan graveyard, playing furiously, surrounded by uncountable balls of glowing blue flame — hitodama, an unmistakable sign of the dead.

The monks spirited the protesting Hoichi back to the abbot, who coaxed the tale of the mysterious samurai visitor and subsequent concerts out of the musician. Hoichi was in grave danger, explained the abbot, bewitched by the spirits of the very clan of whose tale he sang. There was only one way to save him.

That evening, the abbot and his acolytes stripped Hoichi and painted the characters for the Heart Sutra on every surface of his body, even the soles of his feet.

TOOLS OF THE TRADE

The Heart Sutra (Hannya Shingyo in Japanese) is a fundamental Buddhist scripture. Its meaning resists easy analysis, but it begins with the words "form is emptiness, and emptiness is form." The current Dalai Lama translates the sutra's key mantra as:

"Go, go, go beyond, go thoroughly beyond, and establish yourself in enlightenment."

If Hoichi's tale is to be believed, painting the sutra in its entirety on the body of an individual can hide their presence from the dead. Note that this only serves as a visual camouflage; it does not mask sounds. Total silence is a requirement as well.

The abbot instructed Hoichi to wait for the samurai but remain utterly silent and still, no matter what happened, until the warrior went away. The sutra, explained the abbot, would protect him.

The samurai arrived late that evening. He called for Hoichi again and again, but the musician remained silent, his arms and legs folded as if in meditation. But then Hoichi heard the frustrated warrior sigh: "no sign of him save for this pair of ears. I must return them to my lord to prove I have attempted to obey my orders." The abbot had forgotten to inscribe Hoichi's ears with the holy text!

Hoichi felt a pair of iron-cold hands grab his ears and tear them from the sides of his head in a single fluid motion. Even amid the pain and spray of blood, the lute-player remained totally still and silent. The servants found him still sitting in the lotus position the next morning, drenched with the blood from his wounds.

Profusely apologizing for his oversight, the abbot personally nursed Hoichi back to health. And as word of the weird tale spread, so too did Hoichi's reputation. Before long, he found himself a wealthy man, engaged in the activity that satisfied him most; playing his lute for appreciative audiences, who came in droves to see Hoichi the Earless.

Surviving an Encounter…

Lafcadio Hearn, who first reported this tale, claimed that "in former years, the Heike [ghosts] were much more restless… They would rise about ships passing in the night, and try to sink them; and at all times they would watch for swimmers, to pull them down." Note the past tense. Attacks of this sort are unknown today.

Still, it can't hurt to take precautions. A preventative prayer to the lost souls of the Heike at the family grave in Akama Jingu isn't a bad place to start. It's located just a short drive from JR Shimonoseki Station. (We highly recommend doing this during daylight hours.)

In the unlikely event you do find yourself invited to a ghostly party by long-dead samurai, make sure to find a monk who's familiar with the Heart Sutra and handy with a brush and ink. Oh, yeah — don't forget those ears.

YUTEN SHONIN

Name in Japanese: 祐天上人
a.k.a.: Saint Yuten
The Exorcist of Edo
Sannosuke (childhood name)
Gender: Male
Occupation: Part Shaman, Part
Buddhist Priest
Sect: Jodo
Lived: 1637–1718
Lived in: Edo (Tokyo) and others
Method of contact with spirits:
Prayer, ritual, and a willingness to listen
Existence: Historical Fact

Claim to Fame

Yuten Shonin is Japan's most famed exorcist. His most well-known adventure involved appeasing the angry spirits of Orui and her brother Suké, whom you read about in chapter 1. But this was just one of many similar spirit-cleansings he performed throughout Japan. His knack for dealing with the dead came from an uncanny ability to decipher their stories, making him more of a "ghost-counselor" than "ghost-buster." He approached haunting and possessions with the analytical mind of a private detective, interviewing those involved to unravel the story of whatever spirit had taken ahold of the victim.

Word of his exploits spread like wildfire throughout Japan, making him a superstar both during his lifetime and after his death.

The Story

Yuten's inauspicious beginnings are as much a part of his legend as his exorcisms.

Born deep in the Tohoku countryside, at the age of eleven Yuten was sent to apprentice with his uncle in the big city. His uncle served as a priest at Zojo-ji, an opulent temple patronized by the Shoguns of Edo (now Tokyo). But no matter how hard he tried, Yuten couldn't memorize the holy texts he needed to memorize; he couldn't follow the rituals he needed to follow, and he generally made a total fool of himself to the point where his own uncle was forced to demote him from monk-in-training to the equivalent of temple janitor.

Stung by his failure, Yuten fasted for days in an attempt to gain clarity. Eventually the vision of an old man appeared before him, explaining that Yuten's insurmountable mental block was due to karma from previous lives. The only way on earth to resolve it was to fast for twenty-one more days at distant Narita-san Shinsho-ji temple. (Coincidentally, the temple has an interesting history of its own. It was built in 939 as a holy weapon of sorts, designed for prayers and rituals to place a curse upon Taira no Masakado, then still very much alive and on the warpath against the Emperor. See chapter 2 for more about this angry samurai.)

After an arduous journey from Edo to Narita, Yuten reached the temple. Explaining his vision to the monks there, he set about an epic, twenty-one day fast before the temple's giant effigy of Fudo Myoo,

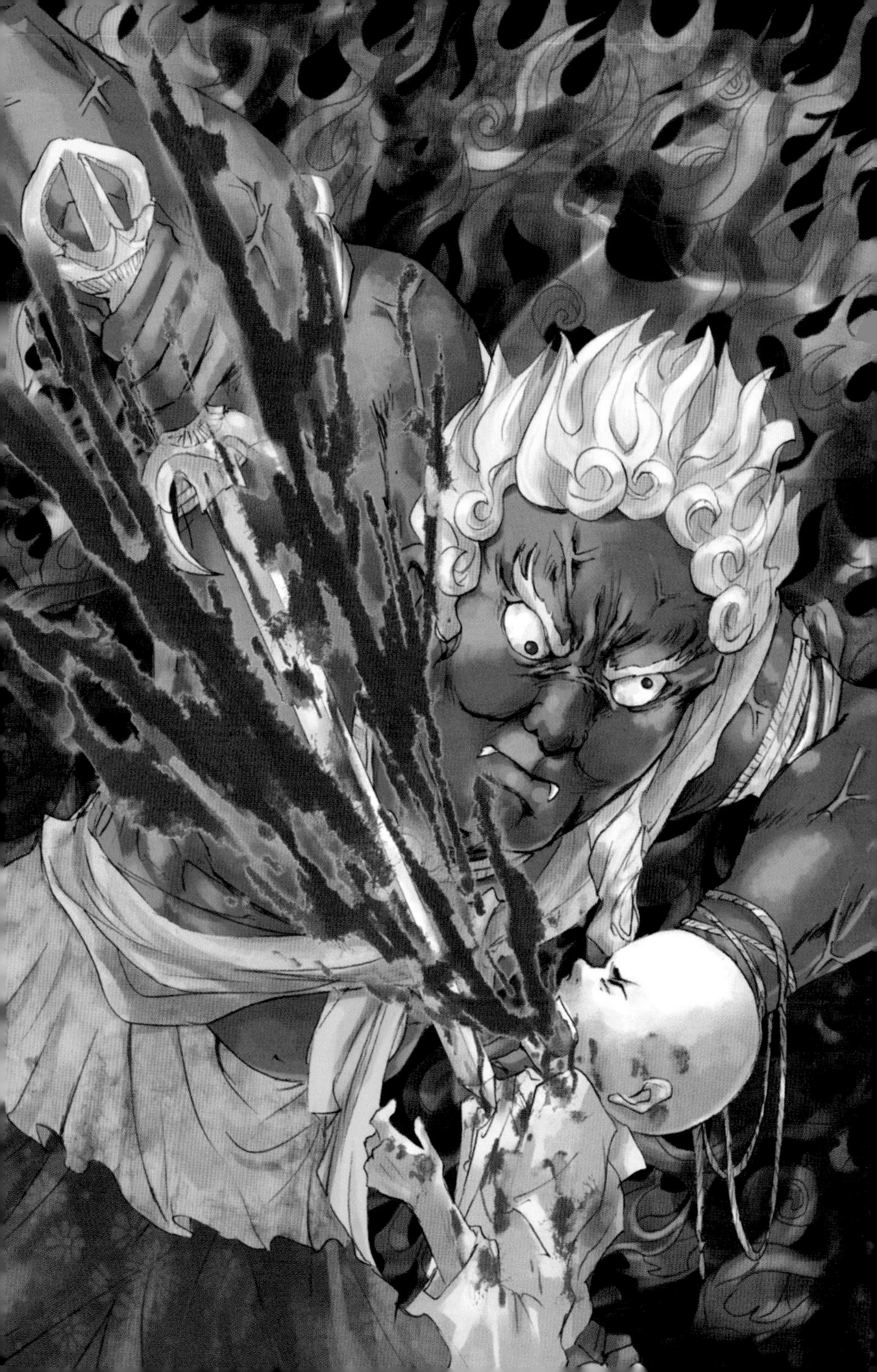

Buddhist sutra written out in Yuten's own hand.

a Buddhist deity also known as Acala.

On the very last day of his fast, the boy looked up — and came face to face with a god. The sight chilled him to the core. Scowling and fanged, powerfully muscular, bearing his customary lariat and broadsword, and wreathed in a nimbus of righteous fire, Acala was more than a match for any human on Earth, let alone a pitifully malnourished and exhausted twelve-year-old.

The god offered the boy a choice. He could go the easy way: die here and be reborn in his next life. Or he could go the hard way: assent to having his bad karma sliced from his soul by force. Yuten didn't even hesitate. He went the hard way.

Switching grip on his sword, Acala plunged the massive blade into the boy's mouth, down, down through his throat and deep into his entrails. Yuten shuddered as his heart seized. Crimson sprayed from his lips as his veins emptied, and with it his accumulated karma. As Acala withdrew the sword inch by painful inch, the child's dry vessels re-filled with fresh blood cleansed by the deity himself. As the receding tip cleared Yuten's mouth, his heart shuddered back to life.

When the monks found the boy's crumpled body laying in a pool of blood before the statue, they mistook him for dead. But Yuten recovered, with new life coursing through his veins — and keen insight through his mind. He was a new man. Literally.

Returning to Zojo-ji, Yuten met with a less than warm reception. The abbot was none too pleased at the boy's having left, no matter his reasons, and refused to accept the story about Acala. For the next six years, Yuten labored in the servants' quarters, studying scripture on the sly. When the abbot of Zojo-ji was promoted to head a larger temple, Yuten interrupted the ceremony with a theological debate that he handily won, shocking the assembled crowd.

Leaving Zojo-ji behind, Yuten took to the roads to help those in need, tracking down rumors of spiritual disturbances that other experts found impossible to explain or address — in essence, a one-man, Edo-era "X-Files." Yuten had a rapport with angry spirits, and in particular angry spirits that possessed women. His battles for the souls of what were then considered

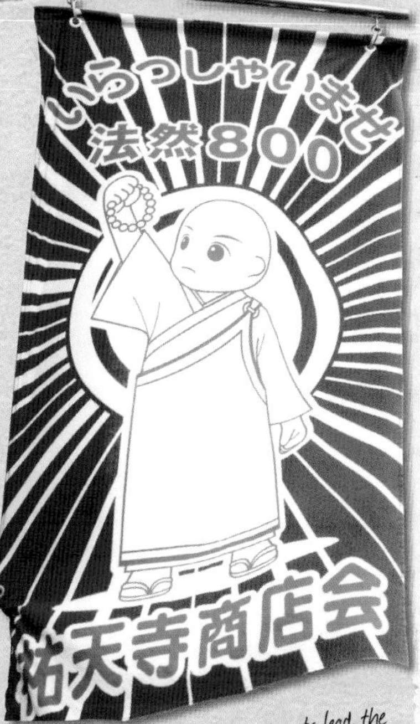
らっしゃいませ
法然800
祐天寺商店会

These super-cute Yuten mascots lead the way to his temple in Meguro!

second-class members of society made him a hero among commoners and a contentious figure among the male-dominated powers that be, but he never wavered from his self-appointed duty to help those most in need — taking cases regardless of their gender, social standing, or background.

Surviving Encounters...

...with Ghosts the Yuten Way: Yuten has long since shuffled off this mortal coil, but you can take a page from his playbook and attempt to learn the stories of the ghosts that terrorize people rather than trying to confront them directly. That said, this method of exorcising spirits isn't for the faint of heart. It's telling that Yuten seems to be the only man in history who successfully pulled it off.

You can also pay your respects to the man himself at Yutenji temple, built by his disciples to honor his memory after his death in 1718. It's located in the Meguro district of central Tokyo, just a ten-minute walk from Yutenji Station on the Tokyu Toyoko line.

RESUME AT A GLANCE

1685: Discovers that the spirit possessing a noblewoman was that of a housemaid her husband had seduced and forced to get a fatal abortion to keep the affair secret. It also becomes clear that this isn't the first, second, or even third time. It's the sixteenth. Husband loses all social standing, joins monastery.

1690: A book recounting several of his most successful cases is published: *A Tale of Salvation for Spirits of the Dead*. It becomes a sensation among the "Ooku," the harem of Edo castle that included the Shogun's mother, wife, and concubines. Yuten's legend continues to grow.

1693: Kurodo Incident. A young man is forced to dump his fiancée for a higher-ranking woman. Decades later, his grown sons begin dying under strange circumstances and his daughter falls ill. Yuten sees a vision of the original fiancée, who died alone several years previous and is now haunting the family. When the husband prays in apology to her soul, the daughter is released.

1711: The Shogun names Yuten the abbot of Zojo-ji, the same temple he'd been kicked out of as a boy.

ONO NO TAKAMURA

Name in Japanese: 小野篁
Gender: Male
a.k.a. Yakyo ("Crazy Ono" – based on another reading of his name's kanji)
Occupation: Court scholar and poet
Lived: 802–853 (Heian Era of Japanese history); Resident of: Heiankyo (Kyoto) (Then capital of Japan)
Form of Attack: N/A. The pen is mightier than the sword, with Ono.
Method of contact: A really, really deep hole
Existence: Historical Fact

Claim to Fame

Europe has Dante. Japan has Ono no Takamura. And while Dante slipped into the afterlife quite by accident in *The Inferno*, Ono made the trip of his own free will — again and again. Every night, in fact. Talk about a literal commute from hell.

The Story

Ono no Takamura is famed as one of Japan's wittiest and most cultivated scholars, a man whose facility with Chinese characters bordered on the superhuman (his grandchildren include one of the six greatest poets and one of the three greatest calligraphers of all time). But don't get the wrong idea. This was no quiet bookworm. Ono had a rebellious streak a mile wide and a sense of humor to match.

Ono served for a time as the court poet to the Emperor Saga, which sounds like a cushy job until you realize that a single misspeak was enough to land you on the Emperor's bad side — or on a boat straight to permanent exile. And Ono wasn't your typical obsequious royal aide.

His most celebrated feat of linguistic prowess is a perfect case in point. Set up by a political rival who cornered him into reading a series of kanji characters that couldn't be uttered aloud without insulting the Emperor, Ono found himself accused of treason. The Emperor asked if Ono had invented the phrase. Ono argued that his unusual ability to read any compound didn't mean that he necessarily composed them. The Emperor put Ono's boast to the test, demanding he decipher a new compound or face the consequences: a nonsense string of twelve characters for "child" in a row:

子子子子子子子子子子子子

You don't need a degree in linguistics to recognize this as an impossible task, but Ono responded with flair, using his encyclopedic knowledge of obscure readings to deliver an amusing interpretation on the spot: "the child of a cat is a kitten; the child of a lion a cub." After a moment the Emperor's glare dissolved into a grin, and Ono was off the hook.

The Story

Perhaps Ono's nonchalance in front of a man as powerful as the Emperor Saga is because he spent his free time hanging out with even more frightening and powerful individuals.

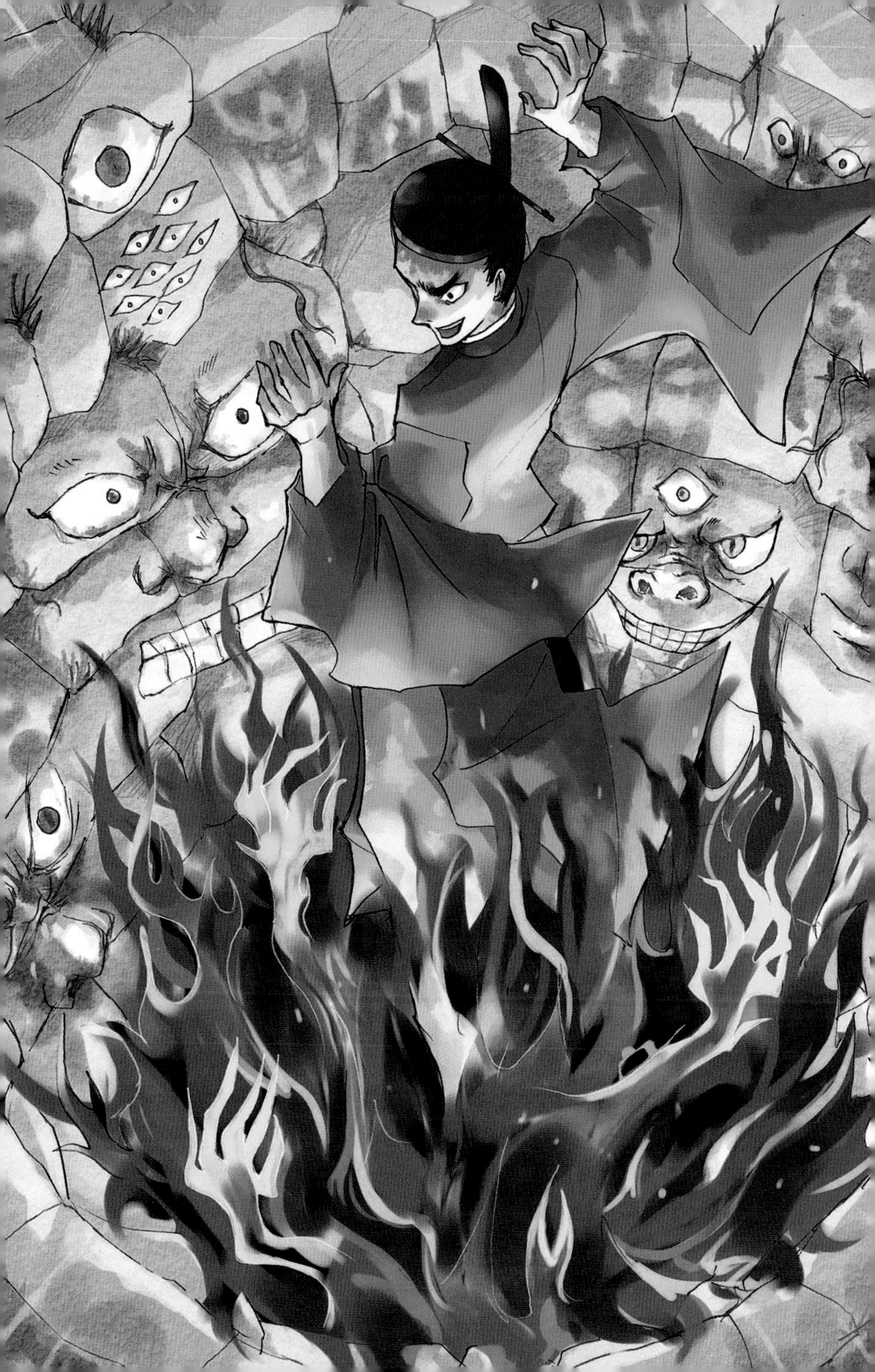

It turns out that this super-scholar was leading a double life. By day he regaled the aristocracy with his sonnets. By night, he snuck out of the palace compound and down a certain well on the grounds of Chinnoji Temple. A well that led directly into the depths of hell.

Chinnoji sat in an area that was then considered the furthest reaches of civilized Kyoto. Beyond its borders lay a literal wasteland where the bodies of everyone from criminals to murder victims were unceremoniously dumped. (In fact, the section of town in which Chinnoji still stands, called Rokuro-cho today, was then known as Dokuro-cho — Skulltown.) Chinnoji sat right on the border between life and death, here and the hereafter.

While Ono kept quiet about his trips among his living pals, it wasn't any secret to the denizens of hell. It seems Ono's wit and erudition was as much of a hit down there as it was up here. But the lid was blown off his nocturnal expeditions in an unexpected fashion one night.

Early in Ono's career, he had been ordered to China as an official study-envoy known as a "Kentoshi." But he couldn't get along with the ambassador, and concocted a fake illness as an excuse not to go. This roiled the entire mission, and seriously compromised Ono's standing. But a friend with connections named Fujiwara no Yoshimi interceded on his behalf, saving the young Ono's reputation.

Little did either know that Ono would have a chance to repay the debt many years later, when Fujiwara fell ill and suffered what we would call today a "near death experience." Fujiwara found himself seated before Lord Enma, the deity who decides the postmortem fate of every human soul. (You'll read more about Enma in the next chapter). But if he was shocked at finding himself in the underworld, he was even more shocked to see none other than Ono no Takamura sitting right beside the fearsome judge!

Ono interjected during the examination of Fujiwara's sins, convincing Lord Enma that the man still had much to accomplish in the world of the living. It's a testament to both Ono's powers of persuasion and the apparent regard in which the Judge of the Underworld held him that Enma sent Fujiwara back to Earth, where he spent many more healthy years.

As you might expect, the next day Fujiwara brought up the incident in the Heian-period equivalent of a water-cooler discussion. Ono swore him to secrecy, but some-how or another the story leaked, and Ono's reputation as the man who had Lord Enma's ear spread throughout the land — a fitting turn for a man who could be said to have pioneered the saying "to hell and back."

A Day Trip to Hell

While you can't climb down Ono's well, you can see it with your very own eyes. Chinno-ji Temple is a twenty-minute ride by bus (take the 100 or 206) from Kyoto Station. Chinno-ji is also home to a pair of statues of Ono and Lord Enma, carved by Ono himself.

What happens when one dies and doesn't turn yurei? Read on for a preview of what lies in store for us all.

CHAPTER SEVEN
The Afterlife

The Afterlife: JIGOKU (HELL)

Name in Japanese: 地獄
Description: Long and complicated, but the main event is coming face to face with Lord Emma (pictured at right).
Existence: We will all find out once we are dead. Read on . . .

You've lived a long and healthy life. Or perhaps not. You died a hero. Or a scoundrel. Or rich. Or poor. It doesn't matter. We all end up here, sooner or later.

Before you start freaking out any more than you already are, being dead and all, let's get a few things straight. This "hell" represents Japanese conventional wisdom on the topic, so it won't map precisely to the one you may be thinking of, were you raised under a Judeo-Christian belief system. It's more of a general realm of the underworld. It is based on a Buddhist belief system, expanded and "localized" over centuries after its import to Japan.

While it is designed to be punitive in nature, it is more like an Earthly prison than it is an eternal fate. Your stay here — and the treatment you receive along the way — is entirely dependent on the sort of lives you lived before you arrived.

Note the plural. Lives. The life you are living now — er, lived up until now — is but the most recent in an endless line extending back through time immemorial.

So you're dead. Assuming you don't have any of the Earthly ties that might bind your soul to the world of the living like the yurei and onryo you've read about up until now, you should find yourself standing on the banks of the River Sanzu — Japan's version of the River Styx. What happens next? Here's what's in store.

1. Meet the "Hag from Hell."

Datsue-ba is a wizened, wrinkled old woman who strips off your clothes and weighs them to determine your amount of sin. Think of this as "entering of evidence."

Some sneaky souls have gotten the idea of showing up naked to slip through the weighing process with a clean slate. Datsue-ba has a special treat in store for them: she peels off their skin and weighs that instead.

2. Cross the River Sanzu.

Now that your sins have been bared, literally, it's time to cross the river.

Unless you're a small child, that is. Dying before ones parents is considered a sin, but children don't go to hell. They stay on the near side of the river, building cairns of stones that get knocked down again and again by the denizens of hell. But a deity called Jizo watches over and gives them refuge. (See the Guiding Jizo, p. 128).

If you're a holy person with a spotless soul, you get to take the bridge across the River Sanzu, followed by a cursory meeting with the powers that be, and an

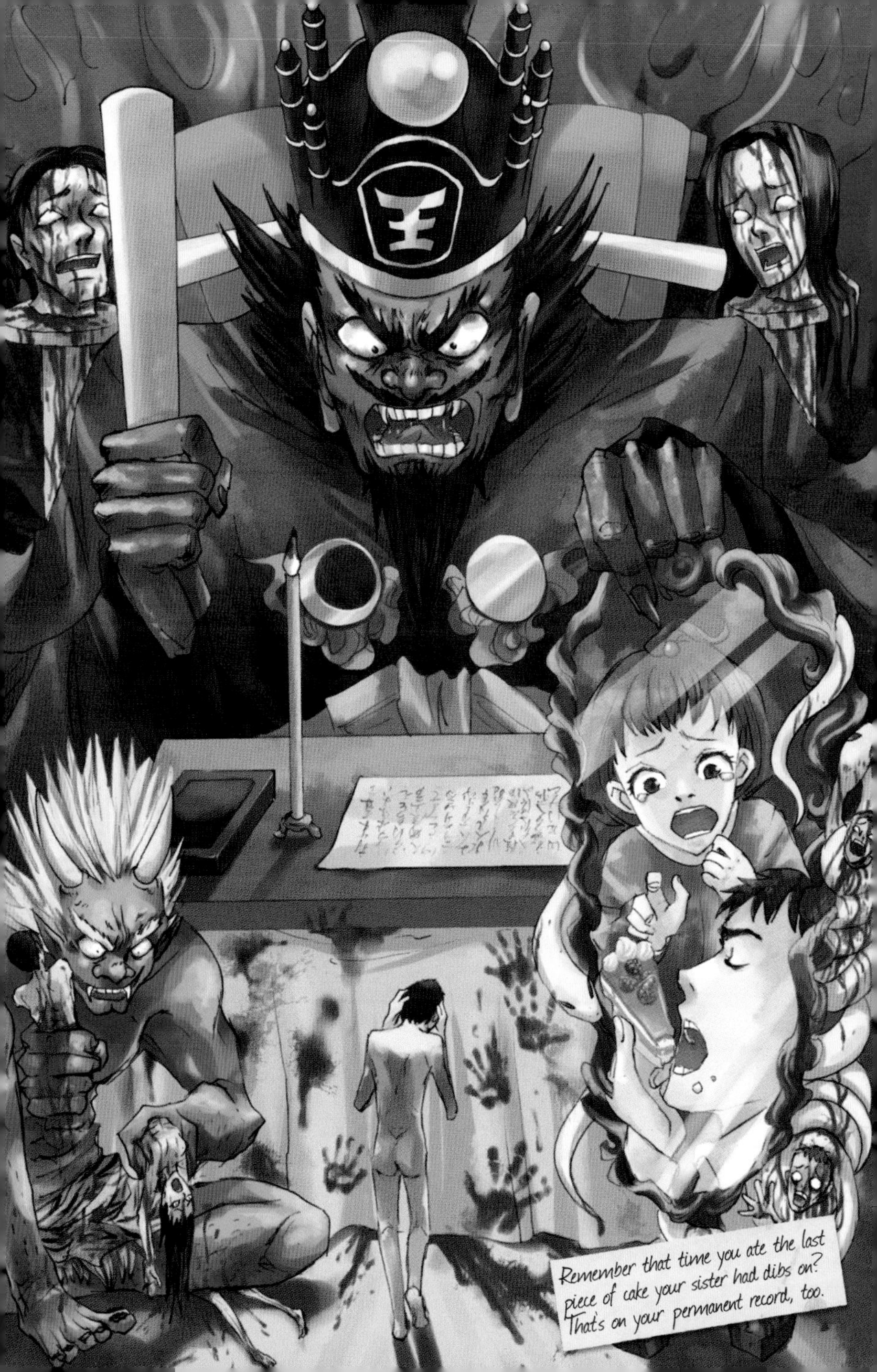
Remember that time you ate the last piece of cake your sister had dibs on? That's on your permanent record, too.

all-expenses paid trip to gokuraku (paradise). The end. Life well lived. Job well done.

Even today, school teachers' grade books are nicknamed Enma-cho (Enma Books) ⇨

For the remaining 99.9999999% of humanity (i.e., you), the trip across is a little rougher. If you're a generally decent sort, you get a rickety boat ride across the turbulent waters. And if you aren't, you're forced to stagger through the freezing waters on foot. There are several crossing points; the very worst offenders are forced to slog more than 250 miles (400 kilometers) to the other shore.

Once you make it across, it's judgment day.

In times of old, it was customary to bury a loved one with six one-sen coins to help them pay for a seat on the ferry across the River Sanzu. These are the same coins the Ame-Kai Yurei used to purchase candy for her baby (see p.78), and the same coins that appear on the banner of warlord Sanada Yukimura (see Ninja Attack!).

3. Meet Lord Enma

According to legend, he is the first mortal human to have lived and died. Ever since, he's been presiding over the Court of Hell as the Lord of the Dead. He isn't actually the first administrator you'll encounter; a variety of sub-judges interview you first in a sort of circuit court to Enma's supreme court.

Lord Enma will ask you to detail your sins yourself. The trick is, he possesses a book that contains a perfect record of the deeds of everyone who has ever lived and died. If your explanation doesn't match up, he'll order your tongue to be yanked out with a pair of tongs. But whatever the case, you'll receive your "sentence" here and...

4. Go to Hell!

Similar to the Western concept of "circles of Hell," Japanese-Buddhist tradition holds that there are eight levels of Hell (see the following page for an artist's interpretation). It's easy to remember them, as they build upon each other in the same way that those endless games of "I'm going on a trip and I'm taking..." you played on long car-trips as a kid did:

1) Tokatsu Jigoku: The shallowest level of hell, reserved for those who have taken any life, no matter how small. Swatted a mosquito? You're a murderer.

2) Kokujo Jigoku: Murderers and thieves.

3) Shugo Jigoku: Murderers, thieves, and degenerates (the latter defined as those who have lain with those other than their married partners, or even thought of doing otherwise).

4) Kyokan Jigoku: Murderers, thieves, degenerates, and drunkards.

5) Daikyokan Jigoku: Murderers, thieves, degenerates, drunkards, and liars.

6) Shonetsu Jigoku: Murderers, thieves, degenerates, drunkards, liars, and blasphemers.

7) Daishonetsu Jigoku: Murderers, thieves, degenerates, drunkards, liars, blasphemers, and rapists.

8) Mugen Jigoku: The deepest level of hell. Those guilty of all of the above, plus whom have killed their parents or holy people, reside here for a lengthy stay.

Oni: Hell's Helpers

The punishments of hell are dished out by creatures called "oni."

Often mistaken for yokai, they are actually a class of creature unto themselves. They are difficult to describe in terms of Western concepts, as they don't precisely slot into categories such as "demon" or "monster." The closest translation is probably "ogre," but even this comes across as far more generic sounding in English than oni does in Japanese. In keeping with similarly unique concepts such as "ninja," "sushi," and such, "oni" is best left as-is: "oni." (Come to think of it, it's smart to let oni be in general, linguistically or otherwise.)

Traditionally, oni are very large, muscular, humanoid creatures with bright red or blue skin. Tiger-striped loincloths are common accoutrements, as are large iron clubs. Their fingers and toes tend to be clawed, their faces snaggle-toothed scowls. Some feature generally human anatomy; others sport grotesque proportions and twisted faces with three or more

A detailed model of an oni's face, based on descriptions from history and folklore

eyes. But the best way to identify these creatures is by their horns, a pair of which are de rigeur for any oni.

In spite of their well-earned reputation as gleeful torturers of the damned, oni are not viewed as inherently malevolent creatures in Japan. Although encounters with oni often end badly for humans, this isn't always the case, and they are less a personification of evil than a personification of powers far beyond human control. A perfect example can be seen in proverbs such as *kokoro wo oni ni suru* — literally, "turning one's heart into an oni" but colloquially meaning "tough love," or *oni ni kanabo* — "giving an oni his club," meaning to "take advantage of one's strength."

TURN THE PAGE TO ENTER HELL!!!

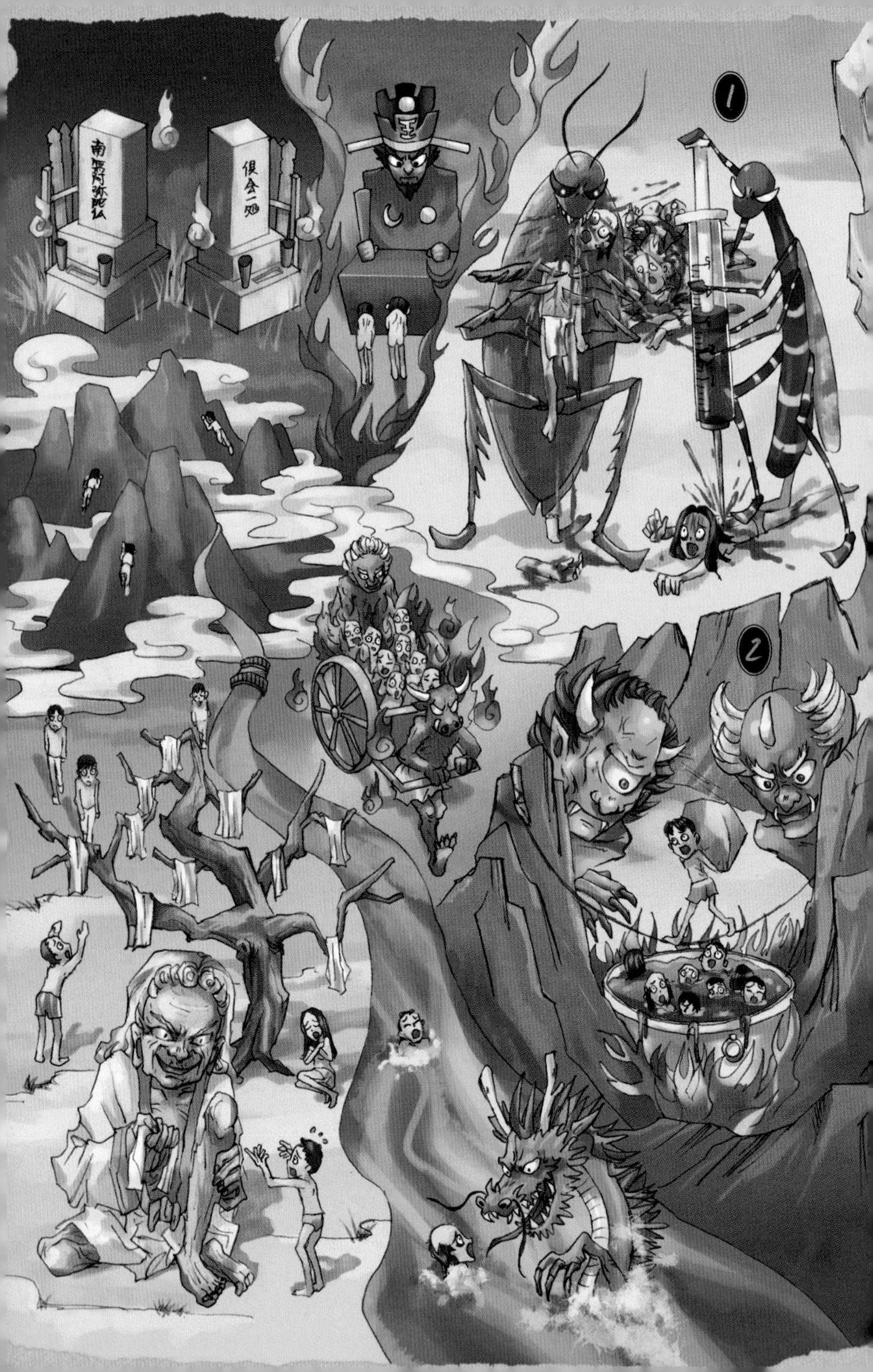
南無阿弥陀仏
倶会一処
王
1
2

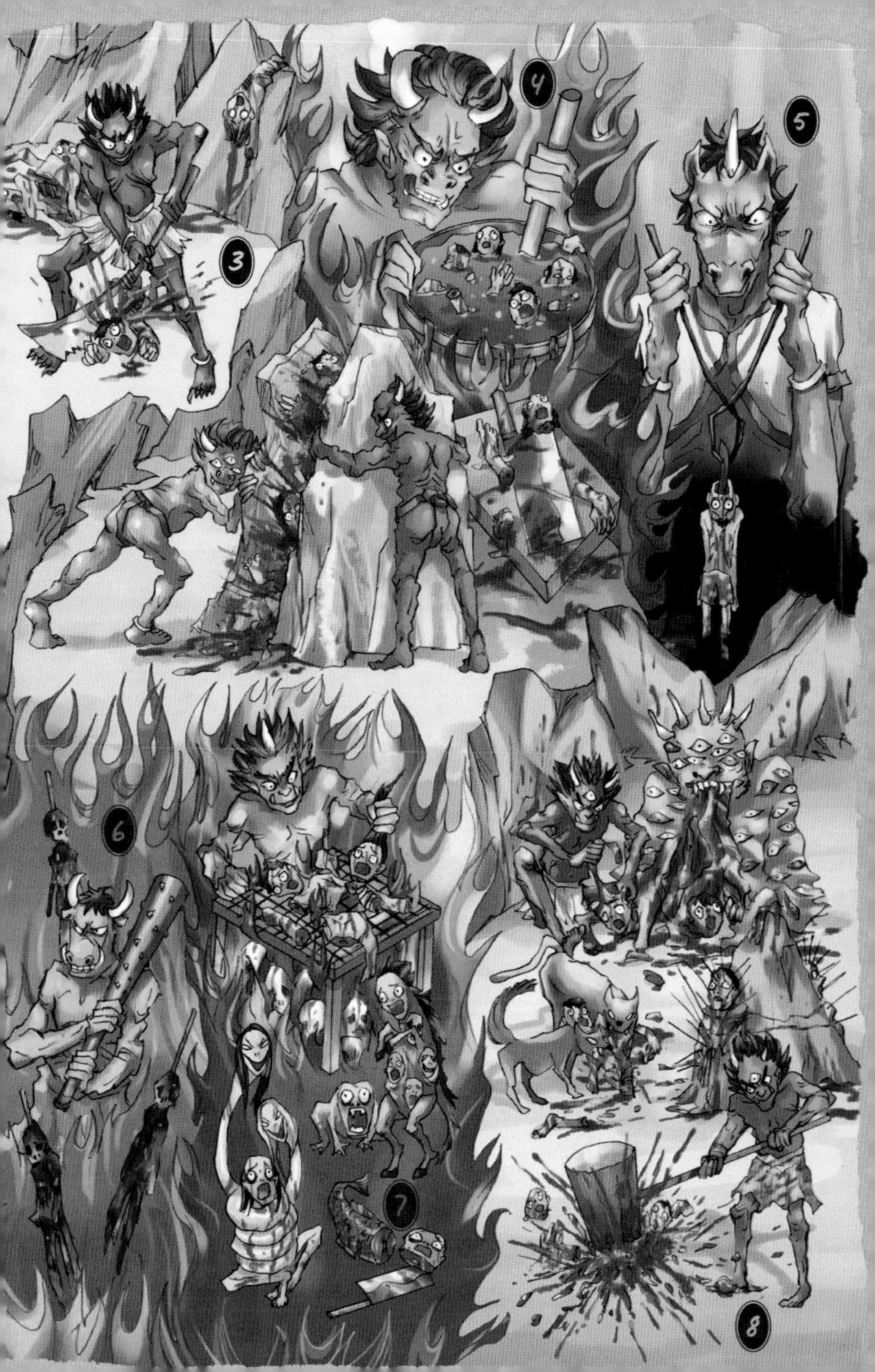
3
4
5
6
7
8

GHOSTLY GLOSSARY

akuryo 悪霊
Literally, a "bad ghost." (As opposed to, say, the spirits of your ancestors, which are nice to have around.)

borei 亡霊
A dead soul whose identity is unknown. Vaguer than "yurei."

eirei 英霊
A "heroic soul." One who has fallen in war.

goryo 御霊
An "honored soul" with royal connections. In practice, often used as a polite way to refer to an onryo.

hinotama 火の玉
A weird fireball that is an indicator of supernatural activity. Similar to what is called a "Will o' Wisp" or "foxfire" in Western folklore.

hitodama 人魂
Visually similar to hinotama, hitodama are considered to be actual souls of the departed. They take the form of fireballs that appear near graveyards and such.

hyoui 憑依
Possession by a spirit or other deity.

ikiryo 生霊
A "living ghost" – the soul of a living individual that leaves its body temporarily. The most famous is that of Lady Rokujo (see p. 28).

jibakurei 地縛霊
The term for a soul that is bound to a specific spot for whatever reason. A ghost responsible for a localized haunting.

kaidan 怪談
Written with the characters for "strange" and "narrative," kaidan refers to ghost stories and other tales of terror. It is sometimes written "kwaidan," which is an archaic pronunciation of the same word.

kami 神
A god or other powerful deity. Not to be confused with yurei or yokai.

noroi 呪い
A curse.

obake お化け
Often conflated with ghosts in colloquial usage, obake (pronounced oh-BAH-kay) literally means "something transformed" and more accurately refers to shapeshifting creatures such as yokai. It is a casual form of the word bakemono.

ofuda お札
A consecrated talisman, often in the form of a slip of paper, that can ward off ghosts and generally keep evil at bay. Procured from Buddhist temples and Shinto shrines. For examples of real ofuda, see p.188.

oharai お祓い
A spiritual cleansing rite performed at shrines. Essentially, a preventative exorcism.

oni 鬼

Powerful creatures that dish out punishments in the afterlife and are occasionally encountered in the human world as well. A symbol of power beyond human comprehension.

onibi 鬼火

Literally "oni-fire." Often used as a catch-all term that encompasses both hinotama and hitodama.

onnen 怨念

A potent mix of anger and/or sadness mixed with an overwhelming desire for retribution. A righteous grudge taken physical form. The fuel for an angry ghost (onryo). For more information, read the introduction to this book.

onryo 怨霊

In its traditional usage, the soul of an enemy of the Emperor returned to wreak havoc on the nation. In modern times, it is used to refer to any angry soul.

power spot パワースポット

Locations that are belived, for a variety of reasons, to be energizing to one's body and soul. Often associated with natural formations or holy sites.

reikan 霊感

The ability to sense the presence of spirits or other supernatural phenomena. Psychics are known as "reinosha" in Japanese.

senrigan 千里眼

Clairvoyance. Often associated with those who claim to be able to see or communicate with the dead.

shinrei 心霊

Another, more generic term for a ghost.

shinrei shashin 心霊写真

Spirit photography. Photographs purporting to contain ghosts or ghostly phenomena. For more information, see p.152.

shinrei spot 心霊スポット

A location known to be haunted.

shoryo 精霊

The soul of a beloved departed relative or friend. Not to be confused with "seirei," which is written with the same kanji characters but actually means something closer to "yokai" or "fairy."

sorei 祖霊

The honored spirit of an ancestor. These are GOOD spirits to have around.

tatari 祟り

A more potent version of a noroi (curse), often resulting from blasphemous behavior. This is what happens when you get the gods angry.

yokai 妖怪

Not a ghost, but a supernatural creature or spirit connected to the natural world. See *Yokai Attack! The Japanese Monster Survival Guide*.

yurei 幽霊

A ghost, usually a frightening one. Read the intro!

TOYS OF TERROR

In Japan, playthings based on demons and ghosts have been popular for decades — even centuries, in some cases. Here are a few of our favorites. Note how none of the manufacturers actually used the term "yurei," opting instead for the cuter-sounding "obake" in an attempt to soften the impact of these often gruesome toys.

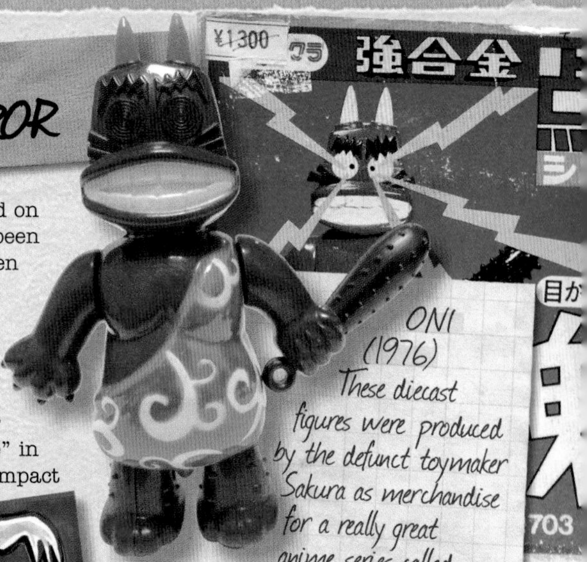

¥1,300
強合金
目が
703

ONI (1976)

These diecast figures were produced by the defunct toymaker Sakura as merchandise for a really great anime series called Manga Nihon Mukashibanashi, or Animated Japanese Folktales. Given that the target audience was children, it isn't surprising that the portrayal of the oni is a bit cuter than you might expect if you've read chapter 7 of this book. The best part: pop in a AA battery and the eyes flash.

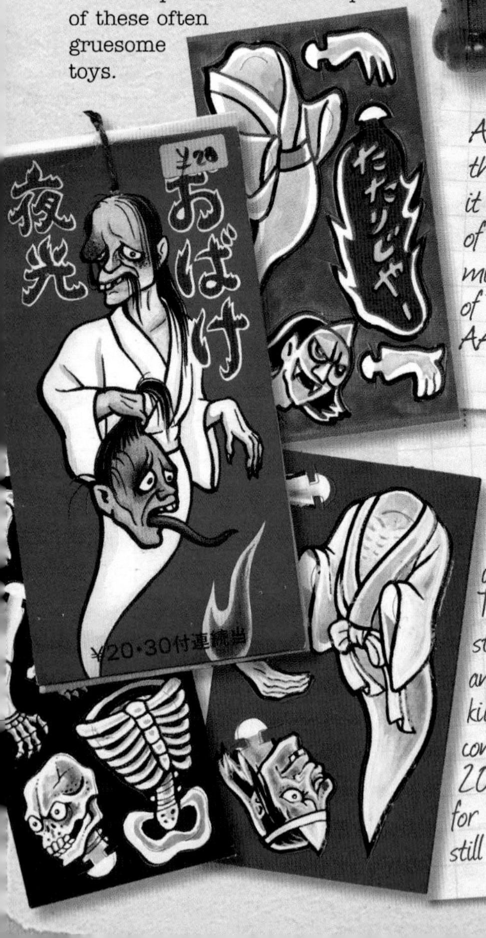

¥20
夜光
おばけ
たたりじゃ
¥20・30付連続当

YAKO OBAKE: "GLOW GHOULS" (1970S)

These paper dolls were sold at dagashiya – "penny candy stores." This sort of product represents the stereotypical dagashiya product: cheap and eye-catching, the better to hook kids into spending their money. The contents consisted of 4 x 8 inch (10 x 20cm) cards pre-printed and punched for easy pop-out and assembly. They're also still glowing strong after all these years.

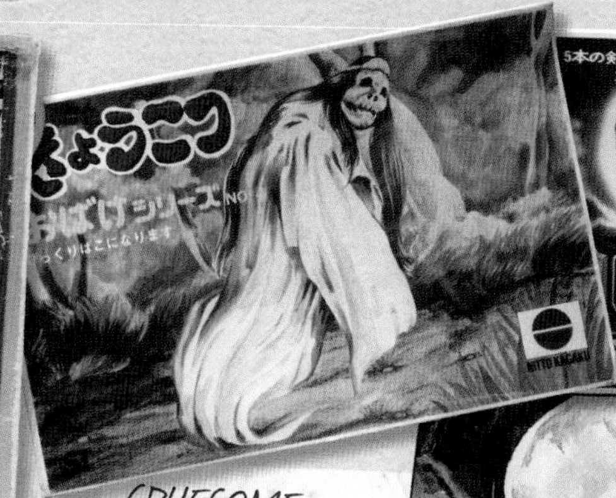
NITTO KAGAKU

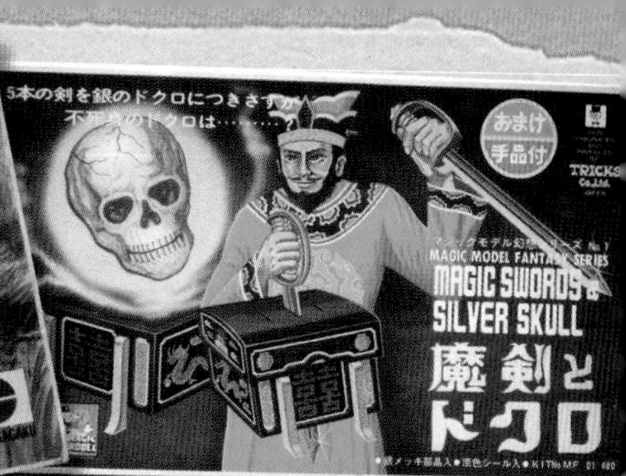
5本の剣を銀のドクロにつきさすが
おまけ
手品付
TRICKS Co.,Ltd.
MAGIC MODEL FANTASY SERIES
MAGIC SWORDS & SILVER SKULL
魔剣とドクロ

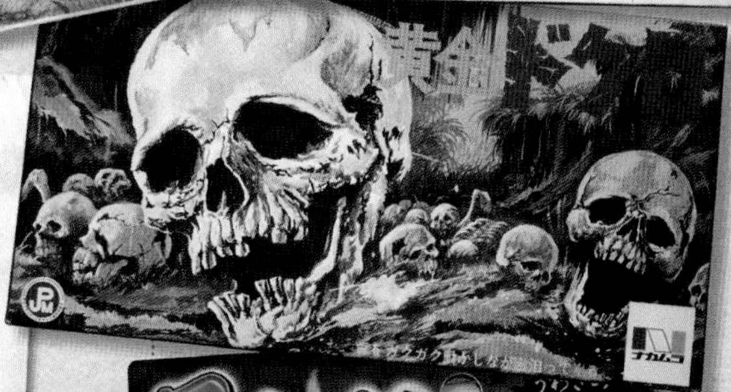

GRUESOME PLASTIC MODELS (1970S)

A variety of plastic model makers, including the long-since-out-of-business Nakamura, produced assembly kits of various spooky creatures back in the 1970s.

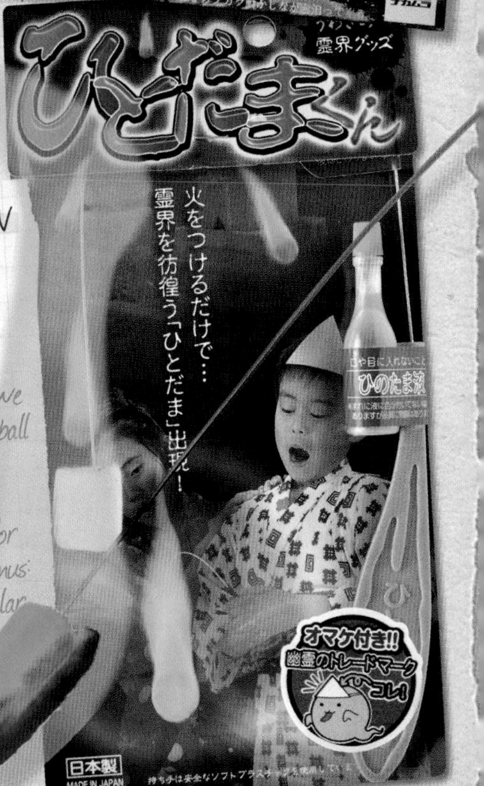
霊界グッズ
ひとだまくん
火をつけるだけで…
霊界を彷徨う「ひとだま」出現！
ひのたま液
オマケ付き!!
幽霊のトレードマーク
コレ!
日本製
MADE IN JAPAN

HITODAMA-KUN (MR HUMAN SOUL FIREWORK)

In the West, we have boring old sparklers. In Japan, they have Hitodama-kun! Simply pour the bottle of liquid human souls – uh, we mean, lighter fluid – on the cotton ball and ignite. Designed to resemble the mysterious fireballs that sometimes appear over cemeteries, they're fun for the whole family, living or not. Bonus: it even comes with a paper triangular funeral headdress, just like any self-respecting yurei wears.

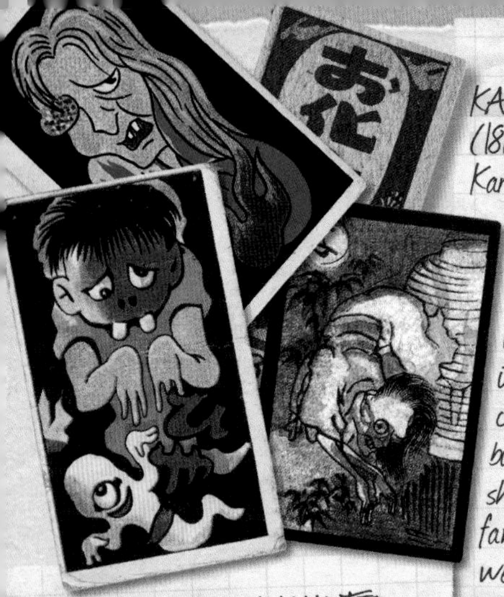
お化

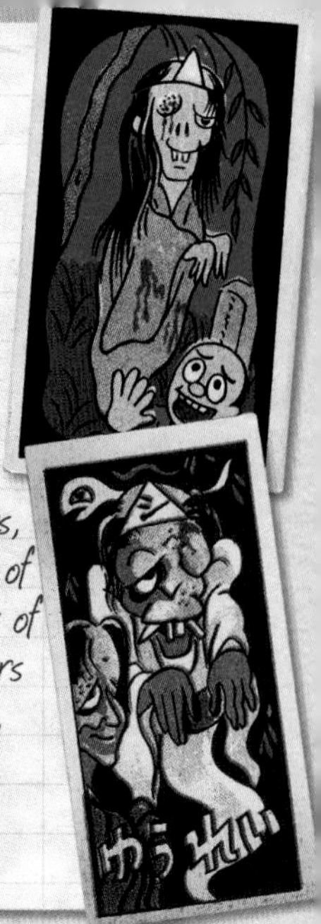
ゆうれい

KARUTA CARDS (1800S – PRESENT)

Karuta, a Japanese word borrowed from the Portugese word for "card," were produced in massive numbers in Japan. The most common are tiny rectangles, but they come in all sorts of shapes and sizes. Portrayals of famous heroes and characters were by far more common, but occasionally enterprising companies produced karuta featuring yurei as well.

OBAKE YASHIKI (HAUNTED HOUSE) SET (1970S)

It's hard to imagine any child wanting to be left alone with these gruesome soft-vinyl figures. The yokai are creepy enough, but the rendition of Oiwa-san from Yotsuya Kaidan must have been enough to cause nightmares. Then again, there's a certain charm to being able to carry around Japan's single most dangerous female ghost in your pocket.

OBAKE HANABI (MONSTER FIREWORKS) 1970'S

Although they're called "obake" (monster) rather than "yurei" fireworks, the art on the package is determinedly ghostly, even featuring a grave.

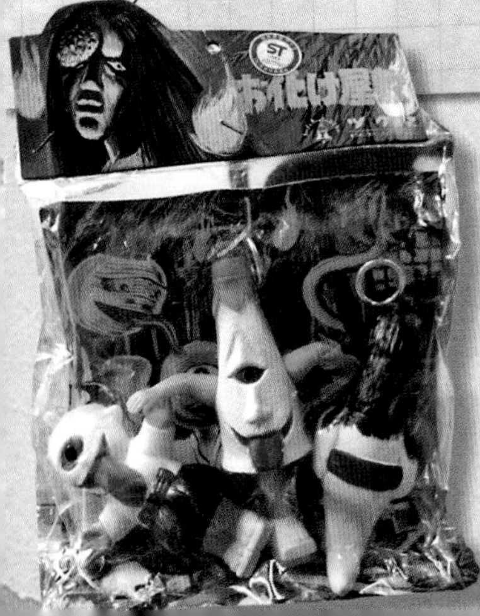
ST

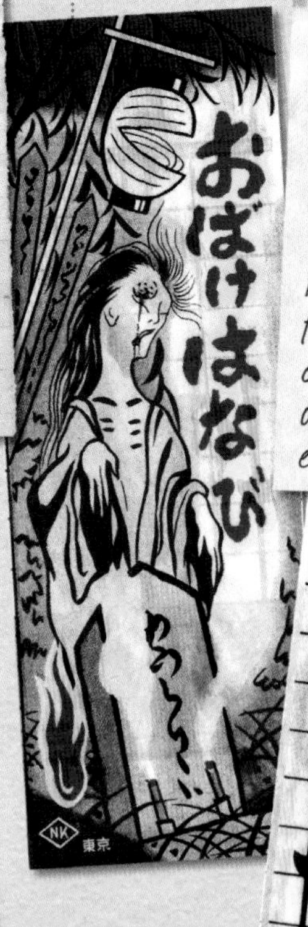
おばけはなび
NK
東京

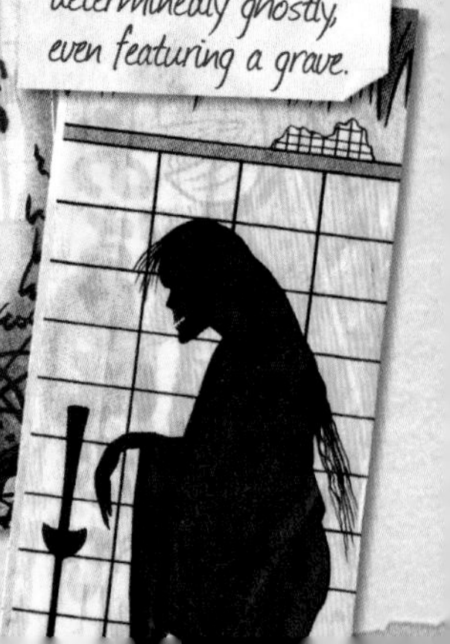

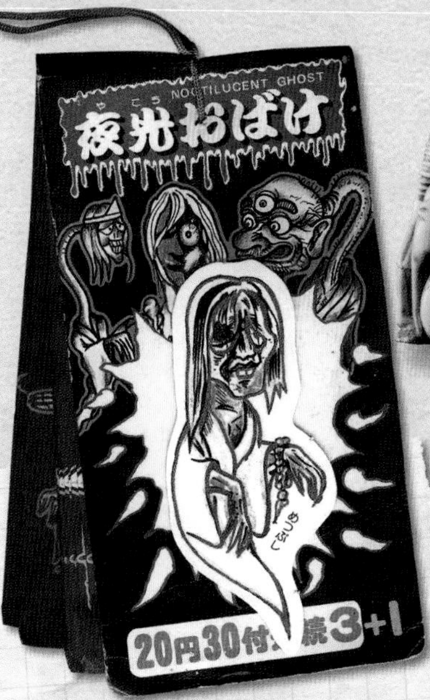

やこう NOCTILUCENT GHOST
夜光おばけ

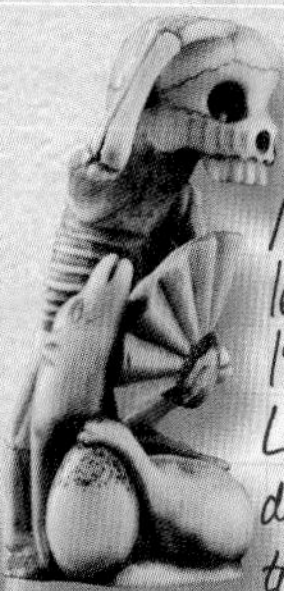

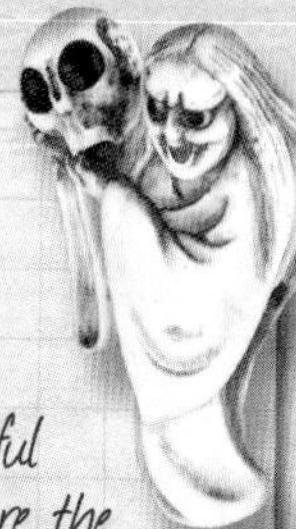

NETSUKE (MID 1600S – EARLY 1900S)

Less "toys" than "playful decorations," netsuke are the traditional Japanese equivalent of cufflinks or tie pins. Carved from ivory or wood, they were used to attach cloth pouches to the sashes of kimono (which have no pockets). Over the years, netsuke evolved from practical necessity to fanciful accessory, with craftsmen turning out increasingly cute, wild, or striking designs. More than a few netsuke feature supernatural motifs, such as these yurei characters.

NOCTILUCENT GHOST MAGNETS (1980S?)

These funky, finger-sized cards feature a variety of yurei and yokai inspired designs. They also have magnetized backs, letting you hang them on your locker or refrigerator. Incidentally, we had to look up "noctilucent" in the dictionary. It's a five-dollar word for "glowing," which they do quite tenaciously even after all these years.

HIKARU OBAKE JIKESHI (GLOWING MONSTER ERASER)

Yet another glowing ghost toy! This pocket-sized Oiwa-san is horrifying AND handy: she's a pencil eraser! She is also a fashion accessory, with a loop on her head for those who want to wear her necklace-style. All this for just 50 yen.

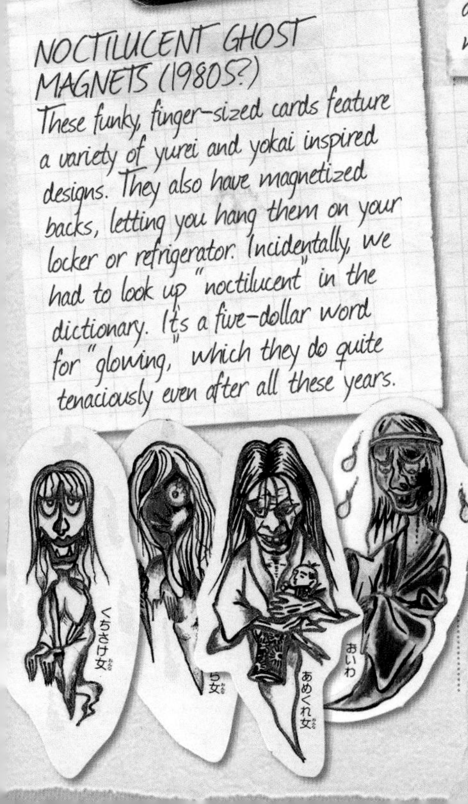

くちさけ女
あめくれ女
おいわ

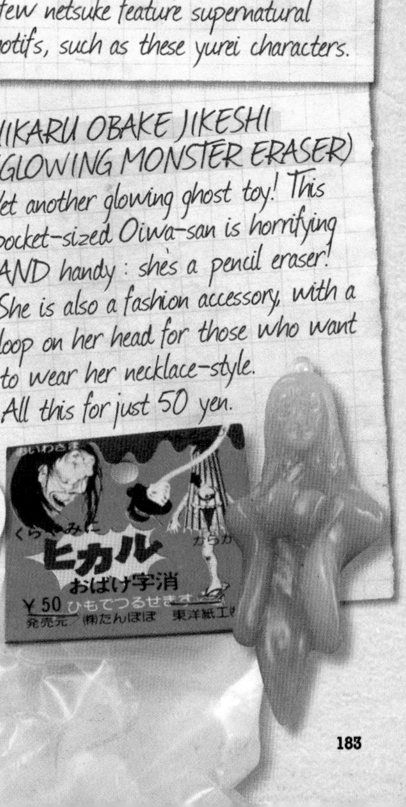

ヒカル
おばけ字消
¥50

YUREI BIBLIOGRAPHY
& RECOMMENDED READING

General Resources

Addiss, Stephen. *Japanese Ghosts and Demons: Art of the Supernatural.* George Braziller Inc., 2001.

Foster, Michael Dylan. *Pandemonium and Parade: Japanese Monsters and the Culture of Yokai.* University of California Press, 2009.

Fujinuma, Ryozo, et. al. *Yokai Yurei Daihyakka.* ("Encyclopedia of Yokai and Yurei.") Keibunsha, 1984.

Hearn, Lafcadio. *In Ghostly Japan.* Tuttle Publishing, 1971.

Hirai, Tadamasa. *Yurei Gashu* (*A Collection of Yurei Paintings*). Zenshoan, 2000.

International Research Center for Japanese Studies. *Ibun Yokai Densho Detabesu.* ("Strange Phenomenon and Yokai Legend Database.") http://www.nichibun. ac.jp/YoukaiDB/ (Retrieved July 22, 2011.)

Mitford, Algernon. *Tales of Old Japan.* Project Gutenberg. Ed. Jonathan Ingram, Sandra Brown. http://www.gutenberg.org/ files/13015/13015-h/13015-h.html (Retrieved July 22, 2011.)

Murakami, Kenji. *Yokai Jiten* (*Yokai Encyclopedia.*) Mainichi Shimbunsha, 2000.

Nakaoka, Toshiya. *Shashin! Nihon Kyofu 100 Meisho* ("Photographs of 100 Famous Scary Spots in Japan!") Futami Shobo, 1983.

National Museum of Japanese History, eds. *Hyakki Yako no Sekai* (*The World of The Demons' Night-Parade*) National Institutes for the Humanities, 2009.

Omori, Akihiro. *Nihon no Onryo* (*Japan's Angry Ghosts*). Heibonsha, 2007.

Smithsonian Institution. *Japanese Masterworks from the Price Collection.* The Arthur M. Sackler Gallery and Shogakukan, 2007.

Tada, Gen. *Kaisetsu Kojiki — Nihonshoki.* (*An Analysis of the Kojiji and Nihonshoki*). Saitosha, 2006.

Oiwa

Brazell, Karen. *Traditional Japanese Theater: an Anthology of Plays.* Columbia University Press, 1997.

Botan Doro

Asai, Ryoi. *Otogi Boko: Shin Nihon Koten Bungaku Taikei.* (*Otogi Boko: New Japanese Classic Literature Collection Edition.*) Eds. Osamu Matsuda, et. al. Iwanami Shoten, 2001.

Lady Rokujo

Shikibu, Murasaki. *The Tale of Genji.* Trans. Arthur Waley. Vermont: Tuttle, 2010.

Bargen, Doris G. *A Woman's Weapon: Spirit Possession in the Tale of Genji.* University of Hawai'i Press, 1997.

Sugawara no Michizane

Brown, Delmer M. and Ishida, Ichiro. *The Future and the Past: a translation and study of the Gukansho, an interpretative history of Japan written in 1219.* University of California Press, 1979

Griffis, William Elliot. *Japan in History, Folk Lore and Art.* Houghton, Mifflin, 1894.

Ito, ed. Rekishi Dokuhon: *Seinaru Jinja Onryo no Kamigami (A History Reader: Holy Shrines and Angry Gods).* Shinjinbutsu Ouraisha, 1991.

Kohada Koheiji

Santo, Kyoden and Sunaga, Asahiko, ed. Gendaigo Yaku *Edo no Denki Shosetsu: Fukushu Kidan Asaka no Numa (A Modern Translation of the Edo Novel: Asaka Swamp: A Strange Tale of Revenge).* Tokyo: Kokusho Kankokai, 2002

Markus, Andrew Lawrence. *The Willow in Autumn: Ryjtei Tanehiko, 1783-1842.* Harvard university Asia Center, 1992

Sumpter, Sara L. *Katsushika Hokusai's Ghost of Kohada Koheiji: Image from a Falling Era.* http://prizedwriting.ucdavis.edu/past/2004-2005/pdfs/sumpter.pdf (Retrieved July 18, 2011.)

Sumpter, Sara L. *From Scrolls to Prints to Moving Pictures:* *Iconographic Ghost Imagery from Pre-Modern Japan to the Contemporary Horror Film.* http://undergraduatestudies.ucdavis.edu/explorations/2006/sumpter.pdf (Retrieved July 18, 2011.)

Sakura Sogoro

Walthall, Anne. *Peasant Uprisings in Japan: a Critical Anthology of Peasant Histories.* University of Chicago Press, 1991.

Aoki, Michiko Yamaguchi. *As the Japanese See It: Past and Present.* University of Hawai'i Press, 1981

Morinaga Shinoh

Onuki, Akihiro. *Kamakura Rekishi to Fushigi wo Aruku (Kamakura Mystery Tour).* Jitsugyo no Nihonsha, 2008.

Miyagi & Isora

Ueda, Akinari. *Tales of Moonlight and Rain.* Trans. Anthony H. Chambers. Columbia University Press, 2007.

Hakkoda

Nitta, Jiro. *Death March on Mount Hakkoda.* Trans. James Westerhoven. Berkeley: Stone Bridge Press, 2007.

Jukai Forest (Sea of Trees)

Gilhooly, Rob. "Inside Japan's 'Suicide Forest.'" *The Japan Times.* June 26, 2011.

Uncredited. *Japan: Suicide Point. Time Magazine.* Jan 28, 1935. http://www.time.com/time/magazine/article/0,9171,748346-1,00.html (Retrieved July 22, 2011.)

VBS TV, Producers. *Aokigahara: Suicide Forest*. 2010. http://www.vbs.tv/watch/vbs-news/aokigahara-suicide-forest-v3--2 (Retrieved July 22, 2011.)

Oiran Buchi

Kobayashi, Kazuo. *Oiran Buchi*. Soubunsha, 2005.

Sunshine 60 Building

Oda, Bunji. *Kanshu ga Kakushi Totteita Sugamo Prison Mikokai Film (Previously Unpublished Film Secretly Taken by Wardens at Sugamo Prison)*. Shogakukan, 2000.

Mt. Osorezan

Yajima, Daisuke. *Diminutive traditional shaman seen in new light*. Asahi.com. Jan 27, 2011.

Michibiki Jizo

Schumacher, Mark. *A to Z Photo Dictionary of Japanese Buddhist Statuary* http://www.onmarkproductions.com/html/jizo1.shtml (Retrieved July 18, 2011)

Smits, Gregory. "Danger in the Lowground: Historical Context for the March 11, 2011 Tohoku Earthquake and Tsunami." *The Asia-Pacific Journal: Japan Focus*. http://japanfocus.org/-Gregory-Smits/3531 (Retrieved July 18, 2011.)

Atwater, Brian F., et. al. *The Orphan Tsunami of 1700 — Japanese Clues to a Parent Earthquake in North America: U.S. Geological Survey Professional Paper 1707*. University of Washington Press, 2005.

Japanese Curses

Seki, Yuji. *Noroi to Tatari no Nihon Kodaishi (Curses in Ancient Japanese History)*. Tokyo Shoseki, 2003.

Kokkuri-San

Inoue, Nobutaka, ed. *Folk Beliefs in Modern Japan*. Institute for Japanese Culture and Classics, Kokugakuin University, 1994.

Nagaoka, Toshiya. *Kokkuri-san no Himitsu (Secrets of Kokkuri-san)*. Futami Shobo, 1974.

Hangonko Incense

Kern, Adam L. *Manga from the Floating World: Comicbook Culture and the Kibyioshi of Edo Japan*. Harvard University Asia Center, 2006.

Shinrei Shashin

Jolly, Martyn. *Faces of the Living Dead*. Mark Batty Publisher, 2006.

Koike, Takehiro. *Shinrei Shashin: Fushigi wo Meguru Jikenshi (Shinrei Shashin: A History of Mysterious Incidents)*. Takarajimasha, 2005.

Yuten Shonin

Hardacre, Helen. *Marketing the Menacing Fetus in Japan*. University of California Press, 1999.

Hell

Yushinari, Isamu, ed. *Nihon Oni Soran (An Overview of Japan's Oni)* Shinjinbutsu Ouraisha, 1994.

YUREI RESOURCES

This section covers some classic books and some of our favorite films of the ghost genre that are highly recommended for anyone interested in spooky tales of the supernatural. Those interested in researching further should refer to the bibliography on the previous pages for a detailed list of books and other references that we consulted in making of Yurei Attack!

BOOKS

Genji Monogatari
by Murasaki Shikibu.
Tales of Moonlight and Rain
by Akinari Ueda.
In Ghostly Japan
Kwaidan
by Lafcadio Hearn.
Japanese Tales
by Royall Tyler.
The Legends of Tono
by Kunio Yanagita.
Rashomon
by Ryunosuke.
Akutagawa

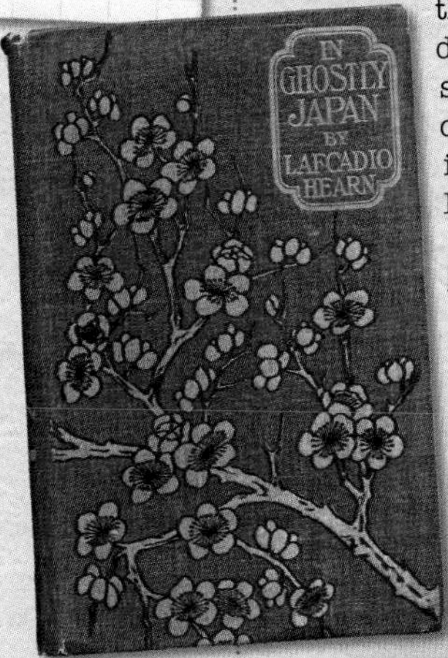
IN GHOSTLY JAPAN
BY
LAFCADIO HEARN

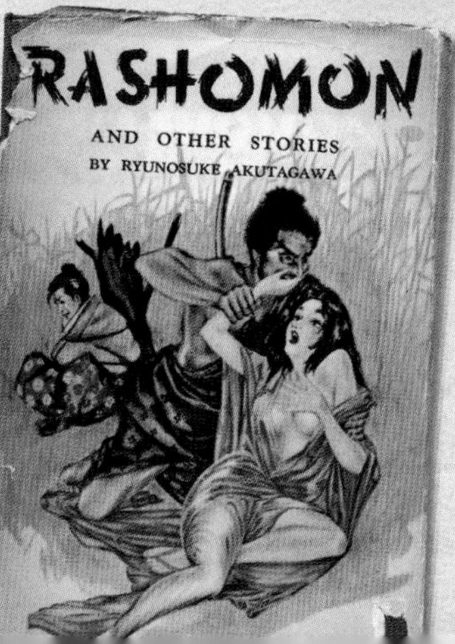
RASHOMON
AND OTHER STORIES
BY RYUNOSUKE AKUTAGAWA

For best results, watch these in the dead of night. completely alone!!

Hiroko & Matt's Top 5 Favorite Japanese Horror Movies

House (1977)
This psychedelic freak-out, set in a haunted house, is considered a classic of Japanese horror filmmaking.

Kwaidan (1964)
If you're going to watch any one Japanese horror movie, make it this one. It contains dramatizations of several of the tales chronicled in this book, including Miyagi and Hoichi the Earless.

Ringu (1998)
The movie that kicked off the "J-Horror" phenomenon. Quite possibly the best portrayal of an *onnen* (angry spirit) ever filmed. The Hollywood version, "The Ring," is OK, but nothing beats the original.

Uzumaki (2000)
Although it isn't exactly a ghost story, this (literally) twisted tale of spirals taking over a town is one of the most abstract yet chilling tales of a haunting ever told.

Ju-on: The Curse (2004)
This "J-Horror" classic proved so popular both in Japan and abroad that Hollywood re-made it several years later as "The Grudge."

OFUDA 御札

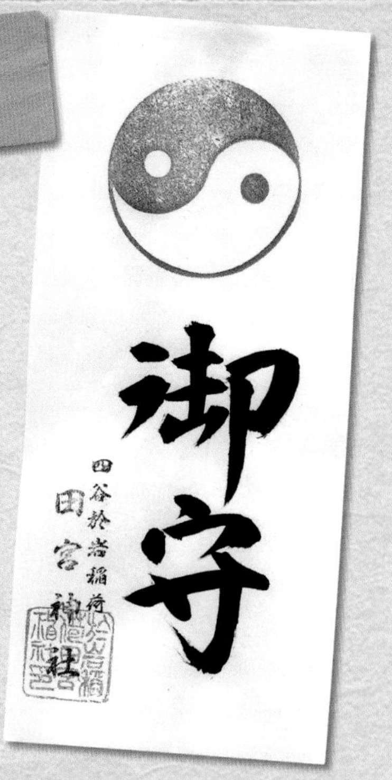
御守
四谷於岩稲荷
田宮神社

Ofuda are paper talismans used to ward off evil of all sorts, ranging from simple bad luck and misfortune to specific ghosts or other supernatural forces. They are widely used as amulets in the religions of Shinto and Shugendo. Generally obtained from Shinto shrines, they take the forms of slips of paper stamped or inscribed with information about from what or whom the owner is being protected.

The ofuda shown here were obtained from Tamiya Jinja Shrine, also known as the Yotsuya Oiwa Inari Shrine. It is located in downtown Tokyo on the site of the former Tamiya residence — the very same one in which the first yurei portrayed in this book, Oiwa-san, lived centuries ago. A visit to this shrine is de rigeur for anyone who writes about or performs material based on this angry ghost's life (or rather, afterlife). These ofuda were given to us and everyone involved in the production of this book after we paid for an *oharai*, or preventative exorcism ceremony, prior to beginning work. (Better safe than sorry.)

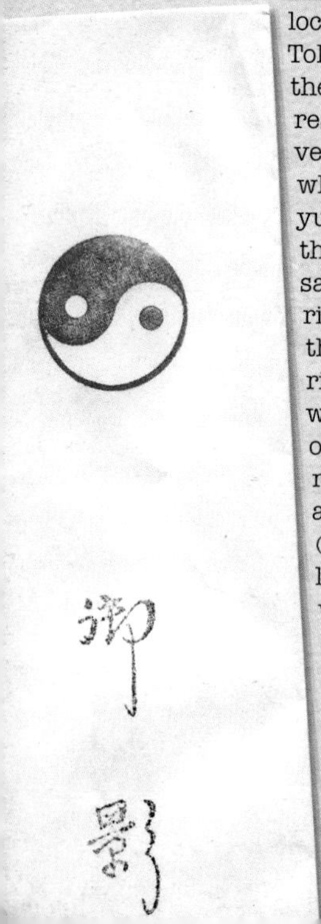
御
影

Ofuda are generally placed on a wall inside one's home. In extreme cases, such as that of the Tale of the Peony Lantern (p.27), many hundreds are pasted on walls and entrances to afford residents protection.

We provide these examples here for those curious about what ofuda look like. Unfortunately, simply copying and pasting up facsimiles isn't believed to be effective; one must visit a shrine and obtain a "live" ofuda for maximum protection. Even "live" ofuda have expiration dates and need to be replaced, generally on an annual basis.

INDEX

PHOTO/ILLUSTRATION CREDITS
Joe Price Collection 9, 10, 190 ; Hiroko Yoda 43, 63, 71, 79, 82, 83, 106 - 7, 110 - 1, 115, 119, 122-3, 127, 130, 142, 162, 167, 187-8; Tomoo Haraguchi 52, 54, 175; Katrina Grigg-Saito 83; Flickr member "Simon le Nippon" 103; Andrew Lee 136 -9, 181 (bottom right); Rob Oechsle 154-5; Matt Alt 80 (Oni diecast); Yoshiko and Naoki Karasawa 180 (Glow ghouls), 182 (Karuta, monster fireworks); Nandemoplamo 181 (Model kits); Gojira-ya 182 (Haunted House Set); Ilja van de Pavert 183 (Saluting skeleton netsuke); Bernard Hurtig 183 (Skull-carrying ghost netsuke); David Keymont 183 (Monster eraser)

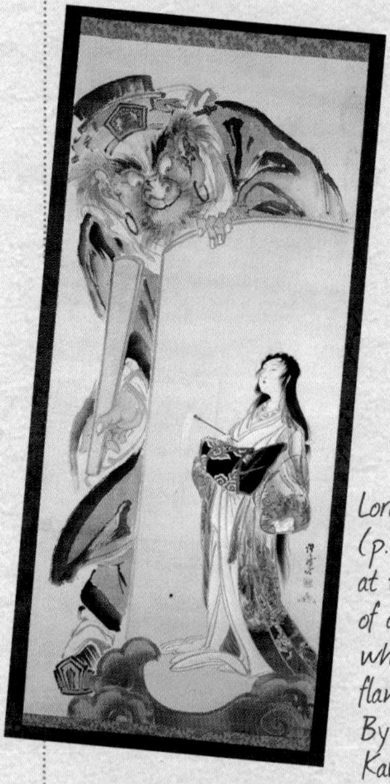

Lord Enma (p. 172) leers at the spirit of a courtesan, who wears a flaming kimono. By the legendary Kawanabe Kyosai.

THANKS TO

First and foremost, we need to single out Gregory Starr for his unflinching devotion to our peculiar set of interests. Without him, *Yokai Attack!*, *Ninja Attack!*, and *Yurei Attack!* would never have sprung into existence. His decision to pair us with the fiendishly talented page-designer Andrew Lee is what made the series what it is.

Another big thank-you is for Eric, William, and all the fine folks at Tuttle Publishing, who took our books under their wing after the untimely demise of our previous publisher.

Very special thanks are due to the individuals who assisted us with various imagery. Legendary art collector Joe Price graciously allowed us to use the ghost paintings that appear in the introduction and on the preceding page. Film director Tomoo Haraguchi loaned us assorted gruesome props. Collector "Nandemoplamo" and toy store "Godzilla-ya" allowed us to use photos of the models and toys from their extensive collections. Manga artists Yoshiko and Naoki Karasawa loaned us imagery of *menko* and *karuta* cards. Photographer Rob Oechsle gave us permission to use vintage photographs from his archive. And Katrina Grigg-Saito graciously allowed us to use a photo of her family's Okiku doll.

Thanks also to all of our friends here in Tokyo who provided valuable ideas, perspectives, and occasionally cold beer, including Andrew Szymanski, Tatsuya Morino, Yutaka Kondo, Konami Chiba, Nobuhiro Arai, Keitaro Hamabe, Masaji and Eri Shiina, Anri Tsutsumi, Susumu Maruyama, and Rintaro Yamamoto.

And thanks, of course, to Oiwa-san and all of the other ghosts who let us make it through the writing of this book without serious incident.

Hiroko Yoda
Matt Alt
Tokyo, Japan
March 2012

Yokai Attack!
The Japanese Monster Survival Guide
Revised Edition with 16 New Pages All in Full-Color for the First Time!
Hiroko Yoda and Matt Alt
Illustrations by Tatsuya Morino
外国人のための妖怪サバイバルガイド
妖怪に気をつけろ!!
TUTTLE
Ninja Attack!
True Tales of Assassins, Samurai, and Outlaws
Revised Edition with 16 New Pages All in Full-Color for the First Time!
Hiroko Yoda and Matt Alt
Illustrations by Yutaka Kondo
外国人のための忍者常識マニュアル
TUTTLE

MAKE SURE YOU ALSO CHECK OUT THESE OTHER BOOKS BY HIROKO YODA AND MATT ALT
Yokai Attack! The Japanese Monster Survival Guide and *Ninja Attack! True Tales of Assassins, Samurai, and Outlaws*

Hiroko Yoda and Matt Alt are a husband and wife team who run a Tokyo-based translation company that specializes in producing the English versions of Japanese video games, comic books, and literature. They are the co-authors of *Yokai Attack!* and *Ninja Attack!*, both originally published by Kodansha International and with new expanded editions coming out from Tuttle Publishing.

Shinkichi is a Tokyo-based illustrator and designer. An active creator of "dojin" (self-pubished manga). Ironically, she's deathly afraid of ghost stories. *Yurei Attack!* is her international debut.